TURN LEFT AT THE DAFFODILS

Elizabeth Elgin is the bestselling author of *All the Sweet Promises*, *I'll Bring You Buttercups*, *Daisychain Summer*, *Where Bluebells Chime*, *Windflower Wedding*, *One Summer at Deer's Leap*, *The Willow Pool*, *A Scent of Lavender* and *The Linden Walk*. She served in the WRNS during the Second World War and met her husband on board a submarine depot ship. She lived in the Vale of York until her death in 2005.

By the same author

Whistle in the Dark
The House in Abercromby Square
The Manchester Affair
Shadow of Dark Water
Mistress of Luke's Folly
The Rose Hedge
All the Sweet Promises
Whisper on the Wind
I'll Bring You Buttercups
Daisychain Summer
Where Bluebells Chime
Windflower Wedding
One Summer at Deer's Leap
The Willow Pool
A Scent of Lavender
The Linden Walk

Writing as Kate Kirby

Footsteps of a Stuart
Echo of a Stuart
Scapegoat for a Stuart

ELIZABETH ELGIN

Turn Left at the Daffodils

HARPER

Harper
An imprint of HarperCollins*Publishers*
77–85 Fulham Palace Road,
Hammersmith, London W6 8JB

www.harpercollins.co.uk

This paperback edition
1

First published by HarperCollins*Publishers* 2006

Copyright © Elizabeth Elgin 2006

Elizabeth Elgin asserts the moral right to
be identified as the author of this work

A catalogue record for this book
is available from the British Library

ISBN 978 0 00 783381 8

Set in Sabon by Palimpsest Book Production Limited,
Grangemouth, Stirlingshire

Printed and bound in Great Britain by
Clays Ltd, St Ives plc

Elizabeth Elgin

29.08.1924

—❦—

03.09.2005

To everyone involved in her publications and her many loyal and special readers, we thank you and hope you cherish this, her final book. Remember her with the love that she put into writing her novels. And, Mum, we hope the ending is as you planned it.

We love and miss you more than words can ever say.

George, Jane, David, Gillian, James, Simon, Matthew, Martin, Tom, Katie, Grace and baby George William, Dominique, Becky, Ellen, Emma (Your 'clan').

O DEUS DA NOITE, BOA BLESS, SONHOS DOCES.

To Betty's second great-granddaughter Grace Mair Elizabeth Hall and her third great-grandchild "Baby" Cheetham, expected in January 2007. Also, to a very dear friend, Mrs Edna Parkinson.

ONE

May 1941

She brought the doorknocker down twice, then prayed with all her heart that Auntie Mim was in because if she wasn't, Nan Morrissey was in deep trouble. And stranded in Leeds.

This morning, she had walked out of Cyprian Court in high old dudgeon; this morning, her suitcases had not seemed so heavy. Now, hungry and tired, she wondered if she had done the right thing – not for walking out on the Queer One and her Georgie – but because maybe she should have thought things out, first. Like how she would get from Liverpool to Leeds when there were few trains into or out of Liverpool, no trams running, and few buses able to get into the city centre. Because of the bombing, that was.

She closed her eyes and whispered, 'Auntie Mim – *please?*' then heard the blessed sound of door bolts being drawn back and the grating of a key in the lock.

'Well, if it isn't our Nan!' Miriam Simpson snorted. 'Left home, have you?'

'Sort of.' Tears of pure relief filled Nan's eyes. Then she took a shuddering breath and said, 'Chucked out, more like. Can I come in, please?'

'And what have you done to make your dad throw you out?' Arms folded firmly, Auntie Mim barred the doorway. 'Got yourself into trouble, then?'

'Me dad didn't throw me out. He's dead. Funeral two days ago.' Her bottom lip trembled with genuine sorrow. 'It was *Her* threw me out, and not because I've got myself into trouble, because I haven't!'

'Come on in then, Nan. I'm sorry about your dad.' She really was. Will Morrissey had been decent to her sister. 'Leave the cases in the lobby and sit yourself down. Heart attack, was it?'

'No. Air Raid. He was on duty at the hospital and it got a direct hit. Them bluddy *Jairmans*! They've made a right mess of Liverpool – I had to get out. And I won't be a bother, honest, if you'll let me stay till I get myself sorted.'

'Oh, all right. But I can't feed you Nan, rationing being what it is, and I don't allow swearing.'

'Sorry. And it's all right. I took my ration book when I left.'

Indeed, she had taken everything she thought to be legitimately hers. Food coupons, her identity card and the large brown envelope marked *Marriage Lines, Birth Certificates, etc.* in her

2

mother's handwriting. And her clothes. Mind, she wished she had left the brown envelope at the back of the drawer, now she knew what was inside it.

'Had words with your stepmother, then?' Miriam filled the kettle and set it to boil.

'Suppose so. Dad ought never to have married her. I couldn't stand her, and that brat. And she couldn't stand me, either. She was weeping and moaning over Dad, like she was the only one who mattered. Not a thought for me losing my father. And then she said she'd have to be the wage-earner now, and that she'd be working full-time and I would have to look after Georgie. That's how it all started.'

'Because you said you wouldn't?'

'Not exactly. But I said I was sick of her kid. D'you know, he wouldn't go to bed on his own and I had to go with him. At half-past six at night, would you believe? And he was three, and still in nappies, and he always has a snotty nose, an' all,' she added, when her aunt remained silent.

'I told her! "I'm sick and fed up of that kid," I said. "I've got my certificate from night school for touch-typing and I want to go to work." And she said nobody would employ the likes of me what couldn't speak proper, and if I wanted to stay in *her* house, I'd do as I was told if I knew what was good for me.'

'So you upped and offed? And now I'm landed with you. Are you sure you're not in trouble?'

'Sure, Auntie Mim. Cross my heart and hope to die. And I won't be stoppin' for long. I'm joining up, see. The Army.'

'Now what do you want to do a thing like that, for? And anyway, you aren't old enough.'

'I'm nearly eighteen and they take you at seventeen and a half. And why shouldn't I join up? What could be worse than stoppin' at Cyprian Court, now me dad's gone?'

'You'd have to take orders and salute people . . .'

'So do all the women in the Forces. What's so special about me?'

'But what would you do, in the Army? You've had no education to speak of and you've never worked.'

'I've got my typing certificate, and I haven't worked because it suited *Her* to keep me at home for a dogsbody. Can't you see, Auntie Mim, that I'd be the same as everybody else, once I'd joined up. Same uniform, the same pay. I'd be – well – *normal.*'

'Oh, dear.' Miriam Simpson felt sorry for her sister's child, even though she had seen little of her these last few years. It couldn't have been a lot of fun, losing a mother when you were a child, then getting a stepmother, a couple of years later – and one who took a bit of getting on with, if what she had heard was true. 'I suppose you're hungry? Get this tea down you, then I'll do you a slice or two of toast and jam. All right?'

'Smashing.' Nan sipped the tea gratefully. 'And I can pay me way, till the Army sends for me. I've got money in the Post Office.'

'We'll have to think about that. I've got a gentleman lodger, see. He's something to do with aeroplane engines and he's gone to Derby on a course for a month. He gives me a pound a week, but you can have his bed for ten shillings if you'll help in the house and do a bit of queuing for me. I can't say fairer than that.'

'It's a deal – and thanks. I won't be any trouble, Auntie Mim.'

'You better hadn't be, or you'll be on your way back to Liverpool before you can blink! And you'd better get yourself to the Food Office in the morning – see about an emergency card for your rations.'

'I will.' And look for the nearest recruiting office, because the sooner she got herself into uniform, the better. She would have to have a next-of-kin, of course. You always did when you joined up, but that was all right, because Auntie Mim *was* her next-of-kin, now.

She thought about it that night as she lay in the bed that was hers for four weeks. It struck her like a thunder clap. What if it took longer than that to get into the Army? Where would she go when the lodger came back? Cyprian Court, would it have to be, tail between her legs?

She pushed so terrible a thought from her mind, closed her eyes and thought instead about her father, wishing he could know she was going to be all right. Poor dad. He hadn't had much of a life. Losing Mum, then getting himself saddled with the Queer One, and Georgie.

And thinking about Mum, what about that birth certificate? But she would worry about it tomorrow. Beautiful tomorrow, when she would present her touch-typing certificate to the Recruiting Officer. Bright, shining tomorrow, when her new life would begin.

May, without any doubt at all, was the most beautiful of months; a green, blossom-filled goodbye to winter; to short days and blackouts that came too early, and fogs and cold houses and everything that was depressing.

Caroline Tiptree leaned on the gate, gazing over the cow pasture to fields green with sprouting wheat, and hawthorn hedges coming to life again and the distant blue haze that carpeted Bluebell Wood.

So precious, this Yorkshire hamlet in which she lived; in which Englishmen had lived since Elizabeth Tudor's time. So comforting to know that wars had come and gone, yet still Nether Hutton remained unchanged. Twenty-one houses, and all of them built of rose-red brick; all of them with flower-filled gardens; most of them with chimney stacks twisted like sticks of barley sugar. She turned to lean her back against the gate, reluctant to go home, to face the recriminations and tears she knew would follow. When she told her mother, that was.

Sighing, she made for Jackmans Cottage, named for the long-ago sea captain who had built it with a purse of gold, given by a grateful queen. A house with low, beamed ceilings and wide fireplaces and two kitchens and small windows. A thick-walled house that had not and would not change.

She closed the gate carefully behind her, standing for a moment to take in the courtyard garden thick with the flowers of late spring, for this was the picture she would carry away with her, if she left it. *When* she left it.

'Hello, darling. You've missed the News,' Janet Tiptree called from the sitting room.

'Sorry.' Carrie hung up her coat, knowing she'd had no intention of getting home to hear it. She'd had enough of gloom and doom, was fed up with the war and living in a rural backwater whilst everywhere else seemed to be getting bombed, and Dover shelled every single day from across the Channel. 'Don't suppose there was anything worth listening to – like Hitler wants an armistice . . .'

Or perhaps two ounces on the butter ration? She would settle for an ounce, even.

'Don't be flippant, Carrie. And why the badly-done-to look? Missing Jeffrey – is that it?'

'Not particularly, mother. After all, he wanted to go.'

'Which was sensible, really. Better to volunteer now for the Navy than wait another year to be

7

called-up and put in the Army or the Air Force. Jeffrey's uncle fought at Jutland, don't forget and with a name like Frobisner – well, what else could he join? And you *are* missing him – admit it – or why are you acting like a bear with a sore head.'

'My head is fine, mother. It's my conscience I'm more bothered about. I've got to accept that working in a bank isn't doing much for the war effort. I'm not pulling my weight.'

'But you are!' She patted the sofa beside her. 'Now come and sit beside your mother, and tell her what's wrong – have a little cuddle, shall we?'

'Mother! I'm too old for cuddles. I'm twenty-one, soon, and I'm *not* doing enough. I'm having an easy war, and it isn't right.'

'Now you're not to talk like that.' Her mother was using her coaxing voice, her talking-to-awkward-daughters voice. 'You have a job, you travel ten miles to work each day, and back, and two nights a week you fire watch for the ARP, leaving me all alone here. But do I complain?'

'No.'

She said it snappily, because doing a clerk's job did not seem at all like war work. The local bus picked her up at eight each morning and got her home by six forty-five each evening, and as for the fire-watching duties – well, there had been no fires; not even an air-raid warning, so what was so noble about that?

'Why you and Jeffrey don't fix a date, Carrie, is beyond me. I mean – you'd get a naval allowance

8

and nobody could make you leave home if you were a married woman. Why all this soul searching? What's brought it on, will you tell me?'

'You wouldn't believe me, if I did.' She turned abruptly to stare out of the window.

'Try me, dear. And please don't turn your back when you speak to me.'

'Sorry – and all right, if you must know . . .' She went to sit beside her mother, then stared at the empty hearth. 'What has brought it on? Seeing everything so beautiful, I suppose. Hutton in the spring and this lovely little village and – and the invasion. Because there's going to be one, and I don't want us to be invaded. All this is worth fighting for, mother.'

'And Jeffrey has gone to fight for it. All the young men in the village, too. Nether Hutton is well represented.'

'Y-yes . . .' Her mother was right – except that there were only two young men of conscription age in the village. And herself, of course. 'And it's going to be better represented,' she blurted, red-cheeked to the brass fender. 'Because I'm going, as well. I'm going to join up.'

'*Join up*! I have never in all my life heard such nonsense! Have you forgotten your duty to me, Caroline?'

'No. But I really am going. Into the Army.'

'But you are all I have!' Janet Tiptree jumped to her feet and began to pace the room. 'Haven't I suffered enough from war? Didn't I lose your father to the Great War, and must I lose my only child to this one? Your father came home a sick man; came home to die of his war wounds and –'

'And Todd's father was killed, trying to get him out of No Man's Land.'

'Todd Coverdale? Why bring him into it after all these years?'

Her mother's red cheeks and trembling mouth warned Carrie to have care, but still she said,

'All these years? It's not all that long since he left.'

'And did you expect me to keep him out of a sense of duty?' she demanded shrilly. 'I couldn't help it if his mother died. Your father, out of gratitude, told Marie Coverdale that she and her son would have a home here as long as she lived.'

'Yes, and out of gratitude she worked in this house like a servant, almost, and – and –'

'And Todd wanted for nothing. Even after your father died, I saw to it that nothing changed. They continued to live here and Todd went to Grammar School!'

'He got a scholarship! Todd was like a brother to me, yet you sent him away, when his mother died.'

'To his aunt, who was willing to have him. But why all this raking up of the past? You said nothing about his going, at the time. And we are talking about *now*, and you leaving home! What is to become of me, when you go – *if* you go.'

'No *ifs*,' Caroline said softly, gently. 'If I pass

the medical, I'm going. And it isn't a question of duty, either to you or to this country. I'm joining up because I want to; because something is telling me I must. Can't you understand? Can't you, for once, think of something other than yourself?'

'Well, now I know you have taken leave of your senses! Me – *selfish*.' The tears left Janet Tiptree's eyes, her jaw hardened. 'Me, who has been father and mother to you, *thinks only of myself*? Shame on you Caroline. Don't make me more upset than I already am! I suggest you go to bed, and wake up tomorrow in a better frame of mind. And apologise for the things you have said!'

'No thank you. I am well past the age of being sent early to bed. But I am sorry if I have hurt you, if I seem ungrateful for all you have done for me. And I am sorry for your loneliness over the years, but please stop treating me like a child?'

'Then stop behaving like one and remember where your duty lies. And I have nothing more to say. I shall go to bed. I have a migraine coming on. Will it be too much to ask that you bring me up a hot drink, and an aspirin?'

She opened the staircase door and without a goodnight, walked sighing to her room . . .

'Oh, lordy!' Carrie whispered when she heard the banging of the bedroom door.

It had been exactly as she thought: the pleading, tears and recriminations. It always was, when her mother wanted her own way. Sometimes her mother had a hard heart, inside that sweet exterior. It was sad she was a widow, but the Great War had left behind many widows – Todd's mother for one, whose husband had crawled into the void between the trenches. Todd's father had been shot by a sniper as he dragged his wounded officer to safety.

Mind, her father had been grateful; given his word that widow and son should be cared for. And her mother accepted it, because she always took the least line of resistance – and because it suited her to have unpaid help in the house.

Carrie looked at herself in the wall mirror; gazed unblinking so her resolve should not weaken, because there was something else her mother wouldn't like, if ever she found out.

Fix a date for the wedding? Not yet. Because Jeffrey had shocked her, shown a side to his nature she had not known to exist, and she had not liked it. She recalled his mouth, sensuously pouted, his eyes narrowed so he need not look at her and his mouth, wet on hers.

'I'm going to the war, Carrie,' he had said, 'and if you loved me, you'd let me. We're engaged, after all. Where's the harm in it? And anyway, you can't get pregnant the first time.'

So she had let him; had lain there unresisting, eyes fixed on the ceiling whilst he pushed and grunted and shoved.

'Told you it'd be all right, didn't I?' He had nuzzled her neck when it was over, then slid off the bed and pulled on his trousers. 'And it'll be better, next time.'

Next time, thank heaven, was at least three months away, and by next time she could well be out of reach. And she didn't want there to be a next time. Not yet. Not until she could talk to Jeffrey about her fears, her feelings, because if that was what doing *it* was like, then she had got it all wrong.

She shrugged and walked to the window, arms folded tightly around her, mouth stubborn, gazing as twilight touched the garden, muting colours, softening outlines.

The wood pigeon that nested in the tree in the lane outside flew past her line of vision, alighting atop the wall, cooing and burbling. It waddled, pecking, then flapped up to its nest. Poor silly, fortunate bird. It didn't even know there was a war on.

But there *was* a war on and she was going to join it, and not all her mother's tears would stop her. Soon, she would have to register for war service so why not choose, as Jeffrey had done, what she would do and in which arm of the Forces. Army, Air Force, Navy – did it matter? Could anything be worse than remaining in Nether Hutton, a dutiful daughter, waiting for Jeffrey to come home on leave from the Navy and marry her, just because that was what everyone expected them to do?

She wished she could talk to her mother about what happened that night she had gone out to play whist and left them alone together. Yet she knew she could not, must not.

She slid home the door bolts and turned the key in the lock. Then she pulled the blackout curtains across the window and went to the kitchen.

A hot drink for her mother, and two aspirins. A little honey in the milk and a glass of water for the tablets. A dutiful daughter again, who would one day be a dutiful wife to Jeffrey.

But not on his first leave. Only when she was ready to be a wife. And on this heart-achingly beautiful May evening, she was not.

'Sorry, mother,' she whispered to the honey jar. 'I've got to have time to sort out my life my own way. And sorry, Jeffrey. I *will* marry you, but not just yet; not until we have talked.' Because something so very important could not be open to doubt, or left to chance.

And tomorrow, no matter what her mother said or threatened, she would go to the recruiting office. She *had* to.

'Let's check to see if we've got it right,' the ATS corporal in the Recruiting Office said. 'Nancy Morrissey, of 16 Farthing Street, Leeds. Date of birth November 22, 1924. And you wish, if you pass the medical examination, to join the Auxiliary Territorial Service – right?'

'Right,' Nan said, just a little chokily. 'And I want to be a typist.' She took the folded piece of paper from her handbag. 'Got a certificate . . .'

'That won't be necessary, at this stage. If you

14

pass, you'll be given an intelligence test,' the corporal smiled.

She had a nice smile, Nan thought; had a ring on her engagement finger, too.

'I – I wouldn't like to be a domestic,' she breathed. 'I want sumthin' better than bein' an orderly.'

'An orderly is not to be looked down upon,' the corporal reproved. 'You will be wearing the King's uniform – something to be proud of, whatever job you do. Oh, and your next-of-kin . . . ?'

'That's me Auntie Mim – Mrs Miriam Simpson, 16 Farthing Street, Leeds. I'm living with her, now, 'cause we was bombed in Liverpool.' No need to mention her stepmother. 'Me dad was killed when they bombed the hospital. I hate them Nazis, rot their socks!'

'Rot their socks indeed.' The corporal raised an eyebrow. 'I'm from London – East End.'

'Aaah,' Nan nodded, a bond between them established. 'And I'd like to get in as soon as possible. Auntie Mim can only let me stay for four weeks, see?'

'I'll do my best, but I can't promise anything.' She handed back the identity card and ration book Nan had offered in lieu of her birth certificate. 'Farthing Street is your permanent address as from now?'

'For four weeks, till the lodger comes back. After that, I can't say. That's why I want in quick.'

'I'll add a note. Your medical will be at Albion

Street, here in Leeds, so that'll be handy. I don't suppose you and I will meet again, Miss Morrissey, so good luck.'

'Thanks. Do you like bein' in the ATS Miss – er – Corporal?'

'Yes, I do. Very much.' She rose to her feet.

'Ta-ra, then – and thanks.' Nan pushed back her chair. The interview, she realized, was over. She was in the ATS – if she passed the medical, that was. No going back, now. 'And you won't forget to add the note?'

'I won't.'

Shakily, Nan made her way to the street outside, blinking in the bright sunlight. Shakily, because it wasn't every day you did something as mind-boggling as joining the Army.

She looked at the clock above the Market Hall. Eleven, exactly, which meant that in the span of two hours, she had changed the address on her ration book and identity card from Cyprian Court, Liverpool, to Farthing Street, Leeds; had obtained an emergency card for two weeks' food and offered herself to the Auxiliary Territorial Service for the duration of hostilities. Strange that only yesterday she had walked out on her old life for ever, and if she didn't get into the Army, heaven only knew what she would do, or where she would go. But she had learned, in her nearly eighteen years, not to look for trouble and anyway, nothing could be worse than being at Cyprian Court with her step-mother and her Georgie. Now dad had gone, there

16

was nothing at all to keep her in Liverpool and if Nan Morrissey had anything to do with it, she would never go back there!

She crossed the road to the Market Hall, in search of a queue. Queuing was part of daily life, now. You saw a long line of patiently waiting women, then hopefully joined on the end of it.

'What's it for?' she asked of the woman in front of her.

'Fish.' The reply was brief. Usually people talked to you in queues, but the one in front didn't seem to want to gossip. Nan turned to the woman behind her.

'Fish,' she beamed. 'Fingers crossed, eh?'

Carrie folded the greaseproof paper in which her sandwiches had been wrapped and put it in her handbag. Paper was in short supply, so you used it again and again. She had made her own sandwiches this morning, her mother's bedroom door being firmly closed, with no answer to her knock and her whispered, 'Tea, mother?'

Janet Tiptree, it would seem, was still asleep, though the minute the bus left the village, Carrie was as sure as she could be that she would be out of bed and downstairs before the teapot had time to get cold.

Carrie brushed the crumbs from her knees and stuck out her chin. Today, in her dinner hour, she had resolved to go to the recruiting office and there must be no going back, now. A short walk would take her there, after which heaven only knew what would happen . . .

Yet that was the way she wanted it, and if her mother tried to block her way by refusing her consent, she would try again after her twenty-first birthday. But she *was* going. Somewhere. Some place out of her mother's reach to do what Caroline Tiptree wanted – *needed* – to do.

All she knew – *really* knew – at this moment was that there was a war on and it was going to last for years and years. Longer than the last one, some said. It was a terrible thought but if, by joining the Armed Forces, her small effort could shorten that war by just one day, then she had to do it, no matter what her mother said. Or Jeffrey, for that matter.

The door of the Recruiting Office was wide open, the room inside bare and empty except for a row of wooden chairs and a desk behind which sat an ATS sergeant.

'Er – hello,' Carrie whispered.

'Hello,' the sergeant smiled. 'Can I help you?'

'Yes please.' She was surprised her voice should sound so croaky.

'Then take a pew.' The sergeant was still smiling.

'That was a lovely supper, Auntie Mim.' Nan wiped dry the pan she had just scrubbed.

'Good of you to get the fish.'

It had been a very small piece of haddock, but her aunt had made it into fishcakes, followed by bread and butter pudding, conjured up from a little milk, the egg from Nan's ration card, the remains of a loaf and two precious prunes, chopped into tiny pieces to resemble currants.

'And good of you, lass, to help with the washing up.'

'Think nothing of it.' Nan had done all the dish-washing and pan-scrubbing at Cyprian Court, with never a word of thanks. She settled herself in the kitchen rocker, pink-cheeked at the compliment.

Miriam Simpson took out her knitting. It was all very cosy, Nan was bound to admit; like it would have been at Cyprian Court if Mum hadn't died. She wondered if the Queer One was having trouble getting Georgie to go to bed on his own, and hoped he was being a right little sod. She waited until her aunt had finished counting stitches, then said,

'There's something I want to ask you – about Mum and Dad . . . Did they have to get married?' The words came out in a rush.

'Nobody *has* to do anything, lass – but what made you ask? I thought you'd have known.'

'Well, I didn't. Not till yesterday. They were married three months before I was born. It was a shock, I can tell you.'

'Does it matter when? You were born in wedlock. That's all that need concern you.'

'Yes, but I didn't think dad was the sort to get a girl into trouble, then take six months to make an honest woman of her. I thought better about him than that, if you must know.'

'Oh dearie me.' Miriam laid her knitting on her lap, then folded her hands over it, staring into the empty fire grate. 'Now see here Nan, you're almost a grown up and for better or for worse, you've decided to branch out on your own and join the Army. So I reckon you should know the truth of it, because I don't want you to think ill of your father – and that was what he became, the minute he married your mother.'

'Became?' Nan whispered.

'That's right. Will Morrissey had always cared for your mother – was willing to wed her. He gave you his name, and you should be thankful for it.'

'So am I to be told who my real father was?' Nan's heart thudded, her mouth so dry it was difficult to speak.

'No you aren't, because we never knew. Your mother refused to tell anyone, even Will, who'd been decent enough to marry her. All I know was that she went to her wedding with a hundred pounds in her pocket and a house full of furniture. She was lucky. A lot of women in her predicament got nothing!'

'Ar.' Still dazed, Nan filled a glass at the kitchen tap and drank deeply. 'A hundred pounds was a lot of money in them days.'

'It still is. Whoever it was fathered you, Nan, was of moneyed folk.'

'And where was Mum when it – when *I* happened?'

'Working for a ship-owning family in Liverpool. She was a sort of companion-help to the old mother, I believe. Didn't you know?'

She hadn't known, but it all added up Nan thought, wiping the glass, returning it to the shelf. A hundred pounds and enough furniture to fill the house in Cyprian Court would mean nothing to the likes of them.

'And nobody ever found out?' she persisted.

'No. Your mother could be the stubborn one. Why she had to go to Liverpool to work, heaven only knows. You're like her, Nan. Rushing off to join the Army, I mean.'

'But I was never like her in looks, Auntie Mim.'

'True. You must've favoured your – the other side. Your mother was fair, as well you know.'

Her sister's child, Miriam pondered, had very little to commend her. If you wanted to be brutal, Nan was very ordinary, but for one thing. She had the most beautiful brown eyes, and lashes so long a film star would have killed for them. Those eyes lifted her out of the ordinary.

'So I won't ever know?'

'Not from me, Nan, and not from poor Will, who knew nothing, anyway. You'll just have to accept – well – that –'

'That I'm illegitimate. A bastard.'

'Now that's enough! Whilst you are under my roof, miss, you will *not* use bad language. And you are *not* one of those! You were born in wedlock, so that makes you legitimate – in the eyes of the law, anyway!'

'So my mother wasn't good enough for my real father – is that it?'

'I don't know, I swear it, Nan, so the whole thing is best forgotten.'

'So if I hadn't asked about my birth certificate, would you have told me, Auntie Mim?'

'No. Don't think I would've, if only out of respect for your father – for Will. He was a decent man.'

'He was. Did any job he could lay his hand to; never had reg'lar work, till the war started. That was when he got a porter's job at the hospital. That's why he was killed that night, him and sixty others. I hate Hitler. And I'm sorry I thought wrong about Dad.'

'Then as long as you think of him as your dad like he intended, I know he'll forgive you. So how about putting the kettle on? I reckon we deserve a cup of tea after all that soul-searching. Only the little pot – and don't go mad with the tea leaves.'

Indiscriminate tea drinking was not to be encouraged on the miserly rations folk had to make do with, but tonight it was medicinal, Miriam Simpson decided.

Nan lit the gas with a plop and put the kettle to boil, busying herself with cups and saucers and all the time thinking about that birth certificate and being stupid enough to land herself with another worry. Because being illegitimate *was* a worry, no matter which way her aunt put it.

'Y'know – it's like I said. Once I'm in uniform I'll be the same as all the others, won't I?'

'You will, so don't be going on about it. None of it was your fault.' She picked up her knitting. 'New beginnings for you, that's what it'll be. And shift yourself with that tea, lass!'

'Mother?' Hesitantly, Carrie Tiptree pushed open the kitchen door. 'My, but something smells good.'

'Very little meat and lots of onions.' She said it without glancing up from the pan she was stirring.

'Can't wait. I'm ravenous. Any letters for me?' She was amazed her voice sounded so normal.

'There was nothing from Jeffrey, if that's what you mean, Caroline. But I wrote to him today. I mean, someone has to tell him what you're thinking of doing. He's your fiancé – he has a right to know!'

'But don't you think you should have let *me* tell him? And yes, he *is* my fiancé, but he can't forbid me to do anything. Not yet. And why is it so awful to think about joining up? Is it wrong, mother, to be patriotic?'

'Patriotism is all very well, but it didn't do a lot for your poor father, did it? But I don't want to talk about it. I had my say last night and I won't budge. You're still a minor and I won't give my permission for you to go.'

'All right, then. But please, let's not you and I quarrel. I'm sorry if I have upset you.'

'Oh, I know you are, darling.' Janet Tiptree was magnanimous in victory. 'Just wait till the Government sends for you, eh? After all, you might well be married before your age group comes up for registration and married women can't be made to do war work.'

'They *can*, mother, but they can't be made to leave home. But I'm going upstairs to take my shoes off. I had to stand all the way home on the bus, and my feet hurt.'

'Do that dear, and wash your hands. I'm going to dish up, now. And try to understand that I only want what is best for you? You are all I have in the world. Don't leave me just yet?'

'I won't. Not just yet . . .' she called.

She took off her shoes and placed them neatly beneath her bedside chair, took off her stockings and wriggled her feet into her slippers. Then she went to the wash basin in the corner of the room and stared into the mirror.

Later, she would tell her mother. She would have to, because she had done something so deceitful that now, when she thought about it, for a few fleeting seconds she wished she had not done it.

But she *had* done it, and anyway, she shrugged, by the time the ATS got around to sending for her, she would be as near to twenty-one as made no matter, so why was she having second thoughts?

24

At lunchtime, at the recruiting office, she had had no doubts at all; not until the sergeant had handed back her application form.

'You will, of course, have to get this counter-signed by your next-of-kin. I know you will soon be of age, but it's best that you do. Just in case we are able to process you fairly quickly, I mean.'

'H-how quickly,' Carrie had asked.

'W-e-e-ll, you did say you can drive and we are recruiting drivers as a matter of priority. That is why we need your father's signature. Is there anything to prevent you joining within a couple of months, say? Always provided you are medically fit, that is.'

'N-no. Nothing. And my mother is my next-of-kin.'

'So take this form home, get her to sign and date it, then post it back to us. I'll give you an envelope – OK?'

And Caroline Tiptree, of the glib tongue and unflinching gaze, had said that would be fine, and tucked it into her handbag and smiled a goodbye, even though it made her heart thud just to think of what she would do.

Mind, it had taken a little courage, when she got back to the bank, to borrow a colleague's fountain pen and write *Janet L. Tiptree (Mother)* beside her own signature, then add the date – 13.5.41. And she had slipped out and posted it in the pillar box outside the bank, just in case she had second thoughts.

'And that,' she whispered to her flush-faced mirror image, 'is that.'

No going back, now. The buff envelope with On His Majesty's Service printed across the top, was already on its way and Caroline Tiptree was a step nearer to joining the Auxiliary Territorial Service.

Now, there was only her mother to tell – and Jeffrey, of course – and that, she thought as she washed and dried her hands, was going to take some doing.

Oh, my word, yes!

TWO

Life at Farthing Street could be a whole lot worse Nan was bound to admit, especially since her aunt managed to put a reasonable meal on the table most days.

'Filling if not fattening,' she had said of the Woolton pie they ate for supper that evening, made entirely of unrationed ingredients. Packed with vegetables, topped with a crust made from the piece of suet Nan had queued for at the butcher's on the corner, and moistened with gravy made from an Oxo cube, it was a triumph of ingenuity.

To Miriam Simpson's delight, Nan was very successful in queues. Since they had decided it wasn't worth her while looking for a job – for who would employ a young woman, knowing she was soon to be called into the Armed Forces? – she was free to hunt for under-the-counter food. It saved Miriam's feet and helped pass the days which Nan mentally ticked off as one nearer her entry into the Auxiliary Territorial Service.

'Shall we have fish and chips tomorrow,' she asked. 'I'll get there good and early.'

Neither fish nor chips were rationed. The government, in one of its wiser moments, had seen to it that they remained so. A housewife who once would never have dreamed of entering a fried fish and chip shop, now queued eagerly for them, especially on Fridays, when rations were running low.

'And you can go to the butcher's on Saturday, Nan.' Her niece did far better out of the old skinflint than *she* had ever done, especially in the under-the-counter suet and sausages department. It was probably, she thought, because the girl looked at him with her big eyes, then fluttered those eyelashes for good measure. 'Tell him that anything at all would be much appreciated.'

'A leg of lamb?' Nan giggled, to which her aunt replied that she had just seen a purple pig fly past the top of the street! Legs of lamb, indeed!

'When do you think you'll hear from the ATS, then?'

'Dunno, Auntie Mim. Once I've had my medical, they might send for me pretty sharpish. I asked the corporal to do what she could for me. Fingers crossed there'll be a letter in the morning.' A buff envelope with no stamp on it, and O H M S printed across the top.

She switched on the wireless, settling herself in the fireside rocker, tapping her toes in time to the dance music, thinking that if she wasn't so set on joining the Army and Auntie Mim had a spare bed, of course, Farthing Street would have suited her nicely for the duration.

Oh, hurry up buff envelope, do!

On Saturday night, the telephone in Jackmans Cottage rang.

'It's for you.' Janet Tiptree, who always picked up the phone, handed it to her daughter. 'Jeffrey,' she mouthed.

'Darling,' Carrie whispered, startled. 'How lovely of you to –'

'Caroline – *listen*! I've been hanging about outside the phonebox for ages waiting for this call to come through and we only have three minutes, so what are you thinking about, joining up! If you must do something so stupid, why not join the Wrens? And why did I have to hear it from your mother? Surely I merit *some* consideration?'

There was a small uneasy silence that seemed to last an age, then she said,

'I – I – well, I was going to tell you Jeffrey and anyway, nothing is settled, yet.'

'I should damn well hope not. We're supposed to be getting married when I've finished my training – well, *aren't* we?'

'Y-yes,' was all she could say, because she could hear his angry breathing and besides, there wasn't a lot she could say to the contrary in three minutes. 'But please don't speak to me like that? And I'm sorry you are upset. I'll write, shall I? A nice long letter . . . ?'

'The only letter I want from you is telling me you've forgotten all about the ATS. Did you have a brainstorm, or something?'

'N-no!' Oh, why did she let him boss her around so? 'And thank you for ringing, Jeffrey,' she hastened when the warning pips pinged stridently in her ear. 'Take care of yourself. I'll write. Tonight.'

The line went dead, then began to buzz. She looked angrily at the receiver, then slammed it down.

'So? Your young man wasn't best pleased?' Janet Tiptree said softly, smugly.

'No, he wasn't. He yelled at me! How *dare* he! And you shouldn't have told him, mother. It wasn't up to you, you know!'

'Maybe not, but someone had to. Perhaps now you'll give a bit more thought to your wedding! You *are* engaged, or had you forgotten?'

'Of course I hadn't!' Being engaged, surely, was something you didn't forget, especially when you wore a ring on your left hand. 'Jeffrey and I *will* be married.'

They would. It was what getting engaged was about. But not just yet. Or would he bluster and bluff and demand, as he did the night her mother was out and they had done – *that*? She hadn't wanted to and it mustn't happen again, or next time she might get pregnant and her mother would have every excuse, then, to get them down the aisle at breakneck speed.

'Ah, yes.' Her mother interrupted her thoughts. 'But *when*?'

'When the war allows,' Carrie answered cagily, which was true, really, because now *her* war had to be taken into consideration.

She closed her eyes, wondering how she would face her mother when the letter telling her to report for her medical arrived; wondered, too, how she was to explain the forged signature on the bottom of her application form.

'Are we going to listen to the news, mother? Shall I switch on? It's nearly nine o'clock.'

It was all she could think of to say, dammit!

On May 24th, the newsreader announced in a graver than usual voice that HMS *Hood*, the biggest and fastest ship in the Royal Navy, had been sunk by the German battleship *Bismarck*, and only three from a crew of almost fifteen hundred had survived.

It was as if, Nan frowned, Hitler's lot could do what they wanted, even at sea. The *Hood* had been sunk, the morning paper reported, by one chance shell landing in the ship's magazine. Dead lucky, them *Jairmans!*

She rounded her mouth and slammed down her feet. She was on her way to the medical centre in Albion Street, and the sooner they pronounced her A1 fit, the sooner she would be in uniform, because this morning's terrible news made her all the more sure it was what she must do.

She pushed open the door. There was brown linoleum on the floor; the walls were green-painted. The place smelled of damp and disinfectant.

Nan was pointed to a cubicle, told to undress to the waist, put on the white cotton smock and wait to be called.

Someone examined her mouth and muttered, 'Two cavities,' and Nan was as sure as she could be that that meant fillings. She had never had fillings. Just to think of them made her flinch, because she had heard they were excruciatingly painful.

A doctor listened to her chest, counted her pulse rate, made muttered asides to the clerk beside him who wrote on a notepad.

She was told to get dressed again, hang the white cotton smock on the hook in the cubicle, then follow the nurse to the ablutions, where there were more cubicles.

'Please give a urine sample. In *this*.' A kidney dish was thrust at each young woman. 'Then you transfer it into *this*.' A small, wide-necked bottle. 'And try not to spill it on the floor. When you have provided your sample, you will take it to the desk, give it, together with your surname and initial, to the nurse there, and she will attach a label to the bottle. Oh, hurry along, *do*!'

Some looked shocked. Others giggled. A few blushed. Nan thought it was a lot of fuss over a bottle of wee, but she supposed they knew what they were doing.

'There was one girl there who couldn't do it,

so they stood her in front of a running cold water tap, but it made no difference,' Nan told Auntie Mim that evening. 'She's got to go back tomorrow and have another try, poor thing.'

'And do you think you have passed?'

'I reckon so. They said if we weren't told to report back within three days, we could take it that we were OK, so it's fingers crossed.'

'And you still want to go, Nan?'

'Yes, I do. Let's hope I'm on my way before your lodger comes back.'

'You'll have to sleep on the sofa in the parlour if you aren't, young woman.'

Nan hoped she would be in uniform before then. The parlour sofa was hard and stuffed with horse-hair.

'Can we run to a cup of tea?' she asked. 'In celebration, sort of, of me bein' half way there.'

'We've been having too many cups of tea lately, miss. But there's cocoa on the shelf, if you fancy that. And make it with dried milk.' Cocoa was unrationed when you could get it, as was powdered milk, in a blue metallic tin. 'Can't get those sailors on HMS *Hood* out of my mind,' she whispered, picking up her knitting which usually soothed her. 'There'll be all those women getting telegrams, poor souls.'

'Yes, but I'll bet you anything you like that Winston Churchill's fightin' mad. I'll bet he's rung them up at the Admiralty, and told them to get that bluddy *Bismarck*!'

'I hope he has, and I hope they do,' Miriam said without even reminding her niece that swearing was not allowed at Number 16. 'Sink it before it can get back into port!'

And could they have known it, the entire North Atlantic fleet was already hunting, enraged, for the German ship, and before four more days had run, *Bismarck* would be sunk. An eye for an eye, people would say it was.

Four days later, Caroline Tiptree picked up the letters that fell on the doormat at Jackmans Cottage.

'Post,' she called, chokily, pushing a buff OHMS envelope into her coat pocket. 'Only one. For you, mother.'

Then she ran up the garden path and down the road to the bus stop, all at once apprehensive. Because the buff OHMS envelope could mean only one thing.

She collapsed on the wooden seat in the bus shelter, asking herself if joining the ATS was such a good idea after all, and knowing there was nothing she could do now, except fail the medical. Which she wouldn't.

She rose shakily to her feet as the bright red bus rounded the corner, wondering where she would be in August when Jeffrey came on leave and praying that it was miles and miles from Nether Hutton.

But it wasn't August she should be worrying

about, was it? It was when she must tell her mother about the buff OHMS envelope. Not tonight, of course. Afterwards, perhaps, when she knew she was medically fit, or perhaps when her calling-up papers came would be the best time, because then her mother wouldn't be able to do anything about the forged signature.

But what had she done? What had made her do such a thing when she knew that soon, anyway, she would have to register for military service? Couldn't she have waited just a few more months?

'No, Caroline Tiptree, you could not,' whispered the small voice of reason in her ear. 'You know that if you are around when Jeffrey comes home in August, your mother will have arranged a wedding, and you will go along with it as you always do!'

But not any longer! Oh, she loved Jeffrey and there *would* be a wedding, nothing was more certain. But when the time came it would be she, Caroline, who would name the day.

Sorry, mother, she said in her mind, I have done the most awful, deceitful thing, and you'll have every right to hit the roof when you find out about it.

And sorry, Jeffrey, too, but just this once I was doing what I want to do. How it would turn out she dare not think, and what Nether Hutton would make of her slipping away to be an ATS girl would take a bit of facing up to, as well. Little villages were like that. People knew everyone, and their ancestry, too. What *The Village* thought was very important, and Mrs Frobisher – as well as her own mother – had left people in Nether Hutton in no doubt that a wedding was in the offing, just as soon as the Royal Navy allowed.

She handed a florin to the conductress, said 'One-and-three return, please,' then stared fixedly out of the window to wonder, yet again, where she would be in mid-August? In uniform, perhaps? Or if she were lucky, driving an Army truck? And thinking about the fuss and bother at Jackmans Cottage there had been when her deceit came to light.

The bus stopped at the crossroads and the young woman who always got on smiled and said 'Morning,' as she usually did, then sat down beside her. The buff OHMS envelope was still in Carrie's pocket. No chance of opening it, now, thanks be.

'Mm,' she smiled back. 'Looks like being a lovely day . . .'

Which was, of course, the understatement of the week!

THREE

On the day the buff OHMS envelope arrived, it lay unopened in Carrie's jacket pocket until ten that morning. Medical in four days' time she read, dry-mouthed, in the privacy of the ladies' lavatory. Friday, May 30 at 12.30. And since her lunch hour began at 12.15, it would save the embarrassment of having to ask the head cashier for an hour off work, and being obliged to tell him why she wanted it! She had wondered where she would be when Jeffrey's leave began some time in August, and now she knew.

The time – ten days from the end of her initial training as a motor transport driver; the place – with the Royal Army Service Corps, somewhere in Wiltshire, and new recruit though she had been, she knew better than to ask for compassionate leave. You only got compassionate when it concerned husbands, or already-arranged weddings. You did not get it, especially in the middle of a training course, for a fiancé or wedding dates that might have been!

There had been a hurt letter from her mother and another from Jeffrey, telling her that the entire village was talking about her behaviour and asking were they or were they not supposed to be getting married? But distance gave her courage and she had replied in sweet relief, telling him that next time she was sure they could both come up with a date to suit everyone – and that she loved him, of course.

So now, on this last-day-but-one of August she stood in Lincoln station, kitbag beside her, respirator over her shoulder and with her, three equally curious ATS privates and a lance corporal. They had met up on the platform. Draft HP4. Report to the RTO on arrival at Lincoln, said their travel instructions.

There was a Railway Transport Office on all main railway stations, their purpose to aid the passage of servicemen and women and goods of military importance from Point A to Point B

'I think I'll see the bod in the RTO,' said the lance corporal, who had quickly ascertained she was the only one with rank up, and even one stripe entitled her to take charge. 'They'll know where we go from here.'

She had quickly returned.

'He says he hasn't a clue where HP4 is. All he said was, "Oh. So you'll be one of *them* . . ."'

He had settled his pencil behind his right ear and pulled out a list from beneath a pile of time-tables.

'All he knew, he said, was that he was expecting a draft of five, and when we'd all arrived he had a number to ring, so we could be collected. And he said to nip out smartly, because the WVS trolley was expected any time now and we were to get ourselves a cup of tea. We might be in for a long wait, he said.'

It was almost an hour after they had eaten beetroot sandwiches and drunk large mugs of tea – offered with the most kindly smiles – that an Army corporal, the stripes on his arms brilliantly white with Blanco, clumped past them and into the RTO, then clumped out almost at once, to confront the group.

'Draft HP4, are you? Let's be seeing your warrants, then!'

'Where are we going?' the lance-corporal wanted to know.

'That, young lady, is not for you to ask, not with one stripe up it isn't. So let's be having you. There's a transport outside, so collect your kit and get on board. The sooner we get going the sooner you'll know, won't you?' he said with the satisfaction of someone who knew something they did not. 'And you're in for the shock of your lives,' he added.

They sat on low wooden benches in the back of the Army lorry, holding tightly to the metal struts supporting the camouflaged canvas roof and had soon left Lincoln behind. Now they drove through open country with hedges and pastures and fields yellow with the stubble of newly-harvested wheat and barley.

Carrie gazed out over the tailboard to see flat countryside and a wide, open sky. Farming country, this, and not unlike the fields around Nether Hutton. She steadied herself as the lorry braked suddenly.

'Hang on!' called the driver, swinging into a narrow lane. 'Nearly there now, girls.'

They dropped speed and climbed a small hill. Ahead was a wood and a church; to their right a gate lodge outside which a sergeant waved her arms. They stopped with a skidding squeal, then reversed.

'How-do, sergeant. Got a load of trouble for you!'

'Have you now!' She stood, hands on hips, glaring into the back of the transport. Wide-eyed, draft HP4 stared back.

'Right, then! I am Sergeant James.' She consulted a pencilled list. 'Tiptree, Morrissey and Lance-Corporal Turner, stay where you are. The other two follow me. This is your billet – for the time being. It's called Priest's Lodge and don't take the downstairs front – that's mine. If you shift your-selves and get settled in, you just might be in time for supper. Hang on a minute,' she called to the driver. 'Won't be long.'

Five minutes later, she swung herself into the back of the transport with the ease of an acrobat.

'OK, driver. Southgate Lodge!'

They bumped downhill and stopped at an even smaller lodge, standing beside gateposts of stone. It was pretty and ornate and everything the private with the Liverpool accent had ever imagined a country cottage to be. Roses grew around the door; late-flowering honeysuckle wound itself around iron railings.

'Ar – innit a lovely diddy house.'

'It's sort of – cute,' the lance-corporal was forced to admit. 'Haven't ever had a billet like this, before.'

'Diddy, cute – well, don't get too fond of it,' the sergeant snapped.

'With luck you'll be in a Nissen hut before so very much longer – where I can keep an eye on the lot of you!'

Instead of, she thought grimly, spread all over the place and out of her reach!

'Now – this is Southgate Lodge. Up that drive is none of our business, because up that drive leads to Heronflete Priory. The lane to your right takes you to the QM stores, the NAAFI, the cook-house, the mess hall and the ablutions. Supper at six, then muster immediately after, so unpack your kit and have everything ready in case I decide on an inspection – OK?'

And with that she strode away, arms swinging, heels hitting the ground purposefully, sending dust flying.

'I think,' smiled the lance-corporal, 'that Sergeant James isn't very happy with the way things are here. And I'm Evelyn Turner, SBO-tele-phones. Evie.'

'And I'm Nan Morrissey, teleprinters. Pleased to meet you, I'm sure.'

'Caroline Tiptree, driver. Call me Carrie.'

'Fine! So shall we take a look?'

The squat front door opened directly onto a small room. On two walls were leaded windows; on another, a fireplace. And taking up most of the space were two black iron beds and two brand-new lockers.

Evie opened a door to her left to find an even smaller room with one window, one black iron bed and one brand-new locker.

'Looks like this one will suit me nicely. You two can kip together. And I get first choice because this,' she pointed to the stripe on her arm, 'says that just sometimes I can pull rank!' She took off her cap and jacket and laid them on the bed. 'Now – what else have we got?'

A low door led into a very small kitchen. It had two shelves, a corner cupboard and a white sink with a single tap, which she turned. At least there was water.

'Let's do a reccy outside.'

At the bottom of a small garden, overgrown with grass and brambles, were two brick sheds. One housed a water closet, the slab floor thick with dead leaves. She pulled the rusted chain and water gushed from the cistern.

'Good grief,' Carrie breathed. 'All mod cons.'

'At least it works,' said Nan who was used, anyway, to having an outside toilet.

'I think, though,' Caroline frowned, 'that we'll be expected to use the ablutions up the lane.'

'Yes, but this one will be smashin' for emergencies. I mean, are we expected to hike up that lane for a wee in the blackout an' all, in winter?'

'I don't think we'll be here, Nan. We'll be moved to a hut before so very much longer, if the sergeant gets her way.' Evie pushed open the second door.

It was a coalhouse. In one corner was a pile of logs; in the other, a small heap of coal. A bow saw hung on the wall, a bucket and shovel beneath it. On a shelf, a clutter of dusty jam jars.

'Hey up! There's a fireplace in our room,' Nan beamed. 'Reckon we'll be able to have a bit of warmth when the weather gets cold. Will we be allowed to, Evie?'

'Don't know, but don't get too fond of this billet. By the time the cold weather comes we could be in a Nissen hut with a coke stove, if we're lucky.'

'Well, I'd rather stay where we are, stove or not,' Carrie sighed. 'Southgate Lodge is a lovely little place.'

'Then let's wait and see. And don't say anything about the coal and logs, or someone will have them carted off sharpish!' Evie said, with a year's knowledge of Army life behind her. 'And I think we'd better unpack and make up our beds. We've got an hour . . .'

*　　*　　*

'All right! Settle down, girls.'

Four ATS privates and a lance-corporal, having eaten toad-in-the-hole with onion gravy, followed by sago pudding, were by now nicely relaxed and willing to give the sergeant their full attention.

'You'll be thinking, I shouldn't wonder, that our circumstances are a little – er – different, and they are. We've been landed on what was some lord's private estate – the War Office having turfed him out first.

'The house is called Heronflete Priory, and before some bright spark asks if you'll be required to act like nuns, let me assure you that the priory was pulled down over a hundred years ago, when the present place was built.

'Round about the estate are various houses, all empty now, and a few cottages and lodges once lived in by estate workers. Life will seem a little complicated at first, but things will be sorted, never fear. So – this far – any questions?'

'Yes, sergeant.' A tall girl whose uniform was in need of alteration got to her feet. 'I don't understand any of it. Just what are we supposed to do, here? What kind of a set-up is this?'

'It's – we-e-ll . . . Now see here, you're going to have to learn to keep your eyes down and your mouths shut. The *set-up*, as far as I can make out, commandeered the Heronflete estate in a bit of a hurry. I don't know who they are, or where they are from; if they were bombed out of London or whether they chose to come here because of the

44

isolation. But the Priory is out of bounds until we are told otherwise. We and the soldiers who guard the place, are here as backup. I've been told the switchboard and teleprinters are now installed, so tomorrow we start shifts.'

'But what is our address? We need to write home.'

'Address – 4 Platoon, D Company, Royal Corps of Signals, c/o GPO London. No mention of this place, or anything. And you will post your letters in the box provided in the NAAFI, unsealed, so they can be censored and –'

'*Censored*? Somebody's going to read our private mail?'

'Yes, but the censoring will be confidential, so don't for a minute think anybody is one bit interested in your love letters, or what you write in them. Nothing will be blue-pencilled unless it refers directly or indirectly to Heronflete. And what is more, you will not discuss this place when you are away from it – not when on leave, nor in pubs, dancehalls or cinemas or anywhere else.'

'So they're going to let us out from time to time, sergeant?'

'Watch it!' The sergeant did not allow sarcasm. 'Of course you'll be *let out*. You'll have your time on shift and your free time, and just as any other out-of-the-way unit, transport will be laid on. The only way in which things are different is that this place seems to be a bit of a mystery, as yet.'

'*Seems*, Sergeant? Don't you know, then?'

'I've been told – *things* – and doubtless I will be told more. But for the time being, watch what you say and what you write. If it's of any interest, your letters will not need stamps. And that's just about it for the time being. I'll show you round. The mess hall and cookhouse you already know, and where the NAAFI is. In the ablutions you will also find facilities for doing your personal washing and drying.

'I do not want to see items of an intimate nature or even shirts hanging on lines behind billets. You can send seven items of clothing to the laundry each week. All else, you will hang in the drying room off the ablutions.

'So chop-chop!' She walked to the door, then turned, eyes narrowed. 'And smarten up! Caps on and look lively, or I'll line you up and you can all march around the place!'

'Y'know, this estate is lovely,' Evie Turner sighed. 'I wouldn't like anyone to take it off me if it were mine.'

'Then, if you ask *me*,' Nan flopped on her bed, 'any feller what has so much deserves to have it took off him!'

'Nan Morrissey! You're a communist!'

'Nah. Just believe in fair shares for all. Them houses we've just seen, f'r instance. It's just like a little village and it all belonged to his lordship. Now me, I come from a grotty dump, with an outside lavvy and muck and soot all over every-thing. It's goin' to be like living in the country as far as I'm concerned, and it wouldn't bother me if I stayed here for the duration.'

Southgate Lodge looked almost lived in, Carrie thought, now beds were made up and photographs arranged on locker tops. And a jamjar filled with roses and honeysuckle on the mantelpiece.

'Well, I'm going to write to Bob,' Evie smiled.

'Your husband?' Nan had noticed the lance-corporal's wedding ring. 'Where is he?'

'RAF. Overseas – the Middle East, I'm almost sure. We got married on his embarkation leave. Seven days of heaven, as the song goes, then back to the ATS again. You two got boyfriends?'

'Not me. Wasn't allowed to go out with fellers. Had to stay at home and look after me brother – *stepbrother* –' Nan amended firmly. 'My real mum died and me dad married again. Then he got killed in the bombing, so I wasn't stoppin'. Shoved off to mum's sister in Leeds. Me Auntie Mim. Best thing I ever did; that, and joining up.'

'So life in the ATS suits you?' Carrie liked the frankly-spoken girl with beautiful eyes.

'You bet! Bed and board and no clothing coupons to worry about. Pay day every fortnight, and every brass farthing of it mine! But what about you, Carrie? Courting, are you?'

'I'm – er – engaged, actually. Jeffrey. He's in the Navy.'

'And he didn't buy you a ring? It's unofficial, then?'

'No. I've got a ring. But there was so much

dirty work to do when I was training that I put it with my identity tag around my neck. Afraid it's still there.'

'Ar. I see . . .'

Nan did not see. If she had an engagement ring, no way would she shove it out of sight. 'And I'll take the letters to the post when you've written them, if you like. I'll just do a quick one to Auntie Mim – let her know I've landed on me feet.'

For never before had Nan Morrissey seen so many trees and hedgerows, nor heard birds singing so loudly and so late, nor picked roses and honeysuckle to scent this diddy little room in this diddy little house, she thought with pure affection.

'It's smashing here, Dad.' She sent her thoughts high and wide. *'You're not to worry about me one bit, 'cause I'm living in the country, now, like I always wanted to . . .'*

She hoped he could hear her. She thought reluctantly about the Queer One in Cyprian Court and about Georgie, then blanked them from her mind as if they had never existed.

Dear Auntie Mim,
    This is to let you know my new address so you can write to me. I think I will be here for some time; wouldn't mind being here for the duration, it is so nice. Just three of us in a billet like a doll's house. I'll write more, later. Please write back to me, soon.
                    Love, Nan X X

'Well, that's mine written.' She laid the envelope on the windowsill. 'Think I'll have a bit of a walk, till youse two have finished.'

Remembering to put on her cap she walked down the front path, taking deep breaths of air, marvelling at her luck, and though she had not grasped just what she would be doing here, she was content to be part of a set-up that was as different as could be from the barracks she had reported to, and the just as awful teleprinter training school. All bull it had been, and everything at the double.

Here, it was as if life had slowed down now the hectic weeks of her training were over, though not even in her dreams had she thought to be sent to such a place.

The gateposts either side of the drive that led to Heronflete were ornately patterned in stone and there had obviously been gates there. Probably, Nan thought, taken away to be melted down for war weapons, like gates and railings all over the country. The government in London took anything they wanted; for the war effort, they said, and if you told them it wasn't on, they took not one blind bit of notice, and accused you of being unpatriotic!

She thought about the lord, and if he had been a bit miffed when the War Office took his house and all the estate, and it made her wonder what had happened to the workers and the farmers and their animals, because they had had to get out, too.

A funny old war, you had to admit, but she was glad she had joined it and met up with Evie and Carrie, though Sergeant James was a bit of a martinet, Nan brooded.

She gazed up a wide driveway with oak trees on either side and which turned abruptly to the left about two hundred yards on. Round that bend she might be able to see Heronflete, even though one big, empty house was probably the same as another. It intrigued her, though, for the simple reason that they had been told it was none of their business, though if it were none of their business, why was she and four others – and the sergeant an' all – here in the first place?

The gravel of the drive crunched beneath her feet so she stepped onto the verge, walking slowly, carefully. The grass was damp with evening dew, and long. Probably because there were no gardeners now, to cut it. Must have upset a lot of people, having to pack up and find somewhere else to live. Not fair, really, but what was fair, when you thought, about a war?

She reached the curve in the drive and crouched in the shelter of the trees. Just a quick peep. See what all the mystery was about.

'You there! Halt!' yelled a voice behind her.

She swung round, gasping at the sight of a soldier holding a rifle, and though he wasn't pointing it at her, she was all at once afraid.

'What are you doing here, then? What's your name, girl?'

'304848 Morrissey N,' she gasped, eyes wide. 'Didn't mean to intrude. Was getting a bit of country air.'

'All right. I believe you. But somebody ought to have told you that up here is out of bounds.'

He jabbed a forefinger at a red and white barrier and the sentry boxes either side of it.

'I'm sorry. You won't say nuthin' to Sergeant James, will you? I'll be in dead trouble if you do.' Nan fixed him with a wide-eyed stare.

'Is that what she's called? Her that goes around thinking she can give orders, you mean? Face that'd crack, if she smiled?'

'That sounds exactly like our sergeant,' Nan breathed. 'I don't want to land myself in trouble, first day here. You'll not tell on me? I won't ever come up here again.'

'You can come up this drive, but only if you have a pass saying it's all right, 'cause you'll have to get past me and my mate over there, and we're very particular who we let in! Now on yer way, girlie, and don't try it on again without permission or you'll be on a charge – see?'

'Yes. Much obliged, I'm sure.'

Nan turned and ran, not caring about the noisy gravel, still shocked by the sentry, and his gun.

'Hey, you two!' She burst breathless into the lodge. 'Up that drive! There's sentry boxes and soldiers and one of them copped me, peepin' through the trees. Came up behind me with a gun, and –'

'Nan, you idiot! Weren't we told it was none of our business? Now you'll be in trouble.'

'No I won't, Evie. He said he wouldn't tell on me – this time. An' he said you can get up there, but only if you have a pass.'

'So did you get a look at the place?' Evie asked.

'No, I didn't, and I'm not trying it on again. I didn't expect to get caught but they're there, where the drive turns suddenly. Barrier across it, an' all.'

'Then it must be very secret if they've got guards there.' Carrie folded the single sheet of notepaper and tucked it into an envelope addressed to Jackmans Cottage. 'I've finished, now. Just quick notes to mother and Jeffrey. Maybe I'll come with you to the post. You finished, Evie?'

'Mm. Just the envelope to see to . . .'

My darling,

To let you know my new address and to tell you that I love you, love you, love you. I'll write, tomorrow, to explain in great and loving detail just how much, and how desperately I miss you and want you.

Take care, Bob. You are so precious to me.

She printed the PO address on the back of the envelope then, placing it to her lips, gave it to Nan.

'Bless you, love. I won't be long from my bed. And I'm not hiking to the ablutions, either. I'll make do with a quick wash at the kitchen tap and a walk down the garden. Don't be too long, will you – just in case the sergeant decides to check up on us.'

'I'm going to like Evie,' Carrie said as they took the right turning to where the cluster of buildings stood. 'Poor love. Just seven days of being married, then heaven only knows when they'll see each other again.'

'So when are *you* getting married, Carrie?'

'Don't ask! I'm already in trouble for not setting a date for the wedding.'

'So why don't you want to get married? And why aren't you wearing your ring? Have you and your feller had a nark, or sumthin'?'

'N-no. It's just that everybody seems to be pressuring me into it, and I want a bit of breathing space.'

'Why?' Nan could think of nothing nicer than being married to a man who was decent enough to buy a ring, and make things official. 'I'd like to be married – when I'm a bit older, I mean.'

'And I want to marry Jeffrey, but when *I* want to. And I want to be one hundred per cent sure.'

'And you aren't?' Nan sensed drama.

'No. About ninety-five per cent, I'd say.'

She wished she could tell Nan why; that she was unsure about the really-being-married side of things, and that Jeffrey hadn't been very considerate when *that* happened. But Nan was little more than a child. Hardly eighteen, if looks were anything to go by. It wouldn't be right to talk about *that* to her. Mind, she had the most beautiful come-to-bed eyes, though she didn't seem aware of it; eyes that could get an innocent like Nan into trouble, if she wasn't careful.

'Then you're nearly there, wouldn't you say,' Nan laughed.

'Almost. Jeffrey's next leave, perhaps. Isn't this the most beautiful evening?' Time to talk of other things! 'If we weren't in uniform, we could be forgiven for thinking that there isn't a war on at all, out there.'

'Ar,' Nan sighed, completely captivated. 'Wouldn't mind stoppin' for ever.'

Here, in a place almost hidden from sight or sound of war, was a different life. Here, there would be no wailing sirens to send fear shivering through her; no crowded, sweaty air-raid shelters nor whole streets blasted into rubble. And no hospitals bombed.

Here, Nan Morrissey was as good as anyone else; her uniform saw to that. Here, no one seemed to worry about her accent nor the way her Liverpool bluntness might be misconstrued as rudeness. This set-up that seemed to baffle even Sergeant James was the right and proper place for her to be. It seemed, on this evening in late August, that Nan Morrissey had truly come home.

'Ar,' she sighed again. 'Just wish me dad could see me now. He'd be made up for me, God love him.'

'I'd like to think mine could see me, too. I never knew him, y'know.'

'Last war was it, Carrie?'

'Mm. He was badly hurt but it wasn't his wounds he died of. It was the mustard gas, really. A slow death, it must have been. God! I hope they never use it this time around.'

'Fighting dirty, poison gas is. Do you think them bods in Heronflete are up to something like that? Secret weapons, and that kind of thing?'

'Back-room boys and boffins, you mean?

'Dunno. But they're up to sumthin' or why all the mystery? You don't need soldiers to guard nuthin'.'

'They'll tell us, perhaps – or maybe we'll figure it out for ourselves. And it looks like Evie has fallen asleep and left her light on.' Carrie nodded in the direction of Southgate Lodge. 'Reckon we'd better see to the blackout, or Sergeant James'll be down on us like a ton of bricks.'

The lance-corporal had not fallen asleep. She lay on her bed in blue and white striped pyjamas, writing pad in hand.

'Hey up, Evie.' Nan made for the window. 'Time them curtains was drawn.'

'Sorry. Got carried away, writing to Bob. Couldn't sleep so I thought I'd write again – tell him about this new posting. What time is it?'

'Still not quite blackout time,' Carrie smiled. 'And I've drawn all the other curtains. Couldn't you sleep,

Evie, or were you waiting for us to get back?'

'No. Just got past it, I suppose. Posted the letters?'

'We did,' Nan beamed. 'There was hardly anybody in the NAAFI – just a few soldiers, playing cards. And had you thought – we're going to need cleaning gear. Better ask the sergeant for a chitty so we can get a brush and mop and things from stores – keep Southgate nice an' tidy, so she can't moan at us.'

'I'll see to it, tomorrow.' Evie placed the cap on her fountain pen. 'Y'know, this pen was Bob's. It's a good one and he didn't want to take it with him when he went. Said I was to have it. I write all his letters with it. And oh,' She closed her eyes tightly against tears. 'I do miss him.'

'Hey, old love, you'd be a very peculiar wife if you didn't.' Carrie took Evie's hands in her own, holding them tightly. 'And if talking about Bob helps, we'll be glad to listen, won't we Nan?'

'Course we will. And we'll send nasty thoughts to Hitler and that fat old Goering.' Especially Goering, because it was him sent the bombers to Liverpool; his fault dad was dead.

'Sorry,' Evie sniffed, dabbing her eyes, forcing a smile. 'You'll know how it is, Carrie.'

'Yes. Lousy . . .'

But was it all that bad? Had Carrie Tiptree ever been reduced to tears, just to think that Jeffrey had gone to war? Sad, granted, but never the obvious pain Evie felt.

Yet it was different for Evie and her Bob. They were husband and wife. Lovers. And that loving was good, it was plain to see by the softness in her eyes when she spoke about him. And Carrie knew when she was thinking about him, too. Perhaps Evie wasn't aware of it, but she often fondled her wedding ring with her fingertips. Carrie Tiptree's ring hung with the identity disc around her neck.

Mind, she was fond of Jeffrey – always had been. They'd grown up in the same village, for heaven's sake, and she knew almost all there was to know about him. No one would be able to say theirs was a hasty marriage.

She shrugged and began to undress. She would get into her pyjamas, clean her teeth and splash her face at the kitchen sink. Then go to bed, even if she lay awake for ages.

And she *would* lie awake, thinking about Jackmans and her mother and Jeffrey, too, because she had let them both down if she were to be completely honest. Her mother had given a little moan, then burst into sobs when told her daughter had had a medical and been accepted by the ATS, and there was nothing anyone could do about it, now.

Carrie remembered that night in vivid detail. A vase of roses on the little table beneath the window, petals reflected pink against the dark wood. An old copper jamming pan, placed on the hearth in the ingle fireplace, full of greenery. The soft armchairs, none of them matching. The fat cushions, made by her mother from remnants of bright material. She even remembered gazing at the ink stain they hadn't quite been able to remove from the hearthrug.

He mother had gone very pale, then moaned softly, a bewildered look on her face. Carrie thought she would faint, but then she had gasped,

'Oh, Carrie – such deceit. How *could* you? Why did you do it? I don't understand.'

Her distress had been genuine. Carrie laid an arm around her shoulders, but her mother had shrugged it off.

'You forged my signature, didn't you, on the form?'

'Yes, I did . . .'

'Then I shall tell them about it; that it's all been a mistake and you won't have to go!'

'It would be a waste of time, mother. I'll be twenty-one long before it's sorted.' Carrie's distress had been genuine, too.

'So tell me, Caroline, just what happened to make you do such a foolish thing, and to be so underhanded about it, too.'

'I don't know. I honestly don't. It was everything in general, sort of, and nothing in particular.'

Which was true, Carrie supposed, even though she had felt vague unease for a long time about the way her life was. And as for nothing in particular – she knew *exactly* what it was; the instinctive need to get away and have time to think; make sure that what her mother and Jeffrey's mother wanted was what she, Carrie, wanted too. The doubts first surfaced the night her mother had gone out to play whist, there was no denying it.

'You are all I have in the whole world, Carrie. Your place is at home, with me. And what am I to tell the village?'

'I don't think it's anything to do with them. It's between you and me and – and Jeffrey, I suppose . . .'

'Then tell me what I am to say to Ethel Frobisher? How will I be able to look her in the face?'

'You won't have to. I'll tell Jeffrey's mother. And as for the wedding – well, nothing was planned *exactly*.'

'No, but it was understood, I would have thought, the day Jeffrey gave you an engagement ring. Weddings usually follow, you know. And I don't feel at all well.'

She hadn't looked so good, Carrie recalled. That evening, there was genuine need for aspirin and a hot drink and it had been awful, afterwards, to lie awake, listening to her mother's sobs.

'Won't be a minute.' Carrie cleared her head of thoughts, making for the kitchen. And when she came back she said,

'Put your slippers on, Nan. That stone floor is cold! And I'll set the alarm for seven – that all right with you, Evie?'

And Evie said it was, but would they mind if she closed her bedroom door, and they said it was fine by them. After all, she did have a stripe up!

They didn't talk, though. Nan curled up in her bed like a contented puppy and was quickly asleep. Which left Carrie to wonder about what was to come and when she and Jeffrey would be able to arrange leaves to allow a wedding – because they *would* get married, she was as sure of it as she could be. Yet only when she had laid out her thoughts and doubts, and only when Jeffrey had truly understood and promised to talk about *things*, so that everything would come right for them. Then Caroline Tiptree – *Frobisher* – would have Evie's look of love in her eyes, too, when she spoke of her sailor husband.

She thumped her pillow peevishly, then settled down to listen to the night sounds because she knew sleep would not come easily. It never did, when you were desperately tired and in need of it.

She tried to think of Jeffrey, still in Plymouth barracks waiting for a draft to a ship, but could not, so instead she turned on her back and stared at the ceiling, telling herself that tomorrow was another day, a bright new start to her life as W/462523 Tiptree C. because that was who she was, now, for as long as the war lasted. A name and number.

Yet instead she sighed deeply and tried hard not to think of Jackmans Cottage and her bedroom with the sloping roof and tiny window – and the pigeon that nested in the tree in the lane outside and made a terrible noise as soon as daylight came.

A tear slipped from her eye and trickled down her cheek and into her ear. It made her annoyed to realize it was the first she had shed since leaving home almost two months ago.

She was not, she supposed, as tough as she had thought!

FOUR

Carrie, in search of Corporal Finnigan, found the motor pool in what had once been Heronflete's stable block. Three-sided, with a cobbled yard and approached through gateposts without gates, of course. On her right was what could only be stabling for several horses; ahead, a coach house with massive, wide-open doors; to her left a drab building with small windows and a low, narrow door. Had grooms once lived there, Carrie wondered, and ostlers and stable lads in the old glory days?

She heard the clump of boots and turned to see the driver of yesterday's transport who had warned them they were going to get the shock of their lives. He looked more human in grease-stained overalls.

'Corporal Finnigan? I – I'm the new driver.'

'You'll be Tiptree C, then?'

'Yes, Corporal. Carrie. And you were right, yesterday. This place *was* a shock, but a nice one.'

'Nice? Stuck at the back of beyond, living in civilian houses and a motor pool that would make a cat laugh! Take a look at that!' He jabbed a finger into the deeps of the coach house. 'One pesky transport, one car – officers-for-the-use-of – and one pick-up truck. You'll be driving that round the estate, Tiptree, collecting girls for shifts, I shouldn't wonder.'

'Yes, Corporal.' It was all she could think of to say.

'And you might as well know that when I arrived here, two weeks ago, I had seen better vehicles in museums! But I didn't let them beat me. "I'll have that lot up to scratch, or my name isn't Frederick Finnigan," I said. Know anything about engine maintenance, Tiptree?'

'Sorry – no. But I can change a wheel and I know about keeping spark plugs clean and what to do if a fan belt snaps. Not a lot, but I want to learn.' She truly did.

'Then you've come to the right place. We'll soon take care of them lilywhite hands! Mind, I never yet met a woman as made a good motor mechanic. Haven't got the strength, see, in their arms. We've got a mechanic here, by the way, only he's gone to sick bay. Toothache driving him mad.

'So here are the rules. You will provide tea, drive when required to, and call me corporal at all times, 'cept when the three of us is alone, when you call me Freddy and him at sick bay is Norman. Norm. Any questions?'

'N-no. Should I nip back to the billet and get into my overalls?'

'No point. Do it when we knock off for grub.'

'So when do I make tea?'

'Every other hour, on the hour. Next brew at ten.'

'That's a lot of tea, corporal. Do the rations stand up to it,' Carrie frowned.

'No. Leastways, not the pesky pittance we get from Stores. But me and the sergeant cook have come to an understanding. You take the small enamel pot to the cookhouse and tell them you've come for Freddy's tea. And it'll help if you smile sweetly.'

'Just like that?'

'Exactly like that, girl. So till then, you'd better take the pick-up for a bit of a run – on the estate roads, I mean. And you'll have to crank it up. Give it a good swing.'

Carrie stared with dismay at the truck, then silently enlisting the help of any guardian angel that might be hovering, shoved in the starting handle and swung it hard.

She heard a grunt and a groan and a cough. Oh, my goodness, she had started it! First try! She grinned at the corporal, who grinned back.

'Not bad, Tiptree. It's the way you hold your mouth as does it. So on your way, then. Let's see what you're made of.'

Carrie engaged first gear, inching out of the coach house. And please, she wouldn't run into one of the gateposts? Not on her first day?

She drove carefully. To her left was the estate office, ahead the cookhouse. Now it was a down-hill run as far as Southgate Lodge. She touched the brake with her foot and thanked the angel fervently for a truck that did indeed seem up to scratch.

Evie and Nan were dressed in overalls, cleaning windows outside the billet. Carrie stopped, and jumped down.

'Goodness!' Evie put down her pad of scrunched-up newspaper and made for the gate. 'Where on earth are you going in *that!*' She was trying, Carrie knew, not to laugh.

'It's a right old rattletrap!' Nan joined them.

'It's old I'll grant you, but there's a pussy cat under that bonnet,' Carrie defended, 'and the gears are like silk. As a matter of fact, I might be driving you all to and from shifts in it – when things are up and running, that is.'

'Then that might well be tomorrow. The GPO bods will be finished by afternoon, and all the shift workers are to give the place a good cleaning. We're in the estate office, did you know?'

'I guessed as much. Saw the green vans outside. I'm next door, in the stable yard with Corporal Finnigan and a mechanic called Norman. So see you! I'll go as far as Priest's Lodge, then I'll have to be back for tea at ten. Looks like I'm in charge, in that department!' she laughed. 'Bye . . .'

'Y'know, she's such a pretty girl,' Evie sighed. 'Pity she doesn't smile more often.'

'Pity she doesn't wear her engagement ring,' Nan said darkly.

'Mm.' Evie thought it a pity, too, but had the good sense not to say so.

Carrie drove past the little church and the end of the wood, her hands relaxed on the wheel, feeling not a little pleased that 462523 Tiptree C was doing what she had joined the Auxiliary Territorial Service to do. She was a driver, at last. And for a bonus, Heronflete Priory – Draft HP4 – was as different as could be from the hectic regime she had experienced in barracks, and at the training camp in Wiltshire. Now, life seemed almost calm again. And all things considered, with a little give and take, of course, she might just get to enjoy Army life. One day.

'I want this place fully operational by Wednesday,' said Sergeant James. 'Also, the powers-that-be have indicated that that is the way they would like it, too.' She inclined her head in the direction of the trees that screened Heronflete.

'So they're alive in there? There really is –'

'Quiet! It is not for me to hazard an opinion. Sufficient to say that cars have been seen heading in the direction of the big house, so I think we can take it that *They* have arrived and will expect us to deal efficiently and discreetly with whatever we have been sent here to do! Now, girls, does Wednesday's date have any significance?'

'Er – September 3?' Evie supplied.

'Good! I'm glad one of you is on the ball. Wednesday, will also be the first day of the third year of hostilities. And tomorrow, A-shift will be here and ready for duty at O600 hours and you, Tiptree, will deliver them promptly. You will also be responsible for ferrying the girls at Priest's, who will be working the opposite shifts.'

'Yes, sergeant.' Carrie had already made a mental note to set the alarm for five-twenty which would give her time enough, surely, to dress, collect the truck from the stable yard, then pick up the shift.

She hoped she would get it right; hoped the alarm clock worked; hoped the truck started first time. Mind, it shouldn't be too bad. September mornings were still light, though what would happen in winter, when blackout began in late afternoon and lasted until at least eight the following morning, she chose not to dwell upon too much.

'I will pin up the duty rosters; one in each billet and one here in the signals office, so no one will have any excuse for lateness. And that especially means you, Tiptree.'

'Yes, sergeant,' Carrie whispered, automatically.

'Right, then. Fifteen minutes for a cookhouse break, then I want you back here for ten-thirty and we'll make a start getting the clobber unloaded and stacked away here! OK, girls!'

'Y'know, it's a funny going-on,' Evie said when they sat with mugs of saccharin-sweet tea in front of them – 'the two-shift system, I mean. I've always worked night shift, as well. I believe men will do the nights for the time being. Maybe they aren't expecting much overnight traffic.'

'Well, we'll soon know what's going on. There'll be teleprinter messages, I mean, and you'll be able to have the odd listen-in, Evie.' Nan blew on her tea.

'I'll be doing no such thing, Nan Morrissey. I could lose my stripe for listening-in!'

Could lose it, she amended silently, if she were *caught* listening-in!

'When I arrived here, I wondered what on earth I was going to do,' Carrie smiled, 'but I'm going to be kept pretty busy. I'll have to collect the late shift, then take the earlies back to billets. And Corporal Finnigan expects me to learn engine maintenance, too. Mind, there'll always be Norman to fall back on. He seems very affable, now he's had his toothache seen to. But shift-working is a seven-day job, and my last run will be at ten at night. I'm not going to get any time off at all.'

'Of course you will,' Evie laughed. 'If men are going to do night-shifts, then maybe your corporal will arrange something for you. It was him collected us from Lincoln, remember. Or maybe the mechanic will do some of the late runs.

'Of course, when we are working from two till ten it means that every other night we won't be able to go anywhere. It could play havoc with your love life, if you think about it. Not that I mind, of course, though Bob doesn't expect me to live like a nun. I'll be going dancing, though I won't be up for dates.'

Her wedding ring would see to that. If asked, she held up her left hand and smiled and said, 'Sorry.' The decent ones accepted it, and it was tough luck on those who thought a young married woman in uniform was fair game.

'I suppose there'll be dances round about.' Carrie loved to dance, though Jeffrey wasn't too keen. 'One of the girls at Priest's told me there's a village not far away. Within walking distance, she heard. Perhaps there'll be a pub we can go to – just for the odd drink and a change of scene, I mean.'

'Suppose we'll give it a try,' Evie was fondling her ring again. 'But had you thought that we'll be on duty from two in the afternoon until ten at night, then next day we'll be on earlies – six till two in the afternoon.'

'A bit much, if you ask me,' Nan grumbled.

'You still haven't got the point. We do a late, followed by an early, then we're off duty till two o'clock the following afternoon. Virtually twenty-four hours off. We could go much further afield than the local pub. There'll be dances and flicks in Lincoln and if Sergeant James allows us sleeping-out passes, we could get a bed at the Y W and make a real night out of it.'

'What,' Nan wanted to know, 'is the Y W?'

'You've heard of the YMCA, surely? Well, the

YWCA is the female equivalent. If you can manage to bag a bed there, it's a good place to stay – and cheap and cheerful, too.'

'Ar . . .' Nan frowned. 'But will *I* be able to sleep out? I'm not eighteen till November.'

'If you're old enough to join up, you're old enough for a SOP – if the sergeant allows them, that is.'

'Seems Sergeant James has the last word, here. Why haven't we got an officer of our own?' Carrie frowned.

'Because in my opinion a few females don't warrant an officer. And maybe the sergeant won't be so bad, once we're in some kind of a routine. And talking of angels . . .' Evie nodded towards the doorway where Sergeant James looked pointedly at her wrist watch.

They worked hard all morning, Carrie driving the pick-up truck piled with supplies from the quartermaster's stores to the estate office which now bore a notice on the door. SIGNALS OFFICE: NO ENTRY.

They cleaned out cupboards then stacked them with teleprinter rolls, stationery, pencils, pens and signal pads. They positioned In-trays and Out-trays, dusted everything that didn't move, polished the sergeant's desk, then swept and mopped the black and red floor tiles.

'Just the windows to clean – inside *and* out,' the sergeant stressed, 'then you can call it a day, girls.'

*　*　*

They ate corned-beef hash and pickled red cabbage at midday, which made Carrie very happy, with rice pudding and a dollop of bright red jam in the middle of it for pudding.

'I'm goin' to have a lazy afternoon. Got a magazine to read,' Nan took the billet key from its hiding place above the front door jamb. 'What are youse two goin' to do?'

'Write to Bob,' Evie smiled, 'then do some ironing. And my buttons and cap badge need a polish. What about you, Carrie?'

'Probably sweep the workshop floor or clean the officers' car and see to the tea, of course. Corporal Finnigan won't be giving me the rest of the afternoon off.'

Which was a pity, really, because she had to – *wanted* to – write to Jeffrey. Letters, redirected from their old addresses, had arrived this morning; one for Nan, four for Evie and two for herself; from her mother and from Jeffrey, still in barracks with never a draft chit in sight.

I am stuck here like a lemon, polishing and cleaning and hardly getting any morse in at all. Which gives me a lot of time to think about how much I love you and miss you and wish you had been there when I had my leave.

Have a photo taken of yourself in uniform – not that I need to be reminded how lovely you are . . .

Jeffrey, she thought, could be quite sweet when he put himself out – or had his loving, longing letter been the result of a run ashore and a few pints of beer?

Then she chided herself for such thoughts, knowing that things between them would be all right, once she caught her fiancé in another loving and longing mood and they were able to talk sensibly and calmly about – *things*.

She had reason, too, to warm towards Corporal Finnigan that afternoon when he said, 'I was having a word with Sergeant James about your duties, Carrie – the last run, I mean. Seems you won't have as much free time as the rest of the girls, so Norman here has volunteered to do the evening pick-up, at ten.'

'Norm! How good of you.' Carrie blushed with pleasure. 'Are you sure you don't mind?'

Private Fowler did not mind at all. He was courting very seriously and wrote home to his girl every evening. He was also saving up for an engagement ring, and the extra duty meant less time and money spent in the NAAFI. He also liked Carrie. She was pleasant and willing and – what was by far the most agreeable thing about her – she now did the tea run which been the bane of his life until she arrived.

'Think nothing of it,' he had said, grinning awkwardly, because it was nice to be appreciated, sometimes.

That was when Carrie looked at her watch and,

without being asked, picked up the small enamel teapot and walked cheerfully to the cookhouse.

Nan addressed the letter to her aunt, wrote *On Active Service* in the top, left-hand corner, then propped the envelope on the mantelpiece, wishing there was someone other than Auntie Mim to send her letters. She wondered what it would be like to have a boyfriend to write to, but in Liverpool boyfriends had been thin on the ground when you had to depend on Georgie's sleeping habits for your free time.

It might be nice to be cuddled and kissed – even once. But she was sweet seventeen, wasn't she, and ran true to form because she had never, to her shame, been kissed. But she would be eighteen in November, and a lot could happen between now and then. Oh, please it would!

Dearest Jeffrey, Carrie wrote,

At last I have time to write to you properly. Things have been hectic these last few days but we seem, now, to have settled into a routine and tomorrow shift work starts for real.

There are very few of us, here. I can't tell you what we do exactly, but I am attached to No.4. Signals as a driver, and though we mark our letters On Active Service, and they are censored, it means nothing more than that I am billeted Somewhere in England at the back of beyond in a a tiny gate lodge with Nan and Evie.

Carrie read what she had written, looking for anything that might not be allowed but decided that so far, there was nothing to invite the censor's blue pencil or scissors. Somewhere in England was a term always used now, and could mean anywhere at all between the south coast and Hadrian's Wall. She wondered who censored their letters. Sergeant James? She hoped not.

I am alone, here, tonight. Nan and Evie have gone for a long walk, in the direction of the village which is about a mile away.

Nan is very young – not yet eighteen – and delighted to be away from her 'wicked step-mother'. Her eyes are enormous and brown, and her eyelashes are the longest I have ever seen. Nan and I room together; Evie, having a stripe up, has the small single bedroom. Evie is married to Bob, who is overseas and she writes to him every day.

Married. So what did she write to Jeffrey about their own wedding? She should tell him, she knew, that she could not wait for the day when they would be able to arrange it but instead she wrote,

I have been thinking about you and me, and if we will have a very quiet, village wedding.

74

Long white dresses and veils are out, now, so if it looks like being a winter wedding, how about us being married in uniform? It would save a lot of fuss and bother and might be rather nice, don't you think? As soon as we can get together, we must have a long talk about it . . .

Talk! Dear sweet heaven, it wasn't the wedding she wanted to talk about! It was *after* the wedding that sometimes had her sick with worry, even to think about it. Oh, they had kissed and cuddled a lot and at times got quite passionate, which had been rather nice, but actually *doing it* . . .

And why did people refer to it as *It*? Wouldn't lovemaking be a better word, though hers and Jeffrey's coupling had been entirely without love. Just a taking, really, and she stupid enough to let it happen!

I think that in about another month, I might be able to put in a request for leave, but will have to talk to Sgt James (our boss lady!) about it.

When you get drafted to a seagoing ship, will you automatically get leave? If you do, perhaps I can try to get a 72-hour pass, so that at least we can talk together about things . . .

It all came down to talking, didn't it? And how would she, when they did eventually arrange leaves together, be able to tell him about her doubts?

'I didn't enjoy what we did, Jeffrey.' Would she, *dare* she, say that? Would her criticism annoy him or would he understand how she had felt and tell her, *promise* her, it would be all right between them, once they were married?

'Oh, damn, damn, *damn!*' Irritated, she walked to the window to stand arms folded staring up the lane, seeing nothing. What a mess it all was! And why hadn't she told her mother about it?

Because she couldn't talk to her mother about such things. Her mother had always been stuffy about what went on between married couples; had told her they found her under the lavender bush at the bottom of the flower garden and even though she had been very young at the time, she had known that babies grew in ladies 'tummies and the district nurse got them out.

She returned to her bed, pushed off her shoes and lay back, hands behind head, wondering if she were making a fuss over nothing; thinking that maybe every bride-to-be had doubts and worries. Maybe even Evie had had them?

Sighing, Carrie picked up her pen and pad.

I think about you a lot, Jeffrey, and miss you very much. But it is all the fault of the war, and there are many couples not so lucky as you and me – Evie and Bob, for one.

I hope you will get a ship, soon. It must be awful for you in barracks. I hated barracks when I first joined up but this place has more than made up for it. Nan and Evie and I get on fine, as I do with Corporal Finnigan and Private Fowler in the motor pool.

She flicked back the sheets and read what she had written. Not much of a letter to write to someone you would almost certainly marry before the year was out; not what a lonely sailor wanted to read. She bit her lip, and wrote,

Take care of your dear self. I love you very much and can't wait for us to be married. When you read this, close your eyes and know that I am kissing you.

She read the letter again then ended it *Yours always, Carrie.*

She supposed that now she must walk to the NAAFI and post it. She wished she had gone out with Nan and Evie and thought that wherever they were, they'd be having a laugh. It made her wish all the more she was with them.

Evie and Nan swung along the narrow road, feet in step, arms swinging, respirators to the left.

Always your left to leave your right hand free for saluting!

'Tell me – did you have bad feet when you joined up?' Nan giggled. 'Gawd – all that square-bashing and them clumpy shoes – I thought I'd be a cripple for life!'

'Mm. I had awful blisters, but you soon get used to the shoes, don't you? And my soft pair will be lovely for dancing in. Do you think there'll be a dance-hall in the village? Or a picture house?'

'Don't think so, but I reckon there'll be a pub. Tell me, Evie, were you miserable when you joined up, because there must be sumthin' the matter with me, 'cause I couldn't wait to get into uniform. And I still like it.'

'Not miserable about being in the ATS. Just unhappy that Bob had to register for military service, and knowing we wouldn't see each other for heaven only knew how long. So I made a vow, the day I waved him off at the station. I was joining up, too. I didn't care which service. The first recruiting office I came to, be it Army, Navy or Air Force, I told myself, would suit me just fine. I worked on a huge switchboard in Eastern Command HQ. There were a lot of us there; it took my mind off being away from Bob, yet now here I am in a little gate lodge in the middle of a country estate and the tiniest switchboard I've ever seen. I'll be able to operate it with one hand behind my back! How about you, Nan?'

'Can't wait for morning. I wonder who my first signal will be from? And just look there.' She pointed ahead as they rounded the corner to where a cluster of houses, a church and public house lay ahead of them. 'Last one there buys the shandies!'

The public house at Little Modeley was called the Black Bull and was small and low-ceilinged and wreathed in cigarette smoke. Heads turned as they entered, then an old man with a pewter tankard in front of him smiled and nodded towards empty chairs beside him.

'You'll be two of them lady soldiers as have comed to the Priory,' he said as they removed caps, gloves and respirators.

'Er – yes. Very nice place,' Evie conceded, dipping into her pocket for a half-crown. 'What are you drinking?'

'A half of bitter and thank you kindly, Miss.'

'She's a Missus,' Nan said when Evie stood at the bar counter, 'so don't get any ideas, grandad. And me name's Nan. I'm not married, and I'm not lookin', either. But how did you know we were at Heronflete?'

'You've been expected. Caused a lot of speculation in these parts when the government told his lordship they wanted him out. Gave him four weeks to pack up, and go. Us thought it would be the Air Force moving in, there being quite a few aerodromes around these parts, but then we heard it would be the Army and civilians . . .'

'What have I missed?' Evie put three glasses on the tabletop.

'Nuthin except that it's probably civvies in the big house and that the lord was given four weeks' notice to get out,' Nan shrugged.

'So what did he call himself when he was at home?' Evie pushed a half of bitter in the man's direction.

'Thanks, Missus, and cheers!' He took a sip then poured the contents of the glass into his tankard, shaking out every last drop. 'He was – still is, I suppose – Lord Mead-Storrow. Took it all very well, so talk had it.'

'You've got to feel sorry for him,' Evie sighed. 'It must have been a beautiful place to live before it was commandeered. Wonder how many staff it took to run the place?'

'Not staff, girl. Servants. That's what the aristocracy employs. And they had to get out an' all. Find other jobs. 'Twas the farmers I was sorry for, though they've been allowed to harvest growing crops. Last of the wheat and barley was cut a couple of weeks ago. Only root crops left, now. Turnips and sugar beet . . .'

'Rotten, innit, when the government can take your 'ouse or your car or your railings and gates without so much as a by-your-leave. Did they give Lord Wotsit another place to go to?' Nan frowned.

'I doubt it. He's got a house in London and another estate in Scotland. Him won't be all that bothered. So what's them civilians doing at

Heronflete and why do they need such a big place to do it in? Must be something of national importance.'

'Do you want to know something?' Evie grinned. 'There are a few guards and ATS personnel billeted in the gate lodges and a couple of RASC bods there, and the cookhouse staff, and having said that, you know as much as we do! I don't know whether it's one of the Services or civilians in the big house. Maybe we'll find out in time, but right now we're as puzzled as you are.'

And that, Evie thought, should have been the end of the matter and the old man should have picked up his tankard and joined the drinkers at another table, but still he lingered.

'I think you two should be warned,' he said softly.

'What about?'

'About,' he tapped his nose with a forefinger, '*things . . .*'

'What things?' To her credit, Nan was instantly on her feet. 'Another glass, grandad?'

'Don't mind if I do.'

'So what things?' Nan was quickly back. 'About Heronflete, you mean?'

'About Heronflete Priory as has been in the Mead-Storrow family for generations. Before my grandad's time, even. It was my grandad as told me. About Cecilia.'

'And who was she when she was at home?' Nan urged, eyes bright.

'We-e-ll, nobody's quite sure who she was, but it was on St Cecilia's day that they found her.' He paused, looking from one to the other. 'So they gave her that name. Had to have a name, see, to bury her decent . . .'

'You mean someone found a dead body at Heronflete?' Now Evie was curious.

'Nah. At the Priory. When they was pulling it down. Them Storrows was rich, so they decided on one of them houses that look like a castle. Knocked down what was left of the priory so they could build another place, grander than the one they were living in – the one that's there, now.'

'But where did they find the body? Came across a grave, did they?' Nan's eyes were rounder than ever.

'Grave? Oh, my word no! Came across a skeleton. Shackled hand and foot. Walled up.'

'Oh, my lor'. A nun, was it?'

'Had to be. Men wasn't allowed in priories. That poor woman must've been there for hundreds of years – before King Henry the Eighth looted the place, then had the roof pulled off. Must've caused great consternation, at the time. Lord Storrow's ancestor got into a right state about it. Thought the terrible way the woman had died would bring bad luck to his smart new house. So he got a priest in, talk has it, and had the spot where she was found blessed, then gave the skeleton a Christian burial.

'You can see the grave, still. About a hundred

yards from the house, with a little stone there. A bit worn now, I believe, but you can still make out the name.'

'That was a very decent thing to do. She'd have been 'appy about havin' a decent grave. But we won't be allowed to go and look at it. We can't get up to Heronflete without a pass.' Nan remembered the soldiers. 'Nice to hear a story with a happy ending.'

'Ar, but it wasn't – a happy ending, I mean. That nun wasn't taking it lying down. Her didn't want to rest! Well, would you have done if you'd died the way she did? To this very day, she reminds folk about it, makes sure they don't forget.'

'Now don't tell me she comes back a-haunting,' Evie giggled, 'because I won't believe it. I have never seen a ghost and I've never met anyone who has!'

'Then you should've spoken to the estate workers around Heronflete. People saw her . . .'

'How many – and were they sober at the time?'

'Folks saw her, that's all I know. A figure in black, and not near the grave, either. Near the stables. People figured that it was in the vicinity of the stables that she died, when you saw plans of what the priory looked like, and took into account where it was set down.'

'Well, I hope it isn't true grandad, 'cause our friend works at the stableyard. It's where they keep the transports, now.'

'We-e-ll, chances of seeing Cecilia are rare. Only

on two dates have folk come across her. In April
– when people felt that's when she might have
been walled up – and on St Cecilia's day, the time
when her was set free, you might say.'

'And when is that?' Evie was still smiling,
completely unconvinced.

'In November, if you must know. When the
nights are dark early.'

'*When* in November?' Nan's tongue made little
clicking noises and she gulped at her drink.

'The twenty-second. Leastways, that's what my
grandad told me.'

'*The twenty-second!*' Nan got to her feet, pulling
on her cap, wriggling her fingers into her gloves.
'Come on, Evie. I'm goin'. Don't want to hear
nuthin' more about ghosts!' She slung her respirator, and made for the door.

'Now look what you've done!' Biting back a
smile, Evie got to her feet. 'Telling such fibs!
G'night Mr-er . . . Nice to have met you.'

'An' you too, Missus. But I wasn't fibbing.
Honest I wasn't!'

And then he began to chuckle.

'Wait on! Don't be upset,' Evie soothed when she
caught up with the indignant Nan. 'You know
there are no such things as ghosts. He was only
teasing!'

'Maybe he was, but they didn't have to find the
nun on *my* birthday, did they?'

'Does it matter when the poor soul was found

84

– *if* she was found, which I very much doubt. You should have seen your face, Nan. The old boy was having the time of his life, inventing a ghost and getting free beer into the bargain!'

'Well, *I* think he meant it. He was real serious about it – couldn't have made all that lot up on the spur of the moment. But there's one way to find out. We've got to ask around and see if anybody has come across a grave with a stone marker. I reckon that guard what came up on me from behind the other night would know.'

'So what do you say to him, Nan? Excuse me, but have you seen a nun's grave on your travels? You'd have to tell him, then, about the man in the pub, and he'd laugh his head off at you! So, repeat after me! There – are – no – such – things – as *ghosts!*'

'All right, then – there are no such things as ghosts. But I'm goin' to find out all I can about that grave. A hundred yards away from the house, didn't he say?'

'Yes. And Southgate is much farther away than that, so it's extremely unlikely that you'll ever see the nun – *if* she exists, that is.'

'Ghosts don't *exist*, Evie. If they existed, they wouldn't be ghosts. And I think we should warn Carrie to be careful of that stable block. As a matter of fact, I wouldn't mind goin' to the NAAFI when we get back – have a big cup of hot cocoa.' Cocoa, Nan reasoned, was safe and sane and helped you to sleep.

'What! Had you forgotten – the NAAFI hut is right beside the stables,' Evie giggled.

'I know it is, but it's April and November that's the hauntin' season so we'll be all right tonight, Miss Clever Clogs. Now, are you goin' to hurry up, or what!'

Nan Morrissey wanted the thick walls of Southgate Lodge around her – and before it got dark, an' all!

Carrie locked the door of Southgate Lodge, placed the key on the door lintel, then made for the NAAFI, Jeffrey's letter in her pocket.

'Hi, there! Have we got news for you!' A breathless Nan at the gate. 'You aren't goin' to believe this in a million years!'

'So tell me,' Carrie smiled, glad to see them. 'You found the village pub and they were giving free drinks!'

'Garn! Better'n that, Carrie. Heronflete's got a ghost! An old feller in the pub told us.'

'Don't take any notice. He was pulling her leg. There are no such things as ghosts. You tell her, Carrie!'

'What? That I don't believe in spirits and ghosts and things that go bump in the night? But I did, once – when I was a kid. But walk with me to the NAAFI. Tell me about it?'

So, breathless and flush-cheeked, Nan told all, and when she had finished and when Carrie had posted her letter she said,

'OK? So do you believe the old feller, Carrie?'

'Well – once I might have, but since you ask, Nan, no, I don't. When I was little, there was a big old house near the village. Empty, and falling down and dangerous. Chunks falling off it all the time. We weren't supposed to go there, but the lads in the village couldn't keep away.

'They didn't want girls with them, so they told us awful tales about headless ghosts and blood-stains on the floor. Said that was why the place was so neglected – because no one would live there because they'd been frightened away by the hauntings. None of it was true, of course. Jeffrey and Todd had invented it all. Stupid of me to have believed them. So – shall we have a mug of tea whilst we're here? My treat.'

And Evie said thanks, she would, and Nan said could she have cocoa to help her to sleep?

'So here's to ghosts,' Evie laughed, raising her mug of tea.

'Don't mock.' Nan sipped her cocoa gratefully. They made smashing cocoa, here; put Carnation milk in it so it was worth the extra penny. 'And you believed once, Carrie, even though it was only a leg-pull. So tell me – I know Jeffrey's the feller you're engaged to, but who is Todd – your brother?'

'No, though we were brought up together. My father owed his father, you see.'

And, with remembering in her eyes, she told

them about how, before he died, her father had made provision for his batman's widow and her young son; out of gratitude, that was.

'Todd was nearly fourteen when he left us. Marie, his mum, died very suddenly of diphtheria so he went to his Auntie Hilda, in Lancashire.'

'Did you miss him,' Evie asked softly.

'I did. He'd always been around, then suddenly there's this lady come to take him away. I wanted him to stay with us, but my mother said she couldn't be held responsible for bringing him up; that it was best he should go to family. I cried a lot.'

'So where is he, now?'

'Haven't a clue, Nan. He never wrote, nor came back to the village – not even to see his mother's grave. I've never been able to understand why, because before he went he said he was going to marry me one day and I told him I'd like that very much. My first proposal – aged twelve . . .'

'Rotten of him not to write, for all that.'

'Mm. I was really upset. And what was worse, I hadn't got his aunt's address and my mother had lost it, so I couldn't write and ask him how he was. Perfidious creatures, men are. I still think about him – sometimes.'

'But of course you do. You always remember your first love. Only natural. But you're happy with Jeffrey, now.'

'Of course I am, Evie.'

'So why don't you wear your ring,' Nan demanded bluntly.

'You know why not. But I promise you that if ever we go out to a dance, or anything, I'll wear it.'

The sun was setting as they walked back to Southgate Lodge. Low and red in the sky promising a crisp September morning, then sun to break through and melt away the early autumn mists.

'Soon be time to draw the blackout curtains.' Evie unlocked the door. 'And this is the first time in my entire Army career that I've ever had the key to my billet! It's so – *different* – here. Too good to last, if you ask me.'

'And why shouldn't it last,' Nan demanded, taking off her cap, unbuttoning her jacket. 'I always dreamed of country cottages but I never once thought the Army would billet me in one. If I have any say in the matter, I'm stoppin' here for the duration.'

'Ghost and all?' Evie teased.

'All right, then. Mock if you want, but it'll be a different kettle of fish, won't it, when I find that grave marker.'

And find it she would or her name wasn't Nancy Morrissey who was a member of the Auxiliary Territorial Service and would be eighteen in November. On the day – or night, most probably – that the ghost walked!

'Er – anybody goin' down the garden to the

89

lavvy before it gets dark? I'll nip down with you, if you are . . .' Nan was nothing if not careful.

'OK. Let's all go,' Carrie grinned. 'We can hold hands. Safety in numbers, I suppose, in case we meet Cecilia!'

Which made Evie remark that she'd had enough of the ghostly nun for one day, and could they please remember there was a war on and tomorrow they were on early shift; their first shift at Heronflete and it began at six in the morning!

It made Carrie remember to make sure the alarm clock was set for 5.20, and Nan to ponder just how much wiser they all would be after that first shift. And it made her feel glad she would be working in the old estate office and not in the stableblock, with Carrie.

And oh, my goodness! If only the Queer One at Cyprian Court could see her now!

FIVE

Sergeant James slammed the flat of her hand on her door marked SIGNALS OFFICE: NO ENTRY then stood, hands on hips, mouth rounded in disapproval.

The blackout curtains on the windows either side of the door were still drawn even though, because of Double Summer Time, it had been light for half an hour. She bought down her hand again, then relaxed a little at the sound of bolts being drawn back and the scrape of a key in the lock.

A man said, 'Oh – hi . . .' He was rubbing the back of his neck, and yawning. 'Sorry, Ma'am. Was having a zizz . . .'

'Please do not address me as Ma'am. I am not an officer.' She stepped inside, followed by Evie and Nan. 'And are you allowed to sleep on night duty? What about the switchboard and the teleprinters?'

'They're fine. I put the alarm bell on the

switchboard and the printer starts up automatically if a signal comes through. Which it didn't. All night.'

'I see. Draw back the curtains, Morrissey, and open the windows.' She glared at a tin lid filled with cigarette ends. 'And will you take that with you when you leave, please?'

'Sure. No problem,' he smiled.

Nan took a sneaky look. He wasn't half bad. Tall, fair, dressed in black pumps and navy trousers and polo sweater. Too old for her, of course. Must be at least thirty.

'I thought there were to be two night operators.' The sergeant took off her cap and jacket and began the process of rolling up her sleeves to the elbow. 'And how do I address you?'

'Well, you are a sergeant and if I were in your mob, I'd be a sergeant too. But in the Navy, I'm a petty officer – P O, I suppose.'

'So that's your name? P O? Fine by me.'

'Well, no,' he smiled and that smile was quite something, Nan thought reluctantly. 'I'm in Signals like yourself but my rank is that of Yeoman of Signals – not petty officer. I'm addressed as Yeoman – or Yeo, when you know me better.'

'Quaint . . .'

'No, sergeant. It's the way it has always been. There were Yeomen and Chief Yeomen of Signals in Nelson's day, so who are we to change it? The Royal Navy floats on tradition, you know.'

'Really? So I take it there wasn't a lot of traffic during the night?'

'Not a sausage.' He picked up the ashtray. 'Ah, well – see you.'

He walked to the green baize door, inspected the two trays – In and Out – that stood on the hatch beside it. Then he pressed the bell push, and turned. 'By the way, there's a kettle in the little kitchen place and tea and sugar. Milk on the floor. Feel free to brew up.'

The door was opened from the inside and briefly Nan glimpsed a row of bells on springs on the wall.

'Looks like there's kitchens through there,' she said as the green baize door slammed.

'Never mind what's on the other side of that door, Morrissey,' said the sergeant. 'Right now there's nothing I'd like more than a mug of tea.'

In the tiny kitchen was a milk bottle in a pan of cold water under the sink and on the wooden draining board an electric kettle, tins marked tea and sugar. And four mugs in need of washing.

'Shall I make a brew, sarge?'

The sergeant nodded, then turning to Evie who was inspecting the switchboard she said,

'So what do you make of it, Turner – Navy bods at the big house, I mean?'

'Don't know, Sergeant. It gets curiouser and curiouser.'

'And very little night traffic . . .'

'Mm. I thought – mind, I don't know why – that they were a load of civilians from some bombed-out government office, but they've got the Army guarding them and here, in this office, and a signals bod from the Navy on the other side of the green door. Combined Ops maybe?'

'Could be, but I doubt it. And why don't you nip to the motor pool, see if Tiptree is still there? Cookhouse won't be operational till seven – ask her if she'd like tea?'

So Evie hurried round the back of the stables, whispering 'Morning, Cecilia,' then called to Carrie who was making for the gateposts.

'Hey! Wait on, Tiptree! Sergeant says do you want a cuppa? We've got a kettle in there.'

'Wouldn't I just? Busy, are you?'

'No, it's dead as a dodo, and a Navy bod – a *Yeoman* he calls himself – doing the night shift. The sarge was a bit sniffy with him, but he seemed all right to me. Quite handsome, if you like them a bit more mature. But don't forget to thank the Sergeant for the tea, then you might get a brew on a regular basis.'

'At six-fifteen in the morning, I'd positively grovel if there was tea at the end of it. Lead on, lance-corporal!'

Nan switched on the kettle then rinsed mugs under the tap. Amazingly, a tea towel hung behind the door. Short of nothing, that lot at the big house, and tea and sugar unrationed, it would seem.

Carefully she spooned tea leaves into a cream enamel pot with a green handle, then leaned against the draining board, feet crossed, arms folded, to await the kettle, and to think.

Think about Heronflete Priory and the diddy little billet. And Evie and Carrie who were smashing and Sergeant James who just might become human, given time.

And she thought about being in this unbelievable place where a lord once lived, and the fields and trees and wild flowers; the peace and quiet of it, too, with only the bombers – *ours* – that flew over, to remind her that somewhere out there, a war was going on.

Then she closed her eyes and smiled, because tomorrow was pay day.

'What will happen, Sergeant,' Evie asked later, 'when we go to the cookhouse for meals? Will you be able to manage?'

'Of course I will, even when you get long leaves – provided you go one at a time. I've been in signals from day one of this war, and teleprinters and switchboards bother me not one iota.

'And if you are reminding me that the cookhouse is open and none of us has eaten yet, I suggest you toss up for who goes first. In fact, the way things are this very minute, I think the three of us could slope off and never be missed!'

She had wondered about the lack of activity; had even thought that the Post Office engineers might have left without connecting things up, had silently fumed about this tuppeny-ha'penny place and longed with all her heart for the bustle and discipline of a properly-run unit on a wartime footing. And girls in Nissen huts!

'You take first breakfast, Turner,' she said absently, standing behind Nan who sat in front of two silent teleprinters, willing one of them at least to cooperate.

'Switch that printer on, Morrissey.'

Nan pressed the start button and with a clatter the black machine came alive, so she hit the answer-back key, and the carriage swung from left to right and back. On the page in front of her came CEN HP4.

'There, sarge! Must be our call sign! HP4, off Central switchboard. We do exist, then.'

'Seems we do. Give it a go, Morrissey – see if it prints.'

Nan cancelled the transmit swich, then typed *The quick brown fox jumps over the lazy dog.* The words appeared speedily, because it was one of the sentences you typed a lot, when you were a learner. If she had a silver shilling for every time that fox had jumped, she would be a very well-to-do ATS private.

'Do you suppose they know we're here, Sergeant? I mean – they're so secretive that maybe they've forgotten to tell the government about Heronflete.'

'Y'know, that wouldn't surprise me at all, Morrissey!'

She sat down at the switchboard, adjusted the

headset, then willed one of the circular, numbered discs to fall, or one of the square flaps of the outside lines to open with a *brrr*, then sighing, fixed her eyes on the second hand of the wall clock, which moved very, very slowly.

The silence became so uncomfortable that Nan said,

'Have you heard about the ghost, Sergeant? The one they call Cecilia? She was a nun that got walled up in the old priory – left there to die . . .'

But the Sergeant continued to stare at the switchboard in silence. She was so browned off that the last thing she wanted to hear about was a stupid bloody ghost!

It seemed that eight-thirty – or 0830 hrs BST – was the magic time and it was as if all those who lived at Heronflete had arisen, bathed and eaten breakfast, and were ready to do whatever it was they had come to Heronflete to do. When both Evie and Nan had breakfasted and Sergeant James had left for the cookhouse, a disc on the switchboard fell. It was No.5. Picking up a plug she pushed it into the hole beneath No.5, said 'Switchboard', very clearly and firmly, and was asked for an outside line.

She pushed in the corresponding plug, said, 'You're thrrrrrough.' Then she turned triumphantly to Nan. 'We're in business, old love!'

'Who was it?'

'Extension five – a man, for an outside line.'

'What's he talking about? Have a listen, Evie?'

'You reckon?' After all, they were alone. 'I shouldn't, you know . . .'

'Ar. Be a devil!'

Evie said, 'Ssssh, then,' and placed the palm of her hand over the mouthpiece of her headset. Slowly and carefully so as not to make even the smallest click, she pushed a switch forward.

'Ha! Wouldn't you know it, Morrissey! They've got the scrambler on!'

'What's that, when it's at home?'

'Some clever-dick device to distort sound so that anybody tapping in on a phone call just hears gobbledygook. Sensible, I suppose, when you think that a spy could climb a telegraph pole and listen in to any conversation he wanted. They do it all the time, I know that for a fact.'

'Ar,' Nan nodded. 'Amazin' what them *Jairmans* get up to.'

'Don't worry. We do it, too. It wouldn't surprise me at all if that lot,' she nodded towards the green baize door, 'aren't up to something similar.'

'Climbing telegraph poles, you mean?' Nan was disappointed.

'No, but they might be listening in. Monitoring air waves, I mean. They might have operators searching for anything they heard in Morse code and taking it down. Telegraphists.'

'Like Carrie's feller?'

'Yes, though I think he's still in barracks, waiting for a ship. Carrie says he's not best pleased about it.'

'Hmm. What do you make of that romance, Evie?'

'None of my business. The fact that Carrie doesn't wear her ring is neither here nor there. I never had an engagement ring. We used the money to open a bank account for when the war is over. But Carrie often gets her hands dirty and greasy. You can't blame her.'

'Yes, but –' Nan bit on her lip, deciding against telling Evie that Carrie wasn't absolutely sure she wanted to get married just yet and said instead, 'Well, if I had a ring, I'd wear it! Not that anybody's offered yet.'

'Give it time, Nan. You're young enough. Have a bit of fun before you settle down.'

And nan was about to say that chance would be a fine thing when, just as the sergeant opened the door, one of the teleprinters came to life with a loud clatter.

'Hey up, Sergeant! A signal!'

They watched as figures in groups of four clicked themselves into columns. They flew across the page.

'That's a good operator on the other end.' The sergeant nodded her approval.

The typing stopped.

'Go on then, Morrissey. Give them a receipt.'

So Nan looked at the wall clock then typed R 0858B/3/9/41 NM, then tore off the message and handed it to the sergeant.

Now she really *was* a teleprinter operator! Her

eyes shone, her cheeks pinked. And one day Nan Morrissey too would be a good operator!

'Hm. HF4 V ZAA. That's Heronflete from ZAA. So who the heck is ZAA?' the sergeant frowned.

She pressed the bell beside the hatch, placed the signal in the out-tray, then waited until a hand took it, clucking at the stupidity of a signals office that didn't need a sergeant to run it. And she longed for the busy office she had left where sergeants had a mess of their own and didn't have to share a gate lodge with privates. And she missed squad drill; girls marching, arms swinging, responding like automatons to commands! But most of all, she missed Joe; missed him so much it was like a pain inside her and what was far, far worse, the cold, stark certainty that she would never see him again.

'Sergeant!'

'Yes, Turner . . . ?'

Monica James tore herself from the memory of a kiss that had been a last goodbye.

'Take a look at this!' The switchboard was criss-crossed with cords and plugs in holes. Heronflete had come to life. 'I – er – I listened in to the first one; an outside line. It was scrambled.'

'Hmm. Try an internal call, Turner.'

Evie covered the mouthpiece and slid a key gently forward, then nodded.

'They're scrambled, too – even inside Heronflete.'

'Which only goes to show that something just might going on in there.'

She nodded towards the green baize door, all at once disliking it, because if the Army girls – herself included – were to be treated like a load of mindless morons who couldn't be trusted to keep their mouths shut, then the sooner she was out of this place, the better! It made her think that maybe volunteering for service overseas might be the best way out – a new start, perhaps?

The bell buzzed again. She walked to the in-tray to pick up a signal, in code.

'Right then, Morrissey – here's one for you to send . . .'

It gave no clue; was merely prefixed *Attention of C in CWA*. A pencilled note attached with a paperclip instructed *Send to LPL CWA*.

The sergeant searched the route-map on the wall that gave all Army teleprinter stations. LPL CWA was not on it, but who damn-well cared!

Nan secured the signal to the holder in front of her, then began to tap the spacebar to alert Central Switchboard – wherever it was – that Heronflete had a signal for someone who was a Commander-in-Chief – that much she deduced without too much effort – but where LPL and WA were, no one was going to tell her.

It bothered her not one bit. Nan Morrissey was sending her first secretive signal; she was at war!

It made her glow with happiness. And for a bonus, she reminded herself yet again that tomorrow was pay day. How good could life get!

*　　*　　*

'I'll be doing the shift-run in ten minutes, Freddy,' Carrie called. 'You'll have to wait for your tea till I get back!'

Pick up B-shift at Priest's Lodge at 1350 hours, deliver them to the signals office, wait outside for A-shift – Evie and Nan – and drive them back to Southgate. It was a piece of cake, though it might make a change, she thought, if she were to get some real driving in. On proper roads.

Lenice and Ailsa made up B-shift. Lenice Cooper's uniform was still in need of alteration but she vowed it would stay that way until she went on long leave when her uncle, a time-served tailor's assistant, could make a proper job of it. Lenice, she had insisted, was not an unusual name at all, but the feminine of Leonard, which was her father's name.

Ailsa Seaton was fair and pretty with a pink and white complexion. Carrie thought she seemed so fragile she should have been named Rose, or something delicately floral. Ailsa was Scottish and homesick for Edinburgh and hid behind Lenice's forceful personality.

Carrie would not, she had quickly decided, cross swords with Lenice who was a bit Bolshie, and was glad the lord had been booted out of his dirty big house!

Yet it took all sorts to make a world, Carrie thought, and all sorts and shapes and sizes to make up the Auxiliary Territorial Service, which was beginning to have its good points.

She called a goodbye to Freddy and Norm who grunted from beneath the bonnet of the officers' car, and thought about Jeffrey's letter which had been cheerful and optimistic. Jeffrey's draft chit into the real Navy – the *pusser* Navy, he called it – had come through and he told her not to write to Barracks again, and wait until she heard from him.

I know the name of my ship, but had best not tell you in a letter, or the censor will cut it out. Sufficient to say that by the time you get this I shall be on my way at last.

Thanks for yours, which arrived this morning.

In haste and high delight. Take care of yourself. I love you.

Jeffrey

Carrie tooted a goodbye as she left the stable yard. The afternoon was pleasant. September days were quite something; still warm, yet without the blazing heat of summer. A mellow time; a small Indian Summer before Autumn finally gave way to winter. Which made her wonder how it would be when the snows came and they had to get from Southgate to the motor pool and the cookhouse and the ablutions. Would they be issued with gumboots, or would Sergeant James have got her way by then, and have them all in a more conveniently placed Nissen hut? With a coke stove, of course.

But she would worry about leaving Southgate when she had to. Right now it was a delight to be driving on the estate roads, making for Priest's Lodge where, she hoped, Lenice and Ailsa would be waiting at the gate.

Carrie thought about Sergeant James who had been on duty since early morning and wondered how long her shifts would be and if they had managed to work out a meals rota. But that was up to the sergeant, whose dislike of the way things were at Heronflete plainly showed.

'Nothing to do with you, Private Tiptree,' Carrie said to the hen pheasant that ran across the lane ahead of her, then made cheerfully for Priest's Lodge.

'Have you eaten, then?' she asked of B-shift as they climbed into the back of the truck.

'Of course. At half-twelve, though it's a heck of a trudge to the cook-house and back,' Lenice grumbled. 'Mind, it'll be a whole lot worse when it rains, had you thought about that, Tiptree?'

'N-no.' Carrie stared ahead, deciding not to mention she had gone one better, and thought about *snow*! 'But we've got our capes – we'll be all right.' Lenice had the makings of a barrack-room lawyer, Carrie frowned; one who always complained – often and loudly. 'And it hasn't rained yet. This far, the weather has been lovely. Looking forward to your first shift,' she asked over her shoulder, turning right at Southgate, making for the huddle of buildings ahead.

'Suppose so. Anything to relieve the boredom, though why I let myself be inveigled into a capitalist war I'll never know!'

Carrie almost told her it was to fight the Fascists, who were far more evil than capitalists, but instead she said,

'Now you know political opinions are forbidden so if you don't mind, Lenice, I want none of them in this truck whilst I'm in charge!'

They completed the journey in silence, then Ailsa whispered, 'Thanks,' as they got down.

It was the first word she had spoken and Carrie thought how awful it must be for her at Priest's and it made her all the more glad that she shared with Evie and Nan who were absolute loves.

'Had you thought,' Nan said with relish, 'Priest's will be doing the early shift in the morning as well, and that Evie and I will be off till tomorrow, at two? Don't know whether to get up for breakfast, or have a lovely lie in.'

'Yes, but Priest's will be free for a trip into Lincoln on Saturday. Norm told me there'll be a transport laid on.'

'So will you be driving, Carrie?' Evie looked up from her bedmaking and the meticulous envelope corners she was tucking in.

'No one has said anything to me.' Now Norm had agreed to relieve her of the evening shift, Carrie supposed she might have no choice in the matter. 'I'll be available from two, so maybe I will. I'll ask Sergeant James to sort it with Freddy.' She had learned that orders came from above and you didn't go over the head of anyone with rank up.

'Did you see the notice in the NAAFI – a dance, on Friday night?'

'What – *here*?' None of the soldiers she had seen at Heronflete looked a likely dancing partner. Nan frowned.

'No. At the aerodrome. Invitation to the Sergeant's Mess. Dancing from seven till ten-thirty. Transport laid on. If we're going, we won't be back here till eleven, at least. We'll have to put in for a late pass,' Evie warned.

'Then I'm game,' Nan beamed, thoughts of a real night out pleasing her. 'Will they have a decent band, do you think?'

'They very often do, in the RAF. Should think it'll be a good hop,' Evie said.' Before I came here, I went to quite a few RAF dances. They often lay on beer and sandwiches.'

'And they send transport? But will it be worth their while,' Carrie frowned, 'for just the three of us, because I don't suppose the sergeant will be going.'

'They'll probably pick up in the villages around – civilian girls, to make up numbers. Is Friday night on, then?' Evie wanted to know.

And Carrie and Nan said it was, and had anybody realised it would be their first night out for ages and ages?

'OK, then. Leave the passes to me,' Evie said.

'And I'm going to the washroom to press my best uniform and wash some stockings. Anybody coming?'

But Carrie said she had to write to her mother, and Nan said she was going to take off her collar and tie and sit outside at the back in the sun.

To think, she supposed, about how smashing it was at Heronflete, even if they were a bit of a funny lot. And maybe to give a little thought to the grave marker, and how she would be able to find it if they weren't allowed up the drive, much less within a hundred yards of the house. Because that's where they'd buried Cecilia, Grandad had said.

My word, but being in the ATS gave you a lot to sit in the sun and think about!

Nan lay on her bed, hands behind head, watching as Carrie put on her make-up. She was very lovely, Nan thought; a nose every bit as perfect as Hedy Lamarr's and high cheekbones, like Lana Turner's. And her hair was thick and fair – more honey-coloured than blonde. But of more importance than Carrie's enviable beauty was the ring. On the third finger of her left hand.

'I'll wear it,' she had said, 'if we go dancing, or anything,' and there it was, sparkling and flashing; three diamonds that must have cost every bit of twenty pounds.

'Something the matter?' Carrie met Nan's gaze in the mirror and turned, smiling.

'No. Was just thinking that's a smashin' ring.'

'Mm. It feels a bit strange, wearing it again. Wonder where Jeffrey is.'

'Maybe on his new ship. Maybe sailing off into the sunset.'

'He could be, but I'm sure he'll be with the Home Fleet. If his ship was going foreign, he'd have been given leave. And talking about leave, we'll have got three months' service behind us, soon, and you're supposed to get leave every three months, don't forget. Must ask Evie about putting in for it.'

'You'll be goin' home, to Yorkshire?'

'Yes, and I'm quite looking forward to it. Be nice to wear civvies again and sleep in, mornings – and see Mum, of course. She's missing me a lot, and it's going to be awful for her when the bad weather comes.'

'Why?' Nan watched as Carrie removed Kirby grips from her pin-curled hair.

'Well, we've got a little car and up until now I've always done the driving. When petrol was rationed, we decided we could manage on foot or on bikes in summer, to save our petrol coupons for winter. And Mum can't drive . . .'

'Then you'll have to give her a few lessons, when you go home.'

'Might be a good idea, though if she'd wanted to drive, she'd have taken it up before now. Mind, if she feels confident, it should be all right. At least she won't have to pass a driving test.'

Tests had been suspended for the duration, which was very convenient, Carrie thought. All you did, now, was to apply for a licence, then start driving, which her mother would refuse point blank to do. She knew it! She already hated the blackout; driving a car in it when winter came wouldn't even be considered. But it was too late now to worry about her mother living in an isolated village miles away from shops of any size; it was only one of the things she hadn't taken into account in her haste to leave Nether Hutton.

'Hi, folks!' Evie's bedroom door opened. 'Got your war paint on, then, 'cause we'll have to get a move on. The transport is picking us up at Priest's at seven. Aren't you putting your lipstick on, Nan?'

'Haven't got one. The Queer One didn't allow make-up. Said it was common.'

'Why do you call your stepmother The Queer One?' Carrie asked as they walked towards Priest's Lodge. 'Hasn't she got a name?'

'Yes. It's Ida. She said I was to call her mother, but it wasn't on.'

'Why not?'

'Because she wasn't my mother. And she didn't like me and I didn't like her. It's why I shoved off when dad died. No way was I stoppin' with that one, and when I'm due for leave I'll go to Auntie Mim's, even if I have to sleep on the parlour sofa. Mind, I just might ask for my travel warrant to be made out to Edinburgh. Always wanted to go to Scotland . . .'

The possibilities, thought Nan, were heady and endless.

The RAF transport they shared with five civilian girls came to a stop at the guard room of the RAF bomber station.

'Five civvies and three Army girls,' called the driver, who was a member of the Womens' Auxiliary Air Force – an aircraftwoman, or a WAAF, Carrie supposed – envying the skill with which she handled the large transport. 'For the Mess dance.'

The red and white barrier was lifted and behind them, as they drove through, they could see outlines of huge hangars, wooden buildings and rows of Nissen huts. They stopped outside one of them.

'Here you are, girls! Sergeants' Mess. And they aren't on ops tonight, so there'll be plenty of partners,' the driver grinned as she let down the tail board. 'Sounds like it's already started.'

They walked towards the sound of the music and drum beats, then pushed through the thick blackout curtain that covered the door to be met with wolf whistles of relief, Evie thought, at the arrival of eight more partners, because, apart from the WAAFs and three land girls already there, women were outnumbered by two to one. There would be no wallflowers here tonight! They threaded through the dancers to find empty chairs where a lone sergeant sat.

'Hi!' Nan beamed. 'Smashin' band you've got.'

'Er – y-yes.' The sergeant blushed, then stared ahead. 'G-good . . .'

The band was playing very professionally. Shouldn't wonder, Nan thought, if some of them had been musicians in civvy street. Her feet began to tap and she smiled at the airman at her side, wishing he would ask her onto the floor.

The music ended with a roll of drums, the couples returned to the chairs that lined the hut.

It wasn't much of a place, Nan thought, hoping that Sergeant James never got her heart's desire. The windows were already thickly curtained, cigarette smoke hung lazily beneath the curved tin roof.

'Is this your billet,' she asked the man beside her.

''N-no. Our m-mess hall, actually.'

'I live in a gate lodge,' Nan confided. 'Real cute.' She dropped her voice, leaning closer. 'At Heronflete Priory.'

'Mm. Know it. F-flown over it loads of – of t-times. B-big place, like a castle. And sorry for the imp – imp . . .'

'Stammer?' Nan offered.

'Y-yes. But only when I t-talk to girls.'

'Why? Girls don't bite.'

'I blush, too. It p-puts them off.'

Nan turned to gaze at him. Young, like herself. Fair-haired and blue-eyed. And tall. Good to look at, really.

'Well, it hasn't put me off, so you'd better tell me your name.'

'Charles Lawson, though most of the blokes call me Charlie.'

'Hm. No. Charles is too stuffy and Charlie makes you sound a real – well you know . . . Think I shall call you Chas. And I'm called Nancy Morrissey, though I prefer Nan.'

'Hi!' He offered a hand, which Nan took. 'N-nice to meet you.'

'Likewise. And I think you'd better ask me up to dance when the music starts, 'cause if you don't, somebody else is goin' to ask me, and I want to talk to you.'

'You do, Nan? You really do?' His cheeks were bright red. 'I'd love to, but I can't d-dance . . .'

'Why ever not! Don't you like dancin'?'

'I'd like to try it, but I can't pluck up the courage to ask. By the t-time I've said I'm sorry, I can't dance but would they like to t-try one with me some other bloke has nabbed them.'

'But you're talkin' to me, and what's more you and me's havin' the next dance, OK? I mean, you're never goin' to learn, are you, if you never set foot on the floor.'

'You'll be sorry!' He smiled for all that, and it was a lovely smile, Nan thought. Nice, white teeth and even, like a film star's.

'We'll see,' she smiled back, 'and shh . . .'

'Ladies and gentlemen!' The pianist got to his feet, placed his pint pot on top of the piano. 'Please take your partners for a Bumps-a-daisy.'

There was a loud groan, but Nan took not one bit of notice and taking his hand, walked onto the empty floor.

'Look at our Nan,' Evie grinned. 'Think she's clicked.'

'Yes, and he's not bad looking either. Hope no one asks me to do this one,' Carrie shrugged. 'It's such a silly dance.'

'Now, this is a good one for a beginner,' Nan beamed. 'It's just a bit of fun. You clap hands, clap each other's hands, do the bumps-a-daisy bit, and then you do four waltz steps, then start all over again. C'mon, now.'

They clapped hands, slapped hands then bumped bottoms.

'That's it! Now – one two three, one two three. Just follow me, Chas. You're doin' fine.'

He was. The waltzing came easily; bumping bottoms with a young ATS girl with mischief in her eyes was something he would never have dared to do.

Other couples took the floor. One waltzed past them, arms waving and said,

'What ho, Charlie! Got yourself a popsie, then?'

'Take no notice.' Chas had gone beetroot red, again. 'He's a bit loud, that's all . . .'

'Is he now?' Nan manoeuvred them alongside the offending male and his partner. 'Excuse *me*!' she hissed, narrowing her eyes, stepping to the

113

side. 'Oh, dear, he's tripped!' she giggled, before gliding away for the next bottom-bumping.

'Did you like that,' she asked when the dance was over.

'I did. I really did. Pity about old Clarry, though.'

'Who's he?'

'Clarence Harris. The one who skidded on the floor.'

'Mm. Serve him right. Didn't like him.'

'Why not, Nan?'

''Cause he called me a popsie and he called you Charlie and grinning all over his face like he'd said something clever. He asked for it!'

'Nan! You didn't – deliberately trip him, I mean?'

'No. Only he was so busy sniggering with that blonde he was dancin' with that he didn't notice his left foot got a bit near my right one, and down he went! Arse over tip!'

'Oh, my goodness! Nan, you are wicked and an absolute love and can I please have the next dance with you?'

'You can, Chas. You can,' she lifted her eyes to his and smiled. And did he but know it, bless him, he hadn't stammered once since they first bumped bottoms! 'And I think *you* are very nice, too . . .'

When they had had the last waltz together, doing one-two-three, one-two-three in the corner of the hut, Chas said,

'I'll walk you to the transport – if I may? This your jacket?'

Nan nodded, taking her cap and gloves from the sleeve she had pushed them into, holding back her arms as he helped her into it. Then she put on her cap, slipped her arm through his and left the hut.

They stood, blinking into the darkness. You always did that, when stepping into the blackout; give your eyes a few seconds to get adjusted. Then they made for the dim outline of the transport.

'You *will* ring me, Nan? You've got the aerodrome number?' He had written it on a page in his diary and she'd tucked it into her skirt pocket. 'If the operator tells you she isn't accepting incoming calls, it means we'll be flying. Security, you know. I won't be able to ring you, either. And you will remember to get the number of your NAAFI phone for me, so I can ring you when you aren't on shift?'

'I'll remember. Promise. Well, g'night, Chas. Thanks for tonight.' They were beside the transport now.

'Goodnight, Nan Morrissey – and the pleasure was all mine.' He leaned closer and kissed her cheek. 'You *will* phone – give me your number?'

'I said I would . . .' That had been her first goodnight kiss. On her cheek. It wasn't good enough. She took his face in her hands, then rose on tiptoe to kiss his mouth, softly, slowly, gently. 'And you take care, mind, next time you're flying.'

115

'I will, Nan. Promise.'

Oh, too right he would! And he'd get home in one piece, too, now that he had Nan Morrissey to come back to.

She was lost to him then in the darkness but he heard her laugh as she climbed aboard. Then he said her name softly as if it were a talisman. 'Nan. Nan Morrissey. And *you* take care too, darling girl . . .'

When the blackout curtains had been drawn at Southgate Lodge and the lights switched on and door bolts pushed home, Carrie said,

'A smashing dance, eh? Great band.'

'Plenty of partners,' Evie beamed, 'though someone not two feet from me got herself an admirer, or I'm very much mistaken. Well, come on then Morrissey – tell!'

'Ar. He's luvley.' Nan took off her tie and collar then unfastened her shirt buttons, eager to tell them about the sergeant who was a navigator in a Wellington bomber. 'But he can't dance, see, so I offered. He's very light on his feet so he'll be all right, with a bit more practice.'

'You're going to see him again, Nan?'

'Hope so. He gave me the aerodrome number so I can ring him in the sergeants' mess. I couldn't tell him what our NAAFI number was, so I'll give it to him, when I ring. He's called Charles Lawson by the way, and he talks real luvely. Y'know – like a frewt.'

'Like a *what*,' asked Carrie who was winding her hair into pincurls.

'A frewt. FRUIT.' She spelled it out. 'Posh, like . . .'

'I see.' Gravely, Carrie logged up yet another Liverpudlian word.

'Mind, I don't call him Charles 'cause it doesn't suit him. The fellers in his mess call him Charlie, but that doesn't suit him, either. So it's Chas. Mind, he blushes and stammers something awful when he talks to girls but he was all right, once him and me got to know each other. He kissed me goodnight and oh, hecky thump! I need to go down the garden! Anybody coming?' She pulled her greatcoat over her pyjamas and pushed her feet into her slippers.

'Not me,' Evie grinned.

'Nor me, but leave the back door open so we can hear you scream!' Carrie teased. 'Oh, for goodness sake! Take the torch. You'll be all right.'

Nan stuck her nose in the air, closed the bedroom door behind her, switched off the kitchen light, then opened the outside door.

Around her, all was stillness, then she blinked her eyes and made her way down the garden path. And of course she was all right! She put Cecilia from her mind and thought instead of Chas, who was lovely and talked posh – and who wanted to see her again.

'Aaah,' she sighed softly into the night, wondering if Chas was thinking about her. She hoped he was.

'You mustn't tease Nan,' Evie scolded, putting on her pyjamas. 'She's only a kid, remember, and it's up to us to look after her.'

'She'll be all right,' Carrie laughed. 'She's in such a state of bemusement that I don't think she'd notice if she fell over the nun! She's real taken with the airman.'

'I think so, too. After all, I don't think she's had many goodnight kisses! I hope, when she rings him, he'll ask her out.'

'I think he will. More to the point, though,' Carrie frowned, 'Nan works shifts, so every other night won't be on – and Chas flies bombing ops. Fixing dates might be a bit awkward. But did you enjoy tonight, Evie? Got plenty of partners, didn't we?'

'Mm. It was good, getting out again. We'll have to try to arrange a trip to Lincoln.'

'I could drive, if Freddy'll let me take the pick-up. Or maybe Norm would take us, and we could hitch a lift back.'

'I'll have a word with the sergeant. Next Saturday it'll have to be – when we finish shift at two. And hi! You all right?' she asked of Nan. 'Locked the back door?'

'Yes, I have. And was you talkin' about me?'

'We were,' Evie said frankly. 'We said we thought your airman was very nice, and we were talking ways and means about getting to Lincoln next Saturday so bear it in mind, when you're fixing a date with your Chas.'

'Mm. I will. Mind, he might not be able to get out, though I'd still like to go to town. Maybe,' she said almost nonchalantly, 'see if I can find a shop that's got a lipstick under the counter.'

Carrie's eyes met Evie's. Carrie winked slowly, saying not a word, and Evie bit her lip on a smile. Nan looking for a lipstick? So she *had* fallen for the airman, bless the girl. Then she hoped with all her heart that Nan wasn't storing up heartache because fliers had a habit of not coming back from ops.

'Think I'll go on a lipstick hunt, too,' Evie said. 'And I wouldn't mind a jar of cold cream, either – or a tin of Nivea.' And she mustn't think about Nan's young man not coming back from night raids over Germany. Not ever! Absently, she closed her eyes and fondled her wedding ring.

Take care Bob darling, wherever you are and God, if you could, take care of Nan's Chas and Carrie's Jeffrey. And oh, damn and blast this war!

SIX

Letters for Southgate Lodge; four for Evie – redirected – one for Nan, and three for Carrie.

'It won't be long,' Evie smiled, 'before they come to me, here. Bob should have my new address by now. Mm. Don't know whether to gobble them up, now, or to save them for when I come off shift tonight – read them before I go to sleep.'

'Bet you can't save them that long,' Carrie laughed, opening the letter she knew to be from Jeffrey's mother.

My dear Caroline,

News is very thin on the ground, here in Nether Hutton. The days grow shorter and the swallows are twittering on the telephone lines, ready to fly away. Taking summer with them, I suppose.

I called on your mother, yesterday. She seems very low and the dreadful cough she seems not able to throw off is not helping.

But don't worry. I will keep an eye on her for you

I hope soon to hear from Jeffrey and that he has got a ship. He seems very restless, in barracks. I do so hope you will be able to marry on his next leave.

'Jeffrey's mother,' Caroline said to no one in particular, 'says mother is depressed and can't seem to get rid of her cold. She didn't tell me she had one.'

'Mothers never do,' Evie soothed. 'And isn't that a letter from Jeffrey?'

'Mm. It'll be his new address.' The envelope carried the red stamp of the censor. She slit it with her thumb and pulled out a single sheet of notepaper.

Darling Carrie,

My new address is Communications Mess, HMS *Adventurer* c/o GPO London.

When I was in barracks I had a photograph taken in uniform. Have you got it, yet?

In haste. Write back at once. Love you,

'Jeffrey's sent a photograph.' More carefully Carrie opened the brown manila envelope with PLEASE DO NOT BEND written large on top. 'Mm. Not bad. Looks as if he's been to the Navy barber . . .'

'Why isn't he smiling?' Nan frowned.

'Probably because, like most men, he doesn't like having his photo taken. He's quite nice, actually, to look at,' she said defensively. 'He's got thick black hair, though you can't see it for the cap' . . . His cap was pulled well forward, regulation style, over his forehead.

All my love. Jeffrey. Nan scanned the inscription then handed the photograph to Evie. 'Don't you ever call him Jeff?'

'No. Never. His mother doesn't like it.'

'Pity for *her*! Ah, well, I'm nippin' up to the NAAFI to phone Chas. Best go while it's quiet. Anybody want anythin' ?'

'You could ask if they've got cigarettes under the counter.' Carrie did not smoke, but they could generally get a ten-packet in the NAAFI, and she bought hers to give to Norm and Freddie, who did smoke. 'And Lenice said she'd heard that once a month, they get a make-up allocation. You just might ask when it's going to be. After all, you *are* in need of a lipstick, Nan . . .'

Nan walked up the lane, arms swinging, a little pulse of pleasure beating behind her nose. Modeley 147 – Sergeants' Mess was what she must ask for – after taking a deep breath to calm her nerves. Because she was just a little apprehensive, worrying that Chas might not be there. Or he might be there and pretend not to be if he didn't want to speak to her because she had been a bit fresh, come to think of it, kissing him on the mouth. Girls shouldn't kiss fellers – not when they hardly knew them.

The NAAFI was empty. There was no queue at the telephone. Nan placed three pennies and a sixpenny piece on top of the coinbox, picked up the receiver, asking for the number.

'Place three pennies in the box please, caller.'

Nan obliged and was asked to wait, then,

'I have 147 on the line. Press button A.'

Nan pressed. The pennies fell with a clatter. The aerodrome answered which meant Chas wasn't flying tonight. And dammit, she was on shift!

'Can I speak to Sergeant Charles Lawson,' she asked, surprised how quickly she was connected.

'Charlie! The call you're waiting for! Your popsie!'

'Hello, Nan,' he said, almost immediately. 'Thanks for ringing.'

'You've been waitin' for this call, Chas?'

''Fraid so. Even though I was sure you wouldn't ring. Look, Nan, you're working tonight, Monday and Wednesday – right?'

'Yes. What about you?'

'Not sure, but I reckon Sunday night just might be on. That OK for you?'

'Should be.' She giggled. 'Reckon we're goin' to be like Box and Cox, you and me. Where, on Sunday? What time?'

'Do you know the Black Bull at Little Modeley?'

Nan knew it. *And* grandad who drank best bitter there, an' all!

'The Black Bull it is, then Chas. At seven?'

'Right! And if I don't make it, will you forgive me and ring me after twelve, on Monday? And what's your NAAFI number?'

'Modeley 618, but it might be awkward, ringing me. If I'm not there, I mean, they can't take messages. Just fingers crossed, eh, for Sunday?'

'Fingers crossed – and N-nan – take care, dear girl.'

'And you, too. See you, Chas . . .'

Reluctantly, she put down the receiver, wishing they could have talked some more – at least till the threepence ran out. Local calls were easy to get. Not like trunk calls you had to wait ages and ages for, and were only allowed three minutes before the operator interrupted and told you your time was up. Rarely was anyone given longer. The war, of course. Even the telephones were at it, the Armed Forces being given priority over the poor old civilians.

She walked to the counter. 'Any ciggies,' she asked of the ginger-haired assistant.

'Any money?' He dipped beneath the counter and brought out a packet. 'A bob gets you ten!'

'Oooh! Thanks, chum.' Nan parted with a shilling and gave him a wink. 'And there's a rumour goin' round that you might have make-up to sell.'

'News to me,' he shrugged, 'but you'd better ask the lady when she's on duty, tonight. She'll know . . .'

Nan hurried back to Southgate. No lipsticks and suchlike in the NAAFI, but she had a date. Sunday, at seven, at the Black Bull! Quite a way to walk, but what the heck? If Chas was waiting there, it would be worth every step of the way. *If.* Oh, please he wouldn't be flying? Not on her first date?'

With a frown, Carrie read what she had written. Just like her mother not to tell her she was ill; just like Jeffrey's mother to make sure she knew!

Why didn't you tell me you were poorly, mother? Please, please, phone Doc Smithson and ask him to call and give you a check-up. And ask him to give you a tonic, too.

There is not a lot of news. Jeffrey, as you will probably know has got a ship at last. HMS *Adventurer* – home waters, I hope. He sent a photograph. He looks very stern, in uniform.

Should she tell her mother about the dance at RAF Modeley and what a good time they had had? Perhaps not. It didn't seem right to be enjoying yourself when your mother was ill – and alone.

Am going to get something to eat, now, before I take the late shift on duty and collect the earlies. This is just a short note to let you know how sorry I am you are not well, and to beg you to send for the doctor.

In haste, but with much, much love.

Her mother – or *Jeffrey's* mother – made her feel bad because she had joined up instead of getting married so she need not leave home to do her war work. But she *had* left home and would only be back to Jackmans Cottage for a week every three months for as long as the war lasted.

Quickly she addressed the envelope. She would post it when she went for her meal when it would have every chance of being on its way by tomorrow.

She looked out of the window and saw a flush-cheeked Nan hurrying up the path, doubtless with news of the utmost importance to tell! It made her wish she were nearly eighteen again, and going on her first real date. But she was twenty-one, or would be at the end of October.

She arranged a smile on her lips as Nan burst into the room and tossed her the cigarettes.

'That's a shillin' you owe me, Tiptree, and guess what! I'm meetin' Chas at the Black Bull on Sunday.'

There was just nothing to say in reply to such bright-eyed, breathless happiness, so Carrie said,

'Thanks a lot,' and gave Nan two sixpenny pieces without further comment, because she knew she had never felt that way on her first real date – nor on any of the many that followed.

'Fingers crossed, mind – flying, and all that.'

Nan collapsed on her bed and lay, hands behind head, gazing at the ceiling as if, Carrie thought, Chas's face were up there, and smiling down at her.

'Nan,' she said softly. 'You know I'm very happy about you and Chas, but don't get hurt, will you? There's a war on, don't forget?'

'Don't think I don't know.' Nan sat bolt upright, the contentment gone from her face. 'And it looks like every date we have will depend on that war, damn and blast it! And he mightn't even be there, on Sunday. He could be flying ops!'

'So you'll walk all the way to the Black Bull, and he mightn't show – then walk all the way back? And it's getting dark earlier now, Nan.'

'It's all I can do. If they suddenly tell them they're off bombing, he can't give me a quick ring, can he? Their switchboard shuts down. No calls out and no calls allowed in. Security, see?'

'Oh, Nan Morrissey! Your love affair is going to be as complicated as mine,' Carrie laughed. 'You and Chas and me and Jeffrey trying to get together, I mean. But if Chas shows on Sunday, surely he'll walk you home?'

'Of course he will. Suppose, if I'd told him how to get here, he'd have met me at Priest's. I was just so glad to be talkin' to him that I didn't think. But don't worry about me, Carrie. I'm a big girl, now.'

'Mm. Old enough to take the King's shilling so I reckon you're grown up enough to go on dates without Evie and me watching over you like mother hens. Sorry, love.'

'Don't be sorry, Carrie. I like being fussed over. It's nice when somebody cares about you – honest it is. And I'm going to give this place a good turn out, so you'd better get yourself back to the stableyard. And if you see Evie in the washroom, tell her not to hurry back.'

She wanted Southgate to herself, Nan thought; wanted to think about and sigh over Chas. And if it meant getting into her horrible brown overall and sweeping and mopping and dusting the place, then it would be worth it, because Chas was very nice to think about, and sigh over. And oh, *please*, let him be there at seven tomorrow night, and not flying into danger in a bomber?

'I'm pushing off now to get some supper,' Sergeant James said to Evie. 'There isn't a lot of traffic – you can manage without me, Turner, till the end of the shift.' It was more of an order than a question. 'I'll be back before ten, to hand over to the night man.'

'We'll be fine,' Evie smiled, wondering how much longer Sergeant James could keep up her long working day – six in the morning until ten at night, with only breaks for meals. Soon, maybe, she should talk about her having more time off. After all, Evie reasoned, she did have a stripe up and more than able to cope with anything the people behind the green baize door might throw at her. 'See you about ten.'

'So you're in charge,' Nan said when the sergeant had left for the cookhouse.

'Yes I am, and since you don't seem busy, how about putting the kettle on?'

Maybe then, Evie thought, they could have a chat about tomorrow night, and was Nan really thinking of walking the mile back alone, if her boyfriend didn't show up, and to keep to the side of the road if she heard anything coming and not stick her thumb out for a lift. That was just asking for an accident. Things like that happened all the time in the blackout with motors only allowed dim lights to drive on.

She stared at the switchboard and thought, soberly, that soon they would have dark nights to endure; blackouts to be in place, in November, by late afternoon, and not one glimmer of light to be shown until next morning. Not even the lighting of a cigarette, out doors. And then there would be winter, and freezing billets and frost patterns on the insides of windows. It made her wonder if they dare light a fire at Southgate and if, on moonlit nights or nights bright with stars, anyone would notice the smoke puffing from the chimney.

'Y'know,' she said absently, 'I was thinking that when the cold weather comes and we're on late shift, we could boil up the kettle and fill our hot-water bottles.'

And Nan said it would be a good idea, but she didn't have a hot-water bottle and surely Evie knew there were none in the shops, now that rubber was a commodity of war, and anything made from it non-existent, almost.

'Well, next time I go on leave I shall bring mine – and the little camping stove and kettle. I'm not looking forward to winter, Nan.'

'Who is?' Nan blew on her tea. 'But what I'm more worried about is tomorrow night – that Chas will be able to make it, I mean.'

'Yes – but if he doesn't, you *will* be careful walking home on your own?' Evie seized the opportunity. 'Keep to the side of the road, because it'll be getting dark, don't forget.'

'Don't worry – I will. But I don't even want to think that he mightn't be there.'

'You're very taken with him, aren't you Nan?'

'We-e-ll, he *is* the first feller that's asked me out. And he's not a bit common and he talks luv'ly. He'll be smashin' when I've taught him to dance. He gets a bit scared talking to girls, so he's never plucked up the courage.'

'But he asked you!'

'Nah! It was me asked him. I told him that if he didn't get up on the floor with me, then some other feller would ask me – and I wanted to dance with him.'

'Nothing if not direct,' Evie laughed.

'It's the way us Liverpudlians are. Straight to the point. No messin'. I had a great time.'

'I know. I was there, don't forget! But you will be careful, Nan? You know what I mean?'

'I think I do. And don't worry. I didn't come down with the last fall of snow, you know!'

And now they were back to snow again, Evie

thought. And winter and sleeping with your undies under your pillow, to keep them warm.

'I wonder,' she said, 'when Sergeant James will get the leave-roster going? I'm not due leave for two months yet, but you and Carrie and the two at Priest's should be thinking about it before so very much longer.'

'They told us when we first joined that leave was a privilege and not a God-given right.'

'Yes, but you always get it, Nan. They like to throw rules and regulations at you, just to show you who's boss. And someone,' she grinned as a small round disc dropped, 'is alive and kicking at the big house. Thought they must have gone into town tonight, to the flicks.'

She picked up a plug, pushed it in and said, 'Switchboard.'

And Nan hugged her mug which was thick and white and shaped like a chamber pot and willed one of her teleprinters to shift itself and click out a signal.

'I think,' Evie said, 'that it's going to be one of those nights. There are times, I've found, when the war seems to take a breather for some peculiar reason. Ah, well, roll on ten o'clock . . .'

At ten minutes to ten, the green baize door opened and the Yeoman said, 'Evening, ladies.' He was dressed in his usual night rig and carried a notepad and pen, his tin-lid ashtray and a packet of cigarettes. 'Busy?'

131

'Nah. Boring, actually,' Nan shrugged. 'In fact, we decided that most of your lot must be out on the town, it bein' Sat'day night. Packed up for the weekend, have they?'

'Wouldn't know. The high-ups don't tell me anything. I'm not that important.'

'Civilians, are they?' Nan asked.

'Some of them.'

'So tell me, Yeoman, why don't they have their own people looking after the teleprinters and switchboard? Why do they seem to need Army people to do it?'

'Your guess is as good as mine, young lady,' he said, walking into the kitchen. 'Either of you want a cup of tea – and where is your sergeant, tonight?'

'She's here!' They heard the door bang, then Monica James emerged from between the thick curtains covering it. 'And why wasn't this door bolted behind me when I left?'

'Good evening, Sergeant. Tea?' asked the Yeoman.

'No thank you.' She walked, shoulders stiff, to the switchboard. 'Everything OK, Lance-Corporal?'

'Fine. Nothing to report Sergeant.'

'Transport's waiting outside. Get your jackets on and off you go, then. And goodnight, Yeoman. See you at six . . .'

'Night, then – but couldn't we all be a little less formal. We're all fighting the same war, after all.

Couldn't you and I throw caution to the winds and call each other Sarge and Yeo?'

He smiled, and it crinkled his eye corners and made him look much less serious, she thought. But still she said,

'No thank you. As you said, we're here to fight a war, so what would be the point in it? See you tomorrow – and bolt the door, please?'

Then she tugged her jacket straight, tweaked the peak of her cap and went to sit beside Carrie.

'Well! The Navy's laying on the charm. Call me Yeo, he said! But it isn't on and don't any of you forget it.' She turned in her seat to glower at Evie and Nan. 'They made it quite clear from the onset. *Their* lot doesn't fraternise with *our* lot, so if they want to play cloak-and-dagger and treat us like we're not to be trusted, then it's OK by me!'

'But Sergeant,' Evie protested, 'he *is* rather nice and he's only trying to be friendly.'

'Yes, an' if we got to talking to him, maybe we'd find out what that lot are up to,' Nan added.

'They'll tell us, if they want us to know. Now, do any of you want to stop off at the NAAFI for a hot drink?'

'No thanks. We've been drinkin' tea all night. An' we're on early shift, tomorrow. Best be off to bed. Thanks all the same,' Nan said.

Nan Morrissey could not wait for tomorrow to come and for her shift to be over. Only then could she wash her hair, press her best uniform and polish her buttons. Then she would have a quick bite in the cookhouse and be off in the direction of Little Modeley and the Black Bull. And Chas, of course. Would be hell though, if he wasn't waiting when she got there.

'Well, that's Private Morrissey on her way!' Evie giggled. 'Bless the girl, she was in a real dither. It's her first real date.'

'I know it is. She told me so. But – well – I wonder if I could have a word with you,' Carrie hesitated.

'Surely. I've written to Bob. Just got my bed to make up, then I'm all ears.'

'It's sort of – *personal*, Evie. About being married. Y'see, I can't talk to my mother about it.'

'Girls rarely can, I believe – talk to their mothers about *things*. So what's bothering you? Getting wedding jitters?'

'No. In fact I said to Jeffrey that I wouldn't mind us being married in our uniforms – especially if it turns out to be a winter wedding. But it isn't that, Evie. It's what happens after that I'm worried about – and if you'd rather not talk about something – well – so personal, I'll understand.'

'Your wedding night, you mean? But haven't you and he talked it over, yet? About whether you want children right away, or do you both want to wait till the war is over – things like that?'

'I never even thought. Just don't seem to be able to get past the when-it-happens-bit.'

'You mean you're worried about it? Oh, but you shouldn't be. It's wonderful, Carrie!'

'Is it? Well, *I* didn't think so . . .' Carrie looked down at her hands.

'So you and Jeffrey have been lovers?'

'Lovers! Is *that* what you call it? And yes, we did it. He wanted to, so I let him. I just laid there, Evie, and looked at the ceiling, and when it was over I felt sick.'

'Hey, come on now – don't get upset. And remember, you don't have to talk about it, though I think it's best you do. Because loving, between two people, can be – *should* be – nothing short of breathtaking. It makes me go peculiar just thinking about it, and what I wouldn't give right now to be somewhere with Bob for just an hour. And if it's any comfort, Bob and I didn't wait for our wedding night, either.'

'Yes, but I bet you wanted to, Evie, and I didn't . . .'

'But why didn't you talk to him about it, afterwards – tell him how you felt?'

'What would have been the point?' Red-cheeked, Carrie walked to the window, staring out, arms folded. 'You don't criticise Jeffrey. He'd throw a sulk. And anyway, I wanted him out of the house – before my mother got back, I told him. But all I wanted to do was wash myself all over.'

'Well, the way I see it is that it's a rum do if you can't discuss things calmly and sensibly with the man you want to spend the rest of your life with – have his children, too. Was it really so awful, Carrie?'

'No. Just not enjoyable, I suppose. I used to think that being able to do that whenever you wanted to must be really nice. But I suppose, if you want children – and I do – I'll have to put up with things the way they are.' She blew her nose loudly, then drew the curtains over the window. 'Sorry if I embarrassed you, Evie. Tell you what – let's nip up to the NAAFI – maybe have a half of shandy, or something? My treat?'

'No thanks, Carrie. You and I need to talk and it's best we do it here! Because you don't have to put up with anything, you know. It should be an act of loving between you – and not you putting up with it. Sorry, love, but I have to say this – in my opinion, that kind of a marriage will be nothing short of a misery, for both of you! So let's you and me have that talk, and then I suggest you write to Jeffrey and tell him what's bothering you and how you can both put it right.'

'*Whaaat!* And have someone here censor my letter – Sergeant James, maybe? Not on your life, Evie!'

'So you'll wait to talk to him when next you are on leave? Is that wise?'

'Suppose not, especially since everybody expects we're going to be married when we can manage to get leave together. My mother – Jeffrey's mother

– the entire village thinks it. Be a bit late for talking, won't it?

'And Evie, since you are acting *in loco parentis*, sort of, I think I'd better get the whole lot off my chest! I didn't have to volunteer. I needn't have joined up till I registered. And my age group hasn't come up, yet. I really think,' she rushed on, eyes on her hands, 'that I joined up on purpose.'

'To get away from Jeffrey, you mean, or to get out of getting married,' Evie demanded, wide-eyed. 'Do you realise how very serious marriage is – and how very wonderful it can be?'

'I'd like to think we could be like you and Bob, but we're not. Do you know that when you talk about him your eyes go all far away, and tender? And do you realise that you touch your wedding ring, too?' Carrie whispered. 'And hadn't you thought that I wear my engagement ring round my neck because I say I don't want to get it greased up?

'And I didn't join up to get away from Jeffrey, or get out of getting married. It was really, I suppose, to get away from the pressure. Everybody seemed to assume that that's how it would be. I wanted time to myself, to think it out.'

The tears came then, hot and salty, and she covered her face with her hands and wept. And Evie sat on the bed beside her, and held her close, and said, 'Ssssh. Seems to me you've been bottling this up for far too long, Carrie Tiptree, and when you are ready, you and I are going to have a good talk about things, before young Nan gets back. And talking about our Nan,' she smiled, offering a clean handkerchief, 'I wonder if her young man made it or if she's on her way back, now – stood up and fed up!'

Private Nan Morrissey turned the bend in the road and saw the Black Bull ahead. No one was waiting there. She glanced at her watch. Ten minutes early, so where should she wait? Inside the pub, or outside? She remembered Grandad and decided to wait in the car park to the left where she wouldn't be so conspicuous – especially if Chas didn't turn up.

She heard the banging of a car door, and footsteps and then, 'Nan!'

'Hi!' she called, hurrying to meet him.

'I was sure you wouldn't turn up.' He took her hands in his, kissing her cheek.

'And I was sure you'd be flying. I decided to give it till half-past, then shove off back. But you're here. I wanted you to be.'

'You did, Nan? Truly?'

'Honest to God. Now – are we goin' inside for a drink, or shall we have a stroll and a chat, before it gets dark?'

'Whatever you want. We could, of course, sit in the car . . . ?'

'The car? You got a motor, Chas?'

'I sort of share one. She's a little darling. Come and meet her?' He led her to a small car, a baby

Austin, with one door tied up with wire and a mudguard missing. 'We call her Boadicea.'

'You call her *what*!'

Nan knew about Queen Boadicea. Indeed, she'd had nothing but admiration for the tribal queen who rebelled against the Romans who shouldn't have been in England the first place!

'But Chas – that motor isn't one bit like a war chariot! Not the one Boadicea drove. Pulled by horses hers was and it had steel blades sticking out of the wheels so anybody that got a bit close got their legs cut off at the knees! That little thing shouldn't be called Boadicea!'

'What, then?' He grinned.

'We-e-ll – something like Violet or Primrose. Something delicate, sort of – and helpless!'

'Sorry, Nan. Boadicea she is.' He patted the bonnet with a gentle hand. 'It was my turn to have her, tonight. She belonged to an air-gunner who didn't make it back, so we kind of took her over.'

'But where do you get petrol from?' Petrol was severely rationed.

'We sort of come by it. You can usually get hold of the odd gallon if you know where to look. And Boadicea goes a long way on a gallon.'

'Y-yes. Well, I suppose we'd better go inside. I fancy a glass of shandy. How about you, Chas?'

'Anything you say. I reckon we've got a lot of talking to do. And I'll run you back in her.'

'Do you know where my billet is – in the dark, I mean, and without lights? And can you find your way back to the aerodrome, from Heronflete?'

'Darling girl, I can navigate my way to Berlin and back in the blackout – and without lights, too. Boadicea might have seen better days, but I trust her implicitly.'

'Then I'll be glad of a lift, only I haven't got a late pass. I'll have to be in by half-past ten or I'll be in trouble.'

'Don't worry. We'll have you home in good time.' He took her hand, pulling it through his arm. 'Like I said, you & I have a lot of catching up to do.'

And Nan let slip a little sigh, and thought how nice it was to be walking arm in arm with a young man who called her darling girl. And, of far more importance, a young man who hadn't stammered once since they met. Now that *really* was something!

'Feeling better now?' Evie asked softly.

'Yes. And sorry I made such a show of myself. I can usually cope with things. I've had to, y'see, me being what you might call a fatherless only child. And you must think I'm dreadful, leaving my mother on her own like I did. But it seemed to be the only way out. And I'm not making a fuss, truly I'm not.'

'You've every right to make a fuss. Getting married is for life, Carrie, and best you sort yourself out now than be sorry, afterwards. And can I just say, that in my opinion, Jeffrey should have been a bit more – well – careful, when it was your first time. Bob was lovely – so gentle – but it seems to me that Jeffrey just rushed in without any talking – y'know, love words – or coaxing and kissing. And touching, too. Touching is very important; makes you want to as much as he does. But then, it might have been his first time, too – had you thought about that?'

'No I hadn't. I suppose it could have been like that for him, too. But why didn't he tell me, instead of just demanding and snatching, Evie? I think I'd have felt a bit better about it if he'd been straight with me.'

'Yes – we-e-ll – you're *both* going to have to be honest with each other, and both of you must try not to be accusing, or bitter. Just try to talk – or write – as friends; loving friends.'

'I'm not writing to him, Evie. I know it would be far the best way because I could set out my feelings more carefully and without interruption, too. But the thought of my letter being censored – oh, no. And it would be the same for Jeffrey, as well.'

'Then what you're going to have to do is write it all in a letter, keeping nothing back, and then stick a stamp on it and post it in a pillarbox like civilians do. We're going to Lincoln on Saturday – surely you can manage to post one without been seen? It's the best way out, in my opinion.'

'I hadn't thought of that, Evie. After all, even if I were caught, it wouldn't be Heronflete I'd be writing about, would it? It would just be –' She hesitated, sighing deeply. 'Well, it would just be about my love life, wouldn't it. Or the lack of it.'

'You'll give it a go, then? All it needs is an un-biased, uncritical letter telling Jeffrey how you felt about what happened that night, and how willing you are to work things out between you so that, when you do get married, everything will be much less embarrassing. You do want your wedding night to be something to remember always, don't you Carrie?'

'Yes, I do.' Just to think of a loving and gentle husband, caring about how she felt and wanting to make things wonderful for them both, made her feel more understanding towards the Jeffrey who had been so uncaring and brash that it had made her almost dislike him. 'Thanks a lot, Mrs Turner. And I wish I'd talked to you like this ages ago.'

'Ages ago, Carrie, we didn't know each other well enough. And bless you for calling me Mrs Turner. I was Mrs Turner for a whole week, after which I became Turner, or lance-corporal again. And heavens! What *is* that awful din outside!'

'Sounds like a threshing machine in pain!'

Carrie put out the light as Evie made for the front door, calling 'Who is it? Who's there?'

'It's me – Morrissey. Who did you think it was?' Nan giggled. 'And it was only Chas turning Boadicea round. She's a bit naughty in reverse gear, he said.'

'*Boadicea?* Have you been drinking Morrissey?'

'No, Evie. We've been talking, mostly. And listen – there she goes, up the hill by the wood.'

They heard the sound of an engine protesting at so steep a hill, then the grating of gears and the parping of a horn.

'That's Chas letting me know he's got her under control again.'

'We'd better get inside. It's turned half-past ten and I wouldn't put it past the sergeant to do a sneaky check on us tonight – especially after all the commotion. And got who or what under control?'

'Boadicea. She's the little Austin they have as a runabout at Chas's place. She's very old and lots of bits have dropped off but they're all very fond of her, so don't mock her. And if I called your pick-up a rattletrap, Carrie, then I take it all back. You don't know what rattletrap means, till you've been driven in Boadicea.'

'So are you going to tell us about it,' Evie prompted, a little alarmed at the flush in Nan's cheeks and the shine in her eyes. 'You had a good time?'

'Luvely. And fingers crossed that we'll both be able to make it on Tuesday. Chas says he'll pick me up at Priest's, so's I don't have to hoof all the way to the Black Bull, and would you mind if I don't tell you, about it just now? So much happened, see, that it would take half the night.'

'But everything was all right?' Evie persisted. 'He didn't – er –'

'Try anything on? Course he didn't. But I hope it's allowed for him to kiss me goodnight?'

'Of course it is – and I'm not quizzing you, Nan. I haven't got the right. I'd like to know, all the same, that Chas acted – well – like –'

'Like a gentleman,' Carrie supplied gravely.

'Of course he did. He *is* a gentleman. And I'll just do a quick nip down the garden.'

'You'll be all right, Nan?'

'Course I will!'

The kitchen door slammed and Carrie said, 'Well, if falling in love makes you *that* brave, then I'm all for it. And mark my words, Nan's in love.'

'Then I hope she doesn't get hurt – after all, Chas does take more risks than most – flying, I mean.'

'She won't get hurt, Evie. She'll be all right. Nan's sort usually have a good guardian angel.'

'Then I hope Chas has one, too.'

Evie really meant it, because Nan was so very young and this was her first falling in love. And probably Chas's, too. Not twenty-one yet, but old enough to fly over Germany.

Evie hoped that Charles Lawson had a very vigilant guardian angel.

SEVEN

Carrie waited outside Priest's Lodge. Three o'clock, Sergeant James had said, after which she would drive to Southgate, collect Evie and Nan, then set out for Lincoln. She drummed her fingers on the wheel, going over her instructions in her mind.

'You can park behind Lincoln Barracks, no problem,' Freddy had told her. 'Best place to leave the truck, then nobody can get at your petrol. And Norm can take the big car to pick up the late shift. What'll you be doing with yourself this afternoon, Carrie?'

'Just having a look at the shops and maybe I'll get something to eat if I can find a café.'

Carrie had felt uneasy. Not about driving through Lincoln for the first time, nor finding somewhere to park, but about the letter she was going to post sneakily in the first pillarbox she came across.

That letter to Jeffrey had not been easy to write. She had torn up several attempts before deciding that pussyfooting would get her nowhere. Straight

145

and to the point it would have to be – and as reasonable as she could make it without seeming to criticise.

Dearest Jeffrey,

This letter will be very hard to write, but write it I must because something has been upsetting me for a long time – since the night mother was out playing whist, in fact – and we did something we should not have done. I was not proud of myself for giving in because I would rather have waited until our wedding night.

What we did made me feel so guilty, Jeffrey, that I did not enjoy it, and I know I should have, so can we talk about it, and will you at least try to understand how I feel, and what a terrible scandal there would have been in the village, if something had gone dreadfully wrong?

I cannot think about our wedding, you see, without remembering that night and how it upset me. And yes, I know I should have said something at the time, but I was too embarrassed and just wanted to forget it.

I do not know what I am trying to say, exactly, except that I want you to put my mind at rest and tell me it will be absolutely wonderful when next it happens – which will be on our honeymoon, I hope.

This letter is not meant to criticise you. I

just think that we were both a bit hasty and spoiled something that should really be very precious.

I think I have put this badly, and I am sorry, but when next we meet I hope we will be able to talk to each other freely and frankly and put things to rights.

I am posting this letter sneakily, so you need not worry that someone had read it, and I hope you might be able to find a way to do the same when you reply to it. After all, things concerning you and me should be read by you and I only.

Write back very soon, and tell me you understand, darling. And tell me I am being an idiot, and that of course our honeymoon will be something I will never want to forget.

With love.

A disjointed, rambling letter with words tumbling out higgledy-piggledy; a letter she wished she need never have written, but one which, now it was in her pocket, she was glad that she had.

'Wakey wakey, Tiptree!' Sergeant James placed her respirator at her feet, then banged shut the door of the truck. 'You were miles away!'

'Sorry, Sergeant. Just thinking that once we get there I'll be all right. Corporal Finnigan told me where to park. It's just a bit awkward, with no road signs.'

'Agreed, but necessary. Can't have the enemy

knowing where he is if he decides to parachute in!'

'But I thought there wasn't going to be an invasion, Sergeant. Not now that Hitler's invaded Russia . . .'

'The rate that man's going at, he'll be in Moscow by Christmas. Mind, it'll be snowing there soon, so heaven only knows what'll happen when everything is frozen over. But chop-chop, girl, and pick up the other two!'

'Yes, Sergeant.' Carrie could see Southgate at the bottom of the hill, and Evie and Nan waiting at the gate.

'And what will you two be doing this afternoon,' the sergeant asked when they had climbed into the back of the truck.

'Me, Sergeant? I've got a date,' Nan offered cheerily. 'Well, I *think* I have. Course, he might be off bombin' and that'll be the end of it. Fingers crossed, eh?'

'An airman, Morrissey? He wouldn't by any chance own a very noisy car that awoke me at half-past ten the other night?'

'Ar, sorry, Sergeant. That would be Boadicea. She's a car he shares with some of the other lads at the aerodrome.'

'Ha!' Monica James was at a loss for words because, in her opinion, someone as young as Morrissey should be told the facts of life before she went on dates and allowed herself to be driven home in the dark in a car that wheezed and coughed – *and* backfired – fit to wake the dead!

But where did your duty as a sergeant end and where did interference take over? And surely Morrissey would have had the usual lectures in barracks during her training? Personal Hygiene, didn't it come under? Keeping your nose clean and not landing yourself in trouble, it amounted to.

'We'll be dancing,' Nan supplied when the silence had become noticeable. 'He can't dance, so I'm learning him.'

'Then mind your young man gets you back to the truck for ten sharp.'

'Yes, Sergeant.' There didn't seem much else to say, especially since Chas mightn't even be there.

'What will you do this afternoon?' Evie asked the sergeant.

'Got an appointment at the hairdressers for a trim and a shampoo and set, Turner. How about you?'

'Carrie – er – Tiptree and I will tag along together – maybe look out for some under-the-counter-make-up.'

For the rest of the journey there was silence; Carrie concentrating on her driving, Sergeant James thinking how embarrassing it was having to mix with recruits so raw they hadn't had their first leave, yet. Except Turner, that was.

She settled down to think about leave and leave-rosters, whilst Nan brooded that it wasn't half awful having to share your transport with a sergeant on your afternoon off.

But Evie gentled her wedding ring and thought how marvellous it would be if she turned a corner and saw Bob striding towards her.

'I can see the Cathedral,' Carrie called. 'Nearly there.'

She found the barracks with no trouble at all, reversed neatly into a parking space, then locked the truck.

'Ten o'clock!' reminded Sergeant James, then strode off in the direction of the High Street and a hairdresser called Maisie.

'Where are you meeting Chas?' Evie asked.

'Outside the Cathedral. I told him I'm not very good at findin' places, so he said I couldn't miss something so big and I was to meet him there. Fingers crossed, eh?' she grinned. 'See you'se both. Have fun . . .'

'Fun!' Carrie grunted. 'All I can think of is this letter. Keep your eyes open for a pillarbox, Evie.'

'You managed it, then? Difficult, was it?'

'After four false starts, but I got it finished in the end. It's a bit of a jumble, but he'll get the message. And I was very reasonable; said I knew things would be fine when we can get together and put things to rights – or words to that effect.'

'So you'll be threshing things out on your next leave – not arranging a wedding?'

'If Jeffrey accepts the way I feel about – you know – *things*, there's nothing to stop us getting a special licence – takes about three days, I believe. Mind, it would be a quiet wedding and a short honeymoon, so if mother is planning a big do, then we'll have to put it off, to give her time. You were married in white, weren't you?' There was a wedding photograph on Evie's locker. 'Don't think I'll be able to run to anything elaborate, especially since I'd have to give coupons for a dress I'd only wear once.'

'You've got clothing coupons?' Evie frowned. 'Didn't you give them in when you joined up?'

'I gave in my food ration book, my identity card *and* my clothing coupons book. But I only left two coupons in it – cut out the rest and they're hidden at home. And I still think being married in our uniforms would be just fine. And I'm lucky. I won't have to have a utility nine-carat ring. Mother said I could have my grandmother's wedding ring. It's quite thick and a bit old-fashioned, but it's the real thing – and hey up, Evie. You take it!'

An officer was approaching them, head on, and would require to be saluted, because there were no convenient shop windows they could turn to look into, no way of getting out of it.

Evie brought her hand up in the smartest salute; Carrie gave an eyes right then whispered, 'Hell!' I hate saluting!'

'You'll get used to it, old love. King's Regulations and all that. Means nothing, really. You're only saluting the rank and not the man. And this place is crawling with officers – let's get out of here, sharpish.'

They made for the street outside and a pillarbox and a café in that order, finding both within yards of each other.

'Good! Just slip it in,' Evie whispered, 'as if you've got every right to. Try not to look guilty!'

Carrie heard the plop as it fell, then relaxed visibly. It was on its way now; no going back. And Jeffrey would understand – of course he would!

'Right! Tea and with a bit of luck, a cake, or something,' Evie grinned. 'You look as if you could do with a cuppa, Tiptree.'

'I could. And thanks a lot,' Carrie sighed as she opened the café door. 'For helping me sort things out. I feel a whole lot better about everything, now.'

They took off caps and pushed respirators under the table, then smiled as a motherly waitress, wearing a brightly flowered pinafore, whispered,

'I've got jammed scones under the counter – strictly for the armed forces, of course. Would you like one?'

And they whispered back that they would, and that it was very kind of her.

'Y'know – it isn't bad, being in the Forces, Evie. People are very kind; they stop to give you lifts and keep jammed scones for you!'

'Life could be a whole lot worse. The only thing about being in the ATS that worries me is when I'll get my demob.'

And there was one other thing that worried Evie Turner, but she never ever mentioned it, becuase no matter how long the war lasted, her husband must come safely home at the end of it – oh, please God, he must?'

And Carrie noticed the sadness in her friend's eyes and the fingertips that gentled her wedding ring and said brightly, 'First things first, Lance-Corporal – I'm talking about Morrissey. Wonder if she's managed to find her way to the Cathedral, yet.'

'It's big enough. She can't miss it. More to the point is whether Chas will be able to make it,' Evie sighed. 'I hope Nan isn't disappointed.'

And Carrie crossed her fingers and gazed through the window to where the honey-coloured towers rose high above the rooftops of ages-old houses and said, solemnly,

'Fingers crossed. No ops tonight . . .'

They hadn't set a time – an *exact* time – for their meeting.

'I should be there before four,' Nan had told Chas. 'It'll depend, see, on how soon we can get away, and how long it takes me to find you.'

And Chas said that it would be all right; that if everything went to plan he would be outside the Cathedral by half-past three, and would wait until she got there. So now, Nan fretted, he would have been waiting ages and ages, because it was ten minutes to four, and she seemed to have gone round in circles, trying to get there.

Then she saw him and her heart gave a

pitty-pat and her cheeks flushed with pleasure. She called his name, hurrying towards him, and he saw her, and held up his hand, and smiled.

'I got lost,' she said breathlessly. 'Sorry.'

'It doesn't matter. You're here, and I'm so glad to see you.' He wished they were not in so public a place, because he wanted to gather her close and hold her tightly, but things like that were not allowed to members of the Armed Forces. Only in railway stations could they get away with it. 'Where shall we go?'

'Anywhere at all,' Nan beamed and stopped herself in the nick of time from adding that as long as they were together it didn't matter one bit.

'Then we'll find somewhere to eat then go to the dance. There's one on tonight. I've never been to it, but I know where it is.'

'Good, because you're doing very well, you know. You can do the silly dances, Chas, and you can waltz.'

'So what's the programme for tonight?'

'I think,' she said very seriously, 'that you're ready for learnin' the quickstep. And if they have a jitter-bug session, I reckon we should try that, an' all.'

'Oops! Don't think I could manage to do that. It's a bit – er – wild, isn't it?'

'Course not. All you need to remember is to keep to the beat with your feet, then you can do anything you want with the rest of you. There's no rules to it. It's fun, Chas. You'll be able to do it, I know you will!'

And because she was the best thing that had ever happened to him he said,

'OK. If you say so, Nan Morrissey. But tell me one thing, will you? Are you going to ditch me when you've taught me to dance, because I hope you won't.'

'Wot! Let you go when I've learned you all I know, Sergeant! I'm not castin' you adrift for the first WAAF that sets eyes on you to snap up. Not flamin' likely!'

'Then you and I are friends – I m-mean we're *c-close* friends, Nan?'

His face was very serious, his eyes troubled and he was stammering again Nan thought, realising that a bit of Liverpool bluntness was called for.

'If you're askin' me to be your girl,' she said very firmly, 'then I'd like that a lot.'

And he laughed and said, 'I'm askin', Nan Morrissey,' and hugged her close and kissed her and didn't give a damn who saw them!

Carrie and Evie were waiting at the truck parked behind the barracks when Nan and Chas arrived. Evie had taken details of where exactly it was, and they were able to find it in the darkness with no trouble at all.

They had decided to see a film and stood in a long queue at the picture house. *Target for Tonight* was being shown and it seemed everyone for miles around wanted to see it.

It was about a bomber, a Wellington – F for Freddie – on a raid over Germany. It had film-makers aboard and was unemotional and under-stated to a high degree, yet it held the audience enthralled. It was as if they flew with the crew, and shared their fear.

'Did you enjoy the flick?' Carrie asked.

'I did. And do you realise, Tiptree, that the men in that bomber weren't actors? It was the actual crew we saw, and everything was real. I'm glad Bob isn't flying.'

'Mm. And I hope Nan and Chas didn't go to see it. That bomber was a Wellington like Chas flies in, had you thought?'

'Well, all I can say's if that's what going on ops is like, it's a pretty dangerous business. And they seem to go every two or three nights. It's asking for trouble. I wonder if Nan realises what it's like and – and . . .'

'How risky it is for Chas you mean; that one night he might not get back? And sssssh . . .'

They heard Nan's laugh and Evie called,

'Coo-eee. Over here!'

'Hi, there. Had a good time,' Carrie asked when two dim outlines joined them.

'You bet. We went dancin'. And have youse two met Chas? Officially, I mean.'

And Evie and Carrie said they had, sort of, but that it was nice to be properly introduced.

'I'm doing very well, with the dancing, Nan says.'

'He is, an' all. And you should see him jitter-bugging. He's a natural. Won't be long before he can go up to any girl he wants, and ask her to dance. Mind,' she added darkly, 'I'll batter 'im, if he does!'

They were laughing so much they didn't hear Sergeant James arrive and she had to cough loudly and ask if everyone was present and correct.

'All present.' Carrie quickly opened the door for her, so Nan and Chas were able to kiss fleetingly and whisper, 'See you,' and 'I'll ring. Take care.'

'Had a good time, then?' the sergeant asked as they drove slowly towards the road.

'Great, Sergeant.' Evie undertook to reply, she having rank up. 'Did you?

'I did. It made a nice change, getting away from it all. But now that it's on my mind, we're soon going to be thinking about leave.'

'But what will you do for reliefs,' Evie wanted to know. 'Will you try to get a stand-in?'

'Someone who can operate both teleprinters and switchboards, you mean? No need, really, when I can do both. It'll mean a bit of doubling up and a spot of give-and-take, but we'll manage. And since you are all in the same boat – except Turner, of course – I reckon you're going to have to draw lots for who goes when. Think that's fair.'

They said it was. Very fair, and that seven days

leave would be smashing. All except Carrie, of course, who was staring into the blackness, wide-eyed. She had never driven in strange territory at night, before. At home, of course, there was little traffic about and she knew every lane-end and cross roads. And at Heronflete, driving was no problem because she had soon become accustomed to the layout. But here, it was different. Not that she wouldn't get used to it, but with the sergeant sitting beside her, and everyone talking about leave, it was difficult to concentrate.

'How about you, Tiptree?' The sergeant had noticed her withdrawal.

'No bother, Sergeant. Either Norm – er Private Fowler or Corporal Finnigan will take over my driving. No need for a relief. But I can't think of anything better than being at home the third week in October. My twenty-first, you see.'

'Then I think that a coming-of-age deserves a bit of consideration. Speak to me later about it, Tiptree.'

And Carrie said thanks a lot and that she would, then continued to stare into the shifting blackness, gripping the wheel till her knuckles showed white.

It wasn't until she had returned the truck to the stable yard and was making for Southgate Lodge that she began to wonder about things.

What if she were lucky and got the leave she wanted – would she tell her mother or would she just arrive, saying wasn't it a coincidence that her first leave allowed her to be home for her twenty-first and wasn't it a pity she had not been able to give her mother – and Jeffrey's mother – a little more notice? Because given notice, what might they not cook up between them?

The banns read in church, perhaps? Or maybe Jeffrey alerted so he could request marriage leave? They almost always gave you marriage leave, Carrie had discovered, if a wedding had been arranged. And her mother and Mrs Frobisher had a wedding all cut and dried, the minute Jeffrey gave her a diamond ring.

Mind, HMS *Adventurer* might be miles away at sea, or escorting merchant ships in the Atlantic or even, heaven forbid!, taking part in convoys to Murmansk and Archangel with the war supplies Mr Churchill had promised the hard-pressed Russians.

She wondered when his reply to her letter would arrive. Four days, maybe, or five? Best not to worry too much about things until then. And anyway, Jeffrey might see the sense in her reasoning, and would send her the reply she wanted to receive. You never knew, with Jeffrey.

A cold, misty September morning with a hint of frost in the air, Carrie thought as she drove to the signals office to drop off Sergeant James and Evie and Nan. But the sergeant remained in her seat, then said,

'I want to go to Lincoln Barracks this morning, Tiptree. Can you make it all right with Corporal

Finigan, then pick me up here at about half-ten?'

'Of course, Sergeant, but will I be back in time for the shift-change?'

'Don't worry. I won't be long. Just want to get things moving regarding leaves; forms and travel warrants and all that. See you at ten-thirty, then, and keep it under your hat for the time being, if you don't mind. And I'll have to get a move on. Must take over the shift officially.'

'Yes Sergeant. And not a word . . .' Carrie murmured as Monica James slammed the truck door.

She was a stickler for things done the official way, Carrie pondered, reversing the truck, heading for the stable yard. She was getting used to it, now, and felt easy driving it. She looked forward to the trip into Lincoln – and returning in daylight. Soon – in about an hour – the sun would break through the morning mist, and another bright day would begin. And still no rain. There had been none, she thought, since her arrival here and there had been no need for waterproof capes, nor the drying out of shoes. Heronflete had been good to them, though she was almost certain she would bring her rubber boots back from leave, and a hotwater bottle, too.

Leave. Would she be home for her birthday and how would she feel being a civilian again for a week? Sleeping late, mornings, would be wonderful and seeing Jackmans Cottage, too, and the stone-flagged kitchens. And what a joy to sink into the saggy armchairs in the low-ceilinged sitting room, toes curling in front of a crackling fire.

Stop it, Carrie! You gave all that up the day you volunteered for the ATS; the day you decided it was the only way out for you. And you got it! Now you have shared billets, a noisy cookhouse to eat in and there'll be the NAAFI for warmth when the dark nights arrive and Southgate Lodge is almost unbearably cold!

But she had Evie and Nan, and the joy of being her own mistress – Sergeant James permitting, of course. And the sergeant wasn't so bad, once you got used to the sharpness of her voice and tried not to be so in awe of her three brilliantly white stripes.

Carrie left the truck in the yard, in readiness for the trip to Lincoln, then, because thinking about Jackmans had made her decide that an empty Southgate Lodge was not to her liking, she tapped on the door marked SIGNALS OFFICE: NO ENTRY.

'Yes? What is it, Tiptree?' The sergeant opened the door.

'I – I wondered if there was a spot of tea going spare. The cookhouse isn't open, yet.'

'Oh, come in, do! And there's no tea. The switchboard's going mad and both teleprinters at it like there's no tomorrow! Someone must have told Heronflete there's a war on! So chop-chop, Tiptree. Set the kettle on, so we can all have a drink!'

'Yes, Sergeant. Thanks a lot . . .'

Carrie filled the kettle and switched it on. Then she washed mugs and placed them, together with the milk bottle and sugar tin, on an old-fashioned wooden tray, thinking it was nice to be wanted – even if only to see to the morning brew!

It occurred to her as she waited for the kettle to boil that by Monday, given luck, there might be a letter from Jeffrey. A letter, that was, in reply to the one she had sneakily posted in Lincoln. If his ship was not at sea, of course. Or if he wasn't working watch-about, which was four hours on duty, and four hours off, right around the clock, with little time to sleep, let alone write a coherent reply.

But he would understand, she knew it, and tell her she was being an old softy and of course their honeymoon would be marvellous. Which made her feel mean for almost insisting on being on leave on the twenty-second of next month, when she was almost certain that Jeffrey's next leave would be no sooner than the end of November!

The kettle began to puff steam. First things first, Carrie. Your twenty-first is more than four weeks away, and anything could happen in four-and-a-bit weeks! There was a war on, wasn't there. Anything *could* happen!

'Won't be long,' she called. 'Tuppence a cup! Have your money ready, please!'

Carrie reached for the iron key and unlocked the door of Southgate Lodge, herself again, and determined to strip the unmade beds, place the three biscuit mattresses one on top of the other, then fold blankets, sheets and pillowcases, and lay them on top. Then, when she had had her breakfast, she would put on her horrible brown overall and clean the billet. Not that Sergeant James would come on the snoop, because the sergeant was going to Lincoln at ten-thirty and Carrie Tiptree was driving her! And that was her own bed neatly stacked! Now for Nan's and Evie's, then fingers crossed that it was sausages and beans for breakfast . . .

Her nostalgic mood was gone, and the sun had come out and was shining through the little windows all at once making everything seem a whole lot better.

For no reason at all, Carrie thought about Leningrad, and last night's news that it was now completely encircled by the German army. And what was worse, they had no electricity and the first snows had already fallen.

So count your blessings, Tiptree! Here at Heronflete the trees are still green and the sun has come out and you do know where your next meal is coming from. *And* your electricity isn't cut off and no one is bombing you.

And there would, she thought soberly, be none of the people in Leningrad going on seven days' leave in October, either. If the Germans had their way, they'd be going nowhere at all!

Oh, damn and blast this war.

* * *

'It's getting to be a regular thing,' Evie said as they stood at the window watching Nan striding up the hill towards Priest's Lodge where hopefully Chas and Boadicea waited. 'Whenever he isn't flying, they're off out in that dratted Tin Lizzie of his! You don't think they aren't getting too thick, the pair of them?'

'Sssh, Evie. You're doing your mother hen again! And they do seem to be seeing a lot of each other, but Nan will be all right. Chas seems to be a decent young man; I don't think he's out for what he can get. As I see it, they're just a couple of kids off dancing all the time.'

'You could be right, it isn't any of my business. And I don't think Charles Lawson is the sort who'd take advantage of her. Reckon he's the type to marry her, first!'

'They're both too young to be married. They're just having fun Evie, that's all. And hasn't it gone dark all of a sudden? Look – raindrops on the window!'

The rain, that had seemed non-existent at Heronflete, was falling in large drops and a wind from the north-west blew it in small squalls against the little house.

'Well, all I hope is that Morrissey isn't still waiting. She'll get soaked.'

'Morrissey's got enough sense to get herself into Priest's Lodge and wait for him inside. And we did need the rain, Evie. The ground was rock hard and it wouldn't surprise me if the potato crop isn't up to scratch when they lift it. Spuds need lots of water,' the country woman in her said.

Potatoes were much valued. A caricature called Potato Pete was the darling of the Ministry of Food, who printed leaflets on how unrationed Pete could be used to the best advantage.

For no reason at all, Carrie wondered how her mother was managing on one ration book. Two ounces of butter and of margarine; half a pound of sugar, one egg and a shilling and tuppence-worth of meat to last a week. Thank goodness their local poacher had suddenly become respectable and was selling rabbits to anyone who had two shillings to offer! She hoped her mother's pride wouldn't stand in the way of a large pan of rabbit stew!

'I took Sergeant James to Lincoln, this morning.' It was all Carrie could think of to say.

'Mm. She told me she was going to sort out leave passes and things. Wonder who'll be the first to be lucky?' asked Evie.

'Lenice! She'll get herself to the top of the queue, I'd take bets on it. She isn't half pushy. But it's OK with me. I'm keeping my fingers crossed for – my twenty-first.'

'So, will Jeffrey manage to wangle a week at the same time? And have you had a letter from him, yet?'

'There was one this morning, but it didn't mention my letter – the one I posted in Lincoln, I mean.'

'You'll be hearing soon, and you'll wonder why you got yourself in such a state about it. It'll all come right, Carrie. I know it will.'

'It'll have to. And I'm going to write to mother. I'm worried about her. Mrs Frobisher told me she had a nasty cold and was very depressed. My fault, I suppose.'

'Look, Tiptree, it isn't your fault she caught a cold and if she's depressed because she's missing you – well, there are loads of women in the same boat; and most of them manage to get on with it. The Russian women, I mean, and Londoners who have to sleep in the Underground because their homes and everything they own have been bombed into rubble. From what I can make out, your mother's pretty safe in the country.'

'She is. That's one thing I don't have to worry about. And she's comfortably off, too. My father saw to that, before he died. But she's had a lonely life, Evie, and me to bring up all on her own.'

'Yes. I shouldn't have said what I did,' Evie said softly. 'None of my business, I suppose. But it does concern me when you are determined to take the blame for it all – and just because you joined up!'

'Sneakily, don't forget. I didn't know I had it in me. I'd never done anything like that before.'

'So are you sorry you joined?'

'No. I'm not. It's better than I ever thought it would be, and I like being able to do what I want, and not having to tell mother where I'm going and when, precisely, I'll be home. Y'see, Evie, my mother always said that a girl's duty lay at home; that no respectable young lady left home unless it was to go to University, or to take up nursing, or go into domestic service.'

'Ooooh! And there you were, Carrie Tiptree, skulking off to join the ATS! You'll never go to heaven, you know! But get on with your letter. Think I'll pop another in the post for Bob. I've given him all the news, but I feel like telling him I love him. I'll probably write a whole page of I-love-yous. Soppy, aren't I?'

But Carrie told her she was not, then thought to her shame that she wished she were every bit as soppy as Evie was and as much in love, too.

She took out her notepad and pen, kicked off her shoes, then propped pillows behind her head.

Dearest Mother,

I hope by now you are feeling better and have seen Doc Smithson as I asked you to.

It is raining, at last. Since I came here the weather has been beautiful – but it couldn't last, I suppose.

There is no news, yet, about leave . . . ,

Oh, liar, Caroline Tiptree!

. . . though I think we should hear something, soon. But there are so few of us here that I think it will be by rota, and that we'll have to muck in to cover for each other.

167

Another lie! Freddy or Norm would cover for her. There would be no problem, in that direction. It was just, she supposed, that she wanted to surprise them all, and walk into Jackmans unannounced.

Evie is sitting on her bed writing to her husband and Nan has gone out with a young airman she is teaching to dance. News is very thin on the ground, though all is peaceful and quiet, here.

I just wanted you to know that I am thinking about you and hoping you are much better by now. Please let me know you are.

Take good care of yourself,

With much, much love

She addressed an envelope. Not much of a letter, and not very nice of her, was it, not to mention there would be leave to look forward to, soon. But if she were truthful it was a case of the old saying, Forewarned is forearmed, and she didn't want to give her mother or Mrs Frobisher the chance to start their scheming and maybe even tell Jeffrey when she would be home. Not that Jeffrey could do anything about it if he was at sea.

But she would feel better about everything when a reply came to the Lincoln letter, and she knew that things were all right between them and there was nothing to stop them getting married as soon as the Royal Navy and the Auxiliary Territorial Service allowed!

'Think I'd better see to the blackouts, Evie. It's gone very dark, all of a sudden. And I'm not going up to the NAAFI to post this till the rain lets up a bit.'

And Evie was about to agree with her when the front door opened and Nan stood there, misery all over her face.

'Goodness! You're soaked to the skin! Didn't Chas turn up? Why didn't you wait in Priest's?' Evie scolded. 'Get those wet things off and put your pyjamas on, and your dressing gown!'

'Chas didn't turn up,' Nan's eyes filled with tears. 'And I couldn't get into Priest's. Door locked. They're all on shift.'

'Well, never mind,' Carrie soothed. 'There was probably a very good reason for Chas not being there.'

'I know. He'll be flying. It's the only thing that would make him stand me up. But we've been lucky till now, I suppose – my shifts fitting in with his, sort of. Hope he'll be all right.'

'Of course he will, and you don't know for sure he's on ops,' Evie said matter-of-factly, removing Nan's wet cap.

'I do. I gave it half an hour, then I went to the NAAFI and rang the aerodrome. The operator told me they aren't accepting calls.'

'But it's pouring down, Nan. Do they take off in weather like this?'

'They take off in everything, Carrie, except thick fog. I wonder where he's going.'

'Now see here, Nan Morrissey. Chas will be all right. Just keep telling yourself that. So dry your eyes and blow your nose and empty your jacket pockets. Carrie and I are going to post letters and we'll take your uniform and shoes and hang them in the drying room – OK?'

'You don't have to go all that way in the rain for me.' Nan fumbled with her buttons, tears running down her cheeks.

'We were going, anyway, so get a towel to that hair, then get yourself into bed. You're shaking with cold.'

'All right.' Nan unlaced her shoes, then peeled off her stockings. 'And I'm sorry to make such a fuss, but he's never not turned up before.'

'Well, there's a first time for everything, so do as you're told. We'll put our capes on. A drop of rain won't hurt us. And Nan,' Evie said softly. 'This isn't the first time he's flown, don't forget. Chin up, old love. Won't be long . . .'

'Poor kid,' Carrie said as they walked to the NAAFI, heads bent against the wind and rain. 'I think she's got it bad, but she'll get over it. It's just that he's her first grand passion. Anyway, he'll be all right. Why shouldn't he be?'

'Because bomber crews have a pretty bad time of it, Bob told me. He said that some crews are lost the very first op. they fly. Nan told me the other day that Chas had done sixteen operational flights, and I believe that's a whole lot more than most.'

'Look, Evie, I didn't mean to sound smug, or anything and I hope Chas will be all right, truly I do. I just meant that – well – he's Nan's first big romance, and she's bound to feel upset. And waiting all that time in the rain, too.'

'Yes, like you say, he's her first love and even if something, God forbid, happens to him tonight and she never sees him again, she'll never forget him. And you'd know what I mean, Carrie, if ever *you'd* been in love yourself – truly in love. So put this letter in the post with yours and I'll go and get these clothes hung up to dry.'

'Evie Turner! How *dare* you say such a thing!' Carrie gasped.

But Evie was striding towards the ablutions block and chose not to reply, because it was as plain as the nose on her face that Carrie wasn't in love with Jeffrey Frobisher – never had been, did she but know it. Probably, she thought darkly, she had yet to fall in love; really in love.

She shook the jacket and hung it on the drying rail, the skirt beside it, then placed the shoes beside the boiler, reluctant to turn round because she knew someone was standing in the doorway, and that it was Carrie.

'Sorry, Tiptree,' she whispered. 'I was entirely out of order and I shouldn't have said what I did.'

'Then why did you say it? What do you know about my feelings for Jeffrey? Having a stripe up gives you the right to interfere in my life, does it?'

'No, it doesn't. And I said I was sorry, Carrie.

Look – let's get back to Southgate and even if you're mad as hell with me, don't let it show in front of Nan because she's really upset.'

'I know she is. And you weren't – *aren't* – interfering. It was me told you about the way things were, remember? And maybe I don't know what real love is, but I hope I'll learn, once we're married.'

She set off down the hill at a pace and Evie hurried after her, thinking how hopeless life could be at times, and that if Carrie didn't know now what being in love was all about, then being married to her Jeffrey wasn't going to help her find out!

'Carrie,' she called, beginning to run. 'Wait on, old love!'

And oh, what a mess it all was. What a damn stupid awful mess!

Nan was in bed asleep when they got back. Or pretending to be asleep, Carrie thought, looking at the pale face and eyelashes still wet with tears. She tucked in the blankets and gently kissed Nan's cheek. Then she whispered,

'Can I get undressed in your room, Evie? Don't want to wake her up . . .' She rummaged under her pillow for her pyjamas.

'If she's asleep,' Evie said, closing the door gently. 'And Carrie, I *am sorry*. Forgive me?'

'Of course I will, and maybe there's a grain of truth in what you said. Suppose it'll all depend on the way Jeffrey takes my letter when he gets it, and understands what I was trying to say.'

'And what if – just *if* – he doesn't?'

'Then only the good Lord Himself knows, Evie, so let's wait and see, shall we?'

And she added, ruefully, that when the letter came they would both wonder what they'd been worrying about, great daft lummoxes that they were!

'Here – hang your stuff on this.' Evie offered a coat hanger. 'And you'd better tiptoe in and get your alarm clock and set it, or Priest's Lodge aren't going to get to work on time in the morning and we've had enough drama tonight to last us a week. Don't want any more!'

Carrie smiled and nodded and thought all over again what a nice person Evie was, and gently opened the door between.

And Evie closed her eyes and silently vowed that she would bite off the end of her tongue before she ever said anything so forthright to Carrie again – even if it were true, and had to be said, so help her!

EIGHT

The leave-rota lay on Sergeant James's desk in the signal office and open to change, by mutual consent of course. Otherwise, that was it!

'Morrissey is last to go, and when she gets back, I'll have a week – if that's all right with you, Turner?'

'Fine, Sergeant.'

'And you can take charge whilst I'm away? You'll be all right?'

'I'll give my stripe an extra dollop of Blanco,' Evie grinned. 'They won't be any trouble. So, Priest's are going first and second, then Carrie. She'll like that. It's her birthday on the twenty-second.'

'No problem, there. They'll cover for her at the motor pool. And isn't she supposed to be getting married?'

'I – I – well, she did say something to me about it,' Evie hesitated, because Sergeant James never talked about her girls other than as numbers, who only had surnames. 'But it's all a question of getting leave at the same time as her fiancé. He's in the Navy.'

'Mm. I knew that.'

'But how, Sergeant. I mean – you aren't supposed to –'

'Sergeants aren't supposed to know anything at all about other ranks? We're supposed to know *everything* about subordinates, but none of it should be personal, if you get my drift?'

'Then how do you know about Tiptree?'

'I've got eyes in my head, for heaven's sake! There are photographs at Southgate, aren't there? You had a white wedding to an airman and there's a photograph of a sailor on Tiptree's locker. And I think it was Corporal Finnigan who told me she's got an engagement ring, but doesn't often wear it. I didn't get three stripes up by being stupid, you know!'

'No one can call you that,' Evie laughed. 'And you are right. Tiptree hopes to get married when the leaves allow. Once they've got everything cut and dried, she'll be able to apply for compassionate. You get it, don't you, for a wedding?'

'Normally, yes. But to change the subject. Has Morrissey got a young man to consider, leave-wise?'

'No. Not a steady. But she's met a boy from the aerodrome at Modeley. She's teaching him to dance.'

'Is he the one who drives that noisy car? Oh, dear. What a funny old war this is!'

'Sergeant?' Evie did not think being separated from Bob the least funny.

'Funny-peculiar, I mean. This place, for instance. I'll never understand what goes on in the big house. Busy, sometimes; sometimes not. And here am I, Turner, in charge of the signals office and still none the wiser. There hasn't been one signal, to my knowledge, in plain language. Everything coded up, and even the telephones scrambled. And we've only seen the back of the house – the domestic offices, sort of. For all we know, Hitler himself might be on the other side of that green door!'

'Morrissey almost got a look. She went up the drive and got stopped. The sentries had guns.'

'Oh, I know about *them*. Corporal Finnigan says they don't seem to know any more than we do. He says that most of them – himself included – are grateful for a cushy number, so why ask questions?'

A disc dropped. Evie picked up a plug. 'Switchboard.'

She was glad of the interruption, because never before had the sergeant been so open with her and it was disconcerting, to say the least. And, fool that she was, she had let it slip that Nan had walked up the drive when they were specifically told not to! And what was even more awful, Sergeant James could thought-read.

'Where *is* Morrissey?'

'Cookhouse, sergeant. For her supper.'

176

'I know that! She's ten minutes late! And where have you been, girl,' she asked of Nan who fumbled through the blackout curtains, smiling broadly.

'Sorry, sergeant. Big queue, in there. One of the cooks has gone on leave, and they haven't sent a relief for him.'

'I'll believe you! And I'll go next for supper. Rather hungry. I won't be long.' She glared meaningfully at Nan.

'Ar!' Nan grinned when the door had closed behind the sergeant. 'She's got eyes in her behind, that one! My fault, though. I rang Chas.'

'But you rang him at midday.'

'Yes, an' I was so relieved he was all right, I nipped into the NAAFI and rang him again. Just to say hello, mind.'

'And he was there? Not flying?'

'Nah! He seemed dead chuffed to hear from me – again. I'm meetin' him tomorrow night, at seven.'

'Yes. You said.' Evie grinned. 'And take a look at the leave list on the sergeant's desk.'

'Mm. I'm goin' on the twenty-seventh of October, for a week. When are you goin' Evie? Your name isn't here.'

'I'm not strictly due, yet. The sergeant wants a week, mid-November, then I'll be going. Are you looking forward to it?'

'Dunno, really. If I go to me Auntie Mim's, sleeping's going to be a bit of a problem. Mind, I'll maybe ask for a train pass to Edinburgh and sleep off at Leeds on the way there – just to let her see me in my uniform. I've never been to Scotland.'

'And there's nowhere else you'd like to go? Liverpool, for instance?'

'No way! I've turned me back on Cyprian Court for good. The Queer One isn't anything to me, nor her Georgie!'

'But George is your half-brother, Nan. Aren't you just a little bit fond of him?'

'No, I'm not. He's a spoiled brat and he's not –'

She stopped in time. Not her half brother she'd been going to say and that would have put the cat among the pigeons, because not for anything was she letting on about that birth certificate!

'– he's not a kid you could get fond of,' she said, instead. 'And that's the bell!' She hurried to the hatch beside the green baize door, relieved there would be an end to Evie's probing. 'A signal. A long one. In code.'

Always in code. Nothing ever in words they could make sense of. But did it matter? Wasn't Chas more important? And wasn't she Sergeant Charles Lawson's girl and hadn't meeting him been the best thing ever to have happened to her? And no matter what went on at Heronflete, wasn't she the lucky one to have been posted here?

She switched on the teleprinter and began to tap up the switchboard, hoping the sergeant would soon be back to check it with her. Three pages of it, all in groups of figures. Somebody behind the green door, Nan thought, must have had a convulsion, turning out a signal that length. Maybe they weren't *all* asleep, there?

There were letters for Southgate Lodge when they returned from early shift. Evie picked them up then said,

'One for you, Carrie; two for me and two for you, Nan.'

'Two?'

She looked at the Leeds postmark. Auntie Mim. But who the heck did she know in Lincoln who had written to her two days ago? Quickly she slit the envelope with her thumb.

Dearest girl,

When I fly over Heronflete tonight, I will think of you waiting there, and know I won't be able to meet you.

So this is to say sorry and to let you know that B. and I will be at the same spot, the same time, when next you are on early shift.

And it is to say I love you, though I am not yet brave enough to tell you so.

Take care of yourself

C

Tears filled Nan's eyes, but she smiled them away and said,

'From Chas. No names, no pack drill, and goodness knows who posted it for him in Lincoln, but d'you know what? He loves me! It's there, in black and white!'

'Mm. Nice to be loved, isn't it?' Evie asked without taking her eyes from her letter.

'And he says he'll see me when I'm on earlies, which is today!'

'So you'll be able to tell him you love him too, won't you? Because I think you do.'

'Aaaaah,' was all Nan was able to say, because there was a singing inside her and a thudding in her ears, which made her high as a kite that soared and flapped over Heronflete and didn't want to come down to earth. At least not until tonight, at seven, when Chas would be waiting for her.

Carrie's letter was from Jeffrey and strangely she wanted to open it carefully and slowly so she might have time to take a deep, steadying breath before she read it, because either way, good or bad, it was going to take some coming to terms with.

If he said he agreed with her entirely and that of course they must talk about such an important thing as their wedding night, it would be bad enough because it would mean he was willing to lean over backwards; to promise anything that would make her agree to marry him on their next leave.

On the other hand, he might be bitingly sarcastic and resentful she had criticised that first time implying that, for want of a better phrase, he was no good at it! It was almost a relief when she read,

Dear Caroline,

I do not intend to make comment on your letter, which took some digesting, I assure you. I am not so fortunate as you are and unable to get past the censor. Therefore, all I am prepared to say is that I will be writing to your mother, asking her to have our banns read in church so that whenever we manage to get leave at one and the same time there need be no delay.

Sorry if I seem a bit sharp, but am not prepared to go into detail about intimate things which should be read by you and me only, even though the censor is faceless and nameless.

Please pull yourself together and stop acting like a child. I really do not know what goes on in your head these days, nor why you are making such a big thing out of something that, to my way of thinking, should be as normal as breathing in and out. What a drama queen you are becoming.

Write back quickly and tell me that you have come to your senses and that you are the Caroline I have known for as long as I can remember.

Ever

So that was it! Nothing to discuss! Making a drama of their wedding night, was she? And why shouldn't she? Wasn't she entitled to expect something better than *normal*? Because what happened that night had been far from normal and not a bit nice.

'From Jeffrey,' Evie asked when Nan had wandered into the garden to read her letter again. 'Not bad news?'

'The worst. He refuses to discuss it and says I am getting to be a drama queen. Oh, yes – and that I am acting like a child and to pull myself together.'

'Is that all?' Evie, being sarcastic.

'No, it damn-well isn't! He's going to write to mother and tell her to get the banns read in church. No by-your-leave or anything! What does he think he is – a Victorian husband?'

'I think,' Evie said softly, 'that your letter came as an embarrassment and the only way he knew to react was to hit out. Like I said, it might have been his first time, too.'

'So why didn't he write back and say he understood; that the first time was a bit of a shock to him, too? And something else he said, Evie. I was to write back quickly and tell him I am the Caroline he has known for as long as he can remember. Well, for two people who have known each other all their lives, he and I don't know each other at all! And he can whistle for his reply. I won't write back to him for a week, I swear I won't!'

The tears came then. Hot and salty and in great jerking sobs, and Evie held her tightly and made little shushing sounds and patted her back and said, 'There, there now, Carrie . . .'

And it wasn't until the sobs had stopped, when Carrie said that if she went on any longer her eyes would go slitty and her nose would go red and blotchy and anyway, letters like that deserved to be treated with the disdain they deserved, didn't they? that Evie said,

'Let's go for a walk as far as Priest's – take a few deep breaths?'

'You're not asking Nan to come?'

'No. She's deep in her first love letter. Best leave her to wallow in it.'

And when Evie called that they were just popping out for a bit of a walk, Nan gave them a smile and a wave that could well be interpreted as saying, 'You two can shove off to Timbuktu on broomsticks as far as I'm concerned – I'm stoppin' here with me letter . . .'

'I wish Jeffrey had told me he loves me,' Carrie said, still a little sniffy as they took the narrow lane towards the wood and Priest's Lodge. 'Nan and Chas haven't known each other for long, yet he manages to get a letter to her when he's off on ops.'

'We-e-ll, there's love and love,' Evie said softly. 'And I think they do love each other, but they aren't *in* love. It's puppy love, to my way of thinking and that's the way I hope it stays. They're much too young, yet, for the real thing – and besides, Chas is flying.'

'I hadn't forgotten – and that it's very dangerous. But all I was trying to say is that I wish it was the same for Jeffrey and me. Uncomplicated, sort of, and fun. And I wish Jeffrey liked dancing. He'll only get on the floor when he's had a couple of pints. Dutch courage he says it is. I'll bet you anything you like that once we're married he'll refuse even to go to dances, and expect me not to, as well.'

'Or he might,' Evie teased, 'be so happy to be married that he takes you dancing every night, just to show you off!'

'Ha!' Carrie shrugged. 'There's more chance of seeing Cecilia leading a Conga chain round the NAAFI! But I'm not going to write back just yet. I want to think things over and get it exactly right, before I do.'

'Is there anything to think over, Carrie? I can't believe things are as bad between you and Jeffrey as you try to make out. And probably he's thinking things over, too, and realising he shouldn't have been so bossy and heavy-handed.'

'No. Not Jeffrey. He's *never* wrong!'

'Oh, dear. Then tell me, please, if there is anything at all you *do* like about him.'

'What on earth do you mean, Evie? I'm engaged to him, aren't I? I'm going to marry him when the war allows. Stands to reason there are things about him that I like.'

184

'Liking isn't the same as being in love. How can you know you are in love with him – *really* in love?'

'You know something, Lance-Corporal, if I didn't know you better I'd think you are playing devil's advocate. And anyway, who can say what real love is like. I can't, so you tell me?'

'All right, Carrie. I would say that real love – being *in* love – happens when you realise you'll go stark staring mad if you've got to spend another night apart. In short, you want him to make love to you and to hell with the formalities. Bob and I were lovers before we were married.'

'Yes. You said. And Jeffrey and I were lovers, don't forget, and I didn't like it at all.'

'Then you've really got to talk it over. Okay – get your mother to see the vicar and have the banns read in church if that'll smooth things over a bit. Write and tell Jeffrey that you think it's a good idea, then he'll know you are willing.'

'But I'm not willing. And I *won't* go stark staring mad if I have to spend another night without him. On the contrary, it's the thought of having to spend a night *with* him that's getting me on edge.' She glared at Evie defiantly. 'There now, I've said it – is that what you want?'

'Not what I wanted to hear, Carrie, but at least you know something isn't right between you, and you're both going to have to meet each other half way – sort things out. It's called give and take, didn't you know?'

'Yes. I do all the giving and Jeffrey just takes like it's his God-given right and if I'm being uptight for saying so, then hard luck, Lance-Corporal!'

'Now listen to me.' Evie stopped walking and laid a hand on Carrie's arm so they stood face to face. 'And look at me, please, because what you're going to hear is really none of my business, but it's got to be said.

'I think, Carrie, that you and your Jeffrey are heading for disaster if you get married just because his mother and your mother want you down the aisle, because I don't think you're in love with him at all. You're just in love with the idea of being a married woman – and having children, of course! And I'll bet you anything you like that you'll put up with his bossiness and his rotten love-making to get those children!'

'Is that it, then? Have you finished,' Carrie demanded petulantly when the silence between them became unbearable.

'Yes. I said my piece, but the more I listen to you the more sure I am that there's a lot of straightening out to be done before you two even *think* of getting married. And having the banns read doesn't mean you've got to go through with it. Agree to it, Carrie, if only to give yourself a bit of breathing space. And shall we go back, now, before it comes to fisticuffs? I'm not sorry for what I said, but I'm sad I had to say it. Please think hard before you take such a serious step – and forgive me for being so direct?'

'You know I will, and I know you meant well, but will you tell me what I'm going to do, Evie, because I'm damned if I know!'

'No one can tell you that, old love – not even Jeffrey. But until you are absolutely sure that there's nothing you want more than to marry him, then it won't do any harm to give it a bit of thought.'

'You're right, and thanks for giving it to me straight. I can talk to you, you know, far easier than I can talk to my mother, which can't be right when you think about it.'

'Depends how approachable she is. My mum is fine – always was – but it seems to me that you are all your mother has had for the best part of her married life, and you can't blame her for being possessive and –'

'And unapproachable,' Carrie flung. 'Because that's what she is, if I'm honest. A talk like you and I have just had simply wouldn't happen, because I'm sure she doesn't care to discuss intimate things – not even with her only child. So it seems it's up to me now, and, let's face it, it concerns *my* life and *my* future, so I'd better get things sorted out – and before it's too late.'

'That's more like it! Just send Jeffrey a loving letter and tell him you'll write home about having the banns read in church. It'll please him no end and it'll certainly please your mother, and his.'

'And after that? Tell me, Evie . . . ?'

'Sorry, but that's as far as I'm prepared to go. What happens after is for you to decide. Most importantly, don't let yourself be panicked into doing something until you know it is what you want, Carrie. And we'd better get back and do a spot of mopping and dusting. It's clean bedding today, don't forget, and laundry bundles tomorrow. Perhaps, when Nan comes down off her pretty pink cloud she'll collect clean sheets and things – maybe wipe the moonstruck look from her face!'

'Don't mock, Evie. If you ask me, Nan hasn't had a lot of love in her life, this far. And I reckon she and Chas make a lovely couple. Just hope they can hang on to it.'

'That's war for you. It brings people together, but it parts them, too. But no matter what, Nan will always remember her first love – or so I am told. Bob was my first and only love, so I'm lucky. Do you remember yours, Carrie?'

'I do, actually. And I remember my first kiss, too. At least I think he must have been my first love – Todd, I mean – because he asked me to marry him. He's my daffodil boy. Can't tell you why . . . Then he gave me a kiss on the cheek and that was the end of the affair. Off he went with his Aunty Hilda, so I know what it's like, being stood up,' she grinned. 'Surprising how easily you get over it at nearly-thirteen.

'And there's Nan at the gate and with her overalls on, too. Let's give her a hand. Evie – can you see I've been crying? Don't want her to start asking questions – not in her state of euphoria.'

'Don't worry. You're back to normal. And do

you want to go out, tonight? Fancy a walk to the Black Bull?'

And Carrie said she did and that blow it, she would write to her mother tomorrow, and to Jeffrey the day after – if she felt like it! It was a lovely late-September evening for a walk, wasn't it!

Nan heard the rattle and groan of Chas's car, long before it turned the corner and wheezed to a stop. Chas wasn't flying. She uncrossed her fingers and ran towards Boadicea and the steam puffing from under the bonnet.

'Hello, Nan. D-did you get my 1-letter?' he asked anxiously.

'Yes, I did, thanks a lot. Came as a surprise. And don't I get a kiss, then?'

She reached on tiptoe, closing her eyes, offering her lips. She liked kissing Chas.

'There you are. One k-kiss as requested. L-like another . . . ?'

'Now see here, Chas – what's to do with you, startin' to stammer again? I thought we'd got over that. Sumthin' the matter?'

'N-no. Just a bit anxious, I suppose.'

'About the letter?'

'Yes,' he nodded.

'And what you wrote in it – that you loved me?'

'Yes. And I m-meant it. I do love you, Nan. D-do you mind my telling you?'

'Not at all, especially if you mean it and I reckon you do, because that makes it twice you've told me.'

'And you're not mad at me – don't think I'm forward for saying it and f-for asking you if you care about me, just a little?'

'Care? I dunno, Chas – if I love you, I mean. It's all new to me, fallin' for a bloke, see? But I do know I cried my eyes out the night you were on ops. And it wasn't because you'd stood me up, nor nuthin' I was real upset you were up there, trying to find your way to, to – where was it you went?'

'Essen.'

'Ar. Well, like I was saying there was you, getting shot at and there was me, safe as houses, and that it wasn't fair that you were flying. And I got soaked to the skin, but I wanted you to be there so much that I never noticed. And when I phoned you next day and you answered, I felt so relieved I wanted to start crying again.'

'You phoned me twice, actually . . .'

'Mm. Wanted to make sure you were still all right and that you'd be here tonight. And you are. And being here with you makes me happy, Chas, and warm inside. And sometimes, even when I'm sending a signal, I think about you when I should be concentratin' on what I'm doing. Is that what it's like, being in love?'

'I think, Miss Morrissey,' he said softly, tilting her chin with a forefinger, kissing her gently, 'that you are showing the first symptoms of love-itis.'

'Must've caught it from you then, 'cause you're the only feller I've ever kissed.'

'Then could you, perhaps, tell me you love me, too?'

'I think I could, if you kiss me again.'

So he kissed her, then held her close, and she said,

'Mm. Seems I love you too, Sergeant Lawson.' Then she smiled shyly. 'Heaven 'elp us! What do we do now?'

'We go into the Bull and ask for champagne to celebrate,' he laughed. 'Mind, we'll have to make do with a half of beer. That suit you, sweetheart?'

'Nah. Tell you what – let's sit in Boadicea and talk, and if it gets a bit cold, then we'll go into the pub.'

So they ran hand in hand to the little car and snuggled close inside, and kissed for a while. Then Nan said, 'What are we goin' to do when I go on leave, Chas? We won't see each other for a week, had you thought?'

'So when is leave?' he whispered.

'Tenth of October till the seventeenth.'

'Nan Morrissey! You little witch! That's when mine is!'

'Honest? I don't believe it!'

'Then you'd better. Where are you going?'

'Haven't decided, yet. I've never been to Scotland so I thought I'd get my rail ticket made out to Edinburgh – stay at the YWCA. Evie says it's cheap and clean and respectable. Mind, I might break my journey at Leeds – call in on Auntie Mim.'

'No! forget Scotland, Nan. You're coming home with me to meet my mother, so you'd best get your rail ticket made out to Shrewsbury – OK?'

'Hey up, Chas! Are you sure? She mightn't like you springin' me on her.'

'She'll be tickled pink I want her to meet my girl who is beautiful and taught me to dance.'

'Old softy! I'm not beautiful, but I must admit I'm quite good at teachin' dancin'. But more to the point, where will I sleep? Has your Mam got a spare bed?'

'She has, and if you want it all cut and dried and above board, I'll ask her to write you a letter, inviting you officially so you'll know you're welcome, Nan.'

'We-e-ll, put like that, I suppose it'll be all right. Shrewsbury, you said?'

'Near there. A little village, but very nice. And mother won't be in the least bit surprised when I tell her you'll be coming home with me. She knows all about you. She was pleased I'd met you, she said, and that you must be really something to get me onto a dance floor.'

'Then best you don't tell her it was me picked *you* up, or she'll think I'm dead common. And Chas – are you really sure? Had you thought that taking a girl home means it's serious?'

'Yes, I'd thought and yes, I *am* serious about you, and I don't ever want to lose you.'

'Don't say things like that. You won't lose me. I won't let you go – not ever – so just be careful when you're flying in the blackout or you'll have me to reckon with!'

'I'll be careful, sweetheart – especially now I've got you to come home to. So now we've taken care of the leaves, how about nipping in for a quick half?'

'OK,' Nan said, though she would rather have stayed snuggled together in the cramped little car. Being close to Chas was nice – better than nice. It made her feel for the first time in her life that she really belonged to someone who cared for her and about her. Being Sergeant Lawson's girl made her feel very special indeed.

'I was getting pins and needles in my legs.' Charles stamped his feet as he helped her out.

'Then you should have shorter legs or get a bigger car,' Nan giggled, taking his hand.

'Get rid of Boadicea? You are talking about the motor I love, Nan Morrissey. Love me – love my car, OK?'

'OK, Chas. And I wonder if Grandad will be in the Bull. Hope not.'

'The old boy, you mean, who kidded you about the ghost at Heronflete?'

'He wasn't kidding, Chas. It wasn't the kind of story he could have made up out of thin air. Somehow, there seemed a lot of truth in it.'

'Even so, you aren't afraid, are you? Ghosts can't hurt you, nor the dead. It's the living you've got to watch out for, Nan. And gremlins, of course.'

'*Gremlins?*'

'Oh my word, yes. I have the greatest respect for gremlins.'

'Never heard of them. What are they like?'

'They live, mostly, in aircraft and when things go wrong it's usually the gremlins wot dun it. I don't know what they look like, mind. But they do exist – I *think*.'

'All right then. You believe in your gremlins and I'll believe in Cecilia the nun. Grandad's not here,' Nan whispered when they had pushed through the blackout curtains over the front door of the Black Bull. 'But there's Evie and Carrie. Shall we sit with them?'

'Hi, there. Can we join you? Care for a drink, ladies?' Chas asked. Asked it without even the sign of a stammer, Nan thought proudly.

'Very kind, but we'd just decided to make our way back.' Evie got to her feet. 'The nights are drawing in – we want to get to Southgate before it gets too dark.'

'Afraid of meeting the nun?' Chas teased.

And Carrie laughed and said not until November, because that was when she was supposed to haunt the stable block.

'Didn't want to play gooseberry,' Evie said as they walked towards the lodge that stood at the top of the lane leading to Heronfleet. 'Aren't they lovely, the pair of them – both in the deeps of first love. Reminds me of when I realised that Bob wasn't the boy next door who walked me to school and back. I suddenly wanted him to kiss me. And I asked him to, would you believe?'

'How old were you, Evie?'

'About eleven or twelve, I suppose. In my first year at senior school. Anyway, we dodged down an alley and he put his arms round me and kissed me on both cheeks, then said, "Oh, Evie, you've no idea how long I've wanted to do that." And we've been in love ever since.'

'I remember when Jeffrey first kissed me,' Carrie laughed. 'It was at a Christmas party and I think he'd been dared to do it. He manoeuvred me towards the mistletoe and puckered up. But I saw it coming and turned my head away, so it landed on my ear. How's that for romance? And oh, I feel so much better about things. I needed a good long walk and a couple of drinks. I'll sleep just fine, tonight. Thanks for listening to my tale of woe, Evie. I'll write to mother and Jeffrey tomorrow. By the way, has Nan got a late pass?'

'No. She'll be in before we're asleep, all pink-cheeked and bright-eyed. We'll hear them, never fear. I'm sure Chas is safer in a bomber than he is driving Boadicea. One of these days, a wheel is going to fly off it, or something.'

It was good to laugh, Carrie thought as they turned into the lane at Priest's Lodge and made for Southgate. And it was good to have Evie, who was almost like a sister now, and Nan, who had become her kid sister. They had both come to mean a lot to an only child like herself. It made her all the more determined to have at least two children – when the time came to have children, that was. But she pushed Jeffrey from her mind and said,

'Think I'll have an early night – got to be up early, don't forget. I'll try not to waken you both – so you can have a lie-in.'

'In that case, I'll go to the ablutions – wash my hair and have a nice hot shower. It'll be getting dark by the time I've finished so nobody should see me nipping back with my greatcoat over my pyjamas.'

'Hmm. Just might come with you. Won't wash my hair, though. It'll take an age to towel dry.'

Carrie thought sighingly about her hair-dryer at home and wondered why she hadn't brought it with her. She must remember to bring it back from leave in October; her gumboots, too.

She felt all at once contented. Being in the ATS was turning out better than she had ever dared hope. She had good friends, a nice billet and would be on leave for her twenty-first birthday. And what was more, she wouldn't worry about writing those letters until tomorrow, which was the best time to write letters, she decided, because tomorrow was supposed never to come.

'Right then.' Evie interrupted her thoughts. 'Let's get a move on so we'll not risk running into Sergeant James when the shift changes. And talking about the sergeant, I wonder why she's so starchy with the Naval bod from the big house? Do you suppose it's because he's one of the Heronflete crowd? I'm as sure as I can be that she resents our lot being kept in the dark – like we aren't to be trusted, I mean.'

'Dunno. She's not bad looking if she'd just let her face relax a bit. Lenice Cooper told me she'd has a nosey round her room at Priest's when she wasn't around, that was, and there was nothing at all by way of photographs – of a man in her life, I mean. Cooper said if she's got a chap, she's keeping him well hidden.'

'Cooper had no right to snoop.' Evie reached for the key and unlocked the door. 'I'd watch her, if I were you. She seems the spiteful sort of me. She'll be going on leave tomorrow, won't she?'

'Yes. I'm picking her up at Priest's – taking her to Lincoln station.' Carrie collected her soap bag and towels from the kitchen cupboard. 'Alison will be on her own, except for the sergeant. Pity we are shift about, or she could nip down to Southgate for a bit of company.'

'Don't worry about her too much. Once Lenice is off on leave, she'll be able to count the days as her own. And when she's seen her folks in Scotland, I'm sure her homesickness won't be so bad. I've known it happen like that in a lot of cases. Got all your clobber, by the way? Fingers crossed that someone hasn't taken all the hot water!'

*   *   *

Next day, Carrie stopped the truck outside Southgate Lodge and hurried up the path.

'Just thought I'd check that you lazy so-and-so's weren't still in bed. Called in for my overalls, by the way.'

'Been to the station with Lenice?' Nan asked. 'I'll bet she was really excited.'

'She was. She had a case and kitbag with her; taking every bit of uniform that needed alterations done. It'll be good to see her with her skirt the proper length. Don't know how she's got away with it for so long.'

Fourteen inches from hemline to ground, King's Regulations said, which made sense, really, especially with a column of women on the march. Would have looked very sloppy, otherwise.

'Well, at least it'll be the last of her grumblings about the way they threw her uniform at her when she was kitted out. She's so tall, you see. No wonder they got her skirt size wrong,' Evie grinned.

'*And* her jackets and greatcoat, too! Bet you anything you like she comes back with crafty zips in her skirts.' Carrie fished clean overalls from the newly-returned bundle of laundry. 'And I'll have to be away. It's nearly ten. Mustn't keep the motor pool waiting for their tea! See you, girls!'

And with that she was off to the stables to where Freddy and Norm must surely be wondering when they were going to get their drinkings from the cookhouse, suddenly remembering the letters she intended to write when Evie and Nan were on shift.

Then she pushed it from her mind. Time enough to worry about it tonight – and surely agreeing to the banns being read would give her breathing space.

'It's OK! It isn't ten, yet!' She waved to Corporal Finnigan who was looking pointedly at his wrist watch. Then she laughed out loud, because all at once, and if her luck held, Caroline Tiptree seemed to be getting the upper hand on the matchmakers at Nether Hutton.

And it was giddy-making!

NINE

'Damn!' Sergeant James said so suddenly that Private Fowler, who was driving the pick-up truck, braked hard, then looked questioningly at the woman sitting beside him.

'I've left the key in the office. You'll have to go back. Sorry.'

'No problem. Got all night . . .'

He had. The longer it took him to drive the late shift back to Priest's Lodge, the less time he would be able to spend in the NAAFI. He reversed the truck then made for the Signals Office.

'Won't be a tick.' The sergeant jumped down then knocked loudly on the door. 'It's Sergeant James. Open up please, Yeoman.'

She heard the curtains being pulled back, then the door opened and she stepped quickly inside.

'Hello again, sergeant?' He closed the door, then switched on the lights. 'Forgot this?' . . . Smiling, he held up the key.

'Yes. Thanks.' She held out her hand, then

stopped, intrigued by the drawing on her desk. 'Who did this?'

'Er – I did. For Molly.'

'Your wife?'

'My youngest daughter. My wife is dead. Molly is three, so she can only read pictures. She loves ducks. That one –' he nodded towards the drawing – 'is called Willie and he's always in mischief.'

'Look – I'm sorry – didn't know. Give me a minute, please?'

She opened the door, closing it quickly behind her against the bright light that streamed out, then pressed the key into Private Fowler's hand.

'Something's come up. You go on. Will you be all right going into Priest's on your own, Seaton? I'll walk back – shouldn't be long.'

'I'll be fine.' Ailsa Seaton had two more late-shifts to work, then she would be going home to Edinburgh! 'Just fine!'

'I'll see her in, Sergeant,' Norman offered. 'Shall I come back for you?'

'No – thanks all the same. The moon's bright. The walk back will do me good. G'night . . .' She hurried back to the office.

'Look – I shouldn't have asked. I know about your wife. Clumsy of me.'

'You weren't to know. Why should you? She was knocked down in the blackout. The driver obviously didn't know he'd hit her. Probably thought he'd bumped into the kerb, so he – or she

– didn't stop. Blame the war. Civilians are in the front line, too.'

'Yes. I know they are.'

Her Joe had been a civilian; a naval architect.

She picked up the drawing. 'So what has Willie done today that was naughty?' At least she could try to make amends.

'He's lost his woolly muffler, and it was new. A red one.'

'I see. And did Molly – er – lose her muffler?'

'No. Her gloves. She won't feel so bad about it, now.'

She heard the smile in his voice, and raised her eyes to his. 'Where is she?'

'With my parents and her sister Lizzie, near Windermere. They're fine. Lizzie is five and a bit and she can read, if I print the words. But Molly loves Willie, because he's mischievous, like she is. Lizzie is the serious one. She remembers her mother, you see. Molly doesn't.'

'I'll have to go, Yeoman . . .'

'You wouldn't like to stay for a mug of tea? I'm not busy.'

'Thanks all the same, but Seaton is on her own, in Priest's Lodge. Better be off. Another time, perhaps.'

'OK.' He switched off the light, then opened the door. 'Sure you'll be all right? It's a fair walk.'

'It'll do me good, and besides, it's as bright as day. A bomber's moon. Goodnight.'

''Night. Do you have a name, other than Sergeant?'

'Monica. What's yours, other than Yeoman?'

'James. Jim. Take care.'

'I always do.' Already, she was regretting the brief intimacy between them. 'Goodnight.'

She tugged her jacket straight, squared her shoulders then set off at a brisk walk, arms swinging as if she were marching. Above her the moon was high and bright, shadowing trees and hedgerows. And how dare everything be so beautiful when there was a war on? Why was the Heronflete she disliked so much silently mocking her, reminding her she might have to spend the rest of the war here? And *why* had she been so tactless just now? Why had she reminded the Yeoman about his wife, when she knew all about civilians being killed?

She hurried on, checking that Southgate showed no lights, then made for the lane crossing and the wood. Ahead she could see the steep roof of Priest's Lodge, dark against the moon.

Oh, damn this war, and Heronflete and bloody stupid billets in silly little houses! What a way to fight a war, all isolated and safe on the requisitioned estate of some peer of the realm! And damn the back-room boys in the big house, and long may they enjoy their splendid isolation! What did that lot know about war, anyway?

She blinked away a tear, then sniffed loudly, all at once angry with herself because she had not only let her guard down tonight in the signals office, but she had let herself remember Joe.

She slammed the gate behind her, then knocked on the door of the lodge.

'It's Sergeant James, Seaton. Let me in, please, and don't take all night about it!'

Southgate Lodge was quiet and still. Carrie, in pyjamas and dressing gown, sat on her bed, pen in hand.

'And that, Caroline, will have to do!' No more writing and re-writing; no more wasting notepaper. 'And you'll post them in the morning, then forget about them – OK?'

You could talk to yourself when Nan was out with her Chas and Evie had gone to the NAAFI. They would both be in, soon. About eleven. She read the letter yet again.

Dearest Mother,

I hope you have seen Doc Smithson, and that your cold is getting better.

Good news. Sergeant James is making a leave-rota, though we don't know, yet, what our dates are.

She told lies, too, but not for anything was anyone going to know she would be home for her birthday. A surprise it was going to be. *Had* to be!

We have had rain at last, and the earth looks much refreshed for it. Today it is bright, though the swallows are gathering on the telephone lines, twittering, making plans to leave us.

I am alone in the billet. Nan has gone dancing with her boyfriend and Evie is making up numbers for a darts match. We are hoping to get to town – she mustn't mention Lincoln! – for an afternoon and I hear that *Gone with the Wind* will soon be showing there. Great excitement. A three-hour film.

Such a stilted letter. Why wasn't she able to write to her mother and talk to her mother without watching every word? It had been far more easy to confide in Evie, a comparative stranger. She sighed, glad the last few lines of the letter were warmer and more affectionate.

Leave. Just think of it. Seven whole days together and more than three months to catch up on. We will be able to catch up on the wedding, too. Jeffrey has suggested we have the banns read in church as it would save time getting a special licence if, suddenly, we both found ourselves on leave at the same time.

If you agree, have a word with Mrs Frobisher, then pop along to the vicarage, and set things in motion. Neither J. nor I will be there to hear them read out in church but it's a step in the right direction, don't you think?

I will leave it to you, dearest, and meantime, take good care of yourself. It shouldn't be long, now, before I am home.

On October 18th actually, but she was keeping to herself the day when she would walk into Jackmans Cottage saying, 'Surprise! Surprise!' Or would that be stretching it just a little bit? Couldn't she phone a couple of days beforehand? That would save cards being posted, and perhaps a parcel, yet it wouldn't give her mother a lot of time to get in touch with Jeffrey and suggest that he ask for. Because he just might qualify for compassionate if the banns had been read.

She fished in her locker for her diary and sure enough, there were three clear Sundays before she went home, so it might be politic not to post the letter for a couple of days. That would put back the first reading for a week! She had the grace to blush as she wrote,

I am so thrilled I will see you soon. There is so much for us to talk about, and plan, though I don't think a white wedding would be possible, now, with all the restrictions. Give it your thoughts,
    With fondest love

She folded the letter and slipped it into the envelope, wondering how she could be so two-faced. Could it be, perhaps, that in the three months she had been away from home, she had learned to think for herself and not fall in with everything her mother wanted for the sake of peace and quiet?

But she had practised her first deceit when she sneaked out in her lunch hour and volunteered for the ATS, then signed her mother's name at the bottom, using someone else's fountain pen. Not a very nice person when you thought about it, was she?

She switched out the light then drew back the curtains. Outside, the moon was full and high and everywhere lit up like a thousand searchlights, were flinging out beams of light.

A bombers' moon. Was that why Chas wasn't flying tonight because didn't a full moon favour enemy fighters more than it did the slow-moving, heavily-laden Wellingtons from RAF Modeley? She switched on the light again then picked up the letter she had written to Jeffrey.

Darling,

I am sorry my letter put you at a disadvantage and it was wrong of me to post it as I did. And I agree with you that intimate things should be read by no one else but you and me.

I have written to Jackmans asking mother to see to the reading of our banns in church because what you suggested makes sense.

Please write back and tell the Caroline you

have known for as long as you can remember that she is forgiven?

All my love, C.

Another tongue-in-cheek letter; another deceit. There must be something very wrong with her if lies tripped off her pen so easily. Wrong? No! She was merely trying, in a roundabout way, she supposed, to get Jeffrey and his mother and her mother, too, to realise that the wedding was going to be when Carrie Tiptree wanted it; when Jeffrey had agreed to talk to her about the intimate things in an understanding and gentle way, and not bully her into doing what *he* wanted. And his mother and her mother, too, come to think of it!

She addressed the envelope to Communications Mess, HMS Adventurer c/o GPO London, then tucked in the flap. She would post it tomorrow, and let the faceless one who censored the letters make of it what he would! Or perhaps what *she* would. Her mother's letter she slipped into her leather writing case, to be posted in two days' time.

She wished Evie and Nan were here, but they wouldn't be in until the stroke of eleven, both with late passes. Then she wondered if she should slip her trousers and battledress top over her pyjamas and go to the NAAFI for a comforting mug of hot cocoa.

But she didn't deserve a mug of hot cocoa because she was a devious madam and as soon as she could get Evie alone, she would tell her without fear of favour, just what an awful person she shared Southgate with!

Or was it, perhaps, that she didn't want to marry Jeffrey? Wasn't she trying every trick she knew to delay it; even to wriggle out of it?

Oh, dammit, of course she wanted to marry him! He had given her a ring and the next step would be the walk down the aisle – in her uniform, she shouldn't wonder. But whatever she wore, the wedding would happen when she wanted it to, banns or no banns!

And why was she making such a drama of it? This was the twentieth century and no one could force her down the aisle with a shotgun in her back. In Jeffrey's back, perhaps, if she'd been stupid enough to let him get her pregnant.

And that had not happened!

'I wonder, Lance-Corporal, if you could start your shift a couple of hours earlier, tomorrow? I wouldn't ask, but I've got to go to Lincoln to see about leave passes and such like, and I had a call from the nursing sister there, asking me when it would be convenient for her to do a FFI on us, or would I be prepared to do it myself?'

Cheek, Sergeant James fumed inside. A free from infection parade, checking for skin infections and head lice. Just like the nit nurse at school. How many more trifling duties would they expect her to take on? Mind, she accepted that a senior NCO was needed at Heronflete, no matter how small her command, but did it have to be her? Wouldn't it be better if she could hand over this crazy set-up to someone in need of a cushy posting so that Monica James could get stuck into the war for real, and not play nanny to the five women in her charge?

'Sergeant?' Evie frowned, wondering about the faraway look in her eyes. 'Of course I can. Would twelve o'clock be all right?'

'Just fine. Tiptree is driving me there. I shouldn't be too long. I rang sick bay and told Sister I was willing to do the FFI myself – if you lot wouldn't mind. Of course, if you prefer a nurse . . . ?'

'Not to worry. I could almost guarantee there'll be nothing for you to find and I'm sure the girls won't mind who looks behind their ears.'

'Good. Mind, we'll all have to go on dental parade before so very much longer, but we'll worry about that when we have to,' she clucked impatiently.

'Is something wrong, Sergeant?'

'Thanks, Turner. I'm fine, except that this posting is a headache. I'm not used to a set-up like this. Give me barracks any day!'

'But it's so beautiful, here, and so safe. No air-raid warnings, no bombing. And if that lot at Heronflete choose to keep themselves to themselves, why should we worry about it? And half of them are civilians I shouldn't wonder. It's a queer set up if you let yourself think too much about it. No one has seen any of them – except the Yeoman, of course, and he isn't exactly a chatterbox.'

'No, but I think it suits him to be at Heronflete. He has good reason to be there and not at sea. He's got two young children. I found out, last night. He'd done a sketch of a duck and I was stupid enough to tell him I thought it was good. And stupid enough, too, to mention his wife, who was run over in the blackout, and killed. I should have kept my mouth shut.'

'But why? He seems a decent sort to me. Why shouldn't you talk to him sometimes? Maybe if you did, we might get to know why there's that green baize door between us and them, and why we aren't allowed up the drive past the sentries. Mind, Morrissey's boyfriend has flown over Heronflete quite a few times. He says it's like a Gothic castle, hidden almost by trees.'

'But I don't want to talk to him, Turner, and I've stopped worrying about what that lot is up to. But I'm keeping you, and Seaton is holding the fort on her own.'

'She's a teleprinter op, isn't she? Can she cope with the switchboard?'

'Yes – if nothing comes up that's urgent, that is. Thanks a lot. See you about twelve?'

And with that she was off at a smart pace, back to the signals office, leaving Evie to wonder what really made the sergeant tick and why she seemed to want to keep the Yeoman at arm's length – and him so attractive, too!

211

'What did the sergeant want?' Nan demanded, pausing from her cleaning.

'Just wanted me to go on duty a couple of hours early, that's all. She's going to Lincoln, and Ailsa's on her own.'

'Mm. Carrie did say she'd be driving her in. Did she tell you what for?'

'To see to leave passes, and things – and to see about an FFI parade. And a dental parade, as well.'

'Hecky thump!' Nan remembered the two fillings she had had in barracks when she joined and had no wish to meet a dental officer again, so soon after. 'Nuthin' else?'

'We-e-ll – keep this under your hat, mind. She spoke to the Yeoman last night!'

'Yer what! A civil word, you mean?'

'Yes. It seems he's a widower with two young children.'

'There you are, see. Knew it wouldn't be long before them two stopped glarin' at each other. Next thing you know they'll be goin' dancin'. Bet you a bob they will! Mind, I'm sorry about his wife.'

'And I've got two bob that says they won't, but don't ask me why. A feeling I've got, I suppose. And if they really wanted to, how are they to manage it? They're on opposite shifts.'

'Suppose you could be right – and the sergeant's a bit of a sourpuss, isn't she?'

'Not when she smiles, she isn't.'

'You've seen her smile?' Nan gasped.

'Of course I have. Lots of times. She's every bit as normal as you and me, except that I get the impression she's not too keen on Heronflete.'

'Then she *is* a sourpuss! Being here is smashin' – and meeting Chas, an' all. Hope I stay at Southgate for the duration!'

'Me too, but somehow I don't think that will happen. A posting like this is too good to be true. It can't last, Nan.'

'Then I've got another bob that says it can, Evie Turner!'

'Same here. Another shilling that it won't!'

'You're throwin' your money about this morning, aren't you? Bit of a gambler, then?'

'I never gamble, Morrissey old love, but I don't mind a flutter on a dead cert,' Evie grinned.

There was no answer to that, Nan thought huffily, so she went into the garden to pick flowers for the jamjar on the mantelpiece.

Leave Heronflete, she frowned as she came upon a clump of ox-eye daisies and sprays of rose hips. Evie must be joking, oh please she must? This was all she had dreamed about and never even thought to see, let alone live near. And more special even than Southgate was Chas, who loved her and wanted to take her home to meet his mother.

And then she told herself she was being stupid, because it was obvious Evie was teasing. Stood to reason, didn't? Nobody in her right mind bet on a loser – not even on a lance-corporal's pay.

'Eejit,' she chided herself, then gazed skywards as a bomber flew low overhead, and then another. Flight-testing were they? Taking off; a short flight to check engines and that the undercarriage mechanism was spot on. Then landing. Circuits and bumps, Chas said it was, which almost always happened if they were flying that night.

She hugged herself tightly, closing her eyes, sending her thoughts winging to the aerodrome, never thinking she could care so much for one person – except her dad, of course. And the warm affection she had felt for him, God-love him, was not the same as the highs of happiness that blazed inside her when she and Chas were together, or the sick feeling inside her, like now, when she was as sure as she could be he would be flying tonight, into danger.

She made for the lodge, whispering, 'Take care, Sergeant Lawson, 'cos if anything happened to you I don't know what I'd do.' Because if one night he didn't come back, it was downright rotten of Whoever-it-was-up-there to let her meet him, grow to care for him, then take him from her. Life wouldn't be worth living.

She slammed the back door of Southgate Lodge, calling to Evie that she was back, filling the jar with water, pushing in the flowers, haphazard.

'The bombers are test flyin'. Must be on ops, tonight.'

'Mm. And isn't that just lucky, Nan? Both you and Chas on shift tonight which means it's a dead cert he won't be flying tomorrow, and you'll be able to meet.'

'A dead cert? You'd bet on it, Lance-Corporal?'

'A week's pay,' Evie grinned, 'so stop your worrying and get mopping under the beds – OK?'

And Nan, laughed and said,

'Yes, Lance-Corporal! Three bags full, Lance-Corporal!' and was all at once as sure as she could be that Chas and Boadicea would be waiting at Priest's Lodge tomorrow night, and that she would close her eyes and lift her mouth to be kissed. And the Angels would sing . . .

Corporal Freddy Finnigan glared at the wall telephone in the coach-house, then hung it up. He wasn't very fond of the daft instrument, since you could only receive calls on it, with no chance at all of having a sly call out to his old woman.

'Norm!' he yelled. 'You seen Carrie about? Is she back from Lincoln, yet?'

'Ten minutes ago. Gorn to the cookhouse for the drinkings.'

'Ah. Well she isn't going to be best pleased when I tell her she's got to go back. Had a call from the RTO's office. There's someone to pick up.'

'Lincoln station, Freddie?' Carrie, with the cream enamel teapot. 'That'll be Lenice, back from leave.'

'Well, get yourself a quick cuppa then off you go, girlie. Whoever it is will be waiting outside

215

the station exit. Waste of petrol, if you ask me. Pity you couldn't have done it all in one trip.'

'But they didn't know I'd be taking the sergeant to Lincoln Barracks, and they couldn't know what time Lenice's train would arrive,' Carrie soothed, pouring tea into mugs. 'Anyway, I like the drive. Getting to know a few short cuts. And the rations have arrived, so you can have sugar, today. One spoon – and level, don't forget.'

'So how's your love life, Tiptree,' the corporal teased when they were settled in the workshop, blowing on their tea.

'As well as can be expected, given there's a war on. But we're having the banns called in church next Sunday, so I suppose we're on our way. The mothers will be highly delighted.'

'And you, Carrie? Won't you be?'

'Delighted? You know I will.' She felt her cheeks flush. 'And with respect, corporal,' she said with mock severity, 'I don't want any more of your remarks about sailors having a girl in every port! Jeffrey will be at the church on time with his boots blacked, never fear.'

He would. The mothers would see to that! They'd be in church on Sunday in the back pew, of course, so they could see everyone's reactions when the vicar intoned,

'I publish the banns of marriage between Jeffrey James Frobisher and Caroline Tiptree, bachelor and spinster of this Parish . . .'

And her mother would pass Mrs Frobisher a

peardrop to suck, and everybody would sit down very noisily.

She could see it all; could hear every word of it, and especially could she imagine the smug smiles that would pass between the mothers; the almost-relief in their eyes that they'd made it at last – or as near as dammit!

'You all right, girl?' A hand passed before her eyes. 'You was miles away.'

'Sorry, Norm. Just thinking about the wedding – w-e-e-ll, you know how it is?' Norm was getting married, soon.

'Oh.' He took a slurping sip of his tea, wondering why, when Carrie was thinking about her wedding – and the wedding night an' all, he shouldn't wonder – she should look as if she'd lost a shilling and found six pence. 'Yes. Sure. Got your wedding dress yet? My fiancée has.' He liked calling her his fiancée. Sounded rather posh and very French. 'And the bridesmaids chosen – Three. How many bridesmaids are you havin', Carrie?'

'Dunno. Haven't thought about it. We'll be having a strictly uniform wedding, I shouldn't wonder – whenever that is . . .'

'But you're going on leave, soon. Can't your bloke put in for compassionate, then? He'd get it, you know, both of you bein' in the armed forces.'

'Not if he's at sea, he can't. As a matter of fact, it's all very much in the air at the moment, even though the banns are being read.'

Mind, she didn't add that she would be at home

for the last of the readings, because it wasn't any of his business, really.

'Ah, well – best of luck, Carrie. Can't wait for my own leave. It's all planned. Was going to Blackpool for our honeymoon, but it seems it's full of RAF bods.'

'Will it matter where you go, as long as there's a nice big double bed,' Freddy Finnigan asked sourly, annoyed at being left out of the conversation, and him with more experience of being wed than both those two put together. All moonlight and roses they thought it was! Just wait till Fowler saw his intended in her curlers and hairnet, and when she started laying down the law about going to the pub with the lads.

'Won't matter at all,' Norm grinned. 'And hadn't you better be on your way, Carrie. Mustn't keep Lenice Cooper waiting! That one has a sharp tongue if the mood's on her.'

'Then hard luck. And I won't be taking any nonsense from her, when *I'm* in charge of the pick-up.' Defiantly she got to her feet and jammed on her cap. ''Bye, each. Won't be long!'

'Oh deary me. The lass is learning, wouldn't you say?' Freddy grinned, refilling his mug. 'And if I was you, Norm, I'd keep off the subject of weddings – when Carrie's around, I mean. To my way of thinking, her isn't as bright-eyed as her should be – about bein' a blushing bride, I mean.'

'And what makes you think that, then?'

'Because for one thing, Private Fowler, I have

the instincts of an older man when it comes to such things and for another, she don't talk about him as much as she should – thank gawd.'

Females who twittered on about white nighties – or black nighties, as the case may be – and lace-trimmed frillies and suchlike bored him to tears, especially when bawling kids had a habit of happening once the daft couple had full and unin-terrupted use of the marital bed!

'Well, she's having the banns read in church, so she must be willing,' Norman defended.

'Ar yes. But is she eager?' Corporal Finnigan played his trump card, then rose to his feet, indi-cating that tea break was over. 'And anyway, Carrie's a gently-reared girl, so watch what you say about weddings and the like. All right, Fowler?'

And Norman collected teapot and mugs, because Carrie wasn't there to see to them, and said not another word.

'Er – a word if you don't mind, Morrissey,' said Sergeant James when she heard the pick-up stop outside the signals office. 'And it's entirely up to you, mind.'

'*Me*?' Nan frowned, because Sergeant James usually gave orders and had never been known to offer options.

'It's Seaton. She goes on leave tomorrow, but she's on earlies. I don't suppose you could stand in for her – just this once? She loses nearly two days of her seven just getting home and back, you see. Mind, it would mean you working right through, so if you've got a date . . .'

'Reckon I won't have. Saw Chas last night and I phoned him this morning and got through. Seeing him tonight, so tomorrow night it looks like I'll be at a loose end.'

'Then if you're willing . . .'

There was a loud bang on the door and Evie went to answer it to B-Shift, both present and correct, with Lenice in a uniform so professionally taken in and let out and taken up that she looked, as if she had been poured into it, and Alison, pink-cheeked, because she knew her leave pass and travel warrant were on the sergeant's desk and before so very much longer she would be taking the train north.

'Hello, Cooper. Had a good leave?'

'The best, thanks Sergeant.' She wasn't telling them just yet about the on-leave soldier she met at a dance and who was stationed not four miles the other side of Lincoln. Just in case nothing came of the promise to meet her there on Saturday night.

'And you, Seaton – all packed and ready for the off?'

'Yes to both, Sergeant.' Her cheeks flushed still pinker. 'Can't wait for tomorrow, at two.'

'Then just to let you know that Morrissey has volunteered to do your early shift, so as soon as Tiptree is free, she'll run you to the station and you'll be able to get an earlier train.'

'But Sergeant, is it allowed – me sloping off when I should be on shift?' She was in such a quiver of excitement that Evie thought she would take off and never be seen again.

'Allowed? It's me gives the orders round here, Seaton, and I've just said it is!'

'Then thank you – both!' Her eyes filled with tears of pure happiness and if it had been allowed in the ATS to fling your arms around your sergeant and kiss her soundly on the cheek, Private Seaton would have done it. 'I'll be home hours earlier.'

'Right, then. Settle down B-shift, and Morrissey and Turner make yourselves scarce. And if you're in a fit state to be trusted with a mug of hot tea, Seaton, I suggest you cut along to the cookhouse and get me one!'

'She's on such a high that you'll probably get a glass of beer,' Lenice laughed, adjusting her headset, settling at the switchboard. 'But couldn't she have put the kettle on in the kitchen?'

'She could have, but the walk to the cookhouse will give her time to blow her nose and stop her snuffing,' Monica James snapped, a tight-mouthed, deady-eyed sergeant once more, indicating that her act of generosity was over and done with and not to be mentioned again.

So Lenice sat with a plug at the ready and thought about the soldier she had met, who was one of the few men she had ever danced with who was taller than she was. And who had thick, curly hair and the loveliest of smiles and was meeting her, fingers crossed, at seven at the bus station on Saturday. A disc dropped and she pushed in the plug.

'Switchboard,' she said sweetly.

That morning there were two letters on Nan's bed and two on Evie's, placed there by Carrie, who had stopped at Southgate on her way back to the stable block, just in case there was a letter from Jeffrey. Just one from her mother, though, who told her how well the first reading of the banns had gone, and what a buzz of excitement it had caused in Nether Hutton.

It had made her realise that did the two mothers but know it, Carrie Tiptree would be sitting in church beside them to hear the third and last reading. But best not think of that, nor mention it in a letter just yet. Best get off to the stable block where Freddy and Norm would be waiting for their ten-minute-late tea. What she did think of, though, was the second of Nan's letters in a thick, cream envelope – obviously pre-war stationery – addressed in unfamiliar hand writing and postmarked Shrewsbury. So who did Private Morrissey know in Shrewsbury, she grinned mischievously. Another beau? Oh, surely not!

'There are letters,' Carrie said as nonchalantly as she could when the shifts had changed and she was driving Evie and Nan back to Southgate. 'Two each . . .'

'*Two for me!*' Nan gasped.

'Well, if your name is Pte Morrissey N, then yes. One from Leeds and the other from –' She stopped, teasingly. 'Oh, dear, I've forgotten. Have you got a secret lover, Nan?'

'You know I haven't.' Nan's cheeks were bright red. 'And get a move on, Carrie. You've got me wonderin', now!'

'You've got us all wondering,' Evie unlocked the door, laughing as Nan pounced on the two envelopes.

'Hey up! Postmarked Shrewsbury. It'll be from Chas's mother. He said she'd be writing.'

'What about?' Evie asked, biting on a smile.

'We-e-ll – I told you, didn't I? About me and Chas havin' the same leave dates, I mean.'

'And that he'd asked you to go home with him – meet his mother?' Carrie prompted.

'Yes – well – it looks like she's written.' Nan's hands shook. 'Wonder what she's said . . .'

'You aren't going to find out, Morrissey, if you don't open it.'

'Reckon not.' Nan slit the envelope with her thumb, pulling out a single sheet of notepaper. 'And innit posh, eh? The paper matches the envelope.'

'Read it!' Evie gasped.

'Ar. But what if she doesn't want me to go home with Chas?' All at once, the flush had left Nan's cheeks. 'Oh, go on, Carrie – be a mate. You read it, eh?'

'You're sure?' She unfolded the letter, looking

223

at it long and hard. 'You're absolutely sure you want to hear what Stella Lawson says?'

'Read it!'

'OK. Be it on your own head, Morrissey. And you can stop looking like a startled rabbit, because it's OK.'

Dear Nan,

Charles has told me your leaves coincide, so I would like very much if you would come home with him. I have heard so much about you that I am longing to meet you.

Please say you will come?

Sincerely,

Stella Lawson

'There you are, you doubting Thomasina!' Carrie thrust the letter into Nan's hand. 'Read it yourself! And if you want my opinion, it's a lovely letter.'

'Mm. And expensive notepaper. You said Chas talked posh, didn't you? Do you suppose his folks are well-heeled?' Evie murmured.

'Chas hasn't got a dad. Said he was killed quite a long time ago.'

'In the Great War, Nan?'

'Nah. Said he fell out of a tree. Broke his neck. Pickin' apples, he was. Leastways, that's how Chas said it happened. And I don't think they've got a lot of money, 'cause the address is Gardener's Cottage. And anyway, I'm not looking for a rich feller. All I want is Chas, and for him to get through this war.'

'That's what we all want,' Evie smiled. 'Our men back safe and sound. And if you've come down to earth again, mind if I read my own letters, you two?'

And they said they didn't mind at all, then Carrie said Nan should write back at once. But Nan said she must ring the aerodrome, see if she could get hold of Chas, and ran out, making for the NAAFI phone, praying silently that Chas might just be in the Aircrew Mess, and not having a sleep on his bed.

'Well, let's hope Sergeant James doesn't see her. Jacket unbuttoned, no cap, hair all over the place . . .'

'Agreed,' Carrie grinned. 'A clear case of being improperly dressed. Should get her a week's stoppages, at least!'

'Then fingers crossed that she gets through to him. Oh, isn't love wonderful,' Evie smiled, fingers fondling her wedding ring.

And Carrie said, 'Is it?' then wished she could have taken back those two trite words and hoped that Evie, reading the first of her letters, hadn't heard it.

Quietly, she closed the door and made for the pick-up truck, wishing with all her heart as she drove towards the stable block that a letter from Jeffrey could bring a look of love to her eyes or make her fondle the engagement ring she never wore. Or even send her rushing to the phone to speak to him.

But she couldn't phone because Jeffrey was at sea and on Sunday would be the second reading of their banns in church. Another step towards a wedding she didn't want.

No! She didn't mean that! A wedding she didn't want *just yet*, she had meant; when she and Jeffrey had talked about *things*, and he had promised her he understood how nervous she was and that their wedding night would be gentle and loving and sweet.

Tight-lipped, she drove between the gateposts and parked the truck neatly. Then she walked through the workshop and, without a word to either Freddy or Norman, picked up the small, cream-enamelled teapot and made for the cook-house.

Nan hurried into Chas's arms the minute he had manoeuvred himself out of Boadicea.

'Darling! A letter from your mother and she wants me to come on leave with you! I didn't think she'd write, honest I didn't!'

'Well, she has, and I hope you have written back and told her you'd love to meet her.'

He tilted her chin, and kissed her gently.

'Course I did. Evie helped me. Wasn't sure what to say, so she gave me a piece of her best blue notepaper and said how about something like,

'Dear Mrs Lawson. I received your letter this

morning and I would love to come. Thank you very much for asking me. I am meeting Chas – er – *Charles* tonight and I can't wait to tell him – y'know, words to that effect. Short and polite. So I wrote just that and ended with Love from Nan XXX. Do you suppose it was all right sending kisses, Chas?'

And he took her in his arms and kissed her again and said that kisses, even paper kisses from Nan Morrissey, were just wonderful, and did she realise that in just five more days they would be standing on the platform at Lincoln station and heading for seven days' leave.

'Oh, flamin' Norah – I've just thought! My civvies are at Auntie Mim's. There won't be time for her to get a parcel to me. I'll have nothing to wear but my uniform, Chas!' she gasped, dismayed.

'So? I love you in your uniform, but if you don't want to wear it all the time, I'm sure mother has loads of togs you could borrow. You look about the same size, to me.'

'And she'd lend me her clothes? Your mother must be a real nice lady, Chas.'

'She is, sweetheart. I adore her. And she is so pleased I've got myself a girl at last. So play your cards right and she might let you wear her mink!'

'*Mink*! She's got a fur coat!'

'No. Only teasing. But I know you'll like her, Nan, and I know she'll like you. And there's a hop in the church hall tonight – just down the road. A couple of chaps from the mess are going. Think it's dancing to gramophone records and the floor isn't up to much, but I'd like to go – y'know, show off all my fancy steps.'

And Nan said it was fine by her, then thought that it didn't matter how awful the floor was nor that they would be dancing, most likely, to a wind-up gramophone. As long as she was in Chas's arms and dancing so close that their cheeks touched, nothing else mattered. She wanted to be close and to touch him all the time – a part of loving him, she supposed.

It was a very nice, very bothersome feeling.

'Do you suppose,' Nan fretted, 'that Mrs Lawson will mind if I do a bit of washing whilst I'm there. I've got two clean shirts and two sets of clean undies and stockings, but they won't last all week.'

'Nan Morrissey!' Evie scolded. 'You're getting yourself into a state about this leave.'

'No I'm not. Not really. It's just that Chas is on ops tonight and I'm a bit jumpy.'

'Yes, well he's going on leave tomorrow – the whole crew are – so they'll get back all right. And if I were you,' Carrie advised, if only to get Nan's mind out of a Wellington bomber, 'I wouldn't travel in a clean shirt. You know how dusty the trains are now. And wear your battledress top. It'll be a lot more comfortable than your jacket.'

Train journeys in wartime were a hit and miss thing: crowded carriages where twelve people, plus kit, crowded into compartments intended for eight; no water in the toilets, which were usually jam-packed with kitbags and cases and respirators and tin hats, anyway. And the train always late, held up because it was carrying passengers and often shunted into a siding so that trains of more importance carrying munitions and tanks and guns could speed past unhindered.

Is Your Journey Really Necessary, demanded posters, making people who used trains and buses feel guilty even about taking the shortest journey. But Nan wouldn't mind. The more crowded the compartment, the nearer she could sit Chas, and snuggle her arm into his and think about them being together for seven whole days with never a worry about whether he would be waiting for her outside Priest's Lodge – or flying. Seven tomorrows, and being able to say the word without crossing your fingers. Absolute heaven. This afternoon's two-till-ten shift would crawl by and afterwards she would be so excited she wouldn't be able to sleep. Thank the good Lord for Carrie's dependable alarm clock.

'Penny for them?' A hand passed in front of Nan's eyes.

'Worth more than that, but if you must know, I was thinking about tomorrow, and how slowly things are going to go till Carrie runs me to the station in the morning.' Then her eyes opened wide and she held her hand to her mouth. 'Oh, sorry, Evie. I shouldn't have said that, when it might be years before you see Bob. And drat me! I shouldn't have said that either. I'm in such a tizzy I don't know what's got into me.'

'Then I think, Nan Morrissey, that you're in love, and being in love is marvellous – well, most of the time – so just enjoy all the good bits and learn not to worry, so much about the bad bits. Just tell yourself, like I do, that your man is going to be all right because you love him so much that nothing on earth could harm him.'

'Yes, I will, Evie, and thanks for bein' such a love and taking no notice of my blether. We said we'd see Carrie at the cookhouse around twelve, so shall we get ourselves off?'

Not that she would be able to eat a thing. Not even if it were toad-in-the-hole with onion gravy and jam roly-poly and custard to follow. Evie was right, though. Being in love *was* marvellous – well, most of the time. And her mind slipped away to this morning when she had phoned the aerodrome and was told, 'Sorry. I'm afraid I am unable to put you through' – which meant only one thing, and that the late shift and the night would pass so very slowly.

Then she straightened her shoulders, placed her cap at a jaunty angle and, falling into step with Evie, walked with swinging arms towards the cookhouse.

'I hope it's toad-in-the-hole,' she said with more conviction than she felt.

'And lashings of onion gravy,' Evie grinned.

'And look over there! Two magpies, Nan. You don't often see two together – not at this time of the year.'

'And is that bad?' Nan whispered.

'Not a bit of it. It's two for joy. Carrie told me that in her part of the world you touched your forelock and said "Good morning, Sir," to it when you saw a magpie on its own.'

'Why?' Nan thought it was a stupid thing to do.

'Well, because in her part of Yorkshire you always do that because the magpie is the devil's bird, and it don't do to upset one. But to see two at the same time is very lucky, so tell them good morning.'

Nan came to attention and saluted smartly, then whispered, 'Good morning Sir or Madam.'

'That's the way. You're learning. Now have a wish, Nan.' Evie wasn't quite sure if that were true, but Nan was in need of a wish right now. 'Go on. Quickly, before they fly away, and don't tell me what you wish.'

And Nan closed her eyes and crossed her fingers and the most beautiful smile lifted the corners of her mouth. Then she said,

'It *is* onion gravy, Evie. I can smell it from here!'

TEN

'It's a crying shame,' Corporal Finnigan brooded.
'A motor like that, I mean.' He stood, arms folded,
glaring at the Humber saloon. 'No respect, that's
what.'

'But Freddy, you said you were satisfied with
it,' Carrie, clad in overalls, soothed. 'And you said
you'd let me have a go driving it, so when can I?'

'Not until I'm satisfied there's nothing more I
can do to it.'

'But it runs like a dream and you said the uphol-
stery couldn't be bettered.'

Norman had found an unopened tin of saddle
soap in what was once the tack room and they
had set to work cleaning the dark brown leather
interior of the officers-for-the-use-of motor. And
the hard and, in places, cracked leatherwork had
responded gratefully to treatment, guzzling in the
soap until it could take no more and was as soft,
Norman said, as a baby's bottom.

'I know, girl, but there's them headlamps to

clean. All over paint, they are! If the bodywork had to be camouflaged, couldn't they have been a bit more careful? Did they have to slap it all over the lamps and the mudguards?'

'Couldn't agree more, Freddy,' Private Fowler said morosely. 'That saloon was once somebody's pride and joy, then the Army nicks it, paints it all over with khaki and black and green, and sends it to us in a terrible state.'

'Vandalism, but who are we to complain.' Corporal Finnigan looked at his wristwatch and calculated that in nineteen minutes they would stop for tea break. 'Now what say you clean the windows and windscreen inside and out, Carrie, whilst Norm and me have a go at these headlamps and bumpers and get that chrome back to the way it should be.'

'But are we allowed to have fancy chrome bits?' Private Fowler was as sure as he could be that gleaming chromium accessories would be frowned upon by Authority. 'Strictly utilitarian everything's got to be, now.'

'Who runs this motor pool?' the corporal growled. 'This here was once a fine vehicle and will be treated with respect, and then, if we have to transport an officer, we're ready.'

'But our lot hasn't got an officer,' Carrie pointed out, 'and rumour has it that those in the big house are mostly civilians – boffins and back-room boys.'

'Be prepared, Tiptree. You never know, so press on with the glass-work – I want it gleamin' – and then it'll be just about time for the Ten o'clock brew.'

So Carrie selected some soft pieces from the government-issue sack of waste rags, took the bottle marked VINEGAR – MOTOR POOL – NOT TO BE TAKEN AWAY and climbed inside the car she was longing to drive.

'Windows gleaming,' she whispered, then thought about Ailsa whose leave would soon be over and about Nan who was busy writing to her Auntie Mim in Leeds, explaining that in view of the sleeping position at Farthing Street, she had decided to see a bit of the country and had asked for her rail voucher to be made out to Shrewsbury, from where she would write a more explicit letter.

Dear Nan, excited as a kitten with a ball of wool and who would be on late shift tonight and worrying about Chas, who would almost certainly be flying.

'I hope it won't be a long op,' Nan had fretted, 'or he'll be late getting back, won't he? And then he'll have to go to de-briefing and have his breakfast and a shave and we could miss the two o'clock train to Derby.' They were to change at Derby, for Shrewsbury.

'Then if you miss it, you'll have to get a later train, or hitch.' Evie quickly took charge of the situation. 'But will it matter as long as you're together and on leave? And anyway, the train is bound to be late into Lincoln.'

There was a war on and trains were always

late. Sometimes they never arrived, so people had to accept it without complaint or be called unpatriotic, and being unpatriotic was almost as bad as being a conscientious objector.

'Yes, but what if, just this once, it's dead on time?'

'Trains are *never* on time now,' Evie had insisted. 'And the connection to Shrewsbury will probably be late, too, so it won't matter.'

'Won't it?' Nan's eyes were wide and troubled.

'No it will *not,* and that's an order, Morrissey!' Evie jabbed a fore-finger at the stripe on her arm. 'So get off to the ablutions and wash and dry your hair before we go on shift. You don't want to meet Mrs Lawson looking scruffy, now do you? And where, exactly, will you be staying?'

'The sergeant's got the address. Gardener's Cottage, Manor Lane, Wadestone, near Shrewsbury. Chas said there's only a bus there every four hours, so we'll have to hitch from the station. Not that I'll worry about that.'

'No. By then you'll have found something else to worry about – like is Chas's Mum going to like you.'

'Hecky thump, I hadn't thought about that!'

'Heaven help us!' Evie had thrust towel and spongebag at a despairing Nan. 'Off with you! Now!'

Smiling, Carrie rubbed the vinegar-soaked rag on the rear window. Soon, she would see Evie and Nan in the cookhouse. And Cooper, too, she shouldn't wonder, grabbing a quick dinner because Seaton wasn't there and the signals office was short on bods. There was quite a change in Lenice Cooper, Carrie considered, since she had returned from leave. Was it because of the now immaculately fitting uniform, or did she know something that no one else knew, and wasn't letting on?

Carrie huffed warm breath on a stubborn spot on the rear window, looking at the distant tractor, small as a toy, that drove slowly up and down a field. Probably lifting sugar beet. The evicted farmers were allowed to salvage standing crops when the estate had been requisitioned and everybody emptied out without a by-your-leave, but what would happen to those fields once they were bare of crops? Left to lay fallow and to weed over? Such a waste of agricultural land when we needed every bit of food we could grow.

Satisfied with the inside windows, Carrie busied herself with the outside, looking at trees with leaves already dulling to autumnal dark green. The sycamores would be the first to fall, and the limes would turn yellow and die, and then it would be the turn of the oaks that lined the drive. Only the beeches would hang on to their browned leaves for as long as tearing winds and frost would let them.

She thought again about winter, not so far away, now. How would this idyllic place be then, the estate roads rutted with frost and Southgate so cold they would have to stuff the rattling window frames with newspapers?

'Hey up! How am I expected to clean the windscreen with you two in the way?' Carrie complained.

'You're not.' Freddy looked at his watch. 'You can finish the job after tea break! He stood back to admire the bumper and the rims of the headlights, already responding to the application of precipitated whiting. Anything other than precipitated whiting would leave scratch marks, Freddy insisted, showing Carrie the texture of the powder and water paste-mix in the saucer he held. 'I wouldn't be surprised if the gent what once owned this motor didn't use this stuff – or his chauffeur. Get a move on. Tiptree!'

Carrie looked at her watch. One minute to ten and the first tea break of the day. She grinned, pulled on her cap, then made for the cookhouse. Then she saw Nan, rolled towel under her arm, walking up the lane.

'Hi!' she called, then stopped to wait for her friend. 'Getting excited? I'll be picking you up at half-twelve prompt tomorrow, don't forget.'

'As if I could! Can't wait to go on leave, but Chas is flying tonight, I shouldn't wonder, and I'm worried he won't turn up. You know what I mean?'

'Don't be an idiot, Morrissey! Give me one good reason why he shouldn't get back safe and sound, especially as he's going home on leave?'

'Sod's law I suppose. I mean – when did anything ever go right for me?'

'Goodness! *Everything's* going right for you, these days – admit it!'

'We-e-ll, I suppose so. I won't sleep tonight, though.'

'Yes you will, but no snoring, mind. Have you ever thought how loudly you can snore, Nan?'

'I know. The Queer One used to bang on the bedroom wall at Cyprian Court.' The hint of a smile lifted the corners of Nan's mouth. 'But I'd better shift meself. Can't be goin' to the cookhouse with wet hair, eh?'

'No you can't! See you, and stop your worrying.'

Dear Nan, she thought as she made for the back door of the cookhouse. In love for the first time and either high on a happy pink cloud because she was meeting Chas, or down in the depths, because he was almost certainly flying ops.

But he would get back all right – probably in the early hours of the morning, when a dozen or so Wellington bombers circuited above Heronflete, waiting for permission to land, and waking everyone around with their din, bless them! Chas *would* get back all right and he'd be meeting Nan at Lincoln station, knowing that not for seven nights would he be taking off into the twilight. What could harm him with Nan's love to keep him safe?

She opened the cookhouse door, then looked for the sergeant who would almost certainly call, 'Well, if it isn't the love of my life, come for a pot of gin!' (Or beer or whisky, as the mood took him) and to which Carrie always replied, 'Best not, Sergeant. There's a war on, don't forget. I'll make do with tea, just this once.'

And they would both laugh at the same silly joke because it couldn't be a lot of fun for the sergeant, worrying about his wife and three sons in London. And what wouldn't Mrs Sergeant Cook give, Carrie thought, to sleep every night in Southgate Lodge and not once be wakened by wailing air-raid sirens or the terrible crash of bombs? And what wouldn't the poor woman give, to sleep in her husband's arms and know she would awaken to a safe new morning.

Carrie thanked the sergeant with her brightest smile and called, 'Thanks a lot. See you!'

Sleeping in her husband's arms, she pondered, as she carried the pot carefully back to the coach-house. Sleeping in Jeffrey's arms, didn't she mean? She wondered if he snored.

There was a letter for Carrie, from Jeffrey.

Dearest Carrie,
    I will be glad when the banns are finally read. Had you realised it will mean that next time I am on leave, you can apply for compassionate, whether you are due leave or not. Won't be too long, now.
    In haste, before I go on watch . . .

So that was it. Second reading of the banns on Sunday, then home on leave and sitting in church, hearing the final reading. And after that, it was anybody's guess. She folded the sheet of notepaper and stuffed it in her pocket and for some strange reason she wondered if Jeffrey slept in the nude.

'So what was so passionate in that letter,' Nan teased, 'to make you blush bright red, Tiptree?'

'I – er – actually, I was wondering if Jeffrey – well, if he snored.' Carrie finished, relieved.

'*Snored?*' Nan laughed. 'I don't believe you! Unless, of course, you're havin' a dig at me?'

'No, I wasn't, Morrissey, and if you *really* want to know,' Carrie flung defiantly, 'I was wondering if he slept in – well, with nothing on.'

'Ha! That's more like it! Thought it'd have to be sumthin' more passionate than snoring to make you go beetroot red! I wonder if there's more to our Carrie than she'll admit, thinkin' such things. And watch it, Evie! That was my shin you've just kicked!'

'Sorry, Nan. Must've been a knee-jerk reaction – talking about men in the nude, I mean.' Evie shot a warning gaze across the table. 'As a matter of fact, Bob doesn't bother with pyjamas. And these peas are as hard as bullets!'

The conversation about nude sleeping partners was firmly closed by Evie, glaring at her plate.

'Was only teasing.'

'OK, Nan – but if you want a lift to Lincoln in my pick-up, you'd better behave yourself, or I'll drop you outside Priest's and you can hitch a lift to the station!'

'You wouldn't do that, Tiptree!' Nan's eyes opened even wider.

'So shut up, the pair of you,' Evie ordered, 'and eat your peas and your soggy steak and kidney pudding! Oh, lordy – the things we girls put up with for king and country! And you'd both better shift yourselves. It's nearly half-twelve – almost time you were on your way, Morrissey.'

On her way. Nan closed her eyes and pushed aside her plate because she wasn't hungry; not even if it had been toad-in-the-hole with onion gravy, was she. All she could think about – teasing apart – was Lincoln station and if Chas would be there. And if he wasn't there, if something really awful had happened, what would she do? Where would she go? Where would she *want* to go? She got to her feet.

'I'm goin' to Southgate to pick up my clobber. See you, Carrie. Does anybody want my pudding?'

She made for the door, wishing she didn't feel so sick with worry; wishing she didn't love Chas so much; wishing she knew how to pray. Because if she did, she would do a deal with the God who let wars happen and men and women and children get killed, when all He had to do was to have had Hitler run over and killed in 1938!

'Please be there, Chas?' she whispered, then tilting her chin, squaring her shoulders, she added, ''cos if you aren't, you're in dead trouble, sergeant!'

*　　*　　*

It was twenty minutes past one when Carrie parked the pick-up at Lincoln station.

'Right then, old love, loads of time to spare. Have a smashing leave, Nan. And look –'

She pointed in the direction of an RAF transport – exactly like the one that picked them up outside Priest's Lodge when there was a dance at RAF Modeley.

The WAAF driver backed it up, then jumped down, hurrying to let down the tailboard calling,

'Come on then, you lot! Let's be having you! And have a smashing leave,' she grinned, as airmen and WAAFs – aircraftwomen, if you insisted on correctness – threw out bags and cases then jumped down after them.

'There he is,' Carrie pointed to the very last airman to leave the transport. 'Safe and sound.'

'He looks tired,' Nan whispered.

'So would you be if you'd been up most of the night! You'll have to make sure you get seats together then he can get a bit of shuteye. Anyway, have a good leave, Nan – and behave yourself!'

And she was off, though Nan still stood there, shaking with relief, willing Chas to look in her direction, and smile at her. And when he did, and pushed his way to her side, she whispered, 'Hello, Sergeant darling.' Said it very chokily because she was still fighting tears.

And he smiled his lovely smile and said, 'Hi there, Nan Morrissey. Going my way, by any chance?'

* * *

Chas slept all the way to Derby, head on Nan's shoulder, an arm snuggled behind her, and she with her hand resting possessively on his knee, even though the compartment was hot and crowded and thick with cigarette smoke. Nan had never, ever, been so happy in the whole of her almost-eighteen years.

'Strange, isn't it,' Evie said, 'without Nan, he should be almost there by now – delays permitting. I worry about her, sometimes.'

'Why on earth? She was really happy this morning when Chas got off the transport at the station. Mind, he looked tired, but I suppose he'll have had a sleep on the train. And had you thought, Evie, that Nan really likes being in the ATS and living in the country and not having to put up with her stepmother, so why the worry?'

'Because she's so besotted with Chas and being taken home to meet his mother, that sometimes I wish things hadn't got so serious between them. Being aircrew is pretty risky. Hadn't you ever thought how it would be for her if anything happened to him? Can't you recognise that they're truly in love? It isn't just infatuation.'

'Meaning that *I'm* not truly in love?' Carrie gave a final rub to the jacket buttons she was cleaning. 'Just because I don't get all starry-eyed over Jeffrey doesn't mean that –'

'Starry-eyed? You? There was a letter today, wasn't there?'

'Yes, and he says that when he gets leave, I'll be able to apply for compassionate, even if I'm not due any leave. Maybe it wasn't such a good idea getting the banns read.'

'It was a very good idea, Tiptree, if you were mad keen to marry the bloke, but you aren't, are you?'

'Now look here!' Flush-faced, Carrie looked up from her polishing. 'I don't think it's any of your business!'

'It wasn't, but you made it my business, didn't you? You told me how things were between you and –'

'I asked for your advice. In confidence. But now you're throwing it back in my face!'

'No, Carrie. Just reminding you what you said to me, and the advice I gave you. Talk it over, didn't I say, and I still hold to that opinion,' Evie said softly, 'because the way I see it is that when Jeffrey gets leave he'll expect there to be a wedding.'

'So what the hell do I do!'

'Look Carrie – you're going home yourself, soon. Next week at this time, you'll be on your way, so why not talk to your Mum about it?'

'I can't. I won't. You know the way things are, there. Mother would refuse to talk about it – probably have one of her migraines and shut the bedroom door on me.'

'Then it's going to be up to you, Carrie. *You* are the one who's getting married, after all.'

'I'm the one who's being *pushed* into getting married by Jeffrey's mother and my mother. They can't seem to think of anything else! Anyway, I don't want to talk about it!'

'Then I'm sorry for you, because unless you are absolutely sure, you're going to have to write and tell him that the way things are here, you can't get compassionate leave – when it happens, that is.'

'But that would be a lie; downright deceitful!'

'Carrie Tiptree, you've been downright deceitful to your Jeffrey for as long as I've known you, so why get yourself all bothered over one more lie? Anyway, you know my feelings on the matter, so let's drop the subject before you and me fall out. And I'm going up to the NAAFI to post a letter. Want to come with me?'

'All right. And I know you mean well, Evie. Sorry if I got a bit sharp, because you are right. I don't know what to think about Jeffrey's next leave, and it isn't only the honeymoon that bothers me.'

'Heaven help us! *Now* what!' Evie drew the blackout curtains.

'What if I got pregnant on our honeymoon? What if Jeffrey did it on purpose to get me out of the ATS, because he would, you know! He was livid when I joined up, so what better way to get me home and under the mothers' thumbs for the duration?'

'Don't you want Jeffrey's baby?'

'No! Oh, of course I want children, but when *I* want to have them and that wouldn't be until the war was over, if I had anything to do with it.'

'But women don't have anything to do with it, Carrie. It's up to the husband to take care of things like that. You'd just have to trust Jeffrey like I trust Bob.'

'I know. That's what's so awful about it. I don't trust him, you see.'

'Then all I can say is you'll have to have a lot of headaches on your honeymoon. That, or postpone the wedding until you are as sure as you can be that that's what you want to do.'

'Oh, dammit. Wish it wasn't such a walk to the Black Bull – see if they've got any gin under the counter. I feel like getting plastered.'

'Well, by the time we've got there, the Bull will be closed, so you'll have to make do on a couple of beers in the NAAFI. Just nip and check the blackout in the kitchen, will you, then we'll be off. And no more wedding talk tonight! Think of other things.'

'Like what?' Carrie shrugged into her jacket.

'We-e-ll – how about Nan and if they've arrived yet. And there's your own leave, soon. Think of having a lie in bed, mornings, and wearing civvy clothes, and –'

'And going to church, Sunday, and listening to the third reading of the banns and giving mother a lemon slice to suck on to take the smug smirk off her face!'

'You can't get lemons, now. And didn't I say no more wedding talk?'

'You did, Corporal. Sorry, Corporal,' Carrie grinned. 'Not another word. Far better to think about Nan, and if she and Chas are still waiting on Derby station for the Shrewsbury connection, poor loves.'

'As long as they're together, they won't care one iota. Whereever they are, they'll be holding hands, or maybe have found a dark corner, somewhere, for a kiss and a cuddle.'

'I can think of worse ways of waiting for a train,' Carrie laughed, 'so let's get up to the NAAFI before the beer runs out!'

'You're here, both of you! At last!' Stella Lawson hurried down the path, arms wide. 'Oh, come here, do, and give me a hug, then come inside so I can see you.' She drew her son to her, not kissing him; just holding him tightly, her cheek on his, then she reached for Nan, hugging her warmly, kissing her cheek, murmuring, 'I am so glad to meet you, dearest girl.'

'I'm glad to be here,' Nan whispered, overcome by such a welcome. Never before had she been so hugged and kissed; not by the Queer One; not even by her real mother, that she could remember.

'Now hurry inside, so I can shut the door and switch on the light. And how did you manage to get here from Shrewsbury? Hitched?'

She snapped on the light and Nan blinked in

the sudden brightness, then took in the hallway. White walls, white woodwork, and a thick dark-blue patterned carpet covering the floor and all the way up the stairs. There were chrysanthemums in a vase beside the telephone on the table.

'Come into the kitchen. It's warm, there. Didn't light the sitting room fire – saving coal.'

'Mother, take a deep breath,' Chas laughed. 'We're here for seven whole days. All the time in the world to talk. And right now, you could have my stripes for a cup of tea.'

'Then tea it is. For three.' Stella Lawson smiled softly and Nan realised how beautiful she was. Pale blonde hair – *real* blonde, not out of a bottle – bright blue eyes and the most beautiful smile. Chas's smile.

'I'll dump the kit, mother. Is Nan in the small front?'

'She is.' Then when they were alone, she said, 'I don't want to make a thing of it, but I just *must* say this. You are so welcome. I never thought to see the day Charles would bring a girl home. And you taught him to dance, too! What a very special young lady you must be!'

'Ar, there's nuthin' special about me, Mrs Lawson. And it was me first asked Chas to dance. I was sitting by him and I told him that if he didn't ask me onto the floor, then some other feller would. I liked him the minute I spoke to him, see. It was me made all the running.'

'Then I'm glad you did. He was terrified of

248

girls, though heaven knows why; it made his stammer worse. And he's right. You *do* have the most beautiful eyes. And ssssh! He's coming . . .'

'Right, Nan. You're in the room at the top of the stairs, next to mother's. I'm in the attic.' Chas beamed.

'You haven't given up your room for me,' Nan whispered.

'No, I haven't. I've always been in the attic. Wouldn't want to sleep in yours. It's all pretty-pretty and floral. I suppose there wouldn't be a slice of toast, or something?'

'There would. I made strawberry and raspberry jam with the sugar allowance we got in the summer. Just a little, but I've saved a jar for you. And that's the kettle. Tea won't be long, now, and forgive me if I talk too much and keep grinning like a cat that's got the cream, but it is absolute heaven having my son and his girl home. You *are* his girl, Nan?'

'Well, I – er – I suppose you could say –'

'She's my girl,' Chas said softly. 'Seriously my girl.'

'Good.' Stella Lawson took a loaf from the pannikin, cutting two thick slices, handing out two long forks. 'Here you are. Toast your own while I see to the tea. No butter on the bread, mind!'

And Nan and Chas sat in front of the glowing coals, each knowing that for a whole week they would be together at Gardener's Cottage and that toasting bread to spread with homemade jam was only the beginning of something wonderful.

'You don't mind, Mrs Lawson, if I call Charles Chas?' Nan ventured. 'They called him Charlie, see, in the Mess, and I wasn't havin' that, and Charles sounded a bit – well – formal.'

'That's fine by me. Anyway, lovers always have pet names for each other, don't they?'

'We aren't lovers!' Nan flung round, toasting fork poised.

'Sorry. I should have said people in love. You *are* in love?'

'Like I said,' Chas said, softly, 'seriously. Daren't think past that.'

'Well, when the time is right, you'll know.' Complacently Stella poured milk into white china mugs. 'Be careful, though . . .'

'Are you giving us your blessing, mother mine,' Chas smiled.

But 'Watch that toast, boy. You're burning it!' was the answer she made. 'And how did you get here from the station?'

'We were lucky. The train was an hour late – no buses – but there was an ambulance outside so I took a chance that it was coming next door, and it was. Two patients for the Manor. We squeezed in with the driver.'

'Next door is a hospital, Chas told me.' Nan offered her toast to be jammed.

'Mm. For convalescents, and glad to be out of the war for a few months. I work there.' Stella sliced the toast into two. 'Go in every day, except Sunday. Some of them are blind – waiting their discharge. Others are waiting for surgery – dreadfully burned.'

'Don't, dearest.' Chas laid an arm on his mother's shoulders. 'She does it because a lot of them are air airmen – some with burns.'

'I do it out of gratitude. Perhaps I think that if I work really hard there, God will keep Charles safe for me.'

'Then that'll be two of us, looking out for him.' Nan saw her distress and was quickly by her side. 'He'll be fine – just you see if he isn't.'

'Yes, of course he will. I suppose I'm being over-emotional, tonight. And I told matron I won't be in for a week and she said that was OK by her.'

So Mrs Lawson trusted in God? Nan bit into her toast, wishing she could be like her. But someone brought up without religion and taught from an early age that heaven helped those who helped themselves didn't know how to trust in any God. And anyway, weren't German mothers praying for their sons who flew at night? Fighter pilots, mostly, trying to shoot our bombers out of the sky. What did God do about a predicament like that, then?

'This jam,' she said, licking her fingers, 'is absolutely smashin.'

The pick-up truck stopped outside the signals office and Private Fowler parped the horn at the exact moment the Yeoman clicked open the green door, placing cigarettes, tin-lid ashtray and notepad on the desktop.

'Hi. Busy watch?' he asked of the sergeant.

'No. We're managing all right this far without Morrissey, but like you, Yeoman, I can cope with the printers,' Sergeant James smiled. 'All straight, here, *and* the mugs, teapot, etcetera are washed. Also, the floor has been swept and mopped, so you should have an easy shift.'

'We call them watches, in the Navy,' he smiled back. 'And thanks for all the effort. As a matter of fact, it's Lizzie's birthday soon, and I want to do her a special card.'

'Like what?'

'There's a little robin comes for crumbs outside my window. A perky little thing. Thought I might draw him for her.'

Evie watched, fascinated, headset in her hands. So they *were* talking, those two? She wondered how far it would go – if anywhere. Somehow, Sergeant James didn't seem the sort to indulge in casual relationships and Lenice had said there were no personal photographs in her room at Priest's, because she'd had a sly peek.

'Which is your window, Yeoman?'

'You can't see it from here. Maybe, when the leaves are down, you'll be able to. Servants' quarters I think it once was. But your transport is waiting – I'll not keep you. Goodnight, ladies.'

And the sergeant and Evie smiled a goodnight

and ducked through the door quickly to avoid a stream of light piercing the darkness outside.

Evie did not have a chance to question her superior further, since the sergeant automatically took the seat beside the driver whilst other ranks were obliged to scramble into the back.

'Evening, Fowler,' then turning round in her seat Monica James said, 'You'll not be on your own, Lance-Corporal, with Morrissey on leave?'

'No. Tiptree will be in. It's past ten, and she didn't have a late pass. She doesn't often go out, except with Morrissey and me.'

'Of course. Getting married, isn't she?'

'Er – well, not on this leave, I'm almost sure. Her fiancé is in the Navy and the two of them are like Box and Cox, at the moment – never on leave at the same time. But they'll work it out.'

'Saturday, isn't it, that she goes on leave? She'll have to take me into barracks to pick up her train pass and ration card. I take it,' she turned to the driver, 'that Corporal Finigan will remember we'll need transport when Tiptree is on leave?'

'All taken care of, Sergeant. Yours truly will be glad to oblige. And here we are. All change for Southgate Lodge! G'night, Lance-Corporal,' Private Fowler called cheerfully over his shoulder, cheerfully because of an extra-loving letter from his intended. He lifted his hand as Evie banged on the side of the truck to let him know she was down, but in the darkness she did not see it.

Carefully she closed the gate, walking eight

steps forward before shoving out a toe to feel for the front door steps. You counted a lot, in the blackout.

'Hi!' she said, turning the key in the lock, pushing home the bolts.

Carrie, hair gripped up in pincurls, was sitting on her bed in pyjamas and dressing gown, addressing an envelope.

'Hi, Turner. Just finished. I made up your bed . . .'

'Bless you. The letter – to Jeffrey, was it?'

'Er – no. To Mother. Mind, I'm not posting it for a couple of days, to make sure it doesn't arrive too early. Don't want her getting in touch with Jeffrey, demanding he gets compassionate leave because I'm home.'

'You're a sly dog, Tiptree. And anyway, how can your mother get in touch with Jeffrey if he's at sea – except by letter, of course?'

'You don't know my mother, and Mrs Frobisher is almost as bad.'

Carrie tucked in the flap of the envelope, then propped it on the mantelpiece.

Evie grinned, unbuttoning her jacket, saying nothing, because Carrie was at it again, making sure that on her first leave, at least, there would be no wedding.

'Think I'll have a quick cold wash in the kitchen, then dive into bed. It was quite chilly, tonight. And I almost forgot! The Sergeant smiled at the Yeoman and he smiled back and told her he was making a birthday card with a robin on it for his little girl.'

'Ooooh. You don't think there's something between those two?' Carrie gasped.

'*Whaaaat*! Sergeant James? Hardly likely. If you were to ask me, I'd say that she just doesn't like men or she's had a bad experience. Take your pick. I'm fed up trying to understand her. Like I said before, she's really pretty when she lets her face relax.'

'Hm. No comment.' Carrie pulled back sheet and blankets and got into bed. 'As far as I'm concerned, she won't be happy till she has us all in a Nissen hut near the signals office. She isn't best pleased about us being in the lodges.'

'We'll worry about that, old love, when there's a Nissen hut for us to move into. Mind, there's an empty cottage up there, but there are soldiers billeted either side of it, so no chance we'd be allowed in it!'

'Let's hope not. Let's hope we stay here, even though it won't be long before it's winter, and there'll be snow and ice and –'

'Shut up, will you! That tap water is like ice already. Don't mention winter, for heaven's sake.' Evie slammed the kitchen door behind her and fished beneath the pillows for her pyjamas. 'And don't forget to bring a hot-water bottle back from leave, and some bedsocks. We're going to need them before so very much longer! And you haven't heard one word I said. You were miles away.'

'Sorry. Actually, I was thinking about home,

and my own bedroom. I really want to see mother and Jackmans again. Wish there wasn't all the bother about the wedding to spoil it.'

'But there doesn't have to be trouble, Carrie. And you'll pardon me for saying so, but don't you think you're being a bit mean not letting your mother know till the last minute that you'll be home for your twenty-first?'

'No. Not a bit! You've got to keep one step ahead of my mother, Evie. She can be ever so sweet, but she's made up her mind she wants me and Jeffrey married. It's all she can think about.'

'Listen, this is 1941, not the Middle Ages. Nobody can make you get married unless you want to. And maybe, when you and he finally get together and straighten things out, you'll maybe realise that you want to be.'

'Maybe.' Carrie pulled the blankets around her and curled into a ball. 'And put the light out, will you?'

'I will. And shall I tell you what my mother always says? She says that the things we worry about most, rarely happen so think about it, eh?'

'OK. Hope she's right. G'night, Evie.'

Things she was worrying about, Carrie thought as Evie closed her bedroom door. Worrying about marrying Jeffrey. Worrying about whether she really, really wanted to. Worrying about the fuss and bother there'd be if all at once she put her foot down and said she would get married when *she* wanted to and if they – and that included

Jeffrey and his mother – didn't stop going on and on about it, she would volunteer for service overseas, then that would be the last they would see of Caroline Tiptree for the duration!

She sucked in a deep breath and held it, letting it out slowly. Deep breathing was supposed to calm you, wasn't it? She took another gulp of air and wondered, briefly of course, just what would happen if Jeffrey met an attractive WREN and fell for her.

Oh, my goodness! More to the point, what would happen if Caroline Tiptree met someone else? It *could* happen. Take Nan and Chas, for instance. Love at first sight that had been, though they hadn't realised it at the time.

'Idiot, Caroline Tiptree!' she whispered into the pillow. Mind, it hadn't been love at first sight for she and Jeffrey. Rather more it happening without them knowing it. Creeping up on them, sort of. She supposed it was like that when two people had grown up together.

And she *would* marry Jeffrey in spite of his bossy ways, because being in the ATS had taught her to stand up for herself and answer back a bit, and he wasn't going to get things all his own way! And she really should wear her engagement ring. She would put it on tomorrow, grease or not!

It was her last conscious thought before she drifted into sleep.

ELEVEN

They sat at the kitchen table, talking, making more toast, more pots of tea as if reluctant to break up the happiness of the evening and go to bed. Only when the last ember flamed brightly, then flickered and died, did Stella Lawson say, 'I don't know about you two, but I'm for bed. Selfish of me to keep you up till all hours, talking.'

'Mother! We always talk and talk on my first night home. But I didn't get much sleep, last night. Reckon we should all hit the hay.'

'Flying?'

'Yes, but a piece of cake, for once. We were on a diversionary raid, actually, dropping window – y'know, strips of metallic paper – to upset their radar. But no more talk about flying for seven days. Shouldn't wonder if Nan and I don't take in a few dances.'

And Stella Lawson smiled across at the girl with whom her son was so obviously in love and sent up a happy little prayer of thanks, not wholly for her son's leave, nor the fact that now he could dance, but for the doe-eyed young girl who had made it possible.

'Night son – Nan.' She got to her feet. 'Don't be too long saying goodnight.'

It wasn't until the whispering outside Nan's bedroom door had ceased and her son had clumped up the attic stairs that Stella got quietly out of bed and tapped on the door of the small bedroom.

'Are you decent? Can I come in, Nan?'

'Of course you can! Was just unpacking. Wish I'd sent to Auntie Mim's for some civvies. Sorry, but you'll have to put up with my uniform.'

'Then if you wouldn't be offended there are some of mine you can wear. Some of them don't fit me any longer, but they are too good to throw away or send for jumble, especially now clothes are rationed. Tell you what – tomorrow morning we'll go through my wardrobe and see what we can find. Will that suit you, Nan?'

'Yes, *please* – if you're really sure you don't mind.'

'Not a bit. What size shoes do you take?

'Five.'

'Good – so do I. One problem solved. Only thing I don't have, is stockings and undies.'

'And mine are at Auntie Mim's, at Leeds. Trouble was, I joined up the week before clothes went on the ration, so I never got any clothing coupons. But I can wear my Army issue undies. Nobody'll see them, thank heaven.' She lifted her skirt to show her khaki knickers, with elasticated legs almost down to her knees. 'Passion killers, we call them. Me granny – if I had one – wouldn't be seen dead in them!'

'Mm. See what you mean. Look – can you keep a deadly secret, Nan, about blackmarket clothing coupons?'

'Why? You got some?'

'I've got twelve. My cleaning lady gave them to me – I didn't buy them. It was cold, last week, and raining, and she didn't have a decent coat to go home in. And the poor woman's husband has been called up and she has four children to keep on what the Army allows her.'

'So you gave her a coat, for the coupons. Don't see anything very wrong in that.'

'No. I gave her the coat but she *insisted* on giving me the coupons for it – brought them with her next time she came. She said Mum was the word, and any time I had anything I didn't want, she'd be grateful. But what I did was illegal.'

'Garn! The poor woman hasn't got a warm coat, but more clothing coupons than she can afford to spend. I'd call it more common sense, Mrs Lawson.'

'Would you? Then if you aren't worried about where they came from, I'll give you four, for two pairs of silk stockings.'

'You're sure?' Nan's cheeks pinked with delight. 'Then me and Chas can hitch into Shrewsbury tomorrow, to the shops.'

'Good. And I'm so glad you're not being stuffy about borrowing my clothes. Only thing is, when you and Charles go dancing, you'll have to watch it if the floor is slippery, Nan. Imagine falling over, legs in the air!'

'Horrible. The sight of 'hem bloomers would frighten the 'orses and put Chas off me for life!'

They collapsed on the bed in peals of laughter and Charles, on the edge of sleep, heard them and was glad that the two most precious women in his life already seemed to like each other.

Carrie awoke with a cry, then sighed with relief that it had only been a dream – and that it was over.

She had been in her bedroom at Jackmans Cottage, trying on a wedding dress, with her mother fumbling to fasten the tiny sleeve buttons. The dress was of white lace, but not new – not even clean. There had been a stain on the bodice which her mother said she could pin a brooch over, to hide. And the hem looked as if it had trailed through a puddle, yet her mother and Mrs Frobisher had clasped their hands in delight and told her how very beautiful she looked.

'I'll pop into the garden and pick a few flowers and tie them with ribbon for a bouquet,' Mrs Frobisher said.

Jeffrey's mother looked awful, her hair in Dinkie curlers and wearing a dress a size too small.

'Oh, hurry do!' Her mother was agitated.

'Jeffrey's bus gets in at two and the wedding is at half-past! And you'll have to remember to carry your flowers so that you don't show, Carrie. Hold your stomach in as much as you can!'

She was pregnant and being hastily married in a borrowed wedding dress and shoes that pinched. She hadn't known how the baby had got there, but it must have been Jeffrey's, or he wouldn't be marrying her! And she didn't want the baby! She wanted to be back at Southgate with Nan and Evie. She wanted the two o'clock bus never to arrive at the village stop so she could run away: run till she collapsed, exhausted, and Sergeant James found her, then told her she would be late for her wedding if she didn't get a move on!

'No!' she had cried. 'I won't! Please don't make me, Sergeant?'

That was when she awakened in the familiar room, and reached for the torch on her bedside locker, shining it on the alarm clock.

Half-past two, the most ungodly of hours, but it didn't matter. She didn't have to wear the awful white dress and she wasn't having a baby!

She plumped up her pillow and snuggled into the blankets again, willing sleep to come, wishing she had a hotwater bottle to hug, or a mug of cocoa to sip for comfort.

But she had neither, and Nan's bed lay empty beside her own. She wondered where Nan was, and where she was sleeping. Dear Nan. So happy.

'Oh, dammit!' There would be no more sleep

and she would lie awake until the alarm jangled at twenty-past five, when she could get up and dress and step back into normality again, forgetting the bad dream. And she would walk in the silent half light, watching as dim shapes became things familiar to her – the lane she would walk up to the stable block, and Priest's Lodge to which she would drive to pick up Sergeant James and Lenice and Ailsa, fresh back from leave.

She ran her hands across her flat stomach and wanted to laugh out loud at the stupidity of the dream, but her eyes pricked with unshed tears and she stretched her legs so her feet touched the cold bit at the bottom of her bed, which made her even more miserable.

So think of Saturday; that she was going home to Jackmans Cottage in six more days, and that soon she would be twenty-one and able to vote and do anything she wanted without her mother's permission. After Thursday she would be in charge of her life.

But she would still marry Jeffrey, and because she would be wearing her uniform she would not be able to carry a bouquet, nor even wear a single flower, pinned to her jacket lapel. And when the time came, she would *not* be pregnant!

She threw back the bedclothes, and shivering in the cold, wriggled her feet into her slippers, drawing back the blackout curtains at the window.

Everything was quiet and still. Here, at Heronflete, there was no war. Only a half-moon dimly lighting the outline of trees and the roofs of distant buildings.

A fox slid out of the hedgeback beside the lodge. It walked on silent pads, its brush trailing the grass. After a pheasant roosting too low, was it? She watched until it disappeared into the darkness at the bottom of the drive, walking with unconcern where those who lived in Southgate Lodge were forbidden to go.

She closed the curtains, feeling her way to her bed to lie there, thinking and brooding until she slammed the flat of her hand on the alarm clock and made her way as quietly as she could to the kitchen for a wash.

She felt miserable. Even thoughts of her leave failed to cheer her, though she would be excited enough, she supposed, when Norman drove her to the station.

She snapped on the light then walked, naked, to the chipped brown sink stone and the single brass tap turned green for lack of polishing, wishing herself into the signals office and the stale, fuggy air – the *warm*, stale fuggy air – and the cup of hot tea that would await her there

She winced as the cold water hit her hands, then made her soap into a lather, washing hurriedly, telling herself to think about Saturday and her own bed beneath the eaves at Jackmans and the little low window that touched the floor, almost.

She let go a sigh of relief then hurried to dress,

glad for the first time of the unglamorous vest and thick khaki knickers. This morning was the coldest ever, the air scented with autumn. She shrugged into her great coat, turning up the collar. Then she turned off the light, closing the front door quietly behind her, standing on the step, blinking until her eyes adjusted to the half dark. Then she walked carefully to the stable block, glad that to her left the sky was streaked with yellow and that another day was about to begin.

She dug her hands deep into her pockets and thought about hot tea, a leave pass and a return ticket to York – and that tomorrow she would post the letter that stood on the mantelpiece at Southgate a day earlier than she had intended. It was, she supposed, a gesture of gratitude; a thank you that it had only been a dream. And she wouldn't tell Evie about it, because Evie had listened to her moans for long enough! In little more than a week, Caroline Tiptree would be of age – *legally*. She wondered, as she shone her torch on the pick-up truck, if her mother would realise that, though she very much doubted it.

She pushed home the starting handle and swung it viciously, then allowed herself a small smile. She was getting good at starting the engine at the first try. She was getting good, she supposed as she climbed into the cab, at quite a lot of things.

She shrugged, driving carefully out of the yard in the glimmer of the blacked-out headlights, then allowed herself another small smile at the accepted adage that you could always tell a driver in the Armed Forces because their eyes stood out like organ stops.

She coasted down the slight incline – taking your foot off the accelerator saved petrol, Freddy said – then turned left and up towards Priest's Lodge, knowing that the minute she parped the horn the front door would open and Sergeant James and Lenice and Ailsa would walk down the path, shoulders hunched against the early morning chill. Only Evie and Nan were still snuggled in bed; Evie because she was on late shift and Nan because nobody in her right mind would get up at this unearthly hour if she were on leave.

Had they arrived safely, Carrie wondered, and were Nan and Chas's mother hitting it off? But of course they would be. Everyone loved Nan of the wide eyes and the bluntness delivered in a thick Scouse accent. Carrie wondered how far things had gone between then, for there was no doubt at all they were deeply in love. Had they gone the whole way? She hoped not because Nan was so very young – not yet eighteen – and if anything tragic happened, her young life would be shattered. Chas was Nan's first love and as far as Nan was concerned, Carrie frowned, he would be her only love. Nan was like that.

Carrie lowered the window, reached for the horn and pressed it twice. It was then she saw the morning star, large and bright and low in the sky, so she fixed it with a stare and whispered,

'I wish for Nan and Chas to have a wonderful leave and for everything to turn out right for them.'

The front door of Priest's Lodge banged shut and three figures emerged.

'Morning, each,' Carrie said with mock cheerfulness, but they said never a word, because this was an inhuman hour to have to turn out for shift and they were still only half awake. So what better to do but think of Nan, and what she was doing this very minute, and hope she was still asleep and not awake and thinking of Heronflete.

Nan Morrissey was not asleep, nor was she thinking about Heronflete. Instead, she lay, familiarising herself with the softness of the strange bed and the warm cosiness of the pink blankets. She had never before seen pink blankets nor walked, barefoot on a carpet that covered the floor from side to side and end to end. Chas's mum was fond of her thick carpets, Nan mused. All over the house she had them, except in the kitchen.

She reached to switch on the bedside light, amazed to find it was half-past seven. Then she smiled smugly, pulled the plankets up to her chin and thought about Chas, hoping he was still asleep and not thinking about RAF Modeley, nor Wellington bombers and calls to briefing.

They would, Nan thought dreamily, have a wonderful seven days and go to as many dances as they could. Chas would be a good dancer one day. Chas was good at a lot of things. Until Chas, no had had kissed her, she thought, yet now it was bliss to close her eyes and part her lips and offer them eagerly. And Chas, now that he no longer stammered nor blushed bright red, was just about every girl's dream man and the most marvellous thing about it was that he belonged to Nan Morrissey.

We-e-ll, not *belonged*, exactly; not in *that* way, but, soon. She wanted them to, especially when they stood close and Chas's lips were hard on hers and her head was swimming in a don't give-a-damn kind of way. That was when she wanted to whisper, 'Love me, Chas?' but had the wit not to, because one of them had to watch it. Stood to sense, didn't it, though what would happen when neither of them watched it she wasn't quite sure, because no one had ever made love to her, before. And Chas, she was almost certain, had not made love to anyone, either.

It would, she thought tenderly, be a bit of a fumble the first time with neither of them knowing what to do yet longing to do it, for all that. Doing *that*, she was well aware, could be the making of a baby and what people who had never been in love called getting herself into trouble. Yet trouble was the last thing she thought about, Nan was bound to admit, when her head began to swim and her senses told her that nothing mattered, except belonging.

She wished she could talk about it to someone. She had thought, once, that Evie who would understand her feelings would be the best one to open up her heart to, yet she knew instinctively that Evie would tell her to talk to Chas about it, and that Chas would have to be the one to be careful. There were ways and means, Evie would say, and the sooner the pair of them had a good old talk about it, the better.

Yet how could you, when you were both stone cold sober, talk about something that was almost magic, without dirtying it? How could she say, 'Now see here, Chas, it's as plain as the nose on your face that one night you and me are going to go the whole hog, and it'll be up to you to see that nothing happens.' How could she when she wasn't quite sure that Chas wanted to as much she did? How could she say such a thing when it might make him think she was a little tart? Because it was the man who should make all the running. Someone had once said that it was a man's right to ask and a girl's to say no – and that would be the end of it.

But Chas hadn't asked. Perhaps it would be for the best, Nan brooded, if he never asked because if he did she would say, 'Yes. Oh, yes, my darling . . .'

There was a knock on the door and she sat bolt upright, fantasies gone.

'Come in,' she called.

'Been awake long?' Chas stood in the doorway, tray in hand. 'Fancy a mug of tea?'

'Yes, please. And I've been awake ages.'

Chas wore a long woolly dressing gown, tied at the waist with a silk cord. His face was still heavy with sleep and his hair looked as if he had combed it hastily with his fingers, which made her love him all the more.

'This one is yours. One sugar.' He placed a gold-rimmed china beaker beside her, then sat down at the end of the bed.

'Best leave the door open,' Nan said softly. 'Don't want your mother to waken and think we're up to naughties!'

'She's already awake. I've just taken her tea. And d'you know something, Private Morrissey. I'd no idea your hair was so long. I've only seen it rolled up at the top of your head till now.'

'Ar, well, I didn't want to have it chopped off, so I've got to put it up. King's Regulations, see. Your hair mustn't touch your collar.'

'Then will you wear it long this leave? It's so beautiful and wavy.'

'If your mother lends me some civvy clothes, I will. And she said, last night, that she would.'

'Then I shall wear my most comfortable old trousers and my scruffed brogues and a sloppy sweater and we'll pretend there isn't a war on and that there won't ever be one. Just for seven days, shall we Nan?'

'We will. But let's drink our tea, 'cause you're looking at me kind of funny. Is it me army-issue pyjamas?'

'No, darling.' He had already noticed that the

jacket of her blue-and-white striped top was only half-buttoned, and had dragged his eyes from the peep of small, rounded breasts. 'I think they suit you.'

'What! These things! Mind, I suppose I'll be glad of them, once winter comes. You wouldn't have a pair of old socks in your drawer, I suppose, that you don't want? Civvy socks, I mean.'

'I might have, but why?'

''Cause we're goin' to need bedsocks to sleep in before so very much longer, and I'd like it if I had a pair of yours.'

'Idiot. Of course you can have some. I've got some new ones, actually. Blue Paisley patterned, would you believe? My godmother gave me them two Christmases ago and I've never worn them. A bit sissy, I thought.'

'Well, I'd like to have a pair you've actually worn, if that's all right with you, Chas. More romantic, sort of.'

'Then you shall have the Paisleys plus an old pair, and when I'm up there, freezing cold over Germany, it'll warm me to think of you in your striped pyjamas, with your hair all over the pillow and wearing my old socks. And darling Nan, I do so love you.'

'And I love you, Chas.' Hastily she reached for her mug, then pulled the blankets up to her chin. 'I think that right now I love you too much, so I reckon we'd better drink our tea, and behave ourselves.'

And he smiled that lovely smile that Nan thought was to die for and said,

'You win, Nan Morrissey – *this* time. But please make sure tomorrow morning when I bring in your tea, that your hair is screwed up into a severe roll and your pyjama jacket is buttoned, right to the top.'

'Oh, my Gawd,' Nan whispered, feeling the colour rush to her cheeks. Then, knowing that the wild moment had passed, she laughed and said that tomorrow morning, if he knew what was good for him, he'd leave the tea at the door.

And he smiled teasingly into her eyes then whispered, 'No way, my darling – unless you bolt it, that is.'

They laughed, then, a little too loudly, but any kind of laughter relieved the tension that both of them knew would never be far away.

Nan raised her eyes to his, then with studied calm said,

'Is it very cold in a Wellington?'

'It is. That's why we wear fur-lined boots and jackets, and if you don't mind we're civilians for a week, so no more war talk – OK?'

'All right, Mr Lawson. But is it all right for civilians to say "I love you?" All the time? Is it?'

'All the time, Miss Morrissey – and I love you, too.'

Love, he thought. What a sick little word to describe the way he felt about her; felt since the first words she had spoken to him.

'Is this your billet,' she had said, and he'd made a mess of it and blushed and stammered like a prune and he'd wanted there to be a big hole beside him he could creep into. Then she said the magic words. 'I think you'd better ask me up to dance when the music starts, 'cause if you don't, somebody else is going to ask me, and I want to talk to *you* . . .'

Even then, she had chosen him, he marvelled and they had done a bumps-a-daisy, which was the silliest, most wonderful dance in the whole world. He shook his head, because Nan was talking to him.

'Penny for them, Chas. You was miles away and your eyes real dreamy.'

'Worth more than a penny, Nan, but you can have them for nothing. I was thinking, actually, of the night we met and what you said, and the very first dance we had. That was when I fell in love with you. Did you know?'

'Not at the time I didn't, but I got the message very soon afterwards. It was the night, I think, that you turned up in that old Boadicea. I got a telling-off from the sergeant, over the noise. But Chas, will you take my mug and go, please, because I'm thinking things I shouldn't – not in your mother's house, anyway.'

'Could it be,' he took the cup and twined his fingers in hers, so she couldn't take her hand away. 'that you really do love me as much as I love you, and want you? I mean *really* want.' Then his face crimsoned and he released her fingers and whispered, 'I shouldn't have said that, should I?'

'Yes you should, Chas, because it brings things out in the open, sort of.' She dropped her eyes to the pink blanket and he saw the fan of her eyelashes on her cheeks, heard the quickness of her breathing. 'I mean – well, I reckon we've got to talk about it, pretty soon.'

'Talk about *that,* you mean, and how I'm crazy for you and if ever it happened, it would be the first time for me?'

'Mmm. Sumthin' like that. We got lectures when I joined up; supposed to be about hygiene, but parts were how easy it was to get babies, and to watch it. And Chas, it would be the first time for me, too, so I've already got around to thinking that we'd probably make a right old mess of it – first time, I mean. Does that make me sound common?'

'No, it doesn't.' He placed the mugs on the floor beside the door then took her face in his hands. 'It makes you sound exactly like Nan Morrissey who is very straight and says what she means, and it's only one of the things I love about you.'

'Don't kiss me, Chas,' she whispered urgently. 'Because if you do I think we'd both be sorry. But you and me are goin' to have to talk about it, 'cause I believe it's up to the man . . .'

'Yes, it is. We got the same old bumf when I joined up. Strictly under personal hygiene, of course, but what it meant was how not to land a girl in the club.'

'The puddin' club. I've heard about that, too. They kick you out of the ATS pretty quick, if that happens.'

'So darling, if – *when* – we both feel the same and the time is right, shall we agree that for once, neither of us is going to count to ten?'

'Agreed,' she whispered, lifting her eyes to his.

'And you'll trust me, Nan?'

'I'll trust you. Sergeant Lawson, 'cause even though we're only a couple of kids, we're old enough to be in uniform and I reckon that entitles us to be treated like grown-ups – if you see what I mean. When the counting stops, that is.'

'When . . .' He laid his cheek on hers, and closed his eyes, praying desperately.

God in heaven, let me get through this war, even though I thought I knew what I was doing when I volunteered for flying. It was all gung-ho, then, and the glamour of being aircrew. But I hadn't met Nan, then, and I love her so much and want her – even if it's only the once . . .

Then he shook the morbid thoughts from his mind and got quickly back to his feet, squaring his shoulders as if he were a rookie on the parade ground.

'I can hear mother, in the kitchen. You're allowed to come down to breakfast in your dressing gown – when on leave, that is,' he smiled.

'Good. So off with you, lad, so I can make

myself decent.' She was still aware of her unbuttoned pyjama jacket.

She threw back the blankets and got to her feet and the thick rug was bliss to sink her toes into. She wished they had a rug or two at Southgate Lodge. Then she walked to the dressing table and watched in the mirror as she fastened the top two buttons. She did it without embarrassment, because now she was a grown-up and had come to an important decision; the most important decision a girl could make. She tossed back her head and brushed her hair behind her ears, tying it with a red ribbon. Then she shrugged into her dressing gown and tied it tightly at the waist.

Important decision? So had her mother once made a decision, and had it landed her in trouble?

Yet Chas wasn't, couldn't be, like the man who had got her mother pregnant then bought his way out of his mistake with a hundred pounds and a load of furniture. Chas wouldn't do such a thing. Chas was lovely and her first love; her last love, too. But what if something, just once, went wrong and what if Chas didn't get back one night to RAF Modeley? What would happen to her when the ATS kicked her out? Cyprian Court would it be, or Auntie Mim's? Neither, she thought fiercely. She would rather go to a home for delinquent girls where they would expect her to give up the baby for adoption, give up Chas's baby and that would be the end of it, because she wouldn't be given a choice.

'Idiot, Nan Morrissey!' She took in a deep breath, then let it go in little calming puffs, because 'Trust me?' Chas had said, so that was the way it would be, and anyway, who said it was going to happen today, tomorrow, this week, even? When the time was right it would be, and they would know, both of them, and everything would come right for them.

'Shift yourself, Nan!' Chas called up the stairs, so she smiled at the girl in the mirror who was a bit of a drip, anyway, and called 'Coming!', then ran downstairs to the kitchen and the smell of porridge and toast. And to Chas, who would one day be her lover, and who would never let her down.

TWELVE

'What I would like to know is –' Evie took off her cap and gloves, then unbuttoned her greatcoat and hung it behind the front door, 'just *what* is going on in the signals office.'

'Like what?' Carrie prompted, all at once interested.

'Like the Yeoman and the Sergeant are in cahoots, that's what. And you know me, Tiptree, I don't gossip but I could be forgiven for thinking that something isn't quite right. They were standing outside the door, heads together whispering. And I listened, but could hardly make out a word. All I heard was, "If you're sure it will be all right, Yeoman, then no one will say anything. I don't want any trouble, I mean."

'And the Yeoman said, "Leave it to the Royal Navy, Sergeant," so what do you make of that? Norman was driving and he left the engine running, so I'm as sure as I can be that he heard nothing at all. You must ask him about it tomorrow morning, Carrie, just to be sure.'

'You mean they've started going out?' Carrie gasped. 'I don't believe it.'

'And why not? I think the Yeoman is quite good looking. He's very like Bob – an older version, of course. And I've said before that when she lets herself smile, the sergeant looks quite human.'

'Well, I still don't believe it, Evie. More like the sergeant has got her own way, at best and is putting the lot of us in one of the empty cottages at the back of the NAAFI.'

'So why should what the Army does be of any interest to the Royal Navy? Our orders come from Lincoln Barracks.'

'Either that,' Carrie ignored Evie's reasoning 'or she's got her own way about the Nissen hut, with the coke-burning stove. Before the cold weather really sets in, I mean.'

'No. I'm right, I know I am,' Evie insisted, 'or why must no one say a word about it? Anyway, if they *are* dating, I'll be the first one to know, because she'll ask me to do her late shift tomorrow night as she has business in Lincoln, or something.'

'And then you think she'll ask Freddy for the use of the pick-up when I've delivered the 6 p.m. shift?' Carrie grinned. 'No. It's got to be something altogether different, I'm sure of it.'

'You've sent the letter to your mother,' Evie conceded defeat, 'and you said you weren't going to send it until tomorrow.'

'We-e-ll, I had a letter to post to Jeffrey, and I fancied a cup of tea, so I thought I might as well. And anyway, she won't get it for a couple of days – Wednesday at the earliest.'

'Well, I don't think you are being fair. Had you thought that your mother just might have posted your birthday cake to you and you won't be here to eat it!

'*What!* My mother waste her precious stash of dried fruit and sugar on a birthday cake? *That* little hoard is for the wedding cake, Lance-Corporal. In fact, it'll be the last reading of the banns the Sunday I'm home, and the minute it's all cut and dried, she'll make that cake, I shouldn't wonder, and put it in a tin with a cooking apple to keep it moist. I'd take bets on it!'

'So is it gradually dawning on you, Carrie, that by Christmas you just might be married? Are you accepting it, I mean?'

'Accepting? It was a fact that when Jeffrey gave me a ring we'd be getting married some day. And we *will* be, only it'll be when *I* want it.'

'You're as sly as a box of monkeys,' Evie grinned.

'Granted. But with a mother like mine, you have to be. I've always had to be a little under-handed, only now I don't feel so guilty about it as I used to. And in ten days I shall be twenty-one, though it won't make a scrap of difference to mother. She'll still order me about, but at least I'll get to find out about my inheritance.'

'You're an heiress, then? You never said,' Evie gasped.

'Yes, but not a filthy rich one. I know my godmother left me a hundred pounds, but what my father left me I've still to find out. It won't be a lot, but it'll help towards a little house, when we're married. If there are any little houses on the market. There have been so many knocked down, in the bombing.'

'Mm. My way of thinking, too. Bob and I hope to buy our first home – get a mortgage, y'know – but if houses are in short supply when the war is over, they're going to be a lot more expensive. But if you and Jeffrey get married soon, where will you spend your leaves?'

'At Jackmans Cottage, I suppose. I don't want to spend them at his place. Mrs Frobisher is a bit bossy and she's like my mother, a widow with an only child. I can't see us living in Nether Hutton, either. Houses hardly ever come up for sale, there.

'But we're talking about years ahead, because heaven only knows when it's all going to end. I mean here we are, clinging on by our fingernails, and Hitler rampaging all over Europe and Russia. Someone said that the Brits only ever win one battle, and that's the final one. Let's hope it turns out like that.'

'Now see here, Carrie Tiptree, that kind of talk isn't allowed in this billet – right? And for my own part, I won't even *think* that Bob and I are going to be apart for years and years. I couldn't bear it, so I tell myself that something awful will happen to Hitler,' Evie said hotly. 'I've wished it so often I've convinced myself that it will.

'After all, he isn't getting things all his own way in Russia. He thought it was going to be a quick run through to Moscow, but the snows are going to start there, soon, and the bitterly cold winter. I'm as sure as I can be that he won't invade us, now – or if he tries it, we'll be more ready for him than we were, after Dunkirk.'

'I'm sorry. I should think about other people before I open my big mouth. I should have remembered that Bob is overseas. Didn't mean to upset you, Evie.'

'You didn't. Not really. When Bob got an overseas posting we both knew it could be as much as two years till we saw each other again. I tell myself that all the time, then if he gets home sooner it's a bonus. Only don't talk about the war going on and on? Don't remind me?'

'Said I was sorry. I suppose I'm lucky that Jeffrey got a draft to a ship in the Home Fleet.'

'*Suppose*, Carrie? Aren't you sure, then? Come to think of it, there are a lot of things you aren't sure about – regarding Jeffrey, I mean.' Evie draped her skirt, and jacket on a hanger, then began to unbutton her shirt. 'And what wouldn't I give for a hot-water bottle to wrap my pyjamas round? It's really cold, tonight.'

'And we're only in the second week of October. What's it going to be like in December and

January?' Carrie was glad to steer the talk away from Jeffrey and Bob – Jeffrey, especially. 'Like we said, we'll have to bring hotwater bottles back with us when we go on leave and fill them at the kettle in the signals office. Lenice is already doing that, then wraps it in her scarf to keep it from getting cold. That's going to be one of the good things about being on late shift; a hottie to cuddle, at night.'

'I'd rather cuddle Bob,' Evie sighed, 'but we're going to have to stop up cracks and things. There's a terrible draught under the front door. We ought to have a look in the shed – see if there's a sack, or something. And we're going to have to stuff the gap in the window.'

'Y'know, it doesn't seem five minutes since we came here. Remember, it didn't rain for ages and the sun was so warm.'

'Happy days,' Carrie. I'm only going to clean my teeth tonight and rub the flannel over my face. Then I'm going to snuggle in bed and think about Bob. That should warm me up a bit.' Evie looked at Nan's empty bed, piled with three biscuit mattresses and folded blankets and sheets. 'Y'know, I miss Nan. Wonder what she's doing now?'

'Either she'll be dancing with Chas, or sitting in front of a blazing fire, toasting her toes, drat her.'

'Or maybe she's in bed already, cuddling a hotwater bottle. Mind, it's just a thought, but we could try the shops in Lincoln. They just might have them to sell.'

'You've got to be joking, Evie! You can't get anything in the shops, now. No vacuum flasks, no cosmetics, no scented soap. Even razor blades are going under the counter. But we could try, I suppose. You won't be on late shift, on Saturday.'

'No. But you'll be on leave or had you forgotten?'

And Carrie blushed and said she had – just briefly, of course. Then she got into bed, curling herself into a ball so her feet should not touch the cold bit at the bottom. And she thought about the woolly knitted hat she always wore at home when it was very cold outside, and the fluffy pink socks she wore in bed in winter and wondered if the Auxiliary Territorial Service allowed its lady soldiers to go to bed in pink socks and a woolly knitted hat.

'Night-night,' she called to Evie in the kitchen. 'Put the lights out, there's a love.'

Then she snuggled deeply into the blankets and thought about Nan, who, whatever she was doing, was almost certainly warm as toast and not shivering in a cold bed in a gate lodge in the wilds of Lincolnshire.

Nan Morrissey was not warm as toast. Hand in hand she and Chas ran, heads down against the driving rain, along the lane that led to Gardener's Cottage.

'I'm soaked to the skin,' she wailed.

'Never mind, darling. We're home, now. Who'd have thought it would come on to rain so heavily?'

And who would have thought, Nan pondered, shaking with cold, that they would have to walk for almost an hour in it before an Army driver heeded their jutting thumbs and stopped to give them a lift.

'Oh, come in, do!' Stella Lawson called from the sitting room as they hurried into the house. 'You're soaked! Go into the kitchen and get those clothes off!'

Nan made for the dying fire and the last glimmer of warmth it gave out, kicking off her shoes, unbuttoning her greatcoat,

'Well, I'm only glad I didn't go out in them dancing shoes, you gave me, Mrs Lawson, and that lovely dress!' she gasped, teeth chattering.

'And I'm glad,' Chas grinned, 'that it was a Forces, only dance tonight, and we had to go in our uniforms. They're going to take a week to dry out.'

'And *I* am glad,' Stella smiled, 'that you've *got* a week to spare. Now pop upstairs, Charles, and get into your pyjamas and dressing gown; you, too, Nan. Put your clothes on hangers and there are warm towels in the airing cupboard to dry your hair with. Want some Ovaltine? I got an extra pint today, from the milkman.'

And Nan said there was nothing on earth she would like more than a mug of Ovaltine, in front of the sitting-room fire – wearing her warm slippers, that was, and her dressing gown and thick Army-issue pyjamas. And with her dripping hair wrapped in a warm towel, sitting shoulder to shoulder with Chas, how much better could life get?

She thought about it that night, snuggled beneath the pink blankets, a hot bottle at her feet and one in her arms, to hug. Such a time they'd had, dancing every dance. It had been a cold clear night when they set out, bright with starlight, and she allowed herself to imagine herself close to Chas, after the dance, his greatcoat wrapped around her. And lovely, lovely kisses and whispering and touchings until she got the swimmy feeling in her head again.

She was so in love; couldn't believe that something so unbelievable could happen to Nan Morrissey from Cyprian Court, and how marvellous it would be if the Queer One could have a bird's-eye view of Private Nancy Morrissey, snuggled in blankets and sheets that smelled of lavender, and being made a fuss of by Chas's mother, who was very beautiful and who spoke real ladylike.

Then she squeezed her eyes tightly shut and disarmed all thoughts of Ida Morrissey and Georgie from her mind. She was done with Cyprian Court for ever; she belonged to Chas, now. We-e-ll, not belonged *exactly*, but she soon would.

*　*　*

Carrie drove carefully to Priest's Lodge, reminding herself not to sound the horn because Lenice and Ailsa would still be sleeping. It was hard luck on the sergeant, Carrie frowned, though she didn't have to work such long days. After all, Evie had rank up and well able to take charge of a shift. Why couldn't Sergeant James delegate a bit more? Made sense, didn't it, when there wasn't a heavy workload in the signals office. Not once had Nan or Evie said they were rushed off their feet. Mind, it would be interesting, this morning when the shift changed, Carrie thought, with Evie keeping an eye on *things*, just in case.

'Morning, Sergeant,' Carrie called, making sure not to sound too cheerful; not at five minutes to six on a morning not yet light.

Unspeaking, Sergeant James took her place in the passenger seat of the truck, placing her respirator and a rolled-up kitbag at her feet.

So, what was she doing with a kitbag, Carrie frowned. Kitbags were for putting things in, so what was Sergeant James going to stuff in hers?

Slowly, because it was still dark, she reversed the truck, mindful of the drainage ditch at the side of the lane. Then she swung the wheel over and coasted downhill to Southgate Lodge where Evie would be waiting, ready to leave herself into the back, then thump on the cab twice – the signal to drive on. Then she wondered how she could tell Evie about the kitbag without the sergeant hearing and decided to wait until she had parked the truck at the stableyard and returned to the signals office where she usually made tea, sometimes for four, sometimes for five if the Yeoman hadn't disappeared behind the green baize door and clicked the lock behind him.

The Yeoman and the sergeant. So what – if anything – was going on between them and why should the sergeant bring a kitbag with her? And wasn't she a fool, Carrie sighed as she came to a stop outside Southgate Lodge, listening for the crunch of Evie's footsteps on the gravel, waiting for the familiar signal. Because what, she pondered, could be going on romantically between the Yeoman who had not long been widowed and the po-faced sergeant who rarely smiled and whose only ambition in life seemed to be to get the girls in her charge out of the two little gate lodges and into a Nissen hut as near to the signals office as made no matter. But they would soon know, Carrie thought as she heard the two thumps, what it was that no one would say anything about.

Carefully, so the truck did not skid on the gravel, she let out the clutch then turned right and on towards the signals office – and the mystery that would soon be explained. A pity, she thought, that the kitbag had complicated matters.

Charles Lawson lay awake in his room in the roof of the cottage, thinking about the previous evening. The dance had been great, but then it was always great to dance so closely to Nan and, when the time for the last dance came, to lay his cheek on hers, their feet moving slowly in waltz time. He had looked forward to the long walk home to Gardener's Cottage, arms tightly linked and stopping, often, to kiss in the darkness.

But there had been no kisses. Only a frantic dash in the sudden downpour of rain. Wet to the skin they had been and there was nothing like rain dripping cold down the back of your collar to put paid to all thoughts of romance.

He wanted Nan so, and even though they had spoken frankly about their need to belong, he knew that if the time ever came, he would not take her. Not because he was afraid of messing things up, but because he loved her too much. Would it be fair to take what she gladly offered as though it was his right? Mind, there was often talk in the mess about such things; about girls some of the fellows had seduced, and thought nothing of it. A notch on the bedpost. Two a penny, those who fell for the glamour of silver wings and protestations of love. Or was it lust, or the fear of going for a Burton before they had sampled what life was all about?

Charles swung his feet out of bed, searching beneath it for his slippers, telling himself he was a fool for not turning over and going to sleep again. That long lie in bed was one of the things you looked forward to when on leave, yet here he was at six in the morning, wide awake and his thoughts in turmoil.

Slowly, carefully, he walked downstairs to the kitchen to find his mother already there, standing beside the stove.

'Hello, son.' She offered her cheek for his kiss. 'Couldn't sleep?'

'Kind of. Couldn't you?'

'Oh, no. Six o'clock is normally my time, nowadays. I like to do a bit around the house before I go to the manor. Got into the habit, I suppose.' She stirred the tea in the pot and without raising her eyes, said, 'Something bothering you, or haven't you recovered from your soaking?'

'Yes to both, I suppose, though the rain annoyed me, last night. Damped my ardour, sort of.'

'Spoiled things a bit?'

'Reckon so. Will there be a mug of tea, and are you available for confessions, mother?'

'Something you can't work out, then?' She offered a mug. 'Put your own milk in . . .'

'Work out? Not exactly.' He dropped a saccharin tablet into the tea then watched it rise fizzing to the top. 'I mean I've worked it all out, have talked about it with Nan. I want us to be – well – closer, I suppose.'

'And Nan?'

'She wants to, as well. We love each other so much, you see. But it isn't on, is it?'

'What do you want me to say, son?' She raised her eyes to his. 'Shall I perhaps tell you that your father and I were lovers before we were married. But there wasn't a war, then. The fighting in the

290

trenches had finished. We felt safe, sort of.'

'You would. Dad was around to marry you, wasn't he? But what if Nan got pregnant and I went missing? What would she do, then?'

'Charles! Nothing will happen to you! You'll come through this war just as your father came through the last one! Never say such a thing again!'

'OK if it upsets you, I won't. But the chances of flyers doing thirty ops are very slim. A lot of aircrew accept they'll go for a Burton, sooner or later. I'm one of the lucky ones. I've just done my thirteenth.'

'Good! And you'll do another thirteen and then some. You've got Nan to come back to, now – and me. Y'see, there are things I'm sure of, deep inside me, and I *know* you'll be all right. I remember the afternoon you came back from Shrewsbury and told me you'd volunteered for flying duties. I didn't know whether to box your ears for your foolishness, or weep with pride.

'But I didn't sleep, that night. You were hardly nineteen and I didn't want to lose you. So I sent my thoughts to your father and he told me not to worry, that you'd be all right. And then he said something that made me smile. "It'll take more than falling out of an apple tree to get that boy of ours." And I believe him, son, so what is *really* bothering you?'

'Getting married, I suppose. I'm not twenty-one, yet, so would you let me – if Nan said yes, I mean?'

'You know I would. You're man enough to go to war, so you're man enough to get married – and with my blessing, too. But what about Nan? Is she old enough to know her own mind, at not quite eighteen? And would her aunt give her permission?'

She rose from the table, scraping the chair legs on the kitchen floor, lighting the gas under the kettle, closing her eyes tightly against tears. And her son sensed her distress and gathered her in his arms, holding her close.

'Mother, mine – I love you. You know that, don't you? And if you say I'll come through this war all right, then that's what I'll do. But I don't want to take advantage of Nan, and I don't know whether her Auntie Mim would let her marry me. Nan has told her about me, but not about how serious things are between us. It's all a bit of a mess, actually. It's just, I suppose, that I don't want to treat Nan like a tart. I love her too much. I'd feel better about everything if we were married, though.'

'Your father didn't treat *me* like a tart, either. We loved each other so nothing else seemed to matter. It was a terrible thing for us to do, in those days. I'd have been whipped out of town for a slut, if I'd got into trouble. That's what they called it then. The girl always got the blame.'

'They still do! Things haven't changed a lot, even now. Unmarried mothers are still given a hard time, and the child, too. I couldn't risk anything like that happening to Nan.'

'Then ask her to marry you and try to behave yourselves till after the wedding. I'm sure Nan's Auntie Mim will give her permission. And a special licence would only take a few days. I'm on your side, Charles. I'll do all I can to help. I just want you both to be happy, and be damned to this war!'

'Do you know something, mother?' He held her at arms' length, then kissed the tip of her nose. 'You're one wonderful lady, and I'm very lucky to have you. Thanks for not telling me to pull myself together and to go and have a cold bath. And thanks for – well – everything.'

'Oh, away with your nonsense. Pop upstairs and see if Nan is awake. I'll make a fresh pot, if she is.'

And they smiled easily at each other, because of the affection between them, and when he had left the kitchen Stella walked into the hall and took the silver-framed photograph in her hands, gazing at the very young soldier from another war, recalling the cold November day when finally it was all over and she knew he would come safely back to her.

'You'll know what we were talking about, darling? Our boy is so in love – just as we were. I want him safely home, no matter how long this war takes, so take care of him for me? Please?'

'It'll be all right for me to have a cup of tea, Sergeant,' Carrie asked as she stopped to deliver the early shift.

'You usually do. What's so different about this morning?'

'Er – nothing. See you, Sergeant . . .'

Nothing? Oh, but something *was* different, and Carrie Tiptree didn't want to miss any of it.

Hurriedly she parked the truck at the stable yard then ran back to the signals office where Evie sat at the switchboard, forefinger over her lips, nodding towards the kitchen door.

'They're in there,' she whispered, 'so don't go in yet, to make the tea.'

'Why not? What's going on?'

'How do I know? I'm not a fly on the wall, Tiptree.'

'Wish you were.'

The kitchen door opened and a smiling Yeoman walked to the desk, picking up his ashtray, his pen and his writing pad.

The sergeant followed, mouth pursed. Then she said, 'Thank you, Yeoman.'

'Not at all. Anything else you might think of – let me know?'

'No! Nothing more, thanks!'

'See you tonight, then.' The green baize door closed behind him and they heard the sliding of a bolt.

Evie picked up a plug, pointing it at the switchboard, because she couldn't think of anything to say. Carrie looked down at her brown shoes.

'Get on with it then, Tiptree, or don't we get tea this morning?'

'Yes, Sergeant. Right away!' Carrie made for the kitchen. 'Won't be long.'

'And Tiptree. In the corner. The kitbag. Bring it in here, please.'

Oh, Lordy. *The* kitbag. Saying not a word, Carrie picked it up, to hear a clanking sound.

'W-what's in it, Sergeant.' She stood uncertainly in the doorway

'Kettles. Electric. One for Priest's and one for Southgate. And if any of you says *one* word about them, we'll all be in trouble. *All* of us, because even now I doubt my wisdom in accepting them!'

'But how did you manage to get kettles for us, Sergeant?'

'I didn't, Lance-Corporal. It was the Yeoman. He saw Cooper filling her hotwater bottle at the end of the shift, then he asked me why we didn't have kettles in our billets. So I told him we weren't allowed luxuries and he said he was very sorry for you all, especially as he knew where he could lay hands on a couple.'

'He didn't steal them?' Evie whispered, shocked, because she quite liked the petty officer who looked so like Bob.

'He did, sort of, and that's why I'm having second thoughts about it.'

'But who did he steal them *from?*' Carrie laid the kitbag on the sergeant's desk.

'I – I suppose, from his lordship. Technically.'

'The peer of the realm they took Heronflete from?'

'Exactly. It seems there's a room – a kind of butler's pantry on the other side of the green door. It wasn't locked, the Yeoman looked in it.'

'And found two kettles?'

'He found all sorts of things, he said. Electric fires, pans, even a vacuum cleaner. Packed from floor to ceiling, as if they'd been shoved in there and forgotten when Lord Mead-Storrow left. But don't stand there gawping, Tiptree. I'm in need of a cup of tea. A *strong* one!'

'Yes, Sergeant!' Carrie placed four mugs in the sink, ready for washing, and called, 'But if the kettles belong to his lordship and we are utilising them, sort of, in his lordship's gate lodges, you can't – technically, I mean – look on them as being stolen. They haven't been removed from Heronflete, have they? Just moved somewhere else on the estate.'

'Oh, just get on with that tea and don't make such stupid remarks. And the first one to blab is in deep trouble, don't forget.'

And Evie said, 'Yes, Sergeant,' and thought about kettles of water for a hot wash in Southgate kitchen.

And Carrie said, 'Yes, Sergeant,' and thought about hotwater bottles and mugs of cocoa – if they had any cocoa, that was – and powdered milk to stir in it, and wondered if she could get both when she went on leave, because neither was rationed. Just hard to get.

She smiled and wiped the tray top, arranging

three mugs on it, feeling all at once light-hearted, then wondered what Nan would say when she got back from leave, to see an electric kettle in the kitchen.

'Where did you nick that from, then?' Dear, funny Nan. Have a good leave, old love. Carrie looked at her watch. 0625 hours. Nan would still be in bed asleep, if she knew what was good for her!

'Tea up,' she called cheerfully. 'Hot and sweet and strong!'

She wished she could wipe the grin from her face.

Nan read through the letter she had written in pencil to Auntie Mim. In pencil because she didn't want to get a blob of ink from her leaky fountain pen on Mrs Lawson's sheets.

Dear Auntie Mim,
    This is to let you know that I am in Shropshire (near Shrewsbury) where I told you I was spending my leave. It wasn't strictly true, because I am not spending it on my own but with Chas at his mother's house.
    I told you about Chas. He is the airman I met at a dance, remember? We are very good friends now and his mother asked me to spend my week at her place as it turned out that both me and Chas were going on leave

at the same time. What you might call convenient.

Mrs Lawson is a widow and lives in a little house called Gardener's Cottage. It is lovely and snug and has carpets and rugs all over the place, and is in a little village in the countryside.

I know I should have told you where I was going before this, but you mustn't worry. Chas's mother is really nice and has made me very welcome. She has even let me borrow some of her clothes so I need not wear my uniform all the time.

I wish you could meet Chas. You would really like him. Trouble is that it isn't easy for us to get time off to come to Leeds, though it might be a good idea if he was to write to you? Would you like that?

Nan nibbled the end of her pencil. Auntie Mim *would* like Chas though it was stretching it a bit to say they were very good friends, because that was something else that wasn't what you might call accurate when they would be much more than good friends, given the chance. But she couldn't tell Auntie Mim that or there would be a furious letter by return of post, demanding that she behave herself and to think, if she had one iota of sense, about what had happened to her mother and what would happen to Nan Morrissey an' all, if she wasn't careful!

But she *would* be careful, and so would Chas, though it didn't seem right for them to do something like that at Gardener's Cottage, because Mrs Lawson was a lovely lady, and you shouldn't lose your virginity by sneaking up her attic stairs in the middle of the night. To Nan's way of thinking it was a bit common, even though she ached for Chas.

So why not take each day as it came; enjoy being together and dancing together and then, when the time was right, they would both know it, and it would be wonderful; something precious and secret to hug to her when she waited at Priest's Lodge and Chas didn't turn up.

I will write to you the minute I get back from leave and tell you all about it. And I hope that when Chas sends you a letter you will reply to it, as he is such a love and such fun to be with.

Take care of yourself. This letter comes with love from Nan x x x

She sighed. It was the best she could do without giving too much away. Folding the sheets of paper she pushed them in the ready-stamped and addressed envelope. Then she got out of bed, shrugged into dressing gown and slippers and opened the bedroom door to almost collide with Chas.

'Nan – you're awake . . .'

'Nan, softie. I'm sleep-walkin' downstairs to see if there's a cup of tea goin'.'

She lifted her mouth to be kissed, then side-stepped him neatly and made for the kitchen, because she knew Mrs Lawson was there. She had heard her get up, a little before six.

'Nan – I want to talk to you,' Chas whispered urgently then said, 'Damn it!' and followed her downstairs, thinking that maybe he should go carefully about asking Nan to marry him and to wait, if they could, till after the wedding. It might be a shock to her. Being lovers was one thing. Waiting until they were married was altogether another.

Perhaps he should pick a better time; when they were dancing, perhaps, and he could whisper in her ear and hold her even more closely. And come to think of it, they had met at a dance; where better to ask her to be his wife – and to wait till their wedding night. Would she agree or would she tell him that marriage wasn't on and wouldn't it be better to take what they could for as long as the Fates allowed, that was . . .

When he opened the kitchen door, Nan was drying the white china mugs and his mother was piling kindling on the fire. It was a memory to take with him as they bumped around the perimeter track towards takeoff, waiting for the green-for-go light. Those few minutes before he knew they were safely airborne were agonising when he prayed – probably they all prayed – that some wonderful person would fire a red flare from the control tower to stop the mission and call them back.

Then, as they climbed through cloud and into a sky bright with stars, the thumping of his heart steadied because he knew they were in with an even chance of making it back to RAF Modeley, and tea laced with rum and the pretty young intelligence officer at de-briefing asking them all manner of questions.

So, he decided, that during those agonising few minutes, he would close his mind to everything save the image of his mother beside the kitchen fire and Nan in blue and white striped pyjamas at the sink, wrinkling her nose at his teasingly whilst loving him with her eyes.

Dearest mother, darling Nan. He didn't want never to see them again; didn't want to be a name on a war memorial, a statistic. And he wished he could be braver, like most of the other bods in the Mess seemed to be and who lived life to the full, and didn't give a damn about going for a Burton when there were popsies for the taking, and tomorrow was an unmentionable word.

But he didn't want popsies. Nan was his tomorrow and all his tomorrows.

'Hey!' Fingers clicked beneath his nose. 'You were miles away,' his mother smiled. 'What were you thinking about?'

'Miles away?' He shrugged, then said, 'w-e-ll, if you must know, I was thinking that – er – we have only got five days' leave left.'

'Then don't think things like that. Tell yourself that aren't we the lucky ones because we've got five more days left till we've got to go back!' Nan grinned. 'Five more nights goin' dancing', five more mornings in this kitchen drinkin' tea like it wasn't rationed and there wasn't a war on!'

'Good for you!' Stella Lawson smiled, thinking yet again how good Nan was for her son, and how easy it must have been for him to fall in love with her. 'And it's going to have to be porridge for breakfast because the fire won't be ready, yet, for toast. And didn't you say, Charles, that you wanted to go into Shrewsbury this morning and get a decent haircut? What say I drive you both there, then Nan can get her silk stockings.'

'No,' Nan said, very firmly. 'I think the two of you should go on your own. You've hardly had any time without me bein' there. And surely you can get my stockings for me – size nine, and both pairs the same colour?'

'But you'd be very welcome . . .'

'No. I have to post a letter to Leeds and if there's hot water to spare, I'd like to wash my hair.'

'Then if you're sure, Nan, once the fire takes hold you pull out the damper, and the water will be hot in no time at all. We won't be very long – a couple of hours, or so. And if you go to the top of the lane and past the bottom of the manor drive, you'll see the pillarbox about ten yards ahead. Oh, and there's a hairdryer in the bathroom cupboard – feel free . . .'

And Nan said thanks a lot and that she would have everything done and dusted and the kettle boiling on the hob by the time they got back. Indeed, she thought, it was only fair that the two of them should be together now and again and anyway, her hair was still hanging in rat's tails since last night's soaking.

'Right then. I'll get dressed, then post the letter and maybe get a look at the manor. Where I'm stationed, you can't go up the drive to the big house. I tried it once, and got my marching orders from a soldier with a gun!'

'There are no guns at the manor, I promise,' Stella smiled. 'Only soldiers and airmen convalescing. And you get a good view from the gates – where the gates once were – I mean. But we really won't be very long and you don't have to be polite, Nan. You'll be most welcome to come with us. Truly you will. You could pop into the hairdresser whilst Charles goes for a haircut – see if they can fit you in . . .'

But still Nan said they should go to Shrewsbury together and she would post the letter, have a look at the manor, then shampoo her hair.

'An' thanks for the use of the dryer, Mrs Lawson. You're very kind.'

And Chas smiled and said she was an easy person to be kind to as he had once found out, and was she sure she would be all right on her own?

'I'll be fine, Sergeant Lawson,' she teased. 'So

303

off you go and get your hair seen to. And don't let the barber cut too much off!'

Nan waved them off at the kitchen door, then hurried upstairs, impatient to pull on the brown corduroy trousers and the matching suede brogues. Then she wriggled into the butter cup, yellow sweater and tied her hair back with a ribbon.

Outside, everything smelled of rain and freshness, though a cherry tree had lost a lot of leaves that lay yellowing in the lane. Autumn, Nan thought. Soon, by the time her birthday came around, the trees would be bare.

She thought about Southgate Lodge and the oak trees that lined Heronflete's drive; thought too about what Evie and Carrie would think if they could see her in these posh civvy clothes.

And then she wondered what they would be doing at this very minute, and knew that Carrie would be in the stable yard and ready, soon, to go for the ten o'clock pot of tea and Evie and the Sergeant would probably have been to the cookhouse for breakfast and would be managing very well without her.

Nan began to walk, arms swinging as if she were in uniform, gazing ahead to the two tall gateposts. Almost like those at Heronflete, she thought, because somebody had nicked the manor gates, an' all, for the war effort.

She stopped, gazing up the drive to a red brick house with white-painted windows and shutters and a flight of stone steps leading to wide doors.

She counted the upstairs windows and concluded that there must be at least ten bedrooms and attics above them.

Then she centred her attention on a tall young man in blue trousers and jacket and a red tie at the neck of his white shirt. Hospital blues, they had come to be known – the uniform of men who had been wounded.

He swung along on crutches, face red with exertion, then called, 'Hello,' to Nan.

'Hello yourself. And be careful.' She began to walk towards him, wondering what she would do if he fell over. 'You're goin' far too quick.'

'I'm fine,' he grinned. 'You're new around here, aren't you?'

'Yes. Stoppin' at Gardener's Cottage with Mrs Lawson. And don't you think you'd better sit down for a rest? Have you come all the way from the house?'

'Yes. I've got a bet on that I couldn't make it on my own to the gates. Didn't think it would be such hard work.' He hopped over to the oak bench at the side of the drive, and sat down awkwardly.

'There now.' Nan took the crutches and laid them at his side, then sat down beside him. 'Well, you've won your bet, soldier. My name is Nan. What's yours?'

'Alan. Nearly lost my legs in a crash. They've been a long time mending. And I know who you are. Mrs Lawson said her son would be home on leave and bringing his girl with him. We miss her. She does a lot for us.'

'Well, you'll get her back when Chas and me go back to Lincolnshire. What does she do, at the manor?'

'Oh, she fetches and carries and smiles a lot. Nothing is too much trouble for her. She comes in six days a week. Must be funny for her, seeing beds in her drawing room and beds in her dining room, and wheelchairs parked in the hall.'

'What do you mean – beds? Wheelchairs?'

'Well, she used to live there before the government took the manor for a convalescent home. She went to live in one of the cottages on the estate. It doesn't seem to bother her a bit.'

'Listen.' Nan felt distinctly uneasy. 'Are you tryin' to say that Mrs Lawson is posh – gentry, sort of?'

'She's a real lady, if that's what you mean. No airs and graces about her. What you'd call breeding.'

'Yes, but Chas never said a word to me about where he lived, only that it was a little cottage in a village near Shrewsbury. Are you sure you've got it right?'

'Oh, yes. Everybody at the manor knows. Weren't you told about it?'

'No, I wasn't. Not a word. Mind, Chas is like that, very – er –'

'Unasuming?' the soldier supplied. 'Exactly like his mother. And are you all right? You look a bit peculiar.'

'No, I'm fine. Just fine. Bit of a misunderstanding, that's all. Want me to walk back with you?'

'Would you? Bet that lot are watching out of the window, making sure I made it. It'll wipe their eyes when they see me with you!'

'Fine by me, and anyway, I'd like to get a closer look at the manor. It must be a big place.'

Nan's mouth had gone very dry. Shock, she supposed, and the realisation that Chas was out of the top drawer, yet was interested in someone like herself; a nobody who spoke broad Scouse and came from Cyprian Court – a place you definitely wouldn't take your young man home to.

'Mm. Quite big. Must have needed a staff of servants to keep it up – in the days when you could get servants. The nurses sleep in the attics and those who can't get upstairs have their beds in the dining room. It's all very grand. Wouldn't mind stopping here for the duration.'

'I work at a big house,' Nan found herself saying. 'A lord once lived there, and the government gave him a month to get out. I work in what was once the estate office, round the back. Sort of secret. Nobody tells you anything . . .'

The sergeant's caution never, ever to mention Heronflete Priory was forgotten. Nan Morrissey had just learned that the airman she was in love with had been brought up in a manor house, yet he had taken up with the likes of *her*, who was born on the wrong side of the sheets and who didn't know who her father was.

'There's an estate office at the manor,' the soldier said. 'And stables and an orangery and loads of greenhouses. Amazing, isn't it, how the other half lived.'

'Suppose it is.' Nan stopped, taking one last look at the house before she said, 'Look – great to meet you Alan, but I'd better be getting back. Chas and his mum – er, Charles and Mrs Lawson – have gone into town and I've got things to do before they get back. Take care of yourself, uh?'

And with that she ran down the drive, pausing only to post Auntie Mim's letter, wondering why Chas had chosen not to tell her he really lived in a posh house; wondering where all the money had come from to pay servants and gardeners, and how much a house like that must cost to keep warm in winter.

She hurried towards the cottage, taking the key from beneath the back door mat, letting herself in, realising she was shaking.

Charles Lawson in love with Nan Morrissey? My, but that was something to think about, and the two of them planning to be lovers. But it stood to sense, didn't it? People like her were fine to make love to, but that was where it ended. It had happened before and everything had been hushed up. The man who was her father hadn't done the right thing and married her mother. People like him never did.

She ran upstairs to the bathroom, pulling off

308

her sweater, combing through her hair before dunking her head into hot water. Then she soaped and rubbed and scrubbed until the shock was out of her, then rinsed and rinsed until her hair squeaked. Breathless she began to rub it dry, dismayed to find herself still unable to make sense of what the soldier called Alan had told her. Surely he was wrong? Surely, if it were true, Chas would have told her about it?

But rich people who lived in manor houses didn't marry beneath them. Her kind of people, Nan thought, people like her mother, were for having fun with. Sowing wild oats it was called.

Chas, why didn't you tell me? she asked of her image in the bathroom mirror.

But it was happening again. History repeating itself. Her mother had fallen for the same sweet talk and landed up in trouble, and the man who was the cause of it all getting away Scott-free. Or almost.

Why had it all gone wrong? Chas must never, ever, know about what happened to her mother, because a girl who didn't know her real father's name didn't even *think* of letting a man who had been born in a manor house make love to her. Not unless she were stupid, that was, and determined to land up in a home for unmarried mothers.

The tears she had been fighting filled her eyes then ran unchecked down her cheeks. She was still weeping when Charles came home.

'Darling, what's wrong? You're crying. What has happened?'

'Nuthin' happened. I got shampoo in my eyes, that's all, and it stings like mad.'

'But they're red and puffy, Nan.'

'And so would yours be, if you'd got shampoo in them. But where is your mother? I don't want her to see me like this.'

'She'll be a while, yet. We met the vicar at the gate and he asked her if she wanted red cabbages for pickling. She's gone to the vicarage to get them and I suppose she'll be asked in for a gossip. So wash your face and powder your nose. And dab your eyes dry, too. Your lashes are all spiky.'

'So I suppose I look awful with me nose all red, an' all?' she flung, defiantly.

'Oh, come down off your high horse, Nan Morrissey,' he said fondly, taking her face in his hands so she was forced to look at him. 'To me, you'll never look awful, not even when your eyes are swollen and your lashes stuck together and your nose is red and sniffy. So let's start with, "Hi, Chas, you're back, and I love you." Let's take it from there, shall we, because I love you and I want to know that nothing has changed between us – or ever will.'

'I – I *do* love you, Chas. I think I always will, but things *have* changed. I've been thinkin', see, about you an' me being lovers, and it isn't on. We've got to behave ourselves.'

'But I thought we'd agreed – that we both wanted to, I mean.'

'Like I said, we can't, and it mustn't . . .'

'Then why, all of a sudden, have you done an about turn? Who put such ideas into your head?'

'My – oh, no one. I just thought it out for myself.'

Oh, not true, Nan Morrissey! 'My mother,' she had been about to fling at him. 'Some toff got her pregnant with me then bought his way out of it. He didn't marry her like he should have done, because she was working-class and he was out of the top drawer.' But she didn't say it, because her stiff-necked Liverpool pride would not allow it.

'So you've gone off me? In the space of a couple of hours, you've come to the conclusion that anything other than friendship between us isn't on? Why, Nan?'

'Because, I suppose,' she looked down at her shoes, not wanting to see the hurt in his eyes, 'I suppose we ought to be sensible about things.'

'So what's sensible about meeting a girl – a girl who laughs a lot and has the most gorgeous eyes you ever did see – and falling in love with her, the minute she asked him to dance?'

'Love at first sight, you mean? But people say it doesn't happen.'

'Then people are wrong, because you've turned my life upside down, Nan. In fact, if I can't have you my life isn't going to be a lot of use, and I might as well go for a Burton on my next op.'

'Charles Lawson! How could you say such a thing! How *dare* you tempt Fate like that? You should be ashamed of yourself! Take it back.'

'All right. I'm sorry. Stupid of me, but I can't imagine losing you.'

'You aren't going to lose me, and I don't want to lose *you*. I want everything to be the same between us, but I can't risk us being lovers. I *can't*.'

'But why can't you?' he demanded, bewildered. 'What bee have you got in your bonnet? I'm away for a couple of hours and I come home to a stranger.'

'No, Chas. Never that. I won't ever change.'

'But you *have* changed. *Why*?'

'Oh, I – I.' She wanted to tell him about her mother, who was working-class, like herself, and how some rich guy got her into trouble and left her high and dry the minute he found out. And she couldn't tell him that she had just discovered that the man she loved was rich, too, and their sort thought girls like her were just a bit on the side. 'I – I think it's too much of a risk. Let's go on havin' fun, and driving Boadicea and dancing, like always. Let's enjoy life a bit more? You aren't of age, yet, and I'm only just-about eighteen.

'And don't look at me all hurt Chas, because you're the one person in the whole world I don't want to hurt. So shall we talk about it later when we've both calmed down a bit and oh, damn damn! That's your mother at the front gate. I can't let her see me like this. I'm going upstairs to powder my nose.'

'OK. But I do love you,' he called softly from the bottom of the stairs, 'and we *will* talk about it later.'

'Good heavens!' He opened the back door to his mother. 'What have you got there!'

'Cabbages, for pickling. Aren't they beauties? I must say that if the vicar ever gave up preaching, he could make a good living any day as a gardener. I'll put them in the pantry, for now. I've got pickling spice, and thank goodness vinegar isn't rationed. So did you give Nan her stockings? Did she like the colour?'

'I – er – didn't get around to it. She'd got shampoo in her eyes and she's upstairs, right now. Probably powdering her nose.'

'And whilst I remember, have you asked her yet – to think about getting married?'

'Not yet, mother. After all, she's still a bit young, and there's still a war on.'

'I'm well aware of that, son. But I constantly remind myself that twenty years after my generation said there would never be another war, we let one happen again, and that's why you should take every bit of happiness you can. Maybe that's not a very wise thing for a mother to say, but I have been young, remember, and very much in love, so I understand. And I know Nan hasn't got a family, but she could be married from Gardener's Cottage. I'd love it, if she was. Tell you what – you put the kettle on, and I'll nip upstairs and see how she is.'

'No! Please don't!' He took his mother's arm, holding it tightly. 'I'm going to talk to Nan, later. Maybe we'll go out later for a walk and have a good old natter. Sorry, but it's something I've got to do for myself!'

'Well, of course it is!' Stella laughed, all at once realising that her son, who flew into danger so often, was man enough to do his own proposing. 'But I wouldn't go out. It'll be cold, and you don't want to risk another soaking. Why don't you make yourselves comfy in the front room – pile the fire up, and have a heart to heart, eh? I shall be in the kitchen washing jamjars, seeing to the vinegar, and shredding those monstrous cabbages. I won't be disturbing you . . .'

'Shall I tell you something, Mrs Lawson? Like I said before, you're one very lovely lady to have for a mother, and I adore you.'

'Yes, but this lady is getting on a bit, and there's nothing she would like more than to see her son married to a girl who's exactly right for him. And maybe I'd like to know there would be grandchildren around the place, too. Heaven only knows, the manor is big enough for two families – if ever we get it back, that is. There are two kitchens. One each. Women who share a house don't fall out if they have their own kitchen.'

'I'm glad you think a kitchen apiece will solve everything, mother. After all, the lady hasn't said yes, yet, and I'm not at all sure she would want to live at the manor.'

'But it's a lovely house. Roomy, but not too big. You could offer it as bait, when you get round to some serious talking.'

'You're right, of course. A kitchen of her own and a share of the manor isn't something to be sneezed at. But I haven't told Nan about it, yet.'

'Whyever not? You could take her up there and show her round. I'm sure Matron would let you.'

'Yes, dearest, but this is between me and Nan, and –'

'Yes, I know. You're a big fellow now, Charles. Oh, but it doesn't seem long since your Pa died. You were only ten, but you said that you would be the man of the house, and would look after me. And you have . . .'

'Well, I'm twenty now, though I must say that asking a girl to marry you is a lot harder than flying over Berlin. Wish me luck, eh?'

'I will. I always do. Every single day, Charles. So nip upstairs to your Nan, and tell her there's some rosewater in the bathroom cabinet, and that she's very welcome to dab some on her eyes. I'll make a pot of tea. I'm dying for a drink. I thought I might have been offered a cup at the vicarage, but all I got was a conducted tour of the vegetable garden to admire the cabbages and sprouts! So off you go, and tell Nan it'll be tea up in five minutes – OK?'

'Yes, Ma'am.' Charles saluted smartly. 'And be a love and don't mention the manor? Leave it to me, eh?'

And Stella winked wickedly, and said she would.

THIRTEEN

'I never thought,' Evie said, 'that I could get so excited about an electric kettle.' It stood, plugged in beside the fireplace in the little room where Nan and Carrie slept. 'Just think of all the lovely hot washes we can have without having to trek to the ablutions.'

'Mmm. And I shall go and see Mr Greensit, when I go on leave. Our grocer. We get our rations from him. He's very good to mother. She gets quite a few things from under the counter. He was a sergeant in my father's regiment in the Great War, you see, so I'll put my uniform on and take my ration card with me, and ask him if he's got a tin of powdered milk or some cocoa stashed away. He'll let me have them, if he has. We could make hot drinks, then.'

'You crafty monkey,' Evie laughed. 'And had you thought how lovely it will be to have a hotwater bottle to take to bed? I think the Yeoman is a sweetie.'

'He said there were all sorts of electrical things in that pantry. I wonder if he could come by a little fire, for us?'

'No! We should be content with what we've got, Carrie. And don't forget the coal and wood, outside. If things got really bad, we could risk lighting a fire. And had you realised that Heronflete provides our tea and sugar and milk? The Yeoman gets them. Do you suppose we could sometimes er – *borrow* – a spoonful or two of tea for here?'

'Good idea,' Carrie grinned, who had long ago learned that if it wasn't nailed down you could take it. 'And I get on very well with the sergeant in the cookhouse. He doesn't spoon tea into pots, you know. He puts it in in handfuls. My mother would have one of her migraines if she saw him.'

'And you reckon you could sweetheart some out of him?'

'I can try. He can only say no. Oh, I'm going to miss Southgate when I go on leave. Being here is turning out much better than I ever thought. I'd like to stay here for the duration.'

'Some hopes, Tiptree. The Army has a nasty habit of moving personnel around. Don't get too smug, just because we've got a kettle.'

'I won't,' Carrie smiled, 'but when I go home, I shall bring my pink bedsocks back with me, and my woolly knitted hat to sleep in. And my gumboots, in case it snows.'

'In case? It always snows in winter, in the north. I reckon we'll be spending quite a bit of time in the

NAAFI, keeping warm, when the bad weather arrives. But let's not think about winter just yet.' Think about Saturday, Carrie, and going home. Nan should be back by then. Wonder what she's doing, now.'

'Dancing with Chas, I shouldn't wonder or sitting by a lovely fire.'

Nan was indeed sitting beside a fire, feet tucked beneath her, snuggled close to Chas.

'Aaah,' she sighed. 'This is nice, innit? Sitting cosy like this, and that lovely smell coming from the kitchen. Like a real home should be.'

'It's mother, spicing vinegar for the pickling. And this *is* a real home, sweetheart.'

He dropped a kiss on the head that rested on his shoulder, loving her so much, wanting to talk things out with her, yet dreading making a mess of it and spoiling everything.

'I know. Lovely and snug, and people bein' nice to each other. Just the opposite of Cyprian Court. I hated it, there. Couldn't wait to join up, after dad was killed.'

'And are you glad you did?'

'Of course I am. Wouldn't have met you, if I hadn't.'

'So meeting me was good? Nan Morrissey?'

'You know it was.' She turned in his arms, meeting his gaze. 'But what is all this leading up to, because you've been like a cat on hot bricks since this morning.'

'This morning, darling, you said you didn't want

us to be lovers after all, and I wish you'd tell me why. Something happened, didn't it, when I was out?'

'Y-yes, I suppose it did. When I went to post the letter, I met a soldier, from the manor, and I stopped to talk to him. And to cut a long story short, he told me your family own that place. It was a shock, I can tell you.'

'So that's what caused all the tears? But why did it upset you so?'

'Well, for one thing you should've told me, and you didn't. And for another, owning a place like, that makes you upper-class.'

'No it doesn't, Nan. I won't *own* it, as you say, till I'm of age, and even then it'll be up to the Army, and when they choose to give it back. And I don't know what you mean by upper-class. We Lawsons aren't landed gentry like the fellow who owned Heronflete. We worked for our money. Nobody handed it down to us. I'm not a chinless aristrocrat.

'Grandpa Lawson had his own carpet factory, and ran it with his two sons, and eventually my cousin and I will run it – when the war is over, that is, and we can go back to making carpets.'

'So what happened to the factory? Did the government take it off you, as well as the manor?'

'No, but they told us that the manufacture of carpets and rugs had to stop. Luxuries, you see. Not allowed. And they said we had to put the factory on war production. We turned over to, making webbing and tarpaulins and camouflage netting, working day and night.'

'So you've got richer than ever?'

'Not me. My share goes to mother, till I'm twenty-one. To be honest, all I've got is my sergeant's pay.'

'But Chas, you're twisting things. You were born in a manor and you're from the moneyed classes. I was born in a little house in Liverpool and we had damn-all to live on. Most times, dad didn't have a job. Not till the war came, and it cost him his life.'

'So you're angry because I wanted for nothing and you didn't have a very good time of it? Is that why, all of a sudden, you've clammed up on me?'

'Yes, I suppose it is, in a roundabout way. You see, it didn't seem to matter when you said you lived in a little cottage. It was only when I thought about it that it struck me that your sort always get their own way with girls, then ditch them when they've sown their wild oats.'

'But that just isn't true, darling. What made you think I was only out for what I could get? I'd never ditch you. You know I wouldn't!'

'Oh, Chas!' sighing she pulled away from him and got to her feet, taking logs from the basket, laying them on the fire. 'This is one awful mess! And I *do* want you, still, but your sort and my sort don't mix.'

'Oh? Well, I think they do. In fact I'm so sure of it that I want to marry you!'

He gathered her to him, holding her closely, needing to feel the nearness of her.

'You *what?* Oh, I thought your sort could be real swines, but I never thought you'd stoop so low, Chas Lawson! You can't have your little bit on the side, so you're asking me to marry you, just to get it!' She struggled angrily against him, but he held her closely, searching with his lips for hers. 'And you can stop that an' all! Kissing won't get me all weak at the knees, so don't be thinkin' it will!'

'Nan, darling girl,' he whispered softly, his lips to her ear. 'Let me tell you something – *please?*'

And because, fool that she was, she liked the little shivers that went through her when he did that, she stood still in his arms and said, 'What, then . . . ?'

'I *do* want to marry you. I know you don't believe me, but you can ask mother, and she'll tell you that I told her about it yesterday morning – asked her opinion, and I need her permission, I suppose. And one thing led to another. I'd told her that you and I wanted to be lovers and she wasn't a bit shocked. Then I thought it wouldn't be fair on you if you got pregnant, and I went for a Burton. But she said that if I was man enough to fight for my country, then I was man enough to get married, and she gave me her blessing. Said the only setback we might have is that your Auntie Mim might not let you, because she's your next of kin, isn't she?'

'Oh, don't, Chas? Don't ask me ever again? Because it isn't just that you lot are out of the top drawer. There's something else, much worse, to stop us,' she whispered. 'We can't be lovers and it's best we don't get married 'cause there are things about me I'm not very proud of.'

'Oh, dear.' He trailed his lips over her cheek, then kissed the tip of her nose. 'You've been in prison for shoplifting?'

'Garn!'

'You earned your living on the streets, maybe?'

'Hey up! Now I know you're skittin' me.' A small smile lifted the corners of Nan's mouth. 'But if I tell you something, you won't tell your mother, will you? And you won't ever throw it back at me, that I'm what I am?'

'You don't have to tell me anything, sweetheart, but I'd respect your confidence if you decided to. Let's sit down again – talk things over?'

So they sat on the sofa and he laid an arm around her shoulders, drawing her close.

'All right, then.' She took a deep breath, gazing into the fireglow. 'I'm what you call illegitimate, Chas. The man whose name is on my birth certificate wasn't my father. He married my mother because he was fond of her and he didn't want people to look down on her for getting into trouble and her not being married, I mean.'

'But why didn't your real father do the decent thing by your mother, Nan? Was he already married?'

'I don't know, and I won't ever know, because my mother told nobody nuthin'. Not even my dad – the man I *thought* was my dad. She didn't even tell Auntie Mim, her own sister. I only found out when I left Cyprian Court. I took Mam's marriage lines and my birth certificate with me. I'd never seen them before, but it was a shock when I did and it didn't add up – them getting married not long before I was born. That was when the penny dropped.'

'But no blame attaches to you. Nan – if blame there must be. Surely that isn't what has been upsetting you – thinking you weren't good enough for someone who lived in a big house? That's a load of nonsense, and you know it.'

'Maybe that partly, sort of. But I've got to admit that when I found out that you was out of the top drawer, it made me think about us wanting to – well you know . . .'

'Be lovers,' Charles supplied, matter-of-factly.

'Yes. We said be damned to it, didn't we, and let's go the whole hog. It didn't seem to matter when you lived in a cottage. It was only then I realised that rich fellers usually got their own way with girls, then ditched them, just like what happened to my mother. And she man who was my real father must've been rich, because someone gave Mum a hundred pounds. A small fortune, in those days.'

'And not to be sneezed at even now, Nan.'

'Yes, and they gave her a load of furniture, an'

all. Good stuff, but old. Come to think of it, it looked out of place in Cyprian Court.'

'So you don't want me, now, because you think I'm some rich bloke, out to take advantage of you? History repeating itself – is that it?'

'I suppose so.'

'Then you're going to have to come with me and talk to mother, ask her if I really did tell her I wanted to marry you. You'll believe, then, that I do. And the only advice she gave me was for us both to behave ourselves till we could get married. Please, darling, talk to her?'

'You think we should?'

'Yes, I do. She's happy about you and me, Nan. With her on our side we'd stand a much better chance with your aunt – if she wouldn't let you marry me, I mean.'

'Makes sense, I suppose. Auntie Mim never got married, see. Never saw the need for it, she said,' Nan frowned. 'She mightn't be very sympathetic. But maybe with your mother on our side . . .'

'Exactly. She can be very persuasive, so let's go and give her the good news – that the young lady has said yes.'

'But I haven't, Chas.'

'No, but you're going to, aren't you my darling? I want to introduce you to everyone we meet as my fiancée. Let's enjoy what's left of this leave and tell ourselves that next time we're here together, you'll be Mrs Lawson.'

'Official, like – your fiancée?'

'Official, though I don't know what we're going to do about a ring.'

'I don't want a ring, Chas. Carrie's got one and she never wears it. It's round her neck, with her dog tags. Waste of good money, even if we could get one.'

'So does that mean that you've said yes, Nan? Will you marry me – as soon as we possibly can? Please?'

'I'd marry you tomorrow, Chas, if I could. I love you very much, an' it's going to be smashin', being your fiancée.'

'Then shall we go and tell mother – make it official?'

'I reckon we should, and I'm sorry I got hold of the wrong end of the stick, and thought you was out for what you could get. Give me a kiss, and tell me I'm forgiven?'

'Forgiven as soon as asked,' he kissed her gently, smiling into her eyes. 'And tomorrow night, let's go to Shrewsbury to the dance, to celebrate? There's always one on a Thursday. Wear that floaty skirt of mother's, and the gold slippers, and your silk stockings?'

'Yes, but you won't have to twirl me round in it or that skirt'll be round me waist and me khaki knickers'll show. And them knickers are frightenin' to behold!'

'Oh, Nan – I do so love you. I always will.'

'Mmm. And I love you, Sergeant. There could never be anyone else. We were meant to meet.'

'We were. And I'm glad I stammered and blushed so much that you took pity on me, and insisted I dance with you. But let's spread the good news?'

And they linked little fingers and made for the pungent, unromantic smell of spiced vinegar. And Stella Lawson – who would be on their side.

Carrie smiled at the conductress who opened the door of the bus for her, then heaved her kitbag onto her shoulder. She had brought very little with her. Shirts, collars and underwear to be washed, her toilet bag and dressing gown. Not really enough to fill a kitbag, so she had pushed in her Army-issue respirator, too. One item less to bother with in the struggle to find a seat on an already-crowded train. Strictly not done, of course. Respirators must be worn on the person at all times, but who was there to notice, she had thought lightheadedly. She was going on her first-ever leave and determined to walk the length of the village with the very unfeminine kitbag over her shoulder, so those who twitched their curtains at the sound of the bus to see who got off it should see her in all her khaki glory.

Mischief on her part was it, or an act of defiance? She wasn't sure but it didn't matter because it was almost dark and curtains would be drawn, now, against the blackout, so there could be never one twitch to let out even the smallest gleam of light. The blackout was sacrosanct, so no one would see her, she was bound to admit as she walked carefully to Jackmans Cottage, remembering where the kerb dipped and the position of the two iron lamp posts, waiting unlit and unseen to break spectacles and bruise faces.

'Walked into a lamp post did you?' was almost as hackneyed a phrase as 'Get that light out!' or 'Got your identity card?' or even 'Don't you know there's a war on?'

She squinted in the darkness to make out the dim outline of the sycamore tree where the wood pigeon nested. Almost home, now. She would use the back door as they always did, because Jackmans stood end-on to the road – the only one in Nether Hutton to do so. A few more steps to the wide, squat door. Was the tingling inside her one of pleasure or apprehension? She would only know when she saw her mother's face.

She blanked her mother from her mind and thought instead of Nan, who should be back from leave, now, maybe even sitting at her teleprinter in the signals office at Heronflete and wondering how seven days could have passed so quickly and how wonderful they had been. Dear Nan. So happily in love.

Carrie reached out for the gatepost she knew to be ahead of her, walked down four steps and she was there, hand on the door sneck, calling, 'Hi! It's me!' closing the door quickly behind her, making for the snug little room they always used when the nights drew in and the weather became colder.

'Caroline!' The door of the snug opened. 'I've been on edge all day, waiting. You never said when –'

'Never mind. I'm here now!' Carrie gathered her mother to her, hugging her tightly, kissing her cheek. 'Oh, it's good to be home.'

'It's good to have you,' Janet Tiptree said huskily, 'but darling, do take off that uniform. It's *awful*!'

'It isn't awful. I think it's smart and I'm very proud of it, mother.'

Oh please – not already at odds? Not from the very moment she walked in? Was she never to be forgiven?

Then she relaxed, because her mother was smiling, returning her kiss. 'You seem taller, child.'

'I'm not.' Carrie took off her cap and tossed it onto the settee.

'You've lost weight, then.'

'I haven't. We're better fed than civilians, even if the food is sometimes a bit stodgy,' she laughed. 'But I'd love a cup of tea, if the ration will run to it – in a china cup, please? Our mugs are like chamber pots!'

Janet Tiptree smiled smugly. China cups? So her wayward daughter *was* missing home comforts?

'Tea tray's set. Won't be a minute. Take your – er – things upstairs.' A glance at the kitbag. 'And wash your hands and face. You look quite grubby, dear.'

'I feel it. Trains are a bit mucky these days, and crowded.'

Carrie did not protest at being sent upstairs to wash. Nothing had changed, it seemed, but it didn't matter. She could put up with being an only chick for seven days, and besides, her mother must have been lonely.

'There is so much to tell you,' she called over her shoulder as she opened the staircase door.

And quite a bit of explaining to do, Janet Tiptree thought. Why her daughter's letters were censored, and why she had sprung her leave on them so suddenly. And it might be as well to find out exactly where she was stationed. C/o GPO London indeed! What kind of an address was that?

Carrie unpacked her kitbag, pushing the respirator under the bed, taking her laundry to the wicker basket in the bathroom, hanging her dressing gown on the familiar peg behind the door. Only when she had unlaced her shoes and pulled on her slippers did she wash her hands and face, gazing into the mirror as she dried them, wondering why her mother found her uniform so distasteful when it was smart and flattering – except for the khaki stockings, that was, which nobody liked wearing, especially when they got faded from constant laundering.

Squaring her shoulders, she pulled her jacket straight, then walked slowly downstairs, preparing herself for the probing and questioning that must surely come.

'Aaah.' She held her hands to the fire. 'Absolute bliss.' She snuggled into the cushions, accepting the forget-me-not patterned cup and saucer – the second-best china – and took a sip. 'Lovely to be home, mother.' She really meant it.

'You need never have gone, but that is in the past, now. I do wonder, though, why your letters have to be censored and where you are stationed,' she murmured, eyes on the teapot.

'Somewhere in England.'

'In London, where there is so much bombing?'

'No. In the country, actually, on what was the estate of a lord, so it's safer there from air raids than most places. Don't worry about me. I'm fine.'

'I see. Which would explain why you are billeted in a little gate lodge?' Janet persisted.

'Yes. With Evie and Nan – that much I was able to tell you, but everything else is secret – or perhaps I should say *secretive*.' Yes, that was the word. You couldn't tell secrets when you didn't really know what the men in the big house were being so secretive about. 'I just drive about the estate and into town sometimes, to the station or the main barracks. And every phone call that comes through Evie's switchboard is scrambled, and every signal Nan passes is in code. That's as much as I know.'

'But *where* is the town and the barracks, Caroline?'

'Somewhere in England, didn't I tell you,' Carrie teased, trying desperately not to send her mother into a huff. 'Look dear, even Corporal Finigan doesn't know what goes on in Heronflete.'

She stopped, dismayed, but it was too late.

'Ah, so that's where you are?'

'No, mother. That's the name of the estate – Heronflete Priory. And I shouldn't have let that slip – you're not to tell Mrs Frobisher, even. Promise?'

'Oh, all right – as long as I know you are safe and not too far away.'

'Not too far,' Carrie soothed, then held out her empty cup. 'That was heaven. You couldn't squeeze another out of the pot? And you couldn't manage a slice of toast and jam?'

'I can do better than that. I've got ham sandwiches on the cold slab. I told the butcher you were coming on leave and he let me have a ham shank from under the counter. "Don't tell a soul," he said. They're keeping fresh under a damp cloth. Oh, if only you hadn't gone away!'

She made for the pantry with tears trembling on her words and Carrie knew she had not yet been forgiven for sneaking into the ATS. And it would start in earnest, tomorrow, when they went to church to hear the final reading of the banns.

'Mother! They look good enough to eat!' Dainty sandwiches, garnished with parsley. 'Home-made bread, is it?'

And her mother said it was, especially for Carrie's leave, because it wasn't worth going to the bother of baking bread now, just for one.

'You seem to have got rid of your cold at last.'

Carrie tried to talk of other things and oh, it

was going to be such a week – starting in the morning when Jeffrey's mother would join in.

Fleetingly, almost longingly, she thought about Southgate and if Nan and Chas were back and had had the most wonderful leave.

'I can't help wondering,' Janet murmured as Carrie bit into her third sandwich, 'why you weren't able to tell me sooner – about your leave, I mean.'

'Because that's the way it is, mother. Leave is a privilege and not an entitlement. My name came out of the hat, and that was it . . .'

She looked at the mantel clock. Less than half an hour at home, and she was already telling lies.

'And have you no say in the matter?'

'None at all. Like I just said, a privilege, though you usually get it, if the war allows.'

'And will they give you leave when Jeffrey is next home?'

'Not unless we've named the day – and I take it you're talking about the wedding? *If* we'd set a date, then I'd probably be given compassionate leave. The Army isn't entirely heartless.'

Carrie looked at the last sandwich on the plate. There was a wish on it, wasn't there? Always a wish on a biscuit or tart or anything last on the plate, so dare she risk one?

'Dearest mother,' she reached for the sandwich, holding it carefully. 'Things will work out, I'm sure of it.' Dammit, she was wishing in a round-about way, wishing to be rid of the worry of it, leave the wedding in the hands of fate, without any pushing and hinting from anyone. 'Leave it for now, why don't we? I was up this morning at half-five to drive the early shift and I've had a long journey on the train.'

'The train from where, Caroline?'

'You know where from. Somewhere in England,' Carrie said softly, 'and I'm tired. There wouldn't be hot water for a bath?'

A real bath. Not a shower behind canvas curtains in the ablutions. One you could lay back and wallow in – if wallowing was possible in six inches of water.

'Of course there would. Isn't there always? Your nightie is on top of the cylinder, warming, and there's a hot bottle in your bed – and Carrie – it's good to have you back.'

'It's good to be back, it truly is.' She laid an arm around her mother's shoulder, then gently kissed her cheek. 'And we'll talk tomorrow – I promise we'll talk about – *things*.'

It was far easier to talk to Evie about *things*, she sighed, inwardly. Evie was in love and sound love making was a delight and not a duty as her mother had often implied.

She looked again at the mantel clock and knew that Evie and Nan – if she were back from Shropshire, that was – would be in the signals office, waiting for the Yeoman to open the green baize door and take over the night shift – or night *watch* – as the Royal Navy called it.

Soon, they would be in Southgate, talking about Nan's leave. And they wouldn't be missing her, Carrie thought, because Norman always drove the late shift. But they would think about her tomorrow, when it would be Norm who pulled up just before six at Priest's Lodge and Southgate, and they would probably say they wondered what that lucky dog Tiptree was doing probably snuggled up in bed, still asleep.

But she was home, now, at Jackmans Cottage, so why was she thinking about what they were doing at Southgate?

Nan knocked on the door of the signals office, calling, 'It's me, Morrissey. Open up, Sergeant?'

'Good heavens. Morrissey. Come inside, and explain yourself. You should have been here to go on duty with the late shift, and it's nearly ten!'

'Trains, Sergeant. Sorry. But I got my leave pass stamped.'

She had. They both had! at the RTO's office on Derby station and again, at Lincoln.

'So how did you get here, from the station?' Sergeant James was still suspicious.

'The bod in the RTO told me there was an Army transport outside, taking a draft of soldiers to Wragby, and I should try fluttering my eyelashes at the driver, then he might give me a lift part of the way.'

'And did he?'

'Yes, Sergeant. I was lucky. He dropped me off

at Priest's. And I'd give a day's pay for a mug of tea? Can I make one, please?'

'Oh, all right, then. The shift is nearly over, anyway. Have you eaten, Morrissey? The cookhouse won't be open, if you haven't, and I don't suppose the NAAFI will have anything to offer.'

'It's all right, Sergeant. Mrs Lawson gave us egg sandwiches for the train, and an apple. A hot drink is all I need.'

'Did Chas manage to get back to camp?' Evie asked, knowing how miserable Nan would be.

'No problem. There were eight of them for the aerodrome, and there was a transport waiting for them.'

With a very attractive WAAF driver, Nan thought, switching on the kettle, wondering if she dare fill the hotwater bottle Chas's mother had given her.

'Want a cup, Sergeant?' she called from the kitchen. 'And will it be all right if I fill my hottie? I've got it here, in my kitbag.'

'No need,' Monica James, standing arms folded in the doorway, said. 'There's an electric kettle at Southgate, now.'

'A real kettle? Does it work?' Nan demanded, eyes wide. 'Where did you nick it from, then?'

'No one er *nicked* anything. As a matter of fact, the Yeoman found two that Heronflete didn't need and very kindly gave them to us. And keep your mouth shut, Morrissey, or we'll all be in trouble – including the Yeoman. OK?'

'Not a word, Sergeant,' Nan whispered, spooning a tiny amount of tea leaves into the small, cream enamelled pot, thinking of the kitchen at Gardener's Cottage and drinking tea from the fluted white china mugs, and already missing Chas so much that it was like an ache inside her. And they'd only had time for a snatched goodbye kiss because she'd had to hurry to the Army transport before it drove away.

'See you, darling,' Chas had called. 'Same time, same place tomorrow night – unless . . .'

Unless they were flying, Nan thought, wishing with all her heart she would hear the cough and sputter of Boadicea's engine at a little before half-past seven tomorrow night. She wrapped her cold fingers around the thick earthenware mug, then went to sit at the teleprinter.

'Been busy?' she asked. 'Much traffic?'

'No, and only ten minutes to go, thank goodness. You'll be ready for bed, Nan?' Evie smiled.

'Reckon I will.'

But for all that, she couldn't wait to tell Evie that Chas had asked her to marry him and that she had said yes, and that all that remained was for her to write to Auntie Mim. Evie would help her with the letter, and if Chas didn't turn up tomorrow night, Evie would be there to tell her that he would be all right, and how about them going to the NAAFI and queuing for their cigarette ration?

Only five apiece, and neither of them smoked,

but how much tea or sugar, or even milk could be exchanged for ten ciggies if you knew where to look, Nan thought, so they could make hot drinks to order at Southgate?

The green baize door opened and the Yeoman arrived to take over the shift.

Nan smiled at him and wondered if she should thank him for the kettle, then thought better of it as she saw the warning in Monica James's narrowed eyes.

There was a thump on the outside door. Private Fowler was there to drive them back to their billets. And he would be there a few minutes before six in the morning, to take them on early shift.

Back in the old routine. How much she missed Chas, Nan thought, rinsing her mug under the kitchen tap. And how very much she needed to tell Evie about everything, and that Nan Morrissey had a fiancé. Dear Evie, who understood what it was like to be deeply in love.

Carrie awoke and squinted into the darkness, wondering if she really was home. Then the feel of the eiderdown and the softness of the mattress assured her she was and she groped for the light switch at her bedside, blinking in the sudden glare, bringing the clock face into focus. Five-twenty, her usual waking-up time. She smiled smugly, switching off the light, plumping her pillows, snuggling the blankets up to her chin.

She was home, sleeping in her own room

beneath the eaves, and she could lie here all day if she wanted to. But you didn't waste your leave lying in bed and besides, there was church this morning. Eucharist at eleven, and you-know-what.

She pushed the banns from her mind and thought instead about what she would wear, and it took no time at all to decide on her uniform. A quick rub to her buttons and cap badge, and her skirt pressed along the seams so it looked slightly pleated, and much smarter. She was quite proud of her uniform and besides, the village would want to see her in it. Villages were like that.

She closed her eyes, unable to sleep. Sighing, she walked to the window, pulling back the curtains, but it was still dark. There was nothing to do but await the light and the burbling coo of the wood pigeons; lie there snuggled and tell herself how she had looked forward to this lie-in, and how Norman would be awake, now, lighting a cigarette before driving the truck to the signals office.

Southgate would be doing the early shift this morning, and Sergeant James, who disliked the night-shift fug the Yeoman left behind, would be impatient to open the door and windows to air the place out.

And Carrie thought of Lenice, who had admitted to dating a soldier with whom it was wonderful to dance, because he was a head taller than herself – a rarity when you were an unfeminine five feet ten inches tall and had earned the nickname Shortie before she had been in the ATS a week.

And she thought of Ailsa, worried, that when she was at last settling down at Heronflete, her parents were urging her to think about applying for a commission. Stupid, really, because Ailsa wouldn't say booh to a goose, let alone rap out orders to a squad of women.

Carrie closed her eyes and thought about Mrs Frobisher, who was as determined as her mother on the wedding. No! No thoughts about that until after church, when the twittering and questioning would start soon enough. She turned her thoughts instead to Thursday, when she would be twenty-one and would go to see the solicitor in York about her inheritance. It would be good to learn that her father had left her some money, though her mother had flatly refused to talk about it and told her she would know soon enough when she had asked on her sixteenth birthday. So she never again mentioned her father's will, because she didn't want her mother to think she was grasping.

Twenty-one, she pondered. Four days from now she would be an adult and legally in charge of her own destiny. Yet she would still be Janet Tiptree's only child and when she married Jeffrey she would be Jeffrey's wife. Being given the vote had not made a woman the equal of a man and even though it was secret a woman usually voted the way her husband advised.

Yet the coming of another war had changed one thing, Carrie supposed. A woman could now leave home which normally they didn't do – unless it was for something very respectable like getting married or going to university, or to be a nurse. And they could, of course, leave home to go into domestic service, if all else failed.

It prompted Carrie to wonder how many servants there had been at Heronflete – indoors and out – and that when winter came and the trees were leafless, maybe they would be able to catch a glimpse of the front of the house; the secretive part of it.

Heronflete. Away from it for just one day, yet thinking about it already, and she knew that when her seven days were up, she wouldn't mind at all going back there to Evie and Nan and Freddy and Norm, and the Priest's Lodge lot. And that even included Sergeant James, restless as she was for the discipline of barracks, and Nissen huts.

Carrie snuggled deeper into bed, pulling the sheet over her head, closing her eyes, closing her mind to all thoughts so she might sleep again. But she did not, because the bedroom door opened quietly.

'Awake, Carrie?'

'Hi, mother. Been awake since half-past five – habit, I suppose.' She switched on the bedside lamp and saw that her mother carried a cup of tea. 'Oh, bless, you. What time is it?'

'Half-past seven. Breakfast at eight.'

Carrie sat up in bed. Breakfast was always at eight, Sundays.

'You know, mother, it seems all wrong, somehow. Here am I, in my own bed, drinking early morning tea like nothing has changed, yet there are people who'll be creeping out of the Underground in London, and wishing like mad for a tea lady from the WVS to be there with her trolley.'

'The *Underground*? Not a very nice place to sleep.' Janet Tiptree had only once taken a Tube train and vowed never to do it again.

'They've got no choice. Their homes have been flattened in the bombing, so there's only the day centres for them to go to till night time, then they go down into the Underground.'

'What an awful way to live. But how do you know all this? Are you absolutely sure you're not in the bombing, Carrie?'

'I'm as safe as can be – I told you – and I know about what goes on in London because the sergeant in the cookhouse's wife and children are there and he's worried sick about them. Probably feels guilty, as I do, about having such a cushy posting.'

'Oh, I hate this war!' Janet Tiptree drew back the curtains, because the blackout was over for another day. 'And I hate Hitler, for starting it! He was only a corporal, you know, in the Great War. Your poor father was a captain. But your father was a gentleman. Hitler is very common, strutting about with his arm in the air and doing

341

exactly what he wants, making a fool of the British Empire.'

'Well, he isn't making a fool of Stalin. The Russians have started to fight back, and Lenice says the snows are going to start there, soon. That'll make a difference, she said. Lenice is one of the girls I work with,' Carrie hastily explained, 'who takes an interest in current affairs – especially what's going on in Russia.'

'She doesn't have Bolshevik leanings, Carrie?' the elder woman demanded, horrified.

'Well, she's what we would call a bit of a barrack-room lawyer, but for all that, if I was really up against it with my back to the wall, I think I'd be glad to have Lenice beside me.'

'Drink your tea, Carrie.' Janet made a hasty exit. Her daughter mixing with Bolshevik sympathisers was most upsetting, and the sooner she was married – and pregnant – the better it would be for everyone.

She set the kettle to boil, all at once in need of more tea, even though it would be weak, almost beyond drinking, when it came out of the pot. But we would see, she thought grimly, what the day brought! Oh my word, yes!

Carrie was glad she had chosen to wear her uniform. The church was cold and smelled of damp, because churches were not allowed fuel for heating.

Mrs Frobisher was already seated in the back pew and slid along it to make room for them.

'Morning, Ethel,' her mother whispered, and Carrie nodded, and smiled, and mouthed 'good morning,' to Jeffrey's mother, then thought what a cold and gloomy place this was to be married in, and felt relieved that when Jeffrey got leave, which could well be around Christmas, she would be glad she was wearing her warm uniform.

Then thoughts came, unbidden, of the shabby lace wedding dress she had dreamed about, and the stain on the bodice and the soiled hem, and she looked at the cross above the altar and said a little prayer of thanks that it had only been a dream.

Many in the congregation turned to smile at her, and she smiled back, impatient for the service to begin, for the banns to be read for the third and last time and for the usual knot of people who would stand outside once Eucharist was over, and gossip as if they hadn't met for weeks.

She would, Carrie knew, be the centre of conversation – she and Jeffrey and the banns – and when would they be getting married, and didn't she look smart in her uniform?

But it did not happen like that at all. When the service was over, as they gathered the gossipers, on the church porch there was a stunned, almost disbelieving silence amongst the huddle of people outside.

Every eye turned to the sailor who walked down the road towards them, smiling and waving.

Jeffrey! On leave, and the banns read! Carrie

stood in shock, trying not to believe it. But this was no bad dream from which she would awaken, and she stood unmoving as Ethel Frobisher hurried to greet her son.

'What ho, mother – the Fleet's in!' he laughed, kissing her cheek.

'Where on earth have you been, son? I expected you last night,' she scolded affectionately.

'Oh, this and that. Trains late. Had to hitch from York. Hello, darling.'

He held out his arms to Carrie and she went into them, lifting her mouth for his kiss, because that was what was expected of her.

'You never said,' she whispered. 'No one told me . . .'

Yet from Ethel Frobisher's beaming smile and the smirk on her mother's face, she knew they had known all along. They had been playing her at her own game!

'We thought we'd surprise you,' he said, an arm around her shoulders, smiling at the vicar and those who had been rewarded with more than a chat this morning. Caroline Tiptree standing there bewildered, and young Frobisher enjoying the consternation he had caused.

'Welcome home, Jeffrey.' The vicar offered a hand. 'I suppose you will both be at the vicarage this afternoon? Plans, eh . . . ?'

'Afraid not this time, sir. I only managed to wangle a weekend pass. I'm travelling back overnight, tomorrow. But I'll be on long leave, soon.'

A seventy-two hour pass. And half the time spent getting here and getting back to his ship. Relief washed over Carrie, and she dug her hands into her pockets, clenching them into fists because they were shaking so.

'Is your ship in, or something?' she asked as they began to walk towards Jackmans Cottage.

'My ship doesn't go to sea, Carrie. *Adventurer* is a shore base.'

'Like barracks?' She was still bewildered, though the words were coming, now, and her feet moving in step with his.

'No. But my watch gets ashore every other night – it's quite a cushy number, even though it's hush-hush stuff. Tell you when we get home. Have you missed me, Carrie? Your letters have sometimes been a bit vague.'

'Yes – we-e-ll – our place is a bit hush-hush, too, and it's always in the back of your mind that letters are censored. You're always aware that someone is going to read every word you write.'

'So who cares? Anyway, we'll have plenty of time to talk things over before I go back – set a date?'

And Carrie said yes, of course they must talk, that she had wanted to for a long time, and it would be better when they could speak freely. Freely? But Jeffrey would do all the talking and she, Carrie brooded, would nod her head in agreement like a toy donkey.

Then she remembered that Evie said being married should be wonderful and was all at once determined to tell Jeffrey what she should have told him the night *That* happened. Tell him firmly that she hadn't liked it one bit and that she hoped things between them would be gentler, and more loving once they were married.

Married. In that cold damp church, some time in December.

'You're quiet, Carrie . . .'

'Still getting over the shock, I suppose. It's been a long time since I saw you.'

'It needn't have been. By rights you should have been home the first time I had leave. But that's all in the past, now. I believe the mothers have combined meat rations and we're all having Sunday dinner at my place.'

'Nice.' Carrie smiled, aware that Mrs Frobisher had caught up with them.

'Now isn't it a pity that Jeffrey's leave couldn't have been a bit longer, Caroline?' she said. 'You could have been married on your twenty-first, dear, but never mind – a Christmas wedding will be worth waiting for.'

'Yes.' Carrie, on the defensive, thought it best to agree. 'And I've made up my mind to be married in my uniform. Lots of servicewomen are doing it, now. Sort of patriotic, don't you think?'

'I wish it could have been different, for all that.' Ethel Frobisher shook her head sadly. 'I have dreamed, since you both were young, of a big wedding and you walking down the aisle in white on a lovely June day, carrying red roses. But it isn't to be.'

'No, Mrs Frobisher, it isn't,' Carrie said more firmly than she had intended. 'Because you can't get wedding dresses now, and if I just chanced on one, where would I get the clothing coupons from? There *is* a war on, you know.'

'My mother is well aware of that,' Jeffrey flung. 'She *is* a widow, had you forgotten, and her only child in the Navy.'

'I – er – I think I'll wait for your mother, Carrie,' Ethel Frobisher said, uneasily. 'You two go on ahead, why don't you?'

'Happy now, Carrie?' Jeffrey demanded. 'I've been home ten minutes and already you've upset mother.'

'Sorry,' she whispered. 'I didn't mean to, but I'm sick of people going on and on about the wedding. And I might as well tell you, Jeffrey, that both your mother and mine have been a bit sneaky about things. They must have known you'd got a weekend pass, but neither of them said a word about it to me!'

'Perhaps they wanted it to be a surprise – hadn't you thought of that, Carrie? Actually, I rang Mum on Thursday night and she told me you were coming on leave. I used up one of my weekend passes, then, because I wanted to see you and I thought you'd be glad to see *me*!'

'Oh, stop whingeing,' Carrie hissed, then walked, arms swinging, to Jackmans, hurrying down the stone steps, taking the key from beneath the doormat. And why, she demanded of her commonsense, was she still in a tizzy? Was it dismay, or was it anger?

Most probably anger, she thought, as she walked into the kitchen to see a tray, set with four cups and saucers and the best rosebud china, too.

'I'll put the kettle on,' she called as she heard footsteps outside. Then she took off her cap and khaki woollen gloves, tossing them on the table, running her fingers through her hair. And after what had just happened, she wouldn't be surprised if they couldn't all do with a cup of tea.

And oh, damn, damn, *damn!* What a mess it all was, and why was she wishing herself back at Heronflete and lining up, right now, with her mug and knife, fork and spoon for Sunday dinner.

Then she felt ashamed of her pettiness, especially when everyone was so pleased about Jeffrey's leave pass, and reminded herself that no one, not even the two mothers, could force her down the aisle – especially after Thursday. And Jeffrey, she thought as she poured milk into cups, must behave himself so there could be no repetition of what had happened in her bedroom, the night her mother was out, playing cards.

'Carrie, darling.' She felt his lips on the back of her neck and he held her from behind, his arms clasped tightly around her waist. 'Come on – let's kiss and make up. I've missed you, you know.'

'Be careful!' She reached for the boiling kettle. 'I'm trying to wet the tea! And watch it. That's the mothers, outside!'

So that was the mood he was in Carrie thought, tight-lipped, as she stirred the tea in the pot, then covered it with the patchwork cosy her mother had carefully stitched, and which was only used on Sundays.

She leaned against the sink stone, arms crossed, waiting for the tea to brew, letting her thoughts slip back to the stable yard at Heronflete, and what Freddy had said, only last Friday.

'If you're a good girl, Carrie Tiptree, I just might let you have a drive of the Humber when you get back from leave.'

So why was she all at once wishing herself back at Heronflete? Was it because she had not bargained on Jeffrey turning up, unannounced, and did it somehow give her strength of mind to realise she was no longer the apprehensive girl who had left to join the war, but was now someone who could be trusted to drive the long-nosed, powerful car that was as good as a Daimler, Norman had said, and almost as good as a Rolls; have all that power in her hands, though she was as sure as she could be it would only be for a drive around the estate and never, ever, on the road beyond Priest's Lodge.

She pushed all thoughts of Heronflete from her mind and carried the tray into the small sitting room where her mother had already put a match to the fire. Then she returned to the kitchen, stirred the tea once more, trying not to admit that she must not allow such wayward thoughts when her fiancé was home.

'Tea up,' she smiled, and was surprised that her voice was back to normal again and that her hand did not shake as she filled the teacups.

Perhaps, she thought, being in the ATS had given her a confidence she never knew to exist, and that when the wedding date came up for discussion, she would stand her corner, even though the odds would be three-to-one against. And to give herself even more courage, she would think about Evie, and the gentleness in her eyes as she fondled her wedding ring. Wedding ring! They hadn't got around to buying one, yet!

'Had you thought, Jeffrey,' she said in a voice so silkily smooth that it couldn't be true, 'that we're going to have one heck of a job finding a wedding ring before Christmas?'

'How come?' he scowled.

'Because only nine-carat rings are allowed now. Seems that pure gold is a weapon of war, or something, and you even have to go on a waiting list for the cheap ones – or try to get hold of one second-hand.'

'Oh, Carrie, I wouldn't want you to be married with a ring some other woman had worn!' Consternation showed in Janet Tiptree's eyes. 'I mean, it might have belonged to someone who had died, or been divorced. There might be bad luck on it.'

'And those nine-carat rings cost under two pounds, I'd heard.' Ethel Frobisher was equally shocked. 'People might think Jeffrey was a skinflint, paying only twenty-nine and sixpence for his bride's ring.'

'Well – let's worry about that later. First, we'll have to agree a date,' Carrie soothed, realising she was almost enjoying the consternation she had caused. 'And anyway, the vicar blesses the ring, doesn't he? That would take care of any jinxes there might be – on a second-hand one, I mean.'

'Are you sure about this, Carrie?' Jeffrey demanded. 'Are decent wedding rings so hard to come by?'

'Quite sure. And even if all we can get is a second-hand one, it's going to be very expensive. Supply and demand, I suppose. But like I said, we can talk about that later. Let's drink our tea, shall we?'

So after a very shaky start, round one had gone to Private Tiptree, Carrie thought triumphantly. And fingers crossed that she would be able to give a good account of herself if push came to shove and she was obliged to tell Jeffrey there must be no more of *That* whilst he was on leave, so he'd better watch himself, especially if her mother popped out for a chat with *his* mother.

She sipped her tea, looking at Jeffrey who lounged on the sofa with a cushion at his head. His hair, she thought, had been cut far too short and it made his face look even more angular. And then she noticed the fingers holding the cup were stained yellow.

'Jeffrey! You haven't started smoking?' she said, shocked. 'You said you never would!'

'I know,' he shrugged. 'But everybody smokes, now. Can't be the odd one out and besides, we get a ration of twenty a day and all they cost is sixpence. Duty free, they are. HM ships only.'

'Well, I must say the Navy is very privileged. We have to queue in the NAAFI for our allowance, and it's only five a day!'

'Well, the Navy *is* the senior service, Carrie. We expect a few perks. And why didn't you join the Wrens? Their uniform is much nicer than yours.'

'Because there was a waiting list for the Wrens when I went to join up. Seems that every girl wanted in and I might have to wait a year they told me, and since they needed drivers in the ATS, that's what I joined! I don't think Wrens look any better than we do. Their hats are the same shape as the velours we wore in winter, to school!' She was angry; so angry that she was unable to stop herself saying, 'And if you ask me, they look like a crowd of penguins, all black and white!'

'Children! What on earth has got into you both?' Janet Tiptree scolded. 'Does it really matter who's got the best uniform?'

'Not to me it doesn't. I happen to like mine, mother. It was Jeffrey who said –'

'Please!' Ethel Frobisher got to her feet, placing her cup and saucer on the table by her side. 'Is that the way for people who are getting married to behave!'

'No, Mrs Frobisher, it isn't, but I didn't like

Jeffrey saying what he did. In fact, I think it was rather childish of him!'

'Look – I'm sorry, but I've got to go. Dinner to see to.' She held up her hands on mock surrender. 'Are you coming, Janet?'

'Yes.' Flush-faced, she got to her feet. 'And we'll expect you for dinner at one, you two, so I hope you are both in a better mood by then! And Carrie – please wash the china carefully?'

'Yes, mother. It's the best set and you inherited it from Grandma Tiptree. I *know*!'

'*Well!*' Ethel Frobisher made for the back door followed closely by Carrie's mother, shrugging into her coat, making little moaning sounds.

Carrie watched them go, thinking that if her mother was going to have one of her migraines she was welcome to have it at Jeffrey's place! Then, as the back door banged she collected cups and saucers onto the tray, carrying it to the kitchen.

'So! What's this all about?' Arms folded, Jeffrey stood in the doorway.

'Well, for one thing, I don't like you making nasty remarks about my uniform, and for another, you should have let me know you were coming on leave. Why didn't you?'

'And why didn't *you* let your mother know you'd be on leave until only a few days before? Two can play at that game, you know.'

Unspeaking, Carrie ran hot water into the papier-mâché bowl in which the best china was always washed, then tipped a small amount of soap flakes into it, swishing the water into a lather. 'Carrie; I said that two can –'

'Yes, I heard you first time. Two can play at that game, you said, but I don't know what you are talking about, Jeffrey. We're both on leave, so let's enjoy it for heaven's sake and not squabble like a couple of spoiled brats!'

He hesitated, then said, 'Shall I dry,' he said by way of retribution.

'No. Best you don't. They're very fragile so I'll see to them. And I'm sorry I was a bit edgy,' she whispered.

'And I'm sorry I don't like seeing you in that uniform.'

'Then you'd better learn to like it a bit more, because whenever it is that we get married, I'll be wearing it!'

To her credit, she managed to issue the warning with a smile on her lips.

'When will it be, darling?'

'Around Christmas, my mother seems to think.'

'Then she's got it wrong. It'll be either the week before, or the week after. It's usual to let married men with children go home at Christmas. Shall we say the week after, then it'll take in New Year's Eve, as well?'

'Fine by me, though you'll have to let me know in good time so I can put in a request to the sergeant.' She concentrated on the cup she was drying, refusing to meet his eyes.

'Then shall we kiss, and make up, Carrie?'

'All right, but only if you'll promise we can have a talk tonight – a grown-up talk – without starting to quarrel again.'

'Of course we can. Mind telling me what about?'

'About – well, about things and by *things* I mean about what happened the night mother went out to play cards. I didn't like it, Jeffrey.'

There! She had said it and her mouth had all at once gone dry.

'In your bedroom you mean?'

'Yes. On my bed. I don't want it to be like that when we are married.'

'Now see here, old love – what's got into you? It's no great deal, these days, having a dummy run before the wedding. Most of the chaps in our Mess have done it.'

'So you talk about such – such *personal* things with the other chaps?'

'Why not? Haven't you told the girls in your billet that *you* have?'

'Yes, I did. I told Evie, the married one, but it was only because I was upset by what you and I did.'

'And what did she tell you?'

'She said it would be wonderful, if you must know. And I think we should leave this till tonight, if that's OK by you. And Jeffrey, will you do something for me? I wrote to you and posted it uncensored in Lincoln, so will you not say anything about it? Like I said, it's a bit hush-hush where I'm stationed and it's been dinned into us to say nothing at all. Trouble is, mother is determined to get to know what I'm doing, and where.'

'But I already know, Cassie. You're a driver and you obviously can get into town. Wasn't it a Lincoln postmark on the letter you sent me? The rather peculiar letter, I'm talking about . . .'

'Look – I said we'd talk about that later. All I'm trying to say is that where I am based has got to be kept quiet. Even Nan and Evie can't work out what goes on, and they're in signals. Everything they send and receive is in code.'

'So am *I* in signals – communications – and everything I pass is in code and what *I* do is most secret, too. Miniature submarines, actually, but I don't mind telling you, Carrie. *Adventurer* is a real ship, but she doesn't go to sea. She's anchored in a sea loch, in Scotland.'

'So you can get ashore, Jeffrey? Is that why you could get a leave pass so easily? And I thought you'd be at sea, most of the time.'

'So didn't I get a jammy draft chit, then? I always fall on my feet, Carrie. As a matter of fact, there's a pay-phone in the Salvation Army canteen, ashore. I phoned mother last Thursday and she told me you were coming on leave.'

'So why have you never phoned me?' His smile was smug, and it irritated her.

'Why didn't you give me a number to ring you on?'

'Because there's only a phone in the NAAFI, and there's usually a crowd trying to phone home, or waiting for calls. Anyway, I don't know the number.'

'But you've got a mate who's a switchboard operator. Couldn't she give you a crafty call?'

'No, and I wouldn't dream of asking her, not that I'd stand much chance. Our sergeant has eyes in her behind, and ears like radar scanners. She's very strict, Jeffrey.'

'Then you should have been a Wren driver.'

''Look, Jeffrey – what's the point in all this?' she said as softly as she was able, because it was obvious he was trying to get her upset again. 'I'm in the ATS for the duration and that'll suit me fine. I like my job and I like my billet and the girls I share it with.'

'The duration? But what if we have a baby, once we're married? Being preggers would get you out of the ATS pretty quickly, hadn't you thought?'

'No, I hadn't, Jeffrey, but I wouldn't be at all surprised if mother has got it all worked out. She wanted me married so the powers that be couldn't send me away from home to do war work, and now you're coming up with the bright idea that if I start a baby I'll be able to get out of the ATS, and I don't *want* to. I want to hang on in till the war is over. And that's another thing you and I have got to talk about, before I even agree to a date for the wedding!'

She stopped, breathing deeply, because she was determined not to get into another argument.

'Well, talk about the modern woman! And I thought you'd want a family once we were married.'

'Of course I want children, but I want mine to

be born into peace and for them to have nice clothes, nappies not to be rationed. Did you know that babies' nappies cost clothing coupons and you can't get a decent pram for love nor money? And you've even got to apply,' she rushed on, determined to have her say, 'to the Board of Trade, would you believe, for a bed for the little thing to sleep in, once it has grown out of its cot!'

'All right! So you've made your point! No babies till the war is over,' Jeffrey flung, petulantly.

'Yes, but I can't do anything about not getting pregnant, so it would be up to you, wouldn't it?'

'And you don't trust me, Carrie – is that it?'

'Since you ask, I really can't say.'

She met his gaze and held it steadily, and saw that his eyes were narrow with pique and his mouth set tightly and she should have known not to thwart Jeffrey. Her fault, she supposed, but now that everything was in the open, she mustn't give way, or the wonderful freedom she had found in the armed forces would be taken from her.

'Jeffrey – please don't look so put out,' she said as evenly as she could, knowing she should have taken it carefully instead of jumping in, feet first. 'Being married is a serious thing and it's for life, don't forget, and that's why we've got to talk about it – get it right.'

'Yes, I'll grant you that, but you've got very bossy, Caroline Tiptree, since you got into uniform. And very self-opinionated. You've changed.'

'Maybe I have, but we aren't going to fall out,

are we? The mothers are planning a meal for us and we don't want to spoil it by glowering at each other across the table. So let me put this china in the cabinet and see to the fire, then we'll nip along to your place. Friends, uh?'

She took his face in her hands and kissed him gently, just to show there was no ill-feeling on her part. Indeed, how could there be, when another round seemed to have gone to Carrie Tiptree? It was heady stuff and a bit giddy-making. Evie and Nan would be proud of her – Evie, especially.

'Oooh. I've been longing to tell you,' Nan said when their early shift was over. 'Last night I was so tired I just crashed the minute me 'ead hit the pillow. And I couldn't get a word in edgewise this morning, with the sergeant hovering. But I've just *got* to say it, or I'll burst me knicker elastic. Me and Chas are gettin' married.'

'But that's marvellous!' Evie's smile was broad as she hugged Nan to her. 'When? Have you decided, yet?'

'As soon as we can. His mother is pleased as Punch about it, but there's Auntie Mim, see, and she'll have to say yes.'

'But she will, Nan. And getting married is far better than – well – taking risks.'

'Couldn't agree more. But will you give me a hand, Evie, to write a letter to Leeds? And do you think I should write to Mrs Lawson and let her know I've got back, all right?'

'Write to her by all means, but make it a thank-you-for-having-me letter. It's the done thing, Nan.'

'That's what I'll do, then, when I've written to Auntie Mim, and I can tell Chas about it when I see him tonight, fingers crossed.'

'So let's get down to it, shall we? I've got a letter to post to Bob, so we can pop them all in the box in the NAAFI where you can buy me a big mug of cocoa, Private Morrissey – by way of favours rendered.'

And Nan smiled broadly and happily and said wasn't she the lucky one, and if she had been blessed with sisters they would have been exactly like Evie and Carrie.

'I'm so happy,' she whispered, feeling all at once tearful. 'Nothing is going to spoil it, is it Evie?'

'Why ever should it, you old softie? It isn't a sin to be happy and in love, and I'm living proof of it. So get your writing pad out, and let's tackle the letters, then you can tell me all about your leave.'

And Nan wondered what she had done to deserve being billeted in Southgate Lodge with Evie and Carrie.

Why, they had even got a kettle!

FOURTEEN

'For goodness sake Carrie, go upstairs and take off that clobber. I've had enough of uniforms for one day,' Jeffrey demanded after lunch, when they'd returned to Jackmans.

'OK. So I know yours is a bit old-fashioned, but mine is very comfortable,' Carrie retorted, nose in the air. Then, by way of meeting him half way, she unbuttoned her jacket and draped it carefully on the back of a chair and began to roll up her sleeves to her elbows as they always had to, when jacketless. And anyway, she wasn't going upstairs for anything – not when her mother was still at Jeffrey's place.

'When did I ever say my gear was old-fashioned?' He stretched his feet to the fire, then clasped his hands behind his head in a relaxed pose.

'I can't remember when but I think it was in a letter when you first joined up and had just got your kit. You said everything went over your head like a horse's harness. Vest, then collar, then long-sleeved top. And you said the bottoms of your trousers flapped when you walked. I felt quite sorry for you.'

'Then don't. And I don't wear trousers. They're bell bottoms, and once you've got the hang of walking in them, they don't flap. And I thought you and I were supposed to be having a talk about getting married – and all that jazz.'

'*That jazz*, is very important to me, Jeffrey. I want us to be absolutely sure we are doing the right thing. It isn't any use talking about it when we're married. If anything went wrong it would be too late, then – and nothing must go wrong,' she said, earnestly.

'So what is really bothering you, Carrie because I don't understand you. You were willing enough for us to be engaged. Was it that you just wanted a ring on your finger, like most girls do?'

'No, it wasn't! You asked me to marry you and I said I would, so you bought me a ring, which is what usually happens.'

'Then why, all of a sudden, are you dithering about setting a date? You still want to, don't you, or has something happened to make you change your mind? Another bloke, perhaps?' He flung, bluntly.

'No.' There isn't anyone else. And I did expect us to be married, once you gave me a ring, but something *did* happen, Jeffrey, which I didn't like.'

'I know what you mean, but I thought you

wanted to! Now you're going on about it as if I'd raped you! Grow up, Carrie! There's a war on and things like that do happen!'

'Rape?' She got to her feet and stood, hands on hips, looking down at him, which made her feel a little better. 'But I agreed to what we did, so it couldn't have been. But when we'd done it, I found I didn't liked it. It was too businesslike, sort of, and I'd always thought that when it happened there'd be kisses and cuddles and things, beforehand.'

'See here, dammit, all we seem to have done since this morning is argue.' He jumped to his feet, and walked to the window, hands in pockets, staring out. 'Maybe it would have been better if I hadn't come on leave.'

'Your words, Jeffrey, not mine.' She made no effort to stand beside him. 'But perhaps if you'd let me know beforehand, it wouldn't have been such a shock.'

'Shock!' He spun round to face her, his cheeks flushed angrily. 'Is suddenly seeing me shocking, like I'm a vampire or something? Damn it all, Carrie, you and I grew up together and as far as I'm concerned – and my mother, too – it was always on the cards that you and I would make a go of it, one day.'

'Yes. I think my own mother was of the same opinion. But this is a tiny village – a hamlet – and there's never been a lot of choice for either of us, has there?'

She knew what she was saying and that it was hurtful, but still she could not stop herself saying it.

'You're quite right, my dear. Only yourself and three lads – two, actually, once Todd Coverdale left.' He did not turn to look at her but she could feel his anger; see it almost, from the set of his shoulders. 'But for all that, you did give me the impression that you loved me, Carrie.'

'Loved? Love – I still do – but mother will be home, soon, and I don't want her to see us like this. I'm sorry if I seem to have hurt you, but I didn't mean to. It's just that we've got to talk – tonight. Mother likes to have the wireless on, Sunday nights, so I don't think she would mind if we went out for a walk. And Jeffrey, getting married to you doesn't worry me, but what happens after the wedding *does*. And it's that we've got to straighten out, not whether we want to get married or not. Please try to understand?'

'Ha! You seem, since you joined up, to have got very peculiar views on marriage that you never had before – like you've been having heart-to-hearts with your girlfriends. What have they been telling you, Carrie?'

'They haven't told me anything! Nan isn't eighteen till November, so she doesn't qualify to give advice, even if I'd asked for it. But Evie is a married woman – happily married – and it was her I talked to.'

'And your Evie put you off me, it seems!'

'No. I was the one with doubts. Evie told me that being married is wonderful. It was she who said I should tell you I was worried about certain things and that she was sure everything would come all right if we talked it over. Evie wasn't playing devil's advocate. She loves being married.' She went to his side, laying a hand on his arm. 'Don't let's quarrel, Jeffrey? Please?'

'Oh, all right, but I'm damned if I can understand you, Carrie. I've come home to a stranger, truth be known.'

'No. You've come home to a woman who is seeing a bit of the world around her – and is accountable only to herself! And in a couple of days, I'll have come of age and I'll be able to make my own decisions.'

'You've made me very much aware of that, Carrie. And when the great day comes, are you going to write me a Dear John letter and give me my ring back?'

'Oh, don't be so grumpy. We had a lovely meal at your mother's. She was so happy to see us together at last. But you travelled overnight and you're tired. Smile for me, please?'

With her forefingers she lifted the corners of his mouth, but he jerked his head away.

'You're right. I *am* tired. Think I'll get my head down for an hour.'

'Good idea.' She plumped the cushions, making a pillow of them. 'Shall I get a blanket for you?'

'No thanks.' He had the grace to smile. 'But if I snore, shake me, will you?'

And she said she would, then kissed his cheek, leading him to the sofa, telling him to close his eyes.

'Go to sleep,' she said softly.

And please, she pleaded silently, wake up in a better mood, because if you don't Jeffrey, heaven only knows what will happen.

'Half-past five,' Evie said as she and Nan posted their letters in the box in the NAAFI. 'The cook-house'll be serving supper, soon. What say we go back to Southgate and get our mugs and eating irons? We'll be first in the queue, if we shift ourselves.'

And Nan said it was a good idea, but why didn't they have a stroll around the buildings before it began to get dark, and talk about her leave and the lovely time she'd had at Gardener's Cottage.

'Fine by me, but we'd better keep a lookout near the stable block, for Cecilia,' Evie teased.

'Garn! It isn't the hauntin' season, yet,' Nan laughed. 'On my birthday, that ghost is supposed to be around.'

And she didn't have to be afraid of the spirit of a poor walled-up nun, Nan reasoned, when Chas's love was with her every minute of the day and night. Sergeant Charles Lawson who would be waiting at Priest's Lodge tonight, at half-past seven.

Nan wondered if she should tell Evie about the manor and that Chas wouldn't be short of a pound or two when he was twenty-one, but decided against it, for the time being. Right now all she wanted to do was say his name, over and over again. Chas – her fiancé.

'I think,' she said as they walked past the cook-house, 'it's going to be bubble and squeak for supper. Can't you just smell the cabbage?'

'Mm. It's Carrie's favourite. Wonder what she's doing, right now?'

'Oh, bein' made a fuss of by her doting mother,' Nan remembered how wonderful being fussed over by Mrs Lawson had been.

'All mothers fuss,' Evie laughed, 'especially when it's an only child.'

But for all that, she hoped Mrs Tiptree wasn't trying to push her daughter down the aisle until she knew that that was what she really wanted. And she would bet her stripe, Evie thought, that Carrie had doubts about a lot of things because she didn't, not by a long chalk, seem to like acting the part of a starry-eyed bride-to-be who might well be married at Christmas.

A pity, really, because Carrie was a lovely young woman – pink-and-white pretty with corn-coloured hair and deep blue eyes. It made Evie wonder just how many men she had dated – or been allowed to date – before she got engaged to Jeffrey. Not a lot, she shouldn't wonder.

'Is Chas going to buy you a ring, Nan?'

'Nah. He did mention it, but I told him I didn't want one. After all, you can't get them in the shops, now, nor wedding rings, 'cept nine carat ones.'

'And you'd like a decent one, Nan?'

'Ar. G'way! I'd marry Chas with a curtain ring! But we'll talk about it tonight, probably. He gets a weekend pass in about six weeks – aircrew get extra leave passes – so we might be married then, with a special licence. But I daren't think about it, Evie. I mean – what happens if me Auntie Mim says I'm too young?'

They skirted the stableyard, and waved a hand to Norman, who was working on the pick-up truck.

'Now why should she? We wrote her a very nice letter, and sensible, too. If she read between the lines, she would understand you love each other very much and don't want to do anything – well, you know – that could land you . . .'

'In the family way,' Nan supplied, matter-of-factly. 'Chas wouldn't let that happen. He isn't out for what he can get, like some blokes. Anyway, he's under-age, like me. He won't be twenty-one till Boxing Day, but Mrs Lawson is on our side. She said it would be nice – me havin' no family, like – if I could get married from Gardener's Cottage. I've fallen on me feet, there. Don't reckon I'll have any mother-in-law trouble!'

And Carrie laughed, and crossed her fingers and hoped with all her heart that nothing would happen to stop Nan and Charles being married when they were both so young and in love, and that a letter would soon arrive from Leeds with good news in it.

Because surely Auntie Mim would say yes?

Carrie put her uniform on a hanger, then hung it on the peg behind the door beside her dressing gown. The buttons needed polishing and she would sponge and press it, she decided, before she put it on again when her leave was over.

She pulled on grey, pin-striped trousers and a cornflower-blue jumper, which her mother said made her eyes look bluer than ever. Then she dabbed her nose with powder and put on lipstick, realising it was almost used up and wondering where she would get a replacement. In York, perhaps, on Thursday when she went to see the solicitor? Might she wear her uniform, because people behind counters seemed extra kind to those in the armed forces; people behind driving wheels, too, who always stopped at the roadside in answer to a jutting thumb.

She ran her fingers through her hair, wondering if she should make an appointment to have it trimmed, when she was in York. It was getting long, and she didn't want Sergeant James to have to remind her that her hair was touching her collar.

She walked quietly to the sitting-room where Jeffrey lay asleep. His hair was ruffled and he was in need of a shave, which made him look strangely vulnerable. Could Evie have been right? Perhaps the night it happened had been Jeffrey's first time too, and Carrie knew that if he admitted it was, she would be more understanding of the way it had been. She might begin to hope that things could even get better, once they were married. After they'd been honest with each other when they talked, that was.

Being married might turn out to be very nice, she thought, though she hoped they would not spend their honeymoon at his mother's place, nor at Jackmans cottage, and wondered if Jeffrey would agree to find a small hotel, somewhere. Not at the seaside, because since the invasion scare, most beaches were trailed with hoops of barbed wire and some, she had heard, even had mines laid on them. And London would be out of the question because of the bombing, so how about Scotland, even though it would be very unromantic to travel there on a crowded, dusty train.

It was then that she thought of the car, standing in the garage at the bottom of the garden. Her mother refused to even try to drive it so surely there must be unused petrol coupons tucked away, somewhere?

Tomorrow, she and Jeffrey would have a look at it, and hope the battery had not gone flat after standing so long. It pleased her to think she knew quite a lot, now, about what could go wrong with motors. Freddy and Norm had seen to that.

All at once the prospect of driving away on their honeymoon, trailing old boots and showered with confetti, did not seem so dismal a thought. Could she, perhaps, be coming to terms with being married – the private, what-happened-after-the-wedding part of it, that was. If Jeffrey would promise to be romantic and loving when they went to bed together, maybe then it could be every bit as wonderful as Evie said.

'Caroline?' Her mother, hanging up her coat. 'Well, that's got everything washed up and seen to. I enjoyed dinner. The same old rationed ingredients, of course, but I always enjoy a meal someone else has cooked, no matter what. Where is Jeffrey?'

'Ssssh.' Carrie put a hand to her lips, pointing towards the sitting-room door. 'Asleep on the sofa. Don't think he got any sleep on the train, last night.'

'Poor boy. Such a long way to come for just two days with you. Have you had a chance to talk about the wedding, yet?'

'It won't be at Christmas. Married men with children get the Christmas leave mother. But it won't matter when, and we'll try to give you as much notice as we can. And a quiet wedding, if you don't mind. I know you and Mrs Frobisher would have liked a big affair but there's a war on, so nothing can be the same. And think of the money you are going to save.'

'It isn't a question of pounds, shillings and pence when your only child gets married. Your father made good provision for me, and I've been able to put money away. But now the pair of you have managed to be home together at last, perhaps you can get things settled before Jeffrey has to go back to his ship.'

'We'll try to. He's getting the six p.m. Glasgow train from York. Actually, it looks like being a decent evening – we might go out for a walk. You don't mind, mother?'

'Not at all! You must get as much time alone as you can,' Janet Tiptree smiled benignly. 'But you'll miss Jeffrey. What will you do with yourself when he's gone?'

'Oh, there's plenty to keep me occupied. My hair needs a trim and I shall have to see Mr Chambers in York. He must be getting on a bit. Is he still working?'

'Solicitors practise, dear, they don't work. And he had no option but to carry on when his son was called up. But I believe he has a lady assistant. His sister's eldest daughter, so at least they're keeping things in the family. Not that I like dealing with women in legal matters. A man is far more dependable – and understanding – than a woman, to my way of thinking. Still, it's your inheritance, so it will be up to you who you choose to deal with.'

'Of course, mother. But I'm sure the lady will be well qualified to see to things, if Mr Chambers is busy. Take me, for instance. I can hold my own now in the motor pool when it comes to engines, that is. And talking about cars, I'll have to take a look at ours. It hasn't been on the road for months and the battery will probably be as flat as a fluke!'

'You know I don't like driving, dear. I'll agree it was a good idea for the car to be left in the garage in summer and to use the bus, or walk or cycle when we could, to save petrol coupons for the winter. And there are ten coupons – ten gallons of petrol, Caroline – going to waste in my desk.'

'Then if the car is all right, how about me taking you for a drive somewhere nice, later on in the week.'

'This is October, dear, and not nice weather for day trips. And are you sure you can do what is necessary? Wouldn't it be better if I rang the garage and asked them to send someone to have a look at it?'

'Mother! Ringing the garage isn't on, these days! Probably both the mechanics have been called up, anyway. Trust me, why don't you? Corporal Finigan has taught me a lot. I can do an oil-change and all sorts of things.'

'But is that right? That kind of work should be done by a man. What about your hands, and your ring, too? I hope you don't get it covered in oil, or risk damaging it?'

'I don't. When I'm doing anything mucky I take it off and hang it round my neck with my dog tags – er – my identity discs – so there's no need to worry. I only wear it, actually, when I go out,' Carrie offered.

'You go *out*? But you're engaged to be married!' Janet was shocked.

'Yes, I go on trips to town and to dances. We all do. Even Evie, and she's married. We didn't become nuns when we joined up, though neither Evie nor I go on dates with men. But this is 1941, don't forget. Women are emancipated, now.'

'*Emancipated!* Where have you learned such nonsense? Certainly not from me! When I was your age, all a young woman wanted was to meet Mr Right and have her own home and children.'

'Well, I don't want children – not till the war is over.'

If Carrie had blasphemed or sworn in her mother's kitchen on a Sunday afternoon, she could not have shocked her more.

'Don't want children! But you take what the good Lord sends, Caroline, as I did. I had to be content with just one. But deciding how many babies you have and when smacks of birth control which isn't nice. Only common women know about *that*.'

'Ssssh, dear, or we'll wake Jeffrey,' Caroline said softly. Not that she was at all worried about interrupting his sleep, but she didn't want to talk about not having babies, now that she had made the matter perfectly clear to Jeffrey. 'Now, I'm going out to bring in the coal and logs. Are we going to bank down the kitchen fire, or let it go out?'

'Let it out,' Janet said weakly. 'And only about six small pieces of coal. The ration isn't due till the first of next month, so we'll have to eke out with logs, till then.'

'OK. Message received and understood!' Carrie smiled. 'And why don't you pop into bed and have a little nap? I'll wake you up in time for the six o'clock news – with a nice cup of tea, shall I?'

So Janet Tiptree allowed herself to be led, sighing, to the staircase door, all the time wondering what had become of her daughter since joining the Auxiliary Territorial Service, and when she was going to marry and settle down and start a family. A Suffragette, that daughter would have been, had she been born earlier.

'Thank you, Caroline,' she said softly. 'It is good to have you home. I have missed you so much.'

'I've missed you too.' She laid an arm round the drooping shoulders, guiding her mother to the bed. Then she hurried downstairs, wondering how anyone could tell such bare-faced lies on a Sunday afternoon, because come to think of it, she had missed her mother very little and only thought about Jackmans Cottage when the longing for the sight of a glowing fire or tea in china cups got the better of her.

First fill the log basket, then place six small lumps of coal in the scuttle as directed. After which you can spread the Sunday paper on the kitchen table and read it from end to end, which won't take a lot of time. Now, newspapers were rarely ten pages in all. Newsprint was in very short supply which meant that these days you didn't get very much for your penny.

And when she had caught up with the war, checked the time at which blackout curtains must be drawn, she'd read, yearningly, in the small amount of space allowed for advertisements, what a beautiful pair of court shoes she could purchase from Lilley and Skinner, Oxford Street, WI for one pound, nineteen shillings and eleven pence – plus five clothing coupons, of course.

Clothing coupons. Rumour had it you could buy them on the blackmarket for five shillings each, which would make your shoes very expensive indeed.

So when she had accepted that members of the armed forces were not given clothing coupons and that her brown leather, flat-heeled shoes were the only type of footwear available to her for the duration, she would close the back door behind her and walk up the lane whilst it was still light, to gaze out over the cow pasture to where fields had been harvested of wheat, and ploughed over. And she would lean on the field gate and think about the day past and of Jeffrey coming on leave, and what they would talk about tonight now that she had made it clear she wanted to stay in the ATS until the day war ended, be it for two years, or three.

This was a picture she would carry back to Heronflete with her, just as she had stood at the very same gate in May, and seen sprouting wheat and hawthorn hedges blossoming white and the blue haze that carpeted the far away wood. View from the Gate would she call her mind's picture? And her mind, unwilling, recalled spring, daffodils, and Todd, long gone.

Oh! Stop your brooding, Carrie and get yourself outside and some fresh air into your lungs! And because she had kept a check on the shifts, she would allow herself just the briefest thoughts of Nan hurrying towards Priest's Lodge at a little before half-past seven tonight, and Evie making for the NAAFI to post her letter to Bob.

Why did she miss them both, so?

At the field gate, Carrie focused her eyes on the pheasants feeding in the far corner. Silly things, she thought. Get yourselves under cover. Don't you know the shooting season has started? Didn't they know there was a war on and that people with more money than sense would pay black-market prices for game birds which weren't on the official meat ration. She let her mind imagine a plump young cock pheasant, roasted in butter and served with bread sauce. But if you were lucky enough to be offered such a luxury, there was no way you could butter-roast it when the ration for one person for a week was only two ounces.

No more hot buttered toast, now, dolloped with home-made marmalade for Sunday breakfast. No more milky coffee, because civilians only got a half-pint of milk a day and coffee beans had disappeared from the shops. And what about rashers of farm-cured bacon, and how long was it since her mother had asked, 'One fried egg dear, or two?'

She thought longingly of pre-war, pre-rationing breakfasts and wondered how people like her mother and Jeffrey's mother managed on the small amounts of food they were allowed each week. Four ounces of sugar; two ounces of margarine and two of butter; two ounces of lard, one egg and four-teenpence-worth of meat from the butcher. They ate far better in the cookhouse at Heronflete, Carrie thought. The needs of the armed forces took precedence over civilians; even a long-distance phone call was hard to get, because the war and Civil Defence had first call on the phone lines. Poor civilians. They were having a rotten time – especially those living in places getting bombed night after night.

'*Aaah!*' She jumped as a hand touched her arm. 'Jeffrey! What on earth are you doing, creeping up on me like that!'

'I *wasn't* creeping. You were miles away, looking soulful. What were you thinking about?'

'About food, actually and how little civilians are allowed. And I was remembering buttered toast, in peacetime. You haven't had a very long sleep.'

'No. Woke up and there was no one around, so I decided to get a spot of fresh air.'

'Well, there's plenty of it here. The wind is coming from the north-east and there's a smell of Siberian snow, on it, if I'm not mistaken. Soon be winter.' She linked an arm in his. 'It's starting to get dark. Let's go home, and get warm?'

'So do you want to talk, Carrie?'

'About you and me and honeymoons? Yes, I do. We were very stupid that night. Had you once thought that what we did could have got me pregnant?'

'Surely not the first time?'

'That's just not true, but! wouldn't the village have had a field day if you and I had had to get married? They count, you know . . .'

'Small minds,' he shrugged. 'They live in a small world. Half of them don't know there's a war on. But are we friends now, Carrie? I know I upset you, but I was off to join the Navy and – and –'

'And you wanted a taste of life before you went?'

'You could be right. And it was the first time for me, too.' He stared ahead as they walked. 'I should have told you.'

'Perhaps,' she whispered, 'it might have been as well if you had. And Jeffrey, now that we're being honest with each other, please tell me that being married – *really* married, I mean – will be every bit as wonderful as Evie says it is?'

'We can try our best, Carrie.'

'And you won't think I'm being selfish if I don't want us to have children till the war is over?'

'If that's what you want.' He was still not looking at her.

'I do want. And even I know that there are ways and means, and that it's up to you . . .'

'So we'll talk about that, too. Tonight.'

'Shall we go for a walk?'

'But what good will that do?' He stopped walking and turned to face her, laying his hands on her shoulders. 'We won't be able to see a thing. It'll be pitch black, and cold. Pity there isn't a pub in Nether Hutton.'

'Never mind. We can find a quiet corner – unless you'd rather stay in and listen to the wireless. And we'd better get a move on. I said I'd wake mother in time for the six o'clock news.'

She kissed him softly then began to walk, shoulders straight, arms swinging, as if she was a new recruit again, and doing squad drill. But they didn't do drills at Heronflete, though the sergeant would have them at it every day, given a valid excuse.

Heronflete. She was thinking about it again. and it wouldn't do. Here and now was what mattered, and getting things right. She slowed her pace and reached for Jeffrey's hand.

'Darling – let's not have a row tonight, about *things?*' She was willing to give in because she dare not risk another argument then have him leave in a huff tomorrow. Nor did she want to invite the silent reproach in the mothers' eyes. Imagine having to endure five more days of hints and asides and sighs? It didn't bear thinking about. 'Let's take it as said, shall we, that we'll both have to take things easily, the first time? A bit of give and take, sort of, on our honeymoon and getting used to being – well – married?' Then she added in a whisper, 'And you won't mind, terribly, if we put off having a family until the war is over? After all, we won't have a place of our own, and I don't think I want to bring up children in someone else's house.'

She was putting it very badly, she knew, but if they could settle it here and now, they could start to behave like an engaged couple who were going to be married, war permitting, in December.

'OK by me, and anyway, you've already made your point Carrie. Let's leave it, and enjoy what's left of this weekend?'

'Yes, Jeffrey. And bless you for understanding.' She was so relieved that things seemed to have sorted themselves out that she flung her arms around him, and kissed his lips.

'That's better, old love. A bit of passion, and no more of the frosty stuff, eh?'

He kissed her hungrily, and she submitted to the hardness of his mouth and the hand on her buttocks that pressed her closer to him.

It really didn't matter, she thought, because he was going back to his ship tomorrow and nothing could happen in so short a time. She could put up with it, till then.

Put up with it? Did Evie *put up* with Bob's kisses when things began to get passionate between them?

'Jeffrey – we'd better stop.' She pushed away his arms. 'You need a shave and my face is going to get all red, if you don't.'

'OK. Please yourself,' he shrugged. 'You usually get your own way, come to think of it.'

'No, I don't Jeffrey! Give and take is what we just agreed on, so let's not start another argument?'

'Of course we won't. And anyway it takes two to argue, and I'm not going to let you goad me into saying something that's going to start another nark. And you are quite right, darling. I *do* need a shave and a hot bath. Friends, uh?'

And she said of course they were, and tucked her arm in his again then wondered if she hadn't just won round three, or if it would be pushing her luck if she didn't accept Jeffrey's apology, because what he had just said amounted to one, even if he hadn't used the word sorry.

'Better hurry,' she whispered. 'It's nearly six.'

'I was right,' Nan said as they made for Southgate Lodge. 'Bubble and squeak and jam roly-poly for afters. An' the custard wasn't lumpy, tonight.' She looked anxiously at the sky. 'Think it'll rain, Evie?'

'Don't think so, but if it does you'll have to find somewhere dry, won't you? The Black Bull, maybe?'

'Reckon we will.' There must be better places to keep dry than the pub at Little Modely, Nan thought, which was always smoke-filled and never seemed to have anything to offer but mild beer and bitter beer, yet even flat beer became champagne when she was drinking it with Chas. 'Ever had champagne, Evie? What does it taste like?'

'Only once, at our wedding. It tasted a bit like

cider, I thought, but the glasses we drank it out of made it a bit special. Why do you ask?'

''Cause I've never had any. Why do people make such a big fuss about it?'

'Probably because it's associated with special occasions, like weddings, and it's nice to hear the corks popping. You haven't got a crafty bottle stashed away for your wedding, Nan?'

'Nah.' Nan didn't let herself think too much about her wedding because it all depended on Auntie Mim and the mood she was in when she got the letter. 'But I reckon that by Friday or Saturday there'll be something from Leeds, fingers crossed.'

'Then I think,' Evie smiled, 'that she's going to give you her blessing when she reads it. Quite a good effort I think it was, and very honest, too.'

A good effort? Nan frowned. That letter she and Evie had composed between them had been nothing short of a masterpiece that no one but the hard-hearted could have dismissed out of hand.

They were deeply in love, she had written, but both she and Charles (she had used his full name, she remembered) did not want to do anything they shouldn't, until they were married. And she knew she would only be eighteen and people said girls of that age couldn't possibly know their own mind when it came to something as important as marriage but she was old enough, she had added, to know that there was no one in the whole world for her but Charles and since his mother had given them her blessing, couldn't Auntie Mim please, *please* (she had underlined the second please) give her blessing, too? And in writing, if she wouldn't mind, so everything would be legal and above board.

'Do you think they'll be on ops tonight?' She pushed the letter from Leeds from her mind.

'Nan Morrissey, what am I to do with you?' Evie sighed. 'You worry about the weather, then you worry about your Aunt Mim's letter, and now you're having the jitters because Chas mightn't turn up tonight! You're a bundle of nerves, I blame the jam roly-poly,' Evie teased. 'So why don't you get yourself ready and off to Priest's Lodge in good time? And I shall know if he's turned up, because that motor of his makes so much noise that I'll be able to hear it from Southgate.'

'Ar, what would I do without you,' Nan demanded tearfully.

'You'd manage,' Evie said crisply in her lance-corporal's voice, because not for anything did she want Nan to weep. 'And your buttons are in need of a clean, Private Morrissey, so shift yourself, why don't you, or you'll have Chas hanging around outside Priest's and thinking you aren't going to turn up! Don't think that just because he's asked you to marry him you can start being late for dates!'

So Nan swallowed hard on her tears and shaped her lips into a smile and saluted her friend smartly and said, 'Yes, Ma'am!' and ran towards Southgate

Lodge, thinking what a wonderful day May 24th had been – apart from HMS *Hood* being sunk, that was. The magic date on which she had walked into the Albion Street medical centre and been pronounced fit for service in the Auxiliary Territorial Service. The start of a new life, with friends like Evie and Carrie and the Priest's Lodge lot. And meeting Chas and falling in love with Chas . . .

The trouble was, she thought, as she followed Evie into Southgate, that she was too lucky by far and that she had better watch it and not make the Fates jealous by being too happy. So she told herself to wipe the smug smirk from her face and to blink away the stars in her eyes and concentrated instead on the polishing of her jacket buttons and the badge on the front of her cap.

'Thanks, Evie,' she said.

'For what,' the lance-corporal frowned.

'Oh, nuthin'. Just thanks, chum . . .'

She rubbed hard on the brass buttons, because she was so full of love and gratitude and happiness that it just wasn't true, and she wished she knew how to pray; how to say a proper thank you to whoever it was up there who had prompted her to leave Cyprian Court and to volunteer her services to King and Country for the duration of hostilities. And for meeting Chas, too. A very special thank you it had to be for Sergeant Charles Lawson who had become her reason for breathing out and breathing in and who, she hoped with all her grateful heart, would be waiting outside Priest's Lodge tonight. At seven-thirty.

'Good morning,' Jeffrey called, walking down the path that led to Jackmans Cottage garage. 'Trouble?'

'Nothing I can't cope with,' Carrie offered her cheek for his kiss.

'So why are you dressed like that at half-past eight in the morning?'

'Because I'm trying to get the car going.' She was wearing old shoes, her mother's pinafore and a scarf tied turban-fashion around her head. 'And would you believe it, the battery isn't flat. After all that time, I got lift-off first try. Trouble is that I've got a puncture.' She kicked a rear wheel in disgust.

'So what will you do, now, darling?'

'It isn't funny, Jeffrey, so you can stop grinning. I'll change the wheel, of course. The spare is all right, thank heaven. All I need, though, is for you to help me get the car out of the garage. Can you give me a push?'

'But wouldn't it be simpler if you turned the engine on and reversed out of the garage?'

'No, it wouldn't,' Carrie flung. 'A tyre as flat as that one affects the steering. If we push carefully, it'll be all right.'

'So are you sure you can change the wheel,' Jeffrey asked when they had manoeuvred the small Morris car into the yard. 'Those wheel nuts look pretty tight, to me.'

'I know what I'm doing, thanks very much. Actually, if they don't respond to hand pressure, I'll clamp a spanner on them and belt it – the spanner, I mean – with a hammer. That should do the trick.'

'Quite the little mechanic, aren't we.' Jeffrey stood, arms folded and waiting, Carrie thought, for her to make a mess of it.

'I can cope with a flat,' she said shortly, 'and what's more, I don't need a gaffer watching me. You'd do a lot more good if you went to see if mother has the kettle on. I could do with a drink of tea.'

'OK. If you're sure you know what you're doing.' He dug his hands in his trouser pockets and strolled in the direction of the kitchen.

'I do,' she said as pleasantly as she was able.

Of *course* she knew, she thought peevishly. It had been part of her training as a driver and she could do without sarcasm from the Royal Navy. All she needed now was a jack and a foot pump and she would show Jeffrey Frobisher how the Army did it!

She had removed the wheel nuts without having to resort to savagery when Jeffrey returned with two mugs of tea.

'Did you know you've left your ring on the kitchen windowsill?' he demanded. 'In full view for any passing tramp to see.'

'Mother doesn't encourage passing tramps but yes, I left it there because I always take it off when

I'm doing a dirty job. Usually, I slip it round my neck with my identity disk. Don't worry, dear.'

'As long as you're careful. That ring cost a lot of money, don't forget.'

'I know, Jeffrey, but I'm worth every penny of it, aren't I?' She grinned, magnanimous in victory. 'And if you speak nicely to me, I just might run you to York station, tonight.'

'Would you, darling? There and back will blow a petrol coupon – if you think I'm worth it, that is? It might be nice to be waved off, though . . .'

And because she was so pleased about changing the wheel without assistance she lifted her mug and said, 'No problem. Cheers, sailor!'

'Ugh!' Nan shuddered as she gazed at her breakfast plate. 'Once this war is over I won't, ever eat another tinned tomato! If I'd known what they'd be dishing up, I wouldn't have bothered and had an extra hour's kip! And the porridge was awful!'

'Something the matter,' Evie asked gently, because Nan was known for her cheerfulness at all times, and it was not like her to grumble.

'No. Oh, *yes*, I suppose so. For one thing, we're on late shift today so I won't be able to meet Chas and anyway, he'll probably be flying.'

'But you met him last night and with luck you'll be able to see him tomorrow, as well.'

'I know, but tomorrow never comes, does it? And last night was so good that I get fed up when I know that even if he isn't on ops I'll be stuck in the signals office tonight. I want to be with him all the time, Evie.'

'And you will be, old love. Like I always remind myself when I get fed up wanting Bob – this war is going to end one day and we *are* going to win it, an' all!'

One day, Nan thought, was every bit as bad as tomorrow. And last night, when she heard the splutter of Boadicea's engine, it had seemed she was the luckiest girl in the world. She always felt good, when she was with Chas.

Last night had been wonderful. They had decided on the Black Bull and the landlord whispered confidentially that he had cider, under the counter and would they like a drop, for a change? And they talked about the letter she had written to Auntie Mim and that there could be a reply – a favourable one – by the weekend.

'Would you like us to have the wedding from Gardener's Cottage?' he had suggested. 'Mother seems keen on it, and we could get a special licence at short notice, she said.'

They had made such plans and played a silly game of 'What if?' What if the war is over next week, and the shops are full of food, and clothes are taken off the ration, and you can buy as much champagne as you can carry away?

'Then I could have a white satin wedding dress,' she had said.

'Yes, and if things were normal, it would be up to the bridegroom to buy your wedding flowers.

What would you want in your bouquet, darling?'

'Red roses,' she said without hesitation. 'And we'll go to Paris for our honeymoon and hire the best bridal suit in town!'

'But what if it happens in winter? I think I should buy you a fur coat as a wedding present. Would you like that?'

'Not half!' she giggled, remembering the naughty joke about fur coat and no knickers and deciding not to comment on it because it wasn't very ladylike, was it? Not if one day you would live in a manor house. 'Can you afford one?'

'Of course. Once this war is over, anything is possible. You can have two, if you want!'

'So what does a girl have to do to get *two* fur coats,' she replied, winking naughtily, and he said he could think of something without too much trouble.

They had laughed a lot and dreamed a lot last night, Nan thought moodily as she scraped her breakfast into the pig-swill bucket, yet now she would have to wait a whole day – *at least* – before she saw him again and kissed him again.

'Win the war?' she said scornfully, forgetting 'What if?' and last night's passionate goodnight kisses. 'D'you know sumthin' Evie, I'd put up with how long it's going to last, and settle for a letter from Leeds.'

'Friday, don't forget,' Evie warned, 'but it will be worth waiting for when it arrives.'

'You're sure?'

'Of course I am. I composed the letter, didn't I? Auntie Mim will say yes, I know it.'

'Ar. You're a good mate, Evie. I'm dead lucky bein' with you – and Carrie. Wonder what she's doing,' she glanced at her watch, 'at half-past eight in the morning.'

'Probably having breakfast in bed, the lucky dog,' Evie laughed. 'And talking about beds, it's clean sheets and towels today, don't forget, so let's get on with it. And we'll get Carrie's bedding for her, too. Never a dull moment, is there?'

And Nan said there wasn't and arms swinging, shoulders back, she made for Southgate Lodge, the place she called home – when she wasn't with Chas, of course.

And what are *you* doing, Sergeant Lawson, at half-past eight in the morning? Nan sent her thoughts high and wide and hoped that he too, was having a long lie-in and thinking about her, wishing she were there with him and snuggled in his arms.

'We'll have to sweep this path,' Evie said, when they got to Southgate Lodge. 'It's covered in leaves. Don't want the sergeant whingeing about it, do we?'

And Nan volunteered to sweep it, and thought how sad it was that the trees were shedding their leaves thick and fast, and that soon it would be officially winter, with cold dark nights and maybe even snow.

Which made her think of the electric kettle, and

hot-water bottles galore and maybe hot drinks, too, if they would nick tea and sugar from the signals office, and if Carrie could sweetheart some milk out of the sergeant in the cookhouse.

She called down a blessing on the nice Yeoman and wondered if ever he would ask Sergeant James out on a date with him.

Ha! When purple pigs flew over Heronflete and if ever Cecilia did her haunting at the stable block.

'What's so funny, all of a sudden?' Evie was glad to see the smile.

'Purple pigs and Cecilia,' Nan supplied, deciding not to mention Sergeant James and the Yeoman, making for the kitchen cupboard where brush and shovel were kept, herself once more and worries, for the time being, forgotten.

Goodbyes said, Jeffrey pushed his luggage in the back of the car then settled into the passenger seat.

'OK?' Carrie tooted the horn then waved to her mother and Mrs Frobisher. 'We'll be at the station well before six – just in case the train is early.'

'Early?' The joke was lost on Jeffrey. 'It'll be late, like always and you might have to drive home in the dark. Would you be able to manage all right?'

'Of course!' She remembered the last days of her training when she had driven in convoy in the blackout and if she could do that, squinting dry-mouthed at the lorry in front and the one behind her, then driving this nice little car the twelve miles back to Nether Hutton would be a piece of cake. 'Pity you never learned to drive, Jeffrey. Why don't you send away for a licence?'

'Because I haven't got a car, and if I had, it wouldn't be a lot of use to me at *Adventurer*. We're inclined to rely on liberty boats and shank's pony up there.'

'Mmm. And talking about up there, Jeffrey, are you sure you should have let on about what you are doing in Scotland? Secret, shouldn't it be? Careless talk, I mean . . .'

'Look – just because you seem determined to be coy about where you are and what you do, Carrie, I don't think it matters one iota about the midget submarines when all the locals have to do is look out across the loch and see them.'

'But we haven't been told officially that the Navy has midget submarines. Are you sure you shouldn't watch it a bit?'

'Oh, for heaven's sake, girl, they're still doing trials. The Italians are much more advanced than we are in that field. And anyway, this place near Lincoln you're stationed at – what can be so secretive about driving army lorries and cars?'

'I don't drive lorries, there. I'm more or less responsible for the pick-up truck. And as for cars, there's a Humber I'm dying to get my hands on. Freddy – er – Corporal Finnigan, says he might let me drive it, I can't wait. There's a lot of horsepower under that bonnet.

'And don't mention Lincoln to the mothers, there's a love? It was only the postmark on the letter I sent you that gave it away. I was lucky not to get caught. There'd have been trouble if I'd been seen using a civilian postbox.'

'But honestly, darling, is that place so very hush-hush?'

'I don't know. I don't know what goes on in the big house. We guess all the time – boffins, or maybe one of those places where secret agents hang out. And neither Evie nor Nan can make head or tail of it and they work in the signals office. But everything is a mystery, there. Do you know.' she laughed, 'that there's supposed to be a ghost, a nun that walks on St Cecilia's Eve – or so they say.'

'You're kidding?' Telegraphist Frobisher was not amused.

'No, Jeffrey. It's what one of the locals told Evie and Carrie in the pub. And I'll have to watch it, because rumour has it that she's been seen in the vicinity of the stable block, and that's where the motor pool is.'

Carrie slowed at traffic lights on the approach to York, reminding herself to remember where they were because they would be easy to miss on the way back: all you saw, now, was a red, amber or green cross of light since traffic lights, full on, would be a dead giveaway to enemy pilots, it was said.

'Not far to go, now,' she smiled. 'Have you enjoyed your weekend?'

'Of course, but I won't be sorry to be back. They're a good crowd of blokes in the wireless office.'

'I know exactly what you mean.' Carrie thought fondly of Evie and Nan and Lenice and Ailsa – even of Sergeant James, who seemed to spend her days in the signals office and only went to Lincoln barracks when Army needs demanded it.

'And tomorrow, darling, I shall ring the solicitor and ask when he can see me. And I must try to find a hairdresser who can cut my hair. Appointments are hard to come by, these days.'

'Well, I don't know why you don't leave it as it is. I don't like your hair so short. It was far nicer on your shoulders.'

'Yes, but King's Regulations say what the length should be, and anyway, short hair is easier to wash and dry – and there's less risk of getting nits.'

'*Nits*! For heaven's sake, Carrie!'

'No. Not in my billet. But public places aren't very clean, now. Take railway carriages. You can easily catch head lice, there. Anyway, we have FFI inspections – free from infection, I mean. Sergeant James gives us the once-over and –'

'But how demeaning! I don't think the Wrens at *Adventurer* have their heads looked at.'

'Maybe not. But I am in the ATS, Jeffrey.' She shaped her lips into a smile, because she wanted desperately for them not to quarrel. Not tonight, when they seemed to have got things sorted. 'And I didn't know you worked with Wrens.'

'There are a couple, in the wireless office. Quite good operators, actually, but usually they do Port Wave – local stuff.'

'Aaah.' Carrie resisted asking why he implied that Wrens were only good enough for local stuff, and enquired instead if they were very pretty and was it true they could wear black silk stockings.

'I really don't know, darling. I'm not in the habit of looking at their legs. I'm engaged, so I don't chat up other women!'

'Don't you?' Carrie teased, still trying to say nothing that might lead to words. 'And there's me thinking that sailors have a girl in every port!'

He did not answer, folding his arms across his chest, staring ahead into the half-dark.

'Here we are!' Carrie said brightly. 'And in good time for your train.'

'Yes. And watch it when you turn left. There's a damn great lorry on your tail.'

'I've seen it,' she said softly, sliding down the window and making a turn-left sign. 'And actually, there's a Waaf driving it, so don't worry. She won't run into us.'

'Want to bet?' Jeffrey scowled. 'Y'know, Carrie, I'm rapidly coming to the conclusion that women are everywhere, these days. What on earth are they going to do when the war is over?'

'Probably be a bit resentful that they'll be expected to be meek and mild women again, I shouldn't wonder. And there's a spot!' She spied an empty space, concentrating on driving carefully into it and wishing she had not made so provocative a remark and grateful that Jeffrey chose not to answer it.

They stood in silence on the railway platform until Carrie asked a passing porter when the Glasgow train was expected.

'On time?' she repeated, disbelieving, and was told more or less on time which meant it could arrive any time between six and seven. 'Never mind. It gives us more time together.'

'Suppose it does.' He took her hand, pulling her closer, then wrapped her in his arms, nuzzling her neck, knowing that although demonstrations of affection were still frowned upon in public, on a railway platform they could get away with it without too many raised eyebrows.

'Still love me?' he whispered, kissing the tip of her nose.

'You know I do.' She pulled back from him, glad she was not wearing her uniform; even more glad that Sergeant James would by now be in the signals office and highly unlikely to ask her what on earth she thought she was doing! Poor old Monica, Carrie thought almost fondly, wondering if she had ever been kissed in passion, or even stood in a clinch on a station platform.

'And what is so funny?' Jeffrey demanded.

'Nothing. Only thinking about our sergeant.'

'Well, you really do take the biscuit, thinking of your dragon-lady sergeant when you ought to be thinking of me, and how much you are going to miss me!'

'I *am* going to miss you, but I was only thinking that it was a good thing I wasn't in uniform, because our sergeant wouldn't take kindly to canoodling on station platforms – if she were here, that is – and Jeffrey, Sssh!' A signal dropped with a clatter and Carrie strained to see the clock in the half-darkness, because nothing was allowed to be lit up on railway stations now, which made it awkward for travellers when you took into account that station names had been removed in order to deny enemy parachutists details of where they might have landed. 'I think it's coming and it's only 20-past six!'

'Probably a goods train,' Jeffrey scowled as the King's Cross to Glasgow train drew alongside the platform and Carrie backed instinctively from the noise and smoke and steam and the smell of hot grease.

'Look!' She pointed to a compartment slipping slowly past them which had empty seats. 'Hurry, Jeffrey.'

They ran towards the open door, eager for a seat, because to stand for the entire journey was not unknown, nor was the sight of sleeping servicemen, heads on kitbags, sleeping the length of the corridor. Trains had become hot and crowded since war started, and infrequent and almost always late.

'Bye, darling!' Jeffrey snatched up his case and

respirator and pushed his way into the compartment. It was like a game of musical chairs, Carrie thought, following his progress from the platform. And he was lucky. Not only a seat, but a window seat, which meant he could not be squashed in on both sides. He looked up, thumb in the air, and she kissed the tip of her forefinger, then blew it towards him.

Love you, he mouthed, then rounded his lips into a kiss.

Lucky Jeffrey, Carrie thought. At least he would be able to sleep in comfort until Glasgow, though how long it would take him to get to HMS *Adventurer* she had no idea because he had not volunteered the name of the sea loch, nor where 'ashore' was.

She smiled and waved until she could no longer see his face then stood until the red tail lights on the end carriage disappeared into the twilight.

She turned to see a soldier and his girl – or was she his wife? – clasped in each other's arms. Someone on seven days' leave, she thought, then caught sight of a young woman, a baby in her arms, and tears running down her face.

'Can I help you?' Carrie whispered. 'Is the baby heavy?'

'A bit. Thanks . . .'

Carrie took the small child and the young woman dabbed her eyes and blew her nose loudly, trying to smile.

'Embarkation leave,' she said, tears still trembling in her voice. 'God knows when . . .'

'Sssssh,' Carrie comforted. 'Look, love, I've got a car – going to Nether Hutton. Can I drop you anywhere?'

'No thanks. I live close by, but thanks for being so kind.'

'OK, then. Chin up. 'Bye.' She returned the sleeping child, smiling gently, feeling sorry for the young woman who would lie awake tonight, thinking of the husband she might never see again.

Carrie made for the car park, wondering why she was dry-eyed, wondering if, deep down, she was just a little relieved that Jeffrey had gone back to his ship and the weekend had been better than she ever dared hope.

She slumped into the seat, turning the key in the ignition, hoping with all her heart she would never stand on a station platform, a baby in her arms, waving Jeffrey goodbye.

'Damn the war!' she said out loud, wiggling the gear lever into reverse, squinting behind her for the pedestrian who might step out, unseen in the darkness. The blackout was responsible for a lot of accidents, Carrie knew. The Yeoman's wife, for one.

'Damn, damn, *damn!*' she said again, and drove carefully out of the station precinct, waiting for a gap in the passing traffic, her right arm stuck out of the window – as, if anybody could see it, she thought moodily, longing to be home beside the snug fire, feet tucked beneath. She tried not to think of the desolate young mother.

Perhaps, Carrie thought, her mother would go to Mrs Frobisher's house with the news that Jeffrey had caught his train and managed to get a seat, and perhaps, stay for a cup of tea, and a gossip. Carrie hoped so. She really didn't feel like talking to anyone, tonight – not because Jeffrey had gone, but because Evie and Carrie were not there to tell it all to. She missed them a lot; missed Southgate Lodge and the motor pool, and everything about Heronflete, because Heronflete stood for freedom and friends; something she had never had, she thought sadly, until the day she got off the train at Lincoln station, more than three months ago.

She left the city behind her, remembering to look out for the traffic lights, then slowed as she realised there was a slow-moving convoy of Anny lorries in front of her; a long line of drivers who always stuck together so no one had any hope of overtaking them. She knew that. She had once driven in convoy.

She sighed, impatiently. She was in for a slow ride home, and driving slowly wasted precious petrol.

She began to wonder why she felt so utterly despondent, but not for the life of her did she know why, because *that* time of the month wasn't due. She fixed her eyes on the dim rear lights of the lorry ahead and said, peevishly,

'Oh, shift yourself, can't you!' then began to

long for Heronflete, even if tonight Nan and Evie would be working shifts and she would be alone in Southgate Lodge. Or maybe in the NAAFI, where it would be warm and there would almost certainly be a game of darts to watch.

She concentrated her thoughts on York and the solicitor, and finding a hairdresser, because if she could not – hairdressing was considered a luxury trade, now, and in no way essential to the war effort – she would have to ask Lenice, who could do absolutely anything she set her mind to – to snip a bit off the ends.

She arrived at Jackmans at half-past eight, blinking her eyes to rest them from the strain of driving in the dark, kissing her mother's cheek and asking if the ration would run to a small pot of tea.

'I expected you home long before this, Carrie. Was Jeffrey's train late arriving?'

'No, mother. Actually, it left York not what you would call late by today's standards. And he got a seat, too, so he'll be able to sleep most of the way there.'

'And you are missing him already,' Janet Tiptree smiled. 'I can tell by the look on your face.'

'No I'm not. Actually I had to follow a convoy most of the way home. It was a long one, and no hope of overtaking in the blackout. That got me a bit fed up, but it was the young woman on York station I won't be able to forget in a hurry. She had a small baby in her arms and she was very upset, though when I tried to help her she said she would be all right.'

'Well, that what's you get for accosting strangers on railway stations, Carrie. Sometimes they misinterpret your concern.'

'Mother! Her husband got on Jeffrey's train and he was going back from embarkation leave, she told me. I shouldn't wonder if she was thinking she might never see him again. And I wasn't accosting her! She looked upset and in need of a bit of sympathy. We should try to help people, don't you think? There's a war on, and we're all in it, and a few kind words cost nothing!'

'Well, if that's the mood you are in Caroline, I shall go to Ethel's and let her know that Jeffrey got his train all right. If you want a drink, you'd better make it yourself, and use the small pot and half a spoon of tea!'

The back door banged before Carrie could say, 'Be careful in the dark. Better take a torch!'

'Oh, please yourself, mother!' she said instead to the empty room, and riddled the fire with the brass-ended poker and put two logs on the embers, when really only one log at a time was allowed.

Then she set the kettle on the gas stove and ran upstairs to undress whilst it boiled, and felt more relaxed in her pyjamas and dressing gown and fluffy pink slippers and more able to curl up in front of the fire, sort out her thoughts and try, very hard, to count her blessings. And she would not think about the young woman at the station, nor about Heronflete, because thinking about Heronflete would get her nowhere at all. Best think, instead, of her birthday on Thursday and how wonderful it would be to do what she liked – within reason, of course – and not be disappointed that she wouldn't be able to have a party nor get any presents, because there was nothing in the shops to buy, now. No bottles of perfume, nor the camera she had always longed for, and her birthday cards – if there were any for sale – would be of poor quality and wouldn't even come with an accompanying envelope! But for all that, she would be twenty-one, so say it out loud, Carrie!

'Twenty-one!'

She heard the whistle of the kettle and hurried to the kitchen, calculating that Evie and Nan would not be working shifts on Thursday night and maybe she could have taken them – Chas included – to the Black Bull and tried to sweetheart something special from under the landlord's counter and hear her friends say, 'Cheers! Congratulations, Carrie! Happy birthday!'

But on Thursday, there would only be her mother and Mrs Frobisher to toast her with the sherry she knew was hidden in the sideboard cupboard and after one glass, they would talk about December, she was sure of it, and did Carrie really have to be married in her uniform, patriotic though it might be?

Oh, roll on Saturday, and the train that would take her back to Lincoln station, and the bod in the RTO's office ringing the motor pool, and having Norm or Freddy come to pick her up. And on Saturday, neither Evie nor Nan would be on late shift, and there would be so much to talk about.

And it wasn't tea she was in need of, dammit! She took the sherry bottle from the back of the sideboard cupboard and poured a generous amount into a tumbler. Then she tilted her head, took the sherry in three gulps and felt better for it, wondering if she should add a small amount of water to the bottle so her mother would not notice that the level had gone down by at least an inch!

So she rinsed and dried the tumbler, poured tea into a mug, and full of sherry-confidence, she planned the rest of her four days at Jackmans, because on Friday, if there was an overnight train from York to Lincoln, she would take it and spend the last official day of her leave in Southgate, in a state of defiant euphoria!

Dare she? Dare she tell her mother she was needed in the motor pool, because Norm – Private Fowler – was going on marriage leave on Saturday, even though it was a downright lie and his leave not due until November.

She forced herself to think about Jeffrey – very sobering, thinking about Jeffrey – and calculated his train would soon be approaching the slow haul over Shap Fell and he would almost certainly be asleep with his mouth open, legs stretched out in front of him, oblivious to the comfort of the other occupants of the crowded compartment.

It was then that her mother opened the back door and Carrie heard the sliding of bolts and the swishing of the curtain that covered the door, to prevent light from escaping and to block out cold draughts.

'There you are! I decided not to stay long at Ethel's. I like to listen to the nine o'clock news and she refuses to have it on because she says it depresses her. Did you make a pot of tea, Carrie?'

'I did. If you add a drop of water to it, you should be able to squeeze out a cup. And would you mind if I went to bed after the news and read my magazine?'

'Not at all, Carrie. I'm used to being alone, or had you forgotten? And did you put the car away and lock the garage?'

'I did, mother.'

'Then why are you not wearing your ring?'

'Because I took it upstairs for safety this morning. Afraid I forgot to put it on, but Jeffrey didn't notice, so no harm done!'

'And are you in the habit of not wearing it?'

'Yes. I told you so. I sometimes have to do dirty jobs. And don't worry, I won't lose it!' She switched on the wireless, hearing the pips before the news began, checking them with the mantel clock that kept perfect time. 'Here's the news, mother.'

Carrie sighed relief, because only something so important as the impeccably-read bulletin could drive thoughts of her diamond ring from her mother's mind.

'We've got a wireless in the NAFFI,' Carrie whispered. 'Everyone listens to the news. It's more popular than dance music.'

'Ssh!' Janet said sharply, because listening to news bulletins was a patriotic duty, even though sometimes it was not to everyone's liking. But dear old Winston always told the truth. Mr Churchill was to be trusted implicitly.

'Sorry,' Carrie whispered and snuggled into the cushions and closed her eyes and thought about Saturday, and being back at Southgate Lodge. And then she thought about Friday, and if she could find a valid excuse to take the overnight train. And look her mother in the eyes as she lied to her!

FIFTEEN

'I hate bein' on earlies,' Nan grumbled, because leaving a warm bed before six in the morning wasn't a bit nice, especially so since their billet was cold, and if she hadn't put her undies beneath her pillow to keep them warm, it would be absolute murder putting on cold brassière and knickers.

'Yes, old love, but early shift means a free evening don't forget,' Evie called from the kitchen where she was washing in warm water, may heaven bless the electric kettle. 'You won't moan when you meet Chas tonight, will you?'

And Nan said she wouldn't, and suspended her stocking tops then slipped on the serviceable brown shoes that once had blistered her heels, yet now were as comfortable as old slippers.

'Kitchen's free Nan, so hurry up. Norman Fowler is always early.'

Not like Carrie who drove first to Priest's Lodge to pick up the sergeant, then stopped at Southgate at five minutes to six, which meant they took up the shift two minutes before. In time for Carrie to disappear into the kitchen and put on the kettle, Nan thought and this morning, if it looked as if the Yeoman had replenished the rations of tea and sugar, it might not be a bad idea if she was to take a little of each and squirrel it away at Southgate Lodge, with hot drinks in mind.

'Wonder if Carrie will manage to get something to bring back,' she called to Evie. 'She did say she was goin' to try for cocoa and dried milk. Be smashin' if she struck lucky.'

'Yes, and I remembered to post her letter last night. Pity we couldn't get a decent birthday card.'

'Ar, but it's the thought that counts,' Nan said, remembering the good wishes they had sent with *DO NOT OPEN UNTIL 23rd OCT* written on the back of the envelope in case it arrived early. 'D'you realise she might be filthy rich when she comes back off leave. She has money coming when she's twenty-one.'

'She didn't think it would be a lot,' Evie cautioned. 'She thinks there might be money from her father, but all she was sure about was a hundred pounds from her godmother, though not to be sneezed at.'

The remark almost prompted Nan to tell Evie about Chas's family having a carpet factory and a manor house to live in after the war, but she had decided not to say a word about it until Carrie was back from leave.

And then she thought about the hundred pounds

her mother had been given by her father's family – her *real* father's family. Conscience money, that's what, and bad cess to the lot of them she thought defiantly, rolling up her hair and pinning it tightly, because Nan Morrissey was in love and was loved, so neither money nor manor houses nor who you were came into it. All that really mattered was Auntie Mim's letter, and that somehow they could manage to get married on Chas's next leave, even though it would only be a seventy-two hour pass.

'Hurry up, Morrissey,' Evie called. 'That was the pick-up on the way to Priest's. I told you Norman would be early, didn't I? And we haven't made up our beds, yet.'

'So who's going to see?' Nan pulled on her cap and reached for her respirator. 'The sergeant's too busy in the signals office.'

She wondered as she walked to the gate if the sergeant would notice they had cleared the path of fallen leaves and knew that she would. That was how you got to be a sergeant, by having eyes in the back of your head!

All at once Nan was happy again, because just to think of tonight and waiting, fingers crossed, in the lane outside Priest's Lodge for Chas to arrive in Boadicea, made her feel warm inside.

She wondered if the off-side door had dropped off yet. It had rattled something awful on Sunday night, but maybe Chas had fixed it with some wire.

She turned to smile at Evie who was reaching

up to put the key on the lintel above the door, then wondered what they would have for breakfast this morning. Fried sausage sandwiches, perhaps, with HP sauce? Oh, bliss!

'Who were you ringing, dear?' Janet Tiptree asked of her daughter.

'Mr Chambers, but he'll be busy in court tomorrow and Thursday, so I had a word with his new assistant. His niece. Her name is Margaret Dutton, and she seemed very nice. Said she could see me tomorrow at two and that she looked forward to meeting me.'

'Pity you couldn't have seen Mr Chambers, for all that. He looked after your father's affairs, you know, watched you grow up. But nothing has been the same since this war started. And talking of your father has reminded me. It's about your ring, actually. You seem always to be taking it off and putting it on. One of these days you'll lose it. Why don't you leave it at home, and I'll put in my strongbox.'

'If you think I should,' Carrie agreed. 'But I thought you were in favour of my wearing a ring on my engagement finger.'

'And so I am. That's why I think you should have your father's signet ring, now you are twenty-one. You could wear that, instead.'

'But don't you think it would be too big for me?'

'No dear, I don't. He wore it on his little finger

411

– men always did, in those days. It should fit you perfectly. And he initials on it me C T, just like yours, so it would be rather nice if you wore it. Would you like to try it on?'

'Yes – before I go back.'

She didn't mind at all wearing her father's ring. What surprised her was the fact that her mother had offered something so precious. But she wasn't handing over her diamond ring the minute her mother suggested it. Indeed, she had no idea at all why she thought her daughter was not to be trusted with three quarter-carat diamonds and wondered just how much Jeffrey had paid for it, since her mother was making such a fuss.

'What are you thinking about, Carrie? You had quite a faraway look in your eyes. Jeffrey, is it?'

'Actually, no. I was working out the shifts, and Southgate will be doing earlies, so they'll be free, tonight. I was thinking about Nan, and if her boyfriend will arrive in his little Austin. He calls it Boadicea, though anything less like a war chariot you couldn't imagine.'

'How come he can run a car, when he's in the armed forces? How does he get his petrol?'

'It isn't Chas's car. It belonged to a tail gunner who didn't make it back from ops, so they all use it. The first one to scrounge some petrol gets the use of Boadicea. Chas is very fond of the old thing, even though one of the doors is hanging off, and the tyres aren't going to be a lot of use when the roads get icy.'

'It's a very peculiar going-on, if you ask me,' Janet Tiptree huffed. 'Don't they know that petrol has to be brought here by sea?'

'I'm sure they do. And it isn't actually petrol. It's crude oil; nasty and black, though I'm sure the merchant navy lads wouldn't begrudge a crafty gallon of petrol. After all, when those bombers take off, it's evens they won't get back.'

'Well, they know what they're doing, I suppose.'

'Yes, mother. They're all volunteers, like submariners, and I don't think you should criticise our fighting men.'

'Well! If you have nothing better to do than lecture your mother, then I think you should clean your bedroom, Carrie and the bathroom, too.'

Her daughter, Janet Tiptree thought, was getting peculiar ideas since joining the ATS: probably from the girl with the Bolshevik sympathies.

'OK,' Carrie smiled cheerfully. 'And I'll fill the coal scuttle and the log basket. There's quite a lot of leaves on the lawn, too. Think I'll rake them up and put them on the compost. I know, it isn't very patriotic to have a lawn, these days. The government is always going on about it. Have you never thought of growing potatoes on it – digging for victory, sort of?'

'No I have not, and the day I plant potatoes like a peasant has yet to dawn, war effort or not!'

'Entirely up to you,' Carrie said softly, tying on an apron, making for the staircase door, thinking her mother's attitude to the war was a very selfish one and remembering the wife of the sergeant in the cookhouse, whose home and everything in it had been smashed into rubble. Bombs had not fallen here. Her mother had not even heard an air-raid warning.

Fiercely, Carrie stripped her bed then heaved the mattress over angrily. This was only Tuesday. Four more days before she could put on her uniform and leave for the station. Yet how about getting the last bus out of the village on Friday night and the midnight train from York? She wasn't at all sure where she should change, but they would tell her at the RTO's office. A bit of a messy journey she shouldn't wonder but worth it, even if it meant losing a day's leave. And what was wrong with a young woman, she demanded of her conscience, who thought about doing a thing like that and who would have to lie through her teeth, and look her mother in the eyes as she did it? But wasn't her mother lonely and didn't she try to cling to the past with nothing to comfort her but memories?

Saturday morning it would have to be. The early bus out, then the first train she could get from York station. And oh, how she was looking forward to seeing Evie and Nan again, and the tiny gate lodge they lived in, and Freddy and Norm and the sergeant in the cookhouse. And how good it would be to gaze up the drive that led to Heronflete, and still be none the wiser about what went on there.

She winked at Carrie-in-the-mirror and thought

about meeting the lady solicitor and maybe even finding a shop with lipsticks under the counter, tomorrow. And the day after she would be of age, and beholden to no one!

Ten o'clock, and Evie and Nan would have had breakfast in the cookhouse, she pondered, after which Sergeant James would reluctantly leave the signals office in Evie's care and have a slice of toast, a cup of tea and a cigarette for her morning break.

Carrie remembered the motor pool and wondered if the task of collecting the ten o'clock tea had been allocated to Norman, and if the sergeant cook missed her.

And tonight, Nan would be waiting outside Priest's Lodge, listening for Boadicea's clatter which would mean that Chas was not flying, and everything was right with her world.

Lucky Nan Morrissey.

'Good afternoon,' the middle-aged receptionist smiled. 'Miss Tiptree, is it? Mrs Dutton is expecting you.'

'Thanks,' Carrie smiled. 'Sorry I'm late, but I got into a queue for cosmetics.'

'Then I hope you were lucky.'

'I was.' A lipstick and a tube of glycerine and rosewater handlotion. And what was more, the lipstick actually suited her which was more than lucky because these days you took what you were offered.

A door opened, and Mrs Dutton smiled and said that five minutes late was neither here nor there when there was a war on, so she mustn't bother to apologise. And might she say that Miss Tiptree looked very smart in her uniform, to which Carrie replied that people behind shop counters were always kind to those in uniform and that she had lipstick and handlotion to prove it!

'Please sit down. There's quite a bit to do. Would you like to open a bank account with your inheritance? It might be handy if you were to have a cheque book.'

But to Carrie, writing cheques was heady stuff and could well get out of hand, so she asked instead if she mightn't be better putting it in the Post Office?

'Actually, there is quite a lot. Of course, you could put some into your Post Office book, but you seem not to understand how much you have come into.'

'I know there's some from my godmother, though what my father left me I was never told, it didn't seem right to ask.'

'Then take a deep breath, because he left you a thousand pounds which my uncle invested for you and which is now worth –' She searched through the papers on her desk then said, 'Fourteen hundred pounds, actually.'

'Good grief! And I was wondering if Jeffrey and I could afford a house when the war is over. All that money would buy one for us, wouldn't it?'

'It would.' The solicitor was smiling. 'But you already have a house – or you will have, as from tomorrow. Your father left Jackmans Cottage to you – didn't you know?'

'I didn't.' All at once she found it difficult to speak because her mouth had gone dry. Running her tongue round her lips she whispered, 'But my mother lives at Jackmans. Surely it should be hers?'

'No. It's yours, but with the proviso that your mother be allowed to live in it for as long as she wishes. The contents were left to her, by the way.'

'Oh dear.' Carrie shook her head and tried to think of something sensible to say, but when you have one thousand, four hundred pounds, plus a hundred, and a house that was suddenly yours, sense didn't come into it.

'The house is worth quite a lot of money,' came the reassuring words of the smiling lady sitting at the desk. 'It's a unique property. Late Elizabethan, I believe.'

'It is. Built in rose bricks and with a slab roof and twisted chimney stacks. And it's all over beams and –'

She stopped, confused, because if it were really true that Jackmans was hers, it was going to take a bit of getting used to.

'Does my mother know about this?'

'I'm sure that she does. She is one of the executors. My uncle usually offered his clients a glass of sherry but we can't get hold of it now, and you look as if you are in need of a drink. Nor can I offer you a cup of tea, rationing being what it is. But try taking a few deep breaths, my dear. You'll get used to it, in time. And will you be able to come in tomorrow? I'll be able to have all the papers ready for you to sign, and have someone here to witness it. At about three, shall we say?'

And Carrie said it would be fine and that she would go quite mad and blow a petrol coupon and drive in, and was Mrs Dutton quite sure about Jackmans and had she any idea why it should have been left not to her mother, but to herself?

'No idea at all. Nor had my uncle. Perhaps you can talk to your mother about its upkeep – you'll be able to pay a share, now, of the cost of lighting and heating it, and the rates and water rates.'

Pay her share? Of course she would! But talking about expenses to her mother would be quite embarrassing and maybe it would keep until tomorrow when Jackmans would be hers, all signed and sealed. She covered her face with her hands and let go a deep breath, then said,

'You are right, Mrs Dutton. I *could* do with a sherry, though I feel light headed enough without it. Reckon I'd better be careful crossing the road, I'm so giddy.'

'Then if you turn right when you leave here, you'll see a little café a couple of doors down. I'm sure they'll be able to let you have a pot of tea. I'll look forward to seeing you tomorrow.'

'Mmm. And I'll keep away from cosmetic

queues, tomorrow, so I won't be late.' She held out a hand, and said, 'See you at three, sharp.'

The café, two doors down, was closed and in the window a hand-printed notice apologised for the inconvenience, because their allocation had run out, but they would be open on Friday at 10 a.m.

Cafés were always 'running out' Carrie sighed. On the small amounts they were allowed it was amazing they managed to keep open at all, though it was a pity she did not know where the nearest British Restaurant was. There was one in every town, required to serve a non-profit-making meal at a ridiculously low price. Subsidised by the government, of course, and very basic and clean, with wipe-down table tops and linoleum-covered floor.

She held her hands to her burning cheeks and decided against window-shopping until bus time, because seeing something lovely on display and all at once having the money to buy it yet no clothing coupons to offer, would make her even more upset than she was.

She decided against trying to hitch a lift outside the railway station which was a good place for hitching, and sat on a bench to wait until four-fifteen, when the bus for Nether Hutton would leave.

Home a little before five, she calculated, and what would happen now she knew that Jackmans was hers, she didn't care to think about. Mind, her mother had known all along about it. She must have, so why had she been so secretive about it all these years?

She had her reasons, Carrie was bound to admit, not looking forward one bit to five o'clock when it would all come into the open. And thank heaven that tomorrow she must go to York again. On her birthday, it would be, but who cared? She would drive there, leaving at two, to be in good time for the three o'clock appointment, when there would be a lot to talk over and explanations given about what she would be signing. Quite a fair slice it would take out of her birthday she thought thankfully, because there would only be her mother and Mrs Frobisher to wish her well instead of Nan and Evie and the Priest's Lodge lot . . .

You are thinking, she told herself silently and sternly, far too much about Heronflete. You are on seven days' leave, Carrie Tiptree, and you will enjoy them if only for your mother's sake and not think again about going back a day early. You ought to be ashamed of yourself for even allowing such thoughts, and you will behave yourself tomorrow and try to be nice to your mother who must be feeling rotten about having to concede that the house she loved so much now belonged to her daughter – her *wayward* daughter!

The red bus drew to a stop, and Carrie watched the passengers get off, wondering how so many had managed to get on it and how many the conductress had allowed to stand, clinging to the luggage rack for dear life, when a notice to the left of the door stated clearly standing room only for four passengers.

But no one would complain. There was a war on, so complaining about anything was not allowed and branded unpatriotic. And Carrie Tiptree would never complain again, not even when her mother had another migraine or when Jeffrey was more than usually stroppy. Hadn't she just come into more money than she had ever dreamed of and Jackmans Cottage too, even though it looked as if she would live in it for all time with Jeffrey!

She jumped to her feet, slung her respirator, then took her place at the end of the shuffling queue, calculating that she might be lucky and get a seat, probably near someone she knew so she could chat all the way home and forget five o'clock and her mother's angst.

But there was no one on the bus to whom she could talk, so she fished for her return ticket, then let her thoughts roam free and was not at all surprised they took her to Heronflete where most probably Evie and Nan would be in the supper queue at the cookhouse, prior to going on shift at six.

Carrie wondered if it would be bubble and squeak, or toad-in-the-hole with onion gravy – two of her very favourites; wondered, too, if there would be bread and butter pudding with creamy custard (creamy custard being ordinary custard but without lumps).

'Tickets, please,' said the lady conductress, glaring at a young girl who had lit a cigarette, demanding, 'Does your mother know you smoke, love, and do you mind putting that thing out, because cigarettes ain't allowed on this conveyance while I'm in charge. They're bad for me asthmatics!'

'Sorry.' The young girl threw down the cigarette and ground it out with the sole of her shoe.

About fifteen she would be, Carrie thought, and was all at once grateful she was twenty-one, now, and past the gawky age. And oh, my goodness – all that money! One thousand, five hundred pounds. It didn't bear thinking about, though when she had told Evie and Nan, she was sure she would get so great a sum into perspective and not let it affect her life even a little bit.

She smiled at the young girl whose cheeks were still burning from the public reprimand, then thought about what she would say to her mother when she got home.

As little as possible about what had happened this afternoon, she decided. Perhaps if she were to ask about her father's ring and agree to leave her own in her mother's care it would break the ice a little. And maybe when she mentioned that Mrs Dutton had suggested she should share the upkeep of Jackmans, her mother would have a better opinion of lady solicitors.

She gazed blankly through the window and thought again about Southgate, then decided to visit the grocer tomorrow – in her uniform, of course – and ask him for cocoa or dried milk, so they could have hot drinks on cold evenings. And then she thought about the secret heap of coal and the logs in the outhouse and tried to imagine how it would be if they were to risk lighting a fire and how cosy in the firelight. Dear little Southgate. She had not realised until she left it how happy she was there.

The bus stopped and a lady, laden with baskets, got on. Automatically, Carrie got to her feet and offered her seat, because she was in uniform, and it wouldn't do to let the ATS down and sit there whilst an older person was obliged to stand.

'Thanks, love. Bless you,' the lady beamed, and her gratitude made Carrie feel just a little better about her bounty and a little less apprehensive about facing her mother.

She still felt confident as she opened the back door of Jackmans Cottage and called,

'Coo-ee. It's me . . .'

'Hello, dear. I heard the bus,' Janet Tiptree said softly. 'So, what have you got to tell me?'

'Nothing you don't already know, mother. But it seems I have a small fortune – as well as –'

She stopped, unable to say the words.

'As well as this house,' her mother supplied.

'I – I suppose so. But why didn't you tell me?'

'Tell you what?' There was a sharp edge on Janet Tiptree's words. 'After all, child, Jackmans may be legally yours tomorrow, but morally it is mine, and I hope you won't forget it.'

'I won't ever. But what really shocked me was being told I have come into fifteen hundred pounds. I'm going to see Mrs Dutton tomorrow, on my official coming-of-age, and I shall ask her to get hold of a few pounds for me to put into my Post Office bankbook. Apart from that, nothing has changed. as far as I'm concerned. I won't tell Jeffrey about dad's will. Be best if it were kept quiet, I suppose.'

'Of course. As you said, nothing has changed, Caroline, though when you are a married woman, I hope you and Jeffrey will look on this as your home, and live here with me.'

'Yes, but I don't want to plan so far ahead. I'm still trying to take in what Mrs Dutton told me. But I *would* like to talk about dad's ring, or must I wait until tomorrow for it?'

'No. Actually, the ring was given to him by his grandmother on his twenty-first birthday. It belonged to his grandfather, so it is very old and precious and it seems right and proper that, now you are of age, I should give it to you. You *will* wear it on your engagement finger, Caroline, and leave your diamond ring with me?'

'A good idea. There'll be no risk of losing it when I won't have to take it off so often.'

'Your losing your engagement ring worried me, dear, especially as Jeffrey hasn't finished paying for it, yet.'

'Not finished paying for it! You don't mean he bought my ring on hire purchase?' Carrie gasped, shocked.

'No, of course he didn't. But he did borrow the money from his mother and I know for a fact that he hasn't paid her back in full.'

'*We-e-ll.*' Carrie took off her cap and gloves and laid them on the kitchen table, trying not to think that when a man asked you to marry him, you were entitled to suppose he would keep a roof over your head and be responsible for taking care of you. Yet it seemed that Jeffrey had had no such inclinations, especially as he didn't have the price of an engagement ring!

'Well, I mean to say! It's a bit much, isn't it? Tell me – could Jeffrey have had an inkling about what was in my father's will?'

'I don't know, but Ethel might have told him. His mother knew that one day you would inherit Jackmans.'

'You told Mrs Frobisher about it, yet you didn't tell me?' Carrie flung angrily.

'Ethel is my friend and very discreet. Anyway, you were too young to know, Caroline. And please don't adopt that tone with me!'

Carrie took note of her mother's flushed cheeks and the pique in her voice and knew that, twenty-one or not, apologies were called for. Either that, she thought, or a migraine.

'Sorry,' she soothed. 'I wasn't meaning to criticise, but I'm a bit shocked that Jeffrey should ask me to marry him, yet he had to borrow to buy my ring. Unusual, don't you think?'

'No, dear. I suppose he wanted you to have the

best, and your ring is quite valuable. That's why I am so anxious that you might lose it. So shall I get daddy's ring, and shall you try it on?'

'Fine by me,' Carrie said, tight-mouthed, realising that for once her mother seemed to be conceding defeat. 'And I really don't care about my ring – wearing it I mean. I think a plain signet ring will be far more suitable, since I'm sometimes up to my elbows in grease and muck.'

'Then I'll get it now and we'll see if it fits. I have a feeling it will and your father, had he lived, would have wanted you to have it.'

'He was a soldier – I wonder if he'd have been proud of me, being in the army, too.'

'I don't know, child, though since you ask,' Janet Tiptree replied softly – *too* softly – 'I have the feeling that if he were still with us, he would not have allowed you to leave home. Your father was a man of principle and would not have wanted to see young women in uniform.' She closed her eyes and sighed dramatically, which prompted Caroline to say,

'Don't get upset, dear. Go and get dad's ring.'

Christopher Tiptree's signet ring did fit. It bore his initials on a dainty oval centre and did not look too masculine for a woman to wear.

'Let me try it, please?' Caroline held out her hand and was pleased it sat well on her engagement finger. 'There now! I'm sure dad would be glad for me to wear it. And isn't it perfect that we both have the same initials. Can I keep it, mother?'

'Only if you promise not to lose it. There shouldn't be any excuse for you to take it off, Caroline. It's eighteen carat gold, so it should stand up to your army activities better than diamonds. And remember that it was on his finger throughout the Great War. Take care of it, won't you?'

'I will, and I won't ever take it off. It's such a perfect fit that I'm sure I was meant to wear it. Thank you for trusting it to me. I think it suits me better than diamonds. It's a lovely ring.'

She thought later that night as she lay in bed that perhaps she had been too enthusiastic about her father's ring. Could it have been that she preferred it to Jeffrey's diamonds, or had she been trying to let her mother down gently, because of Jackmans? Or could it be she was glad to be rid of her engagement ring and the claim it had on her?

'For shame, Carrie,' she whispered into the darkness, then allowed Heronflete back into her thoughts, if only to compensate for tomorrow and the fuss there would be because of her birthday. And wouldn't it have been great to be with Nan and Evie instead, even if they only toasted it with NAAFI beer, or perhaps at the Black Bull with maybe a crafty under-the-counter gin and lime?

She reached for her torch and shone it on the Mickey Mouse clock that had stood at her bedside ever since she was able to tell the time. And the time was now ten o'clock and Nan and Evie would be waiting with the sergeant in the signals office for the green baize door to open and the Yeoman to arrive to take over the night shift.

Silly selfish little tears pricked her eyes, because she wanted so much to be at Southgate, waiting for Norman to drop off Evie and Nan.

She blew her nose loudly, chiding herself that, until six months ago, this had been her home yet now she was impatient to leave it; leave behind her engagement ring, too.

She thumped her pillows and burrowed into them, thinking about the end of December when she could next be on leave. Then she wondered where the courage she had found the day she signed – *forged* – her mother's name at the foot of the application form for the ATS had gone, and which would return in December, because it would be then she would need it most.

Courage? To be with her when she married Jeffrey, or to be with her when she wrote the letter that would tell them at Nether Hutton she had been refused compassionate leave? And she would be, she knew it, because you were not given marriage leave if you didn't ask for it!

Yet dare she? Dare she lie and deceive again as she did when she joined the ATS? What could be the matter with her thinking if she was already planning not to be on leave at the end of December when Jeffrey said he would almost certainly be having his? Was it because she did not want to be married yet, even though Jeffrey had understood her apprehension about *things* and promised to be romantic and loving once they were in bed together and not to hurt her as he had done that first time? Or could it be that being married carried the risk of making a baby and that, no matter what, she did not want children until peace came.

Yet if she truly loved Jeffrey – loved him as Evie loved Bob and as Nan loved Chas – she should want to have his children and not think up excuses for wanting to stay in the ATS until the war ended.

The Mickey Mouse clock ticked tinnily in her ear, and she pulled the blanket over her head, not to shut out the noise which she had always liked and found comforting since she was a little girl trying not to be afraid of the dark. Snuggling under the blanket was her way, she knew, of shutting out the world and all its problems.

Problems? Just how many problems had Caroline Tiptree, who would tomorrow inherit money and Jackmans Cottage, even if it was still morally her mother's? Fifteen hundred pounds. Just to think of it made her giddy, because so much money guaranteed her independence, though she must ask Mrs Dutton if Jeffrey would have any claim to it, once they were married.

But this was 1941 and women could join the armed forces and had the vote, too! What was hers was her own and surely Victorian laws no longer applied?

Yet Jeffrey must have known that, one day, Jackmans would be hers Carrie thought peevishly, because her mother had told Ethel Frobisher about the will. Jeffrey's mother could have every excuse for matchmaking just as enthusiastically as her own mother had?

She clucked impatiently, groping once more for the torch to find it was almost eleven o'clock, demanding irritably of herself how much longer she would lie awake, fretting about things which might not happen, especially if the Navy didn't give Jeffrey leave in December?

But this was not the age of miracles, and telegraphist Frobisher J would get his leave because there was no reason she could think of why he shouldn't, because things always went Jeffrey's way, didn't they?

'Oh, drat!' She threw back the bedclothes, groping with her feet for her slippers, then walked slowly in the darkness to the door and reached for her dressing gown.

Carefully, she tiptoed downstairs to the kitchen, waving her torch around the room to make sure the blackout curtains were drawn, then switched on the light and, quietly as she could, set the kettle to boil and took mug, cocoa and dried milk from the cupboard.

And when she had made her drink, she would curl up on the sofa in the little sitting room and snuggle into the cushions to enjoy what might be left of the fire, then try as hard as she could to look at things sensibly and reasonably because wasn't she an adult, now – *officially* a grown-up who could do as she wanted within reason – and who didn't have to apply for marriage leave in December – unless, of course, things changed for the better.

She bit on a smile, thinking of the to-ing and fro-ing between her mother and Mrs Frobisher, and the exclamations of horror and consternation because yet again Caroline was upsetting the plans and hopes they had nurtured for years and years by not getting leave, and what was poor Jeffrey to do when he came home in December to be married, and the bride hadn't turned up!

She placed her mug on the hearth, poking the last of the dying fire, then took a small log from the basket, laying it on the hot embers, blowing them carefully to help the log catch fire.

She pushed off her slippers, tucked her knees beneath her, then took a fat, floppy cushion to hug to her as she sipped her drink.

'So, Caroline,' whispered the voice of reason that lately seemed to perch on her shoulder like a bad conscience. 'Just what is all the fuss and soul-searching about? Why don't you accept there will be a wedding after Christmas, and since Jeffrey has stopped being selfish and has listened to your worries with more understanding than ever you hoped for, why don't you remember that from tomorrow you will be a very modern, absolutely independent young woman with money of her own, and even allow that Jeffrey can't be accused of proposing marriage once he learned what was in your father's will, because the idea probably came from his mother, aided by your own mother.' And who on the face of this earth could hold out against two determined women who liked getting their own way? Ethel Frobisher and Janet Tiptree made a formidable couple who could be sneaky with it, when necessity demanded.

Poor Jeffrey, who had probably been prodded into asking her to marry him, even though he didn't have the price of a diamond ring to his name, just as she, Caroline, had been cajoled into accepting that ring and later, had given in to Jeffrey's demands even though she knew what they were doing in her bedroom was wrong.

But wrong or not, they had brought it into the open and she had to admit that Jeffrey had taken it better than she had ever dared hope and that things just might work out all right.

Perhaps, when they were married, they would be like Evie and Bob, who each tried to please the other and who put each other first in their thoughts. It could, she frowned, be like that for herself and Jeffrey, because as his wife she would be the most important woman in his life, and his mother would have to take a back place and stop interfering. Her own mother, too.

She let go a small sigh, and hoped fervently that things really would change once they were married; hoped, too, that *things* between them would be gentle and loving and that it might work out all right.

She wrapped her fingers round the fat mug and sipped gently at the comforting drink, closing her eyes, trying to make her mind a blank because tomorrow would be another day, and why worry about it when all she had to do was go to York and sign where Mrs Dutton told her to sign, then see her signature witnessed so that everything was legal, and after which she would ask as tactfully as she could if, when she married, her husband would have control of any part of her inheritance.

She laid the mug on the floor at her side, closing her eyes, wondering if tomorrow, when it came, would see her thinking up excuses for catching the overnight train on Friday so she could be back at Southgate early.

Dare she try it? Could she pretend to have a phone call from Sergeant James, asking her to get back a day early, or, more likely, *ordering* her to do so on the pretext that she was urgently needed because Norman could not go on leave unless she was there because Corporal Finnigan would be unable to manage without her to drive the shifts.

She smiled, knowing that Freddy Finnigan could manage alone with one hand tied behind his back and knew that Sergeant James's phone call, could it possibly happen, must have a more compelling reason than that – like she was being promoted to lance-corporal and being posted to another base?

Carrie Tiptree a lance-corporal? What a laugh and something totally unbelievable, because not even if Freddy put her in sole charge of the offi-cers-for-the-use-of Humber would she be given a stripe to sew on her arm!

She thought about the cosseted car, and how she had longed to be allowed to drive it; thought, too, about the cookhouse and collecting tea in the cream enamelled pot, and the sergeant cook teasing her as he always did. And then she let her thoughts hover above Southgate Lodge and wondered if Nan had met Chas tonight and if he was kissing her goodnight on the doorstep.

'Oh, *phooey*!' she said out loud and told herself that after her birthday was over and done with, she wouldn't have long to wait before she could decently pack her kitbag and head for the train that would take her to Lincoln station at which the soldier in the RTO's office would ring Freddy and tell him there was one ATS private in need of transportation.

She switched off the lamp at the head of the sofa so the room was in darkness, except for the flicker of the dying fire, then laid a cushion at her head, stretched out her legs and hugged her dressing gown to her, content in her mind that nobody, not even Carrie Tiptree, had to do anything she did not want to; content, too, that the end of December was a long way away and that soon she would be back in her biscuit bed in Southgate Lodge, a hot bottle at her feet, because they had a kettle, now. And she must remember to try her best to sweetheart cocoa and dried milk powder out of the grocer and to pack her bedsocks and hotwater bottle when the blessed day came and she went home to Southgate Lodge, because home is where the heart is, didn't they say: though miss it as she did, she must wait out her leave here at Jackmans Cottage because didn't she owe it to her mother not to leave a day early on some false pretext still to be thought out?

False pretext! Another name for the downright lie she would have to tell to get her out of here on Friday night. And was it so awful to stay another day in this ages-old house in which so much must have happened since an Elizabethan seafarer built it four hundred years ago, and to which her mother had come as Christopher Tiptree's bride.

Would another bride return here after her wedding in late December, even though just one week after she would leave it, kitbag over her shoulder, for the gate lodge at the bottom of the forbidden drive?

She smiled to think of Nan, who had ventured up there and been turned back by sentries with rifles. Dear, funny Nan who cared for the diddy 'ouse in the country every bit as much as Carrie Tiptree did.

Mind, Southgate couldn't hold a candle to Jackmans, yet it was Evie and Nan who made their billet what it was, because people made places, didn't they? And if she could leave as early as possible on Saturday morning, with luck she could be with them in time for supper at the cook-house, because the Priest's Lodge lot would be doing the late shift and there would be time for chatter and to catch up with Nan's love life, and hear if the letter from Leeds had arrived bearing good news.

Carrie wriggled herself comfortable and began to calculate Saturday's schedule, deciding to catch the first bus out of the village. At six-thirty, it had always been known as the workmen's bus, and after stopping and starting at five villages along the way, it would be at the railway station an hour and ten minutes later, which meant an early train out and if she were really, really lucky, she would be back in time for a supper of corned-beef hash in the cookhouse with Evie and Nan.

She closed her eyes as she felt drowsiness begin to take her, and decided not to return to her bed beneath the eaves but to sleep here on the squashy sofa and awaken to her birthday and the day on which she would go again to York to see the solicitor, though she would open her birthday presents and cards before she left.

She thought about the letter which arrived yesterday. It had borne the red, Passed-by-Censor mark and on the back was an instruction that it was not to be opened until the twenty-third. In Evie's handwriting and full of news, she hoped, about people she knew and places dear and familiar to her. Better by far than a birthday card, so dare she cheat and read it tonight in the firelight?

No! She closed her eyes and waited for sleep to come, keeping her thoughts in check, because she must not think any more about Heronflete and she did not want to think about her birthday which would be very boring, she supposed and full of wedding talk once the mothers got together, and not one bit like a twenty-first birthday ought to be, though she mustn't be such a grouch and try to be grateful for her good fortune.

She cleared all thoughts from her mind, and concentrated on Saturday morning at six-thirty and the workmen's bus, just two days and a bit away. Lovely, lovely early bus.

SIXTEEN

Heaving her kitbag off the train at Lincoln station felt every bit as good as Carrie had wanted it to be that sleepless night on the sofa before her twenty-first birthday, and here she really was, standing outside on the forecourt, awaiting a lift to Heronflete.

'Can you ring this number, please, and ask for extension 26?' Carrie had passed the piece of paper to the soldier behind a counter piled with railway timetables. 'Corporal Finigan should answer it. Can you tell him that Tiptree needs transport?'

Not long after, she heard Freddy's barked 'Allo! Motor Pool,' and hoped that at four o'clock in the afternoon she was not disturbing his tea break.

'He wants to speak to you,' the soldier in the RTO's office passed the receiver to Carrie.

'Hello, Freddy. It's Carrie. Any chance of a lift? I'm at Lincoln. Just got off the train . . .'

'Then aren't you the lucky one? Fowler has to run some stuff to the barracks in the pick-up. I'll tell him to collect you on the way back. Where'll you be?'

'Outside the station, and thanks a lot.'

'About an hour, then. See you . . . Ta-ra, then, girl.'

She had smiled her thanks to the RTO clerk, then was drawn onto the platform by the clinking of crockery on what had to be a WVS trolley, and there was nothing she needed more than a cup of tea, offered with a smile. The WVS ladies were angels, she thought, and seemed to find the time to be on every station platform in their green uniforms to offer cups of comfortingly hot tea. She hoped they would all get medals when the war was over

'Tea, dear,' asked the motherly lady with the trolley. 'Sorry we've no sandwiches today.'

'No problem,' Carrie's smile was genuine, 'but tea would be great.'

'We've run out of sugar, too. It'll have to be saccharin I'm afraid.'

'Sweetener will be fine, thanks.' Carrie was eager to wrap her hands round the thick white cup. 'What do I owe you?'

'You don't owe anything, and you should know it, dear! I'm going to platform one, now, so leave your cup under the bench near the waiting room, will you?'

With respirator on her left shoulder and dragging her kitbag behind her, Carrie made for the bench near the waiting room, to sip the saccharin-sweet tea that tasted like nectar and to think that in less than an hour the pick-up with Norman at the wheel would be outside and that by seven-thirty, she could be sitting on her bed, which Evie or Carrie would have made up for her, and saying 'Hi' to Nan who should, all things being equal, be ready to go to Priest's to wait for Chas.

First, Carrie thought, she would produce the milk powder and cocoa her mother's grocer had found under his counter, then they would catch up with the news, and how many letters Evie had had in the past week, and maybe that the letter from Leeds had arrived at last, and guess what Auntie Mim had said in it!

And of course Carrie would say thank you for the good wishes they had sent for her birthday, and tell them about her twenty-first birthday party – which shouldn't take long, there being no champagne, nor a lavish cake, nor, because of the war, even a dance in the parish hall!

But wouldn't it be good to be back at that tiny lodge with Evie and Nan.

She blew on the hot tea, watching the train that drew up at the platform opposite, wondering how many servicemen and women on leave would get off it, and how many, leave used up, would reluctantly get on it.

Since the war began, railway stations had become very important; places of great happiness where couples, so long parted, met. Places of sadness, too, which made her think of the young mother on the station at York who had smiled a brave goodbye to the husband whose embarkation leave was over and who might never see him again.

When the war was over, Carrie pondered, someone should write a book about railway platforms and all the things that had happened on them; lovers' meetings, of course, though there would be heartbreaking partings to write about too, though she had not felt particularly bereft when Jeffrey kissed her, then pushed his way on to the Glasgow train.

She ought to have done; ought to have felt desolate as his train drew out of the station, but she had not.

Relief had she felt, not that he was going, but grateful they had had the important talk and that he had taken it better than she ever dared hope. Or relief that he was going back to his ship, perhaps?

For shame, Carrie Tiptree, she thought, still watching the train opposite, hoping it wouldn't draw away from the platform, leaving too much heartbreak behind it.

She glanced at the station clock, calculating that before so very much longer, she would go to the station exit, then wait for Norman who would take her back to Southgate, where she wanted to be.

What is the matter with you, Carrie Tiptree, she demanded of her conscience. You have come into money and the most beautiful old house, yet you are still thinking up ways and means to be one jump ahead of Jeffrey who had arrived on a 72-hour leave pass without so much as a word of warning. Sneakily!

Half an hour later, she heard the sound of the pick-up truck and there was no mistaking the growl it made in second gear and she envisaged Norman turning left off the road, slowly driving into the station forecourt.

She saw the truck and wanted to rush into the road, waving her arms, yelling, 'Hi, Norm! I'm here, and am I glad to see you!'

But she did not do that, because members of the armed forces were not allowed public demonstrations, especially women members, who must behave properly at all times, and not put the service into disrepute.

Instead, she stood there, grinning broadly, lifting her hand and wiggling her fingers.

'Norm. How good to see you,' she said when he drew up beside her.

'Good to see you, too,' he answered. 'You've been missed, girl.'

'So who missed me?' she laughed.

'Me and Freddy, and the sergeant in the cookhouse, an' all. He kept asking me where his little gel with the teapot was.'

'I'll see them in the morning at ten,' Carrie heaved her kitbag and respirator into the back of the truck, then took a first seat. 'Want me to drive, Norm?'

'No, ta. You're still officially on leave till midnight, so take it easy, Carrie. Had a good time? I was talking to Sergeant James and she said you'd be twenty-one while you were home. Had a good old knees-up, did you?'

'You bet!,' She hadn't had a very good party, but why dwell on it?

'Got a lot of presents?'

'Not really, Norman. Nothing in the shops to buy, these days. But I didn't do too badly . . .'

If 'not too badly' could describe her amazing inheritance, of course.

'Well, your lot will be expecting a drink in the NAAFI,' he grinned, pulling down the window and sticking out his right hand. 'They're off tonight, so you'll be able to treat them, eh?'

Norman, who had taken over driving the shifts in Carrie's absence, knew where everybody was, and almost certainly what they might be doing.

'Well, Lenice and Ailsa and the sergeant will be on shift tonight, and I wouldn't be surprised if Nan isn't meeting her boyfriend. Maybe Evie and I will go to the NAAFI for a crafty half, so you and Freddy will be welcome to join us.'

She leaned back in contentment as things familiar came into view. The left turn off the main road into the lane that ran alongside the wood, then past the little cruciform church and right to Southgate, outside which Norman parped his horn.

'You're back!' The front door opened and Evie stood there, arms wide, and Carrie felt a warmth run through her which could only be a feeling of homecoming, mixed with gladness.

'Come on in and stow your kit! My, but it's good to see you!'

'It's good to be back. I missed you both, too. Where's Nan?'

'Gone to meet Chas. If you didn't see her waiting outside Priest's, then he must have picked her up. She's been dead lucky, the week you were away. Chas only flew ops twice and on nights when we were on late shift. And there was good news from Leeds.'

'Auntie Mim said yes?'

'Not yes exactly, but not a downright no. She said she couldn't give permission until she had heard from Chas, so a letter from him would be appreciated. Nan understood her reasoning. After all, it seemed right and proper for Chas to ask to marry her niece – Auntie Mim being the next of kin.'

'So a letter was sent to Farthing Street, PDQ?'

'Oh, *very* damn quick. It was soon in the post, so now we are all on tenterhooks, waiting for the final yes.'

'It'll come.' Carrie tipped the contents of her kitbag on her bed. 'And wait till you see what I've brought!'

Triumphantly she held up cocoa and milk.

'Who's a clever girl, then! And did you bring your hottie?'

'I did, and some bedsocks. Sorry I couldn't

bring you a piece of birthday cake, but mother could only manage a small jam sponge on the rations, and that soon got eaten. Mind, she'd hoped for a big do – a dance and long evening dresses, and all the village there. Poor mother.'

'Did you get many presents, Carrie?'

'No. Jeffrey's mother gave me a silver teapot. Second-hand, of course, but it was good of her. And there was half a bottle of sherry in the sideboard, so we polished it off between the three of us. Mrs Frobisher got quite pink-cheeked and giggly, though not even the sherry could make mother feel better about not being able to get food and drinks for a real party. She did give me dad's signet ring, though.'

'So *that's* what you are wearing on your left hand? You haven't lost your diamond ring, Carrie?'

'No, it's in mother's strongbox. She didn't want me to lose it. Dad's ring will stand up better to dirty jobs in the motor pool. I shouldn't need to take it off so often.'

'When I first saw it, I thought you'd got married,' Evie grinned.

'We-e-ll, I just might have done. Jeffrey was home, but only on a 72-hour pass. We had a good talk, by the way . . .'

'So Jeffrey was all right about er – things?'

'He was. Mind, I was dreading it, but he was quite understanding. He even admitted it had been the first time for him, too, which surprised me because usually he'll never admit to being wrong or at fault. He was very nice about it, actually.'

'So you don't feel so badly now, about we-e-ll, you know?'

'No, I don't, but he agreed there would be no babies until I wanted one, though when I mentioned to mother that I wanted to put off starting a family, she was quite shocked and said we ought to take what the good Lord sent. She went quite vinegar-faced when I mentioned birth control. Her generation think it isn't quite nice. I felt a bit embarrassed, actually.'

'Then don't! This is the twentieth century, and women aren't coy these days about birth control.'

'Or even about joining up, you mean? The best thing I ever did, Evie, even though mother was so upset about it.'

'Maybe because she wanted you married and a grandchild on the way.'

'Not really. She wanted me married so the government couldn't make me leave home to go on war work. Tell you something, Evie – when I finally do get round to starting a family, I'll make sure I don't have an only child, and I won't be possessive, either, like mother and Mrs Frobisher are. Guess I thwarted their plans by sneaking off into the ATS. Don't suppose they'll ever forgive me for it.'

'Poor Carrie. Look – have you eaten? The cook-house will be closed, now. Want to nip to the NAAFI for a mug of tea and a wad?'

A wad. Army-speak for the thick, wholesome

sandwiches on sale at most NAAFI canteens.

'I'm not really hungry. Mother gave me egg sandwiches to eat on the train and if I feel like a hot drink, we can make our own, now. My, but this is a cushy billet, especially since we got the kettle.'

'Mm. I said I'd fill Nan's hottie and wrap her pyjamas round it, and slip it in her bed. Hope she gets in on time. I worry about her when she's late. One night the sergeant is going to catch her and then it'll be goodbye late passes. Anyway, talking about passes, how come Jeffrey managed to fiddle a 72-hour pass?'

'Haven't a clue, but I got the shock of my life when he walked down the street. We'd just come out of church – went to hear the last reading of the banns and I had this awful premonition that mother would try to get us married whilst he was home but a hurried wedding on a weekend pass couldn't have been very much to her liking. She wanted the whole shebang for my twenty-first and she and Mrs Frobisher have got a white wedding into their heads, though how they're going to manage it, I don't know. Wedding dresses are a luxury, now, so there aren't any in the shops and if there were, how am I to get the clothing coupons to buy one?'

'Tell you what, Carrie, you and I are about the same size, so why don't you borrow mine? It's hanging there, taking up half my wardrobe at home and I'd love it to have another outing. You'd be welcome and lots of women borrow wedding dresses, these days. It's considered patriotic.'

'I suppose it is, but how much more patriotic to be married in my uniform. I'd kind of got used to the idea of walking down the aisle in khaki.'

'Well, at least you seem to have got used to the *idea*! At one time, it seemed to me you weren't all that keen on the aisle at all.'

'Mmm. Admitted I wasn't looking forward to the wedding night, but Jeffrey and I have got it sorted, now. I'm pretty sure I've convinced him that a bit of kissing and cuddling beforehand will be a good thing. I think he'll try to improve on our first effort. I'd hate to think it would be like that again.'

'It won't be, Carrie, as long as you don't go all frigid on him. Give him a bit of encouragement, why don't you, because it seemed poor Jeffrey hasn't had a lot of experience in that direction.'

'So what do you suggest, Mrs Know-all?'

'A flimsy nightie might help. I went the whole hog and wore a black one, with shoelace ties on the shoulders and lace edging.'

'Flimsy nighties cost clothing coupons and extra clothing coupons aren't allowed to buy a trousseau with, not even if you put in a written request to the Board of Trade. And I haven't got anything suitable, at home. My nighties are all serviceable brushed cotton with long sleeves, and my Army pyjamas would put any man off – just like our long khaki knickers would.'

'Oh, dear, Tiptree, you're still determined not to enjoy your wedding night. Perhaps a few gin and limes beforehand might help.'

'Did *you* have a few drinks, Evie?'

'No. Didn't need 'em! Truth known, I was so desperate to sleep with Bob that I almost dragged him to the bedroom. Shameless, wasn't I?'

'Don't think so, Evie. The way you two love each other I think it would have only been a question of who dragged who,' Carrie smiled, trying not to think of dragging Jeffrey by his shirt tails into a big, sinful double bed, though she *did* think of it and it made her shudder, because something so unlikely just wouldn't be on the cards.

'Sssh!' She heard whispering outside. 'Somebody's there.'

'Don't open the door,' Evie called. 'It's most likely Chas and Nan on their third goodnight. Don't be a spoilsport!'

'Hope it is. At least she's not going to be late in.' Carrie checked the time on her watch, looking forward to seeing Nan, cheeks flushed and eyes bright with love. Dear, funny Nan.

She heard a knock on the front door, and hurried to open it to hear a whispered 'Night, darling. Take care of yourself. Love you,' followed by the sound of another last lingering kiss.

'*Carrie*. You're back! What's news then,' Nan hugged her, and closed the door behind her.

'Yes and I've got cocoa and milk powder, so we'll be able to make hot drinks.'

'Ar, an' I nicked tea from the signals office. It's in a jamjar in the kitchen cupboard. So tell us about your birthday, and all the presents you got. Bet you had a smashin' time.'

'We-e-ll – things being what they are, I didn't expect presents. Jeffrey's mother gave me a silver teapot and Mum gave me dad's signet ring. I was very touched, really. He wore that ring right through the Great War. I'm surprised mother could bring herself to part with it.'

'Ar, glad you told me. I got a shock when I saw it.' Nan's eyes were fixed on Carrie's third finger, left hand. 'You didn't loose them lovely diamonds?'

'No. My ring is at home, so don't worry, old love. It's in mother's strongbox. But now we're all together, I think I'd better tell you about the other present I got. I got money on my twenty-first. My father left it to me.'

'Hey up, Carrie. A lot, was it? You once said you thought you'd been left a hundred pounds.'

To Nan Morrissey, a hundred pounds was a sinful amount of money, since her mother had sinned to get so vast a sum.

'There was more than that, Nan, so I hope the two of you won't be too upset. Actually, my father left Jackmans Cottage to me, with the proviso that mother be allowed to live in it.'

'An 'ouse! Carrie Tiptree, you got an 'ouse!'

'I did. I came all over queer when the solicitor told me.'

'But Jackmans is a cottage,' Nan persisted.

'Yes, but it's rather a special cottage, for all that.'

'Then how big is it?' Nan's idea of a cottage, was like the one on boxes of chocolates, with little leaded window panes and roses growing around the door.

'How big? Well, there are three bedrooms and a bathroom and two small rooms beneath the eaves. I sleep in one of them. And we've got two kitchens and a dining room and two sitting rooms. One of them is very tiny, so we call it the snug. We use the snug a lot, these days, because it doesn't take a lot of heating.'

'Flamin' 'eck. Carrie! That's a lot of rooms for a cottage! And it's yours, now! Aren't you just the lucky one? Does it have a garden?'

'Not at the front. The house stands on the street, but at the back there's a walled garden, which, I love, and then some more, where we grow flowers and vegetables.'

'I don't wonder you came all over queer,' Evie laughed. 'Imagine being given something like that, on a plate?'

'Only the house, The contents were left to mother, though I'll never understand my father's thinking, leaving Jackmans to me, and money, as well.'

'*Money! How much?*' Nan demanded bluntly.

'He left me a thousand pounds, which was invested over the years, then it grew by four hundred pounds. And my godmother, my Aunt

Adeline, left me a hundred pounds of savings bonds, so they've been cashed, and the money is being put into my Post Office book.'

For a moment Nan was stunned into silence. Then, 'Well, you'd better not tell Lennice,' Nan nodded sagely. 'You know she don't like inherited money. It's against her religion.'

'Religion my foot. Lennice is Church of England, though her politics don't allow her to look kindly on money you haven't worked for.'

'She's a little bit Bolshie, isn't she?'

'Not really,' Evie soothed. 'She's got more of a fair-shares-for-all outlook. There's no harm in her, anyway. I've often thought that if I were up to the eyes in trouble with my back to the wall, it would be Lennice I'd want at my side. I've found her to be very kind.'

'So I don't reckon she would refuse if I offered to buy her tea and a wad next time we're in the NAAFI out of my inherited wealth?'

'Well, you better hadn't tell her,' Nan advised. 'After all, it's none of her business! Why don't we make ourselves a cup of cocoa to celebrate with?'

'Well, the bottles are in the beds, so why don't you tell me about your Auntie Mim's letter, Nan, and if Chas has written to her, yet?'

'*Written*? That letter was a work of art. Took us a lot of composing, but Chas went to a lot of trouble to get it exactly right. Y'see, me Auntie Mim has a thing about handwriting. She can't abide men who write all spidery and spindly. Says you can judge a man's character by his writing, so I told Chas he'd better make that letter good. He wrote it with his fountain pen that's got a broad nib, so you can't do spidery with a thick nib, can you? And for the finishing touch, he got a bottle of black ink, because thick looks good if it's in black. Very manly, I'd say.'

'Oh, Nan Morrissey, as if handwriting will make a difference!'

'But it will, Carrie. I know me Auntie Mim and her funny ideas. When she gets that letter from Chas, she'll come up with a yes!'

'Oh my goodness!' Carrie gasped, unable to stop laughing, because things had come to a pretty pass when a bottle of black ink could make such a difference to Chas and Nan and their future together. 'Aren't you just the sly one, Nan Morrissey? Does your young man know what a devious woman he's getting?'

'Ar, g'way,' Nan giggled. 'Want me to make us that drink?'

'Please, old love, and blend the cocoa and milk powder together with a drop of water, so it'll be nice and creamy,' Carrie instructed. 'And I'd better nip up to the signals office and let Sergeant James know I'm back so she won't think I've gone AWOL.'

'Then you'd better tell her that Nan is in. We don't want her checking up on us when her shift is over,' Evie grinned.

Nan and Evie were sitting propped up in bed,

pyjama-clad, drinking cocoa, when Carrie got back.

'Everything all right?' Nan wanted to know.

'It is. They didn't seem to be busy, but then they never are. Sometimes I can't help thinking the war has forgotten Heronflete,' Carrie sighed.

'Bet it has, an' all, and it's Heronflete's fault. They go out of their way to be mysterious about things.'

Nan was remembering the guard at the turn in the drive who pointed a rifle at her. 'Would break their hearts to send a signal in plain language that our lot in the signals office could make sense of! Y'know, Carrie, if this war goes on as long as the last one did, we still won't find out what goes on behind that green door. I'd like to know what they'up to. Bet they're all civilians and back-room boys. Scientists, inventin' things.'

'We won't ever know,' Evie offered, 'because I think they're not at all sure themselves. Mind, they could be something to do with propaganda – inventing useless snippets to confuse Hitler – maybe training paratroopers to disguise themselves as nuns.'

'You mean that Heronflete could be one of those secret places where they train spies – secret agents to drop into occupied Europe?'

'Don't think so.' Carrie stirred her drink. 'I've often seen cars passing Southgate with men and women in civilian clothes in them. Big cars, and not painted all over with camouflage, like ours have to be. The people in them looked quite normal and ordinary.'

'Spies usually do,' Nan said scathingly. 'That's why they can get away with spyin'. But had you thought, they might have foreign royalty there what escaped to England when the Jairmans marched in and took their countries over.'

'A safe house – is that what you're getting at, Nan?'

'It could be, though I often think it's just something the government has thought up to give cushy jobs to their friends – them who are sick of bein' bombed every night in London. Jobs for the boys, sort of. You just can't begin to imagine who might be there, and what is goin' on.'

'Well, the Yeoman is one of that lot. He's got a key to that green door. Why don't we try asking him?'

'Now listen you two!' For once, Evie pulled rank. 'It's not for us to reason why, don't forget. We're here to do as we are told, and like the sergeant said, keep our eyes down and our mouths shut!'

'I got a real old grilling when I was home,' Carrie laughed. 'Mother was a bit concerned that we wrote On Active Service on our envelopes when we write home and wondered why letters were censored. She seemed determined to find out where I am, and what I'm doing. I managed to convince her I was in no danger, though when I wrote that letter to Jeffrey – remember Evie? –

and posted it uncensored in Lincoln, the postmark gave things away. But as far as my mother knows, I am stationed in Linolnshire. She would have the time of her life ferreting out what goes on at Heronflete, and believe you me, she would!'

'Ar. When she gets to the bottom of it, I hope she tells us,' Nan giggled. 'Your mother, Carrie, sounds a bit hard-faced, just like the Queer One at Cyprian Court. Clever of you and me, wasn't it, joining the ATS, even though we got landed with Sergeant James.'

'She's not a bad old stick,' Evie, who had experienced many hard-faced sergeants during her two-and-a half years in the service, defended.

'Ha! just think of it,' Nan chortled. 'Sergeant James and my step-mother in a head-on collision. Tell you what, I'd put my money on the sergeant, any day of the week!'

'So, have you told your stepmother that you and Chas want to be married?' Carrie asked.

'What – and risk that one turning up at me weddin' and her Georgie with her! Not likely!'

'Poor Georgie. What's wrong with the little lad?'

'*Wrong*, Evie? He's a right little whinger, and his nose is always snotty. Can't abide the spoiled brat! Him and his Mam would ruin my wedding. Don't want either of them there.'

'So she can't stick her oar in and prevent you getting married?' Carrie teased.

'No, she can't, she's nuthin' to me! and don't say such terrible things, Tiptree. As far as I'm concerned, the only invites I'll be sending out is to me Auntie Mim and to youse two.'

'And will you be married from Auntie Mim's house, Nan?'

'Don't think so. Mrs Lawson said she'd like us to be married in her church and she would love to have the wedding from her house. She's a lovely lady, you know. I've struck lucky, getting her. And when the letter from Leeds arrives, I know it'll be one great big yes, because Auntie Mim won't be able to refuse. Not when Chas told her he would have a job to come home to, when the war is over. Auntie Mim remembers the Great War, and heroes from the trenches having to beg. A lot of them sold bootlaces and matches – hawked them on the streets. She never forgave Lloyd George for not providing them heroes with homes and jobs, so she'd have been real impressed when Chas told her he had a job guaranteed, and a house for us to live in.'

'Lucky Chas. Is he like Carrie? Has someone left him a house?'

Nan closed her eyes and took a shuddering breath, because just to think about Chas's expectations made her feel a traitor to the working classes she belonged to.

As she opened her mouth to tell them, she took a sudden decision not to tell Evie and Carrie what she had discovered about Chas – that he was going to inherit a carpet factory and a huge Manor house with stables and greenhouses and everything, because that wasn't something she wanted to tell the others, not yet. They might think the worst of her and not understand that it was Chas she loved for himself and not for all those things.

Now, Nan Morrissey, she scolded herself, how can you think such things about Evie and Carrie when you know they wouldn't think anything of the sort! They've never been anything but smashin' to me and to Chas, and they're so happy for us now that we're getting married.

All the same, she didn't want to say anything just yet. Something in her was afraid that they might think differently about the whole affair if they knew that Chas was out of the top drawer and was going to marry Nan Morrissey from Cyprian Court, who was not even legitimate if the truth were known, although she would never tell anyone other than Chas about what she had discovered in the envelope marked 'Marriage Lines'.

'Is everything all right, Nan?' asked Evie, concerned. She had noticed the younger girl's expression and the long time it was taking her to say anything in reply.

'Ar,' said Nan, at last, smiling. 'I was just thinking about how peculiar it is that I'm going to be a married woman soon, if Auntie Mim says yes, that is. An' Chas's mother says we can live with her for as long as we need to and he can go back to his old job from before the war, in a carpet factory. It's making tarpaulin and camouflage webbing at the moment, but once all this is over it'll go back to making carpets and Chas can work there again.'

She felt a flush creeping up her neck because she was not being entirely honest with Evie and Carrie. Chas wouldn't just have a job at the carpet factory. He would own it outright once he turned twenty-one after Christmas, along with his cousin, that was. And saying that she would be living with Chas's mother didn't exactly reveal that it would be in an enormous manor house with at least ten bedrooms if the windows outside were anything to go by.

'Well, that's wonderful,' said Carrie warmly. 'It's a great advantage to know what you'll be doing when this blasted war is over and we can all go back to being normal again. Lots of young men are going to find it hard to know how to get back to living civvie life again, and no doubt there'll be hundreds looking for jobs. Lucky Chas to have something to do so he can support you both.'

'Yeah, I reckon,' mumbled Nan, feeling more and more guilty that she wasn't coming clean. Hadn't Carrie told them about *her* expectations, about the cottage that didn't sound much like any cottage Nan had ever heard of with its two sitting rooms, and all that money as well?

'I know you're officially on leave till midnight, Carrie,' said Evie briskly, 'but we're not, so Nan and I had better get to sleep.'

Carrie looked at her watch and whistled. 'Gosh, my leave's almost over! I'd better get to sleep as well. It's the usual five-twenty start tomorrow. I won't know what's hit me after a week of sleeping in till eight o'clock.'

'And we're on earlies as well,' added Evie, 'so it's not exactly a lie-in for anyone.'

'Thank goodness I brought my hottie and my bedsocks back,' Carrie said. 'I can feel a real chill in the air now. It'll be the first of November in a few days. Hasn't time flown by? It's only going to get colder once winter has really arrived.'

'Thanks for remindin' us!' rejoined Nan. 'You're the one with the bedsocks!'

'And you're going to turn eighteen,' said Carrie with a smile. 'And maybe you'll even be married soon after that.'

Nan felt a warm glow round her heart as she thought of Chas, her reason for living, and the delight that flooded her every time she was near him. To think of being married to him was the happiest thought she could have.

'Just before we turn in,' Carrie said, her face suddenly serious, 'I wanted to say something to you, Lance Corporal Turner and Private Morrissey. All the time I was away at home with Mother, I kept thinking about you both – and the others as well. Freddie and Norm, Sergeant James, and even Lenice and Ailsa, and how much I was missing you all. I would imagine what you were doing at different times of the day – going to the NAAFI, or being driven by Norm up to the signals office for your shifts, and how things were going in sweet little Southgate Lodge. I really missed you all. I even thought about coming back early.'

'And missin' a whole day of leave?' squawked Nan, shocked that anyone could think about giving up long lie-ins and cups of tea and warm fires if they didn't have to, even though she was as fond of Southgate and the girls as anyone.

'I know, silly, isn't it? But I did. And I've been happier here than anywhere. I mean it. That's in no small amount due to you two. So thank you both. I've been so lucky meeting the two of you.'

'Ah,' said Nan, her eyes glistening suddenly. 'I know what you mean. I feel the same.'

'Me too,' said Evie with a smile. 'You're both the most smashing girls I've ever met. But if we don't get our eyes closed, we're going to regret it tomorrow! Good night, all.'

'Good night,' the other two echoed.

The lights went out and Southgate Lodge was quiet at last.

SEVENTEEN

'One for you, Nan – postmarked "Leeds". Wonder what it can be about?' Carrie dropped the letter on to Nan's biscuit bed with a grin. 'And two for Evie. One for me.'

Nan pounced on the flimsy envelope with a little shriek. 'Oh my Gawd. This is it. It must be from Auntie Mim.'

She couldn't imagine why she was suddenly feeling so sick inside. Why would her aunt deny her permission to marry Chas? There was no reason at all – not only did her aunt want her to be happy, but once Nan was married Auntie Mim could hand over responsibility for her to Chas. He would be her next of kin after that, and the one to take care of her and support her. But of course Auntie Mim had never met Chas and wasn't to know that he was the best man in the world and the only one she could ever dream of marrying; she would suppose that Nan had stars in her eyes and might not be able to see the real man underneath all the sweet talk and romancing. *Oh*, it was frustrating. It made her want to run to the train station and go straight back to Farthing Street to explain to her aunt in person that Chas was truly decent, a man who loved her as deeply as she loved him. She could only hope that Chas's letter, written with that black ink and thick-nibbed pen, had done the trick.

'Aren't you going to open it?' asked Carrie, seeing Nan's hands shaking a little as she held the envelope. 'Or would you rather I went away?'

'No, oh no, I don't mind. I'm sure she's gonna say it's all right and that we have her permission. But – oh dear – what if she doesn't?'

'There's only one way to find out, and that's to open it.'

Nan took a deep breath and ripped open the envelope, extracting the letter inside. She read it hastily.

Dear Nan,
I've received the letter from your young man and I have to say that he comes across from his writing as a very decent bloke. I liked him very much at once and it seems to me that you've made a good choice there. In ideal circumstances, I would prefer to meet him first but I understand that life isn't what we would wish at the moment, so I'm willing to trust that you know your heart and mind. It's always better for young

people to marry than to take silly chances in life.

So I am very pleased to say that I give my permission for you and Charles Lawson to get married as soon as you may like.

Please write and tell me when your wedding is to be, if you can. If it's at all possible I would like to attend, in the place of your dear mother who would have loved to see that day.

With love
Your Aunt
Miriam Simpson

Nan felt hot salty tears well up and spill down over her cheeks.

'What is it?' cried Carrie anxiously. 'Did she say no?'

'Oh, oh,' sobbed Nan. 'Yes, I mean, no. I mean . . .'

'Which is it?'

'She says . . .' Nan gulped back another huge sob. 'She said yes. She said I can marry Chas.'

'She does? So why are you crying? That's marvellous news, isn't it? Just about the best. Chas's letter must have been a winner.'

Nan nodded. She wiped the tears away with her hand and reached for a handkerchief. 'Sorry, Carrie, you mustn't mind me. Oh hecky thump! You must think I'm a right one, cryin' my eyes out like this. It's just . . . I'm so happy that Chas and I can get married. But at the same time, I'm sad and I don't know why.'

'Nothing to do with Chas, I hope?'

'No, no. Nothin' at all. Just that, not so long ago, I was Nan Morrissey without a mother, having to live with the Queer One and her kid, thinkin' that this might be all there was for me. Then my poor dad was killed by them *Jairmans* and it was worse than ever. And now, I've joined the Army and found you lot, and fallen in love with Chas. It's wonderful! I don't know why I'm cryin' so hard. I'm gonna be married. But my mum isn't here to see it, and dear old Auntie Mim has said she'd like to come if she could. I reckon that's what's makin' me blub like this. She's my only real family, you see. It would be so lovely if she could be there . . .'

'I'm sure she could if you gave her the right notice. Are you not going to be married in Leeds?' said Carrie gently.

'No, Chas's mother said I could be married from Gardener's Cottage and I'd like that. If you could see it . . . it's a really dinky little house and so sweet. I had the best time there and somehow I already feel like it's home for me. More than Leeds, anyhow, even though Auntie Mim was so kind to me and took me in.'

'I'm sure she could get a train from Leeds to Shrewsbury. Wouldn't it be lovely if she could be there? I wish we could all be there, but I can't see that happening unless Sergeant James has some kind of conversion and starts handing out leave-passes left, right and centre, not caring if there's anyone here to run the signals office and drive the shift workers about or not.'

'Yeah, it's a shame,' agreed Nan. 'I can't think of anything nicer than havin' you two there. You could be my bridesmaids! Well, you could. I s'pose Evie would have to be a matron of honour, seeing as she's the married one. But it will be you too, soon, Carrie, won't it? Then we'll all be old married women together.'

'Yes.' Carrie smiled awkwardly and rushed on. 'Now, when are you seeing Chas again?'

'Tomorrow night. But I can't wait that long! I wish I could see him right now and share the news with him. Auntie Mim says she's written to him as well, so he might have his letter from her as well.'

'Why don't we walk up to the NAAFI and you can telephone the mess at RAF Modeley and talk to him?'

Nan looked at her watch. 'Ooh, I'd love to. But it's so late already and I'd much rather tell him in person. We're on earlies tomorrow. The time will pass real quick and then he'll turn up as usual in Boadicea and we can talk about it all we like. It's never the same over the lines, not when you know someone's listening in, even if they don't give a monkey's if you're talking to your fiancé or not.'

'All right then. Evie'll be back in a moment. How about I make a cup of cocoa each with that powdered milk I managed to sweetheart out of our grocer and we can celebrate? You're truly an engaged woman now! And in six weeks' time, you'll be Mrs Lawson.'

'Lawks,' breathed Nan. 'That don't half make it sound serious. I can't help thinking of Mrs Lawson as Chas's mother. She's so beautiful and polished – I can't imagine ever being like her.'

'You don't have to be. You only have to be yourself. After all, that's who Chas fell in love with, isn't it?'

'Yeah.' Nan grinned at her. 'You're right. Now, what about that cocoa? I could do with something to warm me up! It's getting freezing in here.'

'It certainly is. We'll have to do something about it before it gets much worse. I think Evie has some plans up her sleeve. Thank goodness for bedsocks and hotties, that's all I can say. Now I'll go and make that cocoa.'

The next morning was the coldest they had yet known at Southgate Lodge. In mid-November, the weather suddenly took on the icy chill of winter and bitter blasts of air were coming through the gap in the window and wide chink under the door. A frost had crisped over everything outside and the window panes were covered in a lacy pattern of ice both inside and out. Carrie boiled the kettle in the tiny kitchen, thanking heaven that the Yeoman had been as kind as he had to get it for them and that the sergeant had been sensible enough to overcome any of her official scruples and accept it. And where was the harm really? It wasn't as though they were stealing it – it wouldn't leave Heronflete, just spend a bit of time in Southgate Lodge providing a bit of much-needed comfort for some ATS girls in an hour of need and that couldn't be wrong. Grateful for the warm water, Carrie had a quick wash, brushed her teeth and then dressed hurriedly. It was still pitch dark outside, so she took her small torch to light the path on the way to the motor pool.

'Hello, there! If it isn't Private Tiptree, back from her leave in the lap of luxury!' It was Corporal Finnigan, alerted by the sound of Carrie stamping on the ground outside the stable block to warm her feet up. 'Did you have a good time?'

'Hello, Freddie. Yes, I certainly did. It was lovely, thanks.'

'Good. Are you off to get the early shift?'

'Yes – won't be long before they're due, so I'd better get cracking.'

'Well, once you've done that, you'd better get some breakfast at the cookhouse and then we'll get started. I've got something in mind for you today . . .'

'More than getting the tea?' enquired Carrie with a good-natured grin.

'We've missed you on the tea run,' said Freddie. 'Norm tries his best but somehow it just isn't the same. You must be very good at sweethearting that extra bit out of the sergeant.'

'I'm glad you missed me. I'll see you when I'm back.'

Despite the cold, Carrie managed to get the truck started on the first turn. I haven't lost the knack! she thought with pleasure, as she pulled slowly out of the stable yard on her way back to Southgate to pick up the girls. Evie and Nan would be by now, she thought, all sleepy and unwilling to be in the cold air.

As she motored along the lane, she was filled with happiness to be back at Heronflete. She had missed it so, had spent almost every minute of her leave in Jackmans Cottage wondering what was going on here and wishing she could think of an excuse to get back early. She hadn't in the end, but now she was back she was overjoyed. It was funny to think of – lots of people would consider this just about the worse thing, having to get up so early in the freezing cold and start driving shift workers about, before going on the tea run and doing goodness know what else. If she knew anything about it all, she'd probably be changing tires and cleaning out muck before the end of the day. But for Carrie, it was wonderful. She had never known a freedom like it, even with all the rules and restrictions of army life, because she was free to be herself and just like anyone else.

Of course, the truth was she *wasn't* quite like anyone else. She was an independent woman now, who had come of age and inherited quite a lot. An Elizabethan cottage and £1600 was not to be sniffed at, and it guaranteed her ability to look after herself.

Carrie thought back to her interview with Mrs Dutton on the day of her twenty-first birthday when she had gone to the solicitors' office to sign all the papers that would bring her into her inheritance at last. As they were signed and officially witnessed, Carrie couldn't help feeling that the whole world was open to her now, although something was still niggling on her mind. Once they were alone together, Mrs Dutton said, 'Well that about covers it for today, Miss Tiptree. Many congratulations. I'll arrange for the amount of money you requested to be transferred into your Post Office account, and if you have any further requests, you only have to write. Now, is there anything else I can help you with?'

For a moment, Carrie wasn't going to say anything and then she realised that this was her last chance to put her mind at rest. Taking a deep breath, she said, 'Actually Mrs Dutton, there is something . . .'

'Yes?' The older woman looked at her seriously over the top of her spectacles. 'Fire away.'

'The thing is, I'm engaged to be married.' Carrie saw Mrs Dutton's gaze fly to her engagement finger and a look of puzzlement at the heavy gold signet ring that was there. 'Oh, this isn't my engagement ring. This was my father's and it's much more appropriate for me to wear it as my job in the ATS means I'm always working with grease and muck. The other ring, the diamond one, is in my mother's strongbox at home so that it won't be damaged. Actually, that's what my question is really about because I found out that my fiancé hasn't finished paying for the ring and it occurred to me that if he were in any financial straits and we were married . . . well . . .' She trailed off awkwardly. Suddenly it seemed like a dreadful thing to say about the man she was planning to marry, that he might as good as rob her of her money. But she had to ask!

'You mean, if you were married, could he have access to your money and spend it as he wished?' asked Mrs Dutton bluntly.

'Y-y-yes,' stammered Carrie, grateful for the lawyer's straightforwardness. 'I suppose that's it.'

'You're very wise to think about these things beforehand. Afterwards, it's often a case of "repent at leisure", when it's all too late. There's no harm in thinking carefully about the business side of things. No one sensible would do anything less, particularly where your security is concerned.'

'I wouldn't want you to think that I don't trust Jeffrey,' said Carrie hastily. 'And of course, when we're married, I wouldn't hold anything back from him. Once we are married, obviously, we will share all our possessions just like any couple . . .' She felt a blush creeping hotly over her face.

'Of course,' soothed Mrs Dutton. 'But it is perfectly within your rights to know what the situation is. You're not the first woman to bring more into the marriage than her intended, and the law has recognised that for some time. Many people think that a husband has full control over his wife's assets once they are married, but I'm glad to say that that Victorian attitude is long gone. The Married Woman's Property Act of 1925 means that your property remains your own and your husband would not be able to dispose of anything without your permission.'

'Well, that's all right then,' said Carrie, relieved to have all her worries put to rest.

'But – yes, there is a "but", I'm afraid. That's the theory. But in practice you may find it somewhat different. In truth, if your husband wished to have access to your money, he would not find it all that difficult. It would be very easy for him to become a joint signatory on your bank account. Even if you didn't want to do it, you might find yourself unable to refuse, particularly if he mounted a long-term campaign of persuasion or bullied you into it. The truth is, society is on his side. It is perfectly normal for a man to control the family's finances and to decide how money is to be spent. An unscrupulous or innocent bank manager could well allow him to raid an account without permission from you. And I've heard once of a husband putting up a house for sale that was in his wife's name, in the hope of pocketing the proceeds.'

'Oh my goodness!' gasped Carrie. 'I'm sure Jeffrey would never do anything like that!' She felt as though she were labelling poor Jeffrey a criminal and virtually accusing him of trying to steal her money. It felt very low and sneaky indeed.

'Of course not. Those are extreme cases. But I'm simply saying that if you have any doubts at all – even the smallest – then you need to be very careful.' The lawyer leaned forward. 'Can I speak frankly, Miss Tiptree?'

'Please do,' replied Carrie, aware of her scarlet face.

'You seem like a fine, upstanding young woman and your father clearly thought a lot of your judgement to leave you this money at such a comparatively young age. I'm sure that the man you've chosen to marry is just as excellent as anyone would hope. I think it is very much the wise course before your marriage to discuss all this candidly with him, and tell him that you intend to retain control of your assets. I'm sure he will be more than happy to agree to that. Most men prefer to go out and earn their own livings anyway. We could even draw up a document to that effect, if you wished.'

'We-e-e-ll, I don't know.' Carrie couldn't imagine Jeffrey's response to such a conversation and the suggestion of a document to be signed, but she felt instinctively that he wouldn't take too kindly to it. He would not like any suggestion that she was limiting his power over her, she knew that.

'Just think carefully, Miss Tiptree, that's all I

ask. I am, after all, acting in your interests. And any man worth his salt would not mind a jot. But I can only advise – it is in your hands.'

'Thank you, Mrs Dutton. You've given me a lot to think about.'

The older woman smiled. 'Not at all. Oh, and by the way – happy birthday.'

Carrie had headed home to the small birthday party her mother had arranged, a great deal richer and not a little confused about what she should do. Did she, in her heart of hearts, trust Jeffrey? After all, he had not let on that he'd known what her prospects were, even though her mother had as good as said that Jeffrey had known all along that she had money and a house coming to her.

There's no point in even thinking about it, Caroline Tiptree, she told herself firmly. You're going to marry Jeffrey, it's already been decided. It's just a question of when, that's all. Perhaps I *will* talk to him about it. After all, he was quite good in the end when we discussed what happened between us and how I didn't like it. He didn't quite promise me that it will all be wonderful after we're married, but I'm sure he will.

Nevertheless, she couldn't quite shake the worries at the back of her mind.

Once she had dropped a very sleepy and shivery Nan and Evie at the signals office, and got herself some hot breakfast, Carrie drove back to the motor pool.

I wonder what Freddie's got in mind for me, she thought idly, as she turned into the stable yard. The sun had risen now, though it was still cold and foggy. She went towards the dimly lit stable room that served as a garage.

'Hello, Norm! How are you?' she called as she caught sight of Private Fowler's feet. He was under a truck, servicing the brakes.

'Hi, Carrie,' came the muffled reply. 'Doing well, thanks. Yourself?'

'Fine. Glad to be back.'

'Enough of all this chitchat,' said Corporal Finnigan, coming out of the darkness, wiping his hands on a greasy rag. 'If I'm not much mistaken, it's going on for tea time.'

'Want me to get the brew?' said Carrie, reaching for the cream enamelled teapot. 'As if I need to ask.'

'That'll do us nicely,' said Freddie, 'then you can see what I've got in store for you.'

When Carrie got back with the steaming teapot, she was surprised to see that the Humber had been driven out on to the front yard. It looked beautiful, its chrome polished with precipitated whiting to a mirror shine, its glass crystal clear, and the bonnet gleaming with wax and tender care.

'Gosh!' she cried. 'It looks wonderful! Didn't you do well?'

'She's running like a dream, as well,' said Freddie, pleased at her praise. 'She's purring like a cat that's had the cream. Do you want to have a spin?'

'In the Humber? Really?' Carrie was stunned. 'Isn't that a waste of petrol?'

'Strictly speaking, it might be,' Freddie agreed. 'But she's got to have a run around occasionally or she'll seize up, so it's all in her best interests. And she can always be requisitioned then, if she's needed. Not that I'll be telling anyone about her, and nor should you, she's far too good to be treated the way officers treat their transport. She's class. She's only for the best.'

'And you'd really let me drive her?' breathed Carrie. She walked over to the car and smoothed a hand over the softly shining bonnet.

'Well, I hear you've had a birthday, so this is like our little present to you.'

'Oh, thank you Freddie! It's the *best* present!'

Moments later, she was sitting in the luxurious leather seat and steering the beautiful old car down the lane. She would do a circuit, past Southgate, down to Priest's and back. Driving the Humber was incredibly smooth after the juddering and jarring of the army trucks and vans she was used to – it almost felt like floating rather than motoring, or as though at any minute the wheels would lift gently from the road and she would find herself soaring effortlessly over the countryside, looking down at Heronflete from above just like the boys in their planes as they returned to base.

I wonder, she thought mischievously as she went, if *I* could afford one of these now? How much would a top car like this cost? Hundreds, probably. I'd have to be a millionaire, I should think. I'm not *that* rich! This will be the closest I ever come to that kind of life.

Still the independence made her almost giddy. Twenty-one! she thought. With a house and money and everything before me. I've got my independence now. I must be careful to value it.

As she turned on her way back to the motor pool she knew absolutely that there wouldn't be a wedding to Jeffrey in a few weeks' time. It didn't matter if the Navy gave him the leave because she wouldn't be applying for any, so there was no way they could be married.

I don't want to yet, she told herself stubbornly. Some day, yes. But not yet.

Nan's kiss that night from Chas was the tenderest she had ever known from him.

'My darling girl,' he said softly, when they'd parted from their embrace. 'We're really and truly going to be married! Can you believe it? I had my letter from your aunt today.'

'I had mine too,' said Nan, wanting to start crying again. 'Gar, what's happened to me? I'm like a baby these days, sobbing my heart out at the slightest thing! Isn't Auntie Mim terrific?'

'I think she might possibly be the most wonderful human being alive,' said Chas solemnly. 'Come on, darling, let's go the pub and get ourselves something to celebrate with. We're properly engaged now, after all.'

Boadicea doesn't get any warmer! thought Nan wryly as they chuntered down to the village. A bitter blast of cold air came through the side door, freezing Nan's legs so that she could barely feel them. It couldn't make her feel any less happy, though.

They went into the pub together and sat down with their drinks, both bright-eyed with excitement.

'Do you realise what this means, Nan? I've got my weekend pass in just a few weeks – I could apply to add compassionate leave on to it, and you could apply for yours at the same time. Then we can get the special licence – it only takes a few days. After that, we'll be married in no time.'

They were both quiet for a moment as they thought about what it would mean. It seemed incredible – Nan Morrissey and Charles Lawson married, properly husband and wife.

'You do want to be married from Gardener's Cottage, don't you?' Chas asked anxiously. 'I know my mother said it would be wonderful but I don't want you to feel pushed into anything, or that you don't have any say in the matter.'

'Oh, no, I can't think of anything nicer,' Nan said quickly. 'It's what I've been imagining. Me, coming out of Gardener's Cottage on our wedding day and the two of us going back there afterwards for tea and maybe some toast and jam, if your mother's managed to keep any jam back from our last visit.'

'Nan, Nan . . . tea and toast for a wedding breakfast! This war's changed life so much, hasn't it? Once it would have been cold salmon and chicken and everything, followed by wedding cake with champagne. I'm sorry you won't be getting the best, darling. It's what I want for you.' Chas held her hand softly and gazed into her eyes.

'Well, Chas Lawson, I don't know – next you'll be telling me our honeymoon won't be in Paris, and that we'll be back on duty in no time!'

Chas laughed. 'You're so wonderful. Of course it's only what everybody has to do. And I suppose we'll be getting married in uniform, as well.'

'Maybe,' said Nan mysteriously. 'We'll see.'

'Don't tell me you've got clothing coupons for a wedding dress! Armed forces don't get any coupons, so I don't see how you could . . . and you wouldn't have time, or fabric, to make anything. What have you got up your sleeve?'

'Ask no questions,' said Nan, still looking mysterious. 'And you'll –'

'Be told no lies, I know, I know. Hmm, there's more to you than meets the eye. And what meets the eye does me just fine, I can tell you that.' Leaning in, he gave her a quick peck on the cheek and then they both looked round anxiously. Kissing in public was not done, particularly if you were in uniform. A tearful farewell at the station might just be allowed but other than that, it was best behaviour when you were representing the King's Armed Forces and wearing his uniform.

Nan drew in a breath sharply. 'Oh my gawd. Look who it is.'

Chas looked round. 'Is it your sergeant? Who?'

'Over there, with the beer glass. That old man. It's Granddad! The old man who told me about the ghost of Cecilia. You remember, the poor old nun who was shackled and locked away all those years ago. She's had a proper Christian burial now, thank goodness, but all the same, she's supposed to walk abroad round Heronflete. It used to be a priory, you see, long before it was turned into the home of a peer of the realm.'

'But it's all a load of nonsense, isn't it? Old wives' tales, to add a bit of spice.'

'I s'pose so. But it doesn't half sound real when he tells it. Oh, look, he's seen us.'

'Evenin' young lady. You're back again, I see!' called the old man from the nook near the fireplace where he was nestled in, keeping his elderly bones warm against the stones that had captured the heat from the smouldering logs in the hearth.

'Aye, aye, Granddad!' called Nan cheerily. 'It's a cosy place to be on a cold night.'

'Who's this? Your sweetheart?' The old man nodded at Chas.

'This is my fiancé,' Nan said proudly. 'Charles Lawson. We're gonna be married in a few weeks.'

'Congratulations,' he said, grinning and revealing a row of broken and yellow teeth. 'It allus does us good to see some young love about the place. You're an airman, I see. Brave boys, you are. Brave boys.'

'Thank you,' Chas said politely.

The old man turned his attention back to Nan. 'Now you haven't forgotten, have you? What I told you about the poor girl?'

'You mean Cecilia.'

'Aye, that's right, I do. It's coming up to the time, isn't it? Didn't I say?'

'Yes, I remember.' Nan could hardly forget, though she'd tried to put the old man's stories out of her mind. But it wasn't difficult to remember that the ghostly apparition of a long-dead nun was supposed to appear on the very same day as her birthday – the 22nd November. 'St Cecilia's day,' she offered.

'That's right. Just a few more days and she'll be walking. Poor lass. She'll be wanting to remind folks of what happened to her.'

Nan felt a horrible shiver of cold pass over her.

'Don't listen to him,' chided Chas quietly, seeing her pale face. 'It's all just old stories, you know that.' He turned to the old man. 'Can I get you a drink? A bitter, perhaps? And then we'll hear no more of these stories. You're frightening my fiancée half to death!'

'Sorry, I'm sure. And you're very kind, I'll take a glass if I may. I shan't say another word about the goings-on at the Priory, don't you worry.' He chuckled to himself.

'There,' said Chas. 'All forgotten. Happy now, Nan?'

'I suppose so,' she said. I don't want anything to spoil this, she thought. It's the happiest time of my life.

'Then let's talk about the wedding, once I've got these drinks,' he said. 'I'm going to write to Mother tonight so she can get the preparations under way.'

Nan tore her thoughts away from dead nuns walking on bitter winter nights and remembered instead why she was so happy. Auntie Mim had said yes! It was all sorted out, she had her permission and now she was going to be married to the only man in the world for her. How much luckier could she be?

When Chas dropped her home again, they spent long minutes unable to tear themselves away from the soft kisses and tender embraces.

'You drive me wild, Nan,' Chas breathed into her ear, stroking a soft hand over her hair. 'You're the woman of my dreams.'

'Soon I'll be the woman of your days an' nights too,' she said gently, feeling daring that she was even voicing these thoughts. 'An' I'll be all yours.'

'I don't know how I can wait,' he said longingly. 'All I can think of is what it will be like to make love to you at last. I feel like we've waited for ever.'

'So do I. But it won't be long now, just a few more weeks and then we'll always belong to each other.'

They kissed again before Nan pulled away with a sigh, saying she really had to be getting in now, and they bid farewell again.

As she heard the clattering, crashing noise of Boadicea hurtling back down the lane to RAF Modeley, she whispered, 'Goodbye, Chas Lawson. Take care. It's not long now, darling. Then we will truly belong to each other.'

EIGHTEEN

Sergeant James found the imploring eyes of young Private Morrissey difficult to look into. They reminded her somehow of herself, when she was younger and in love and full of that excitement and optimism. That was before she lost all her hope in life and began to devote herself to her army career in order to find a purpose for herself. She got satisfaction now in running an efficient outfit that did the job it had to do as well as possible and to the standards expected by the British Army.

'Compassionate leave, Morrissey? To get married?'

'Yes, please, Sergeant. If possible. The last week of November, if I can.'

'Did you know you can get up to twenty-eight days' compassionate for a wedding?'

Nan gasped. 'Really, Sarge? That's nearly a month! I won't need that long. Chas has only got a weekend pass.'

'Did he apply for compassionate?'

'I dunno. I don't think he likes to be away from flyin' too long.'

'Well, that's a fine example to set. Plenty would leap at any opportunity to escape their duty. I only wish everyone was like him. Why don't you apply for a week? After all, you'll never have another wedding leave.' Sergeant James paused for a moment as though remembering that Nan was going to marry an airman, whose chances of surviving were precarious, and rushed on, 'So I'll put the application in for you and we'll hear in a few days. I shouldn't think there will be a problem. We can cover for you without much trouble while you're away. Speaking of which . . .' Sergeant James nodded at the teleprinter. 'You'd better get back to work. The Yeoman told me that there was a fair bit of traffic in the night. Things are hotting up a bit and we have to be on full-alert.'

'Yes, Sergeant,' said Nan obediently, and went back to her post.

'My goodness!' cried Evie as she came into Southgate Lodge. 'This place is freezing!'

They'd stayed in the cookhouse for as long as they could, lingering over steak-and-kidney and sago pudding for ages before heading back to the billet. None of them wanted to go to the NAAFI, deciding instead that some peace and quiet and letter-writing would suit them all better.

Carrie stamped up and down and rubbed at her

arms. 'Brrr, how does one little house get so cold?'

'It's all outside walls, isn't it? Poor little Southgate stands on its own, and the walls don't look all that weather-tight to me. And then there are all the gaps in the window and the door, and the fire that never gets lit . . .' Evie frowned for a moment and then said, 'Well, I don't think anyone could blame us for trying to get a little bit of blessed warmth in this place. Honestly, I'm beginning to wish that the sergeant could get her way and bag us some nice warm Nissen huts with coke stoves.'

'You can't wanna leave this dinky place!' said Nan, horrified. Then she wrinkled her nose. 'But you're right. It's awful cold.'

'Right. Then let's go out to that shed and get that wood and coal and get the fire going. And Nan, you bring in a sack or two and we'll stuff up the gaps wherever we can.'

Still in their greatcoats and caps, the three girls crept down the path by the muted light of Carrie's torch.

'No one's gonna see us, though, are they?' whispered Nan. 'Golly, my fingers are freezing off.'

'No point in taking in any chances,' hissed back Evie. 'Come on, let's get what we need and get back inside as quick as we can.'

The shed was even messier and dirtier than they remembered. Carrie put some lumps of coal and logs into a tin bucket while Nan found some sacks near the floor, hoping as she picked them up that enterprising rats had not decided to make their beds in them, because she didn't know what she'd do if an enormous great rodent suddenly appeared, flicking its nasty fleshy tail and showing bright yellow teeth. Luckily there were no signs of any pests making their homes there.

Too cold even for them, I should think, thought Nan grimly. Is it going to go on like this till Spring? I don't know how I shall stand it!

'Come on,' called Evie, in a low voice, 'I reckon we've got everything we can from this place. Let's get back inside.'

Southgate felt a little warmer in comparison to the bitterness outside, and Nan set to at once, cleaning out the little grate in her and Carrie's room, while Evie checked the blackout to make sure not a glimmer of light was escaping through the windows. Carrie stuffed the sacks as best she could under the door and ripped one up to make small rags to jam into the window gaps. Soon a little fire was flickering away, while Carrie boiled the kettle and made them all cocoa. They sat on Nan's bed, the closest to the small fireplace, and tried to warm their toes, while their hotties, with pyjamas wrapped round them, were tucked down inside their beds.

'It's more picturesque than anything else isn't it? I can't feel any heat at all from those little flames,' said Carrie. 'Oh well. It makes us feel a little better, doesn't it, even if we're not getting any warmer.'

'It always takes a while for fires to get goin',' said Nan. 'They're always at their best just before we all go to bed, aren't they?'

'It's lovely,' Evie said stoutly. 'Poor old Priest's I bet Lenice and Ailsa don't have this, especially with Sergeant James there to keep an eye on them and make sure everything's done according to regulations. So, Nan, have you applied for your compassionate?'

'Oh yes. Now that Chas has permission from Auntie Mim, there's nothin' to hold us back. Sergeant James said I could have up to twenty-eight days, can you believe it? But I've only gone for a week, 'cos Chas isn't going to get that long and I can't see any point in staying away without him when he'll be back here, and so will you lot.'

'So no time for a honeymoon?' asked Evie, with a grin.

'We'll get a wedding night or two,' said Nan, flushing. 'We don't need much more than that and we can always take a proper honeymoon when the war is over. Imagine – we might even go to Paris or something, once them nasty *Jairmans* have been sent packin'.'

There was a pause while they all thought of a day when the war was over.

'Bob will be home,' said Evie dreamily.

'Chas and I can live happily together in Gardener's Cottage,' said Nan, smiling, 'and he can go back to the carpet factory.'

'I suppose I'll be married to Jeffrey,' added Carrie

in a small voice. 'Perhaps we'll have children.' Her own dream didn't seem much compared to the others – they obviously couldn't imagine anything nicer, but Carrie just couldn't imagine anything else. She quickly changed the subject away from herself. 'What are you doing for your wedding, Nan? Will there be cake?'

'Cake! I shouldn't think so. How does anyone get enough butter and eggs for cake these days?'

'Sometimes people pool their rations,' Evie said, wrapping her fingers round her cocoa mug to warm them through. 'That's what we did. All my aunts and neighbours and everyone put something in and even though it was a mix of margarine and butter and oil and powdered egg, with a bit of sugar and dried fruit, my mum managed to make a very good cake – two tiers! And she iced it – but only the tops, not the sides. And my uncle Stan had a bottle of sherry, so we all had something to toast with. It was a lovely day. Bob looked super in his uniform. Oh, I do miss him.' For a moment, Evie's face took on a sad, far-off expression and it looked as though she might weep. Then she quickly got control of herself and jumped up. 'Tell you what, Nan, why don't you try my wedding dress?'

'Have you got it with you?' asked Nan, surprised.

'No, but I'll write to Mum and she can send it in a parcel. It'll be here in no time. What do you think?'

489

'Well, I don't know . . .' Nan said doubtfully. 'Is it good luck to wear someone else's wedding dress? I always dreamed of something new.'

'That was before there was a war on, Nan,' Evie said. 'It's positively good luck now, not to say patriotic.'

'Besides,' added Carrie, 'you couldn't ask for a wedding dress that carried more love and happiness in it than Evie's, could you?'

'No,' Nan agreed. Her face brightened and she gave a huge smile. 'You're right, Carrie. Thanks ever so much, Evie, I'd love to try on your wedding dress, and won't it just give Chas the hugest surprise ever when I walk in wearing a proper dress. He won't believe it.'

'Good, that's settled. I'll write to Mum tonight and it will be here as soon as you like. Now, I don't know about you two, but I'm sure that fire is getting warmer. Isn't it lovely?'

They finished their cocoa as they watched the last log burn away to soft, glowing embers.

'Is it necessary to smoke quite so many cigarettes on the night shift?' asked Sergeant James crossly, as she came into the signals office. The Yeoman was just tidying up in preparation for going off shift, back to where he came from behind the green baize door. 'It's too cold to open the windows for any length of time these days. I don't want to live with this ghastly fug all day. I don't know how you can stand it.'

'Sorry,' said Yeo blithely. He was far too used by now to Monica James's sharp moods to be bothered by them. They always passed. 'If it's any comfort, it's been quite quiet – it should stay like that most of the day, if it's anything like usual.'

'Turner!' snapped Sergeant James. Evie jumped to. She'd been smiling at Yeo and leaning against the door. 'If you've nothing better to do, you can get the kettle on. I need a cup of tea.'

'Yes, Sergeant,' said Evie obediently and went in to the small kitchen to brew up a pot from the supplies that she was sure were topped up by Yeo. There must be lots of goodies behind that green door – not just kettles but lots of lovely things, food as well. Imagine if there were a heater and a box of chocolates! That just about summed up all of Evie's fantasies these days – apart from a kiss and a hug from Bob, which she'd give up all her treats and luxuries for in the batting of an eye. As she made the tea, she kept an ear open for the conversation going on in the other room, and heard the Yeoman saying something like, '. . . If you fancied it one evening?'

'No thank you, Yeoman,' was the sharp reply.

'I thought you were going to call me Jim,' protested the Navy signalman.

'All right – Jim. It's quite out of the question. I don't take evening passes, I'm needed here. And once Private Morrissey goes on compassionate, I'll be busier than ever. It's just not possible.'

'Suit yourself,' said Jim, without a trace of

annoyance in his voice. 'But if you ever do feel like it, just let me know. Now, I'd better be getting to my bed.'

'Yes, well . . . thank you, Yeo . . . I mean, Jim. I appreciate it. I hope you understand my position, though.'

Ahhh, go on! thought Evie, willing the sergeant to unbend just a little. Go out on a date, it'll do you good! But she would never dare say any such thing.

'Where is Private Morrissey?' called Sergeant James to the little kitchen where Evie was just putting the hot water over the tea.

'Cookhouse. She'll be about five minutes.'

'Good, then you can go, Turner, all right?'

'Yes, Sergeant.'

'And get yourself as much as you can – I have a feeling it's going to be a busy day. Don't ask me why.'

Evie came back in with the teapot and mugs. 'It's not looking too good out there, is it?'

'We've always got to be positive, Turner, you know that. You must have heard what Churchill said just the other day: never give in. Never, never, never. No matter how bleak it looks, we've got to press on and believe that we will win. Yes, the Germans are advancing in Russia, besieging cities and causing huge suffering. But they're facing a winter over there now, and the spirit of a people who, like us, won't be defeated. The Germans can't win. I believe that, Turner. Do you?'

'Yes,' said Evie, thinking of Bob and wondering where he was at this very moment, and sending a prayer for his safekeeping.

'Good. That's the spirit. Now let's get on.'

She's not so bad, thought Evie, taking up her position at the switchboard and waiting for the first disc to fall. But I still think that her going out on a date with the Yeoman is the best idea I've heard in a long time! She never will, though. She's too stubborn.

It was definitely harder to work in winter, thought Carrie. All the cold and dark – it was the devil's own work to get out of bed. Leaving the cosiness and warmth of her blankets for the chill of the room and the icy water and getting dressed was almost impossible and she couldn't help moaning when she finally had to brave the cold.

Much worse for people in Leningrad or places like that, she told herself. You've got a warm cookhouse and a hot breakfast to go to. Think of all those poor people suffering and dying from cold and hunger, with no help able to get through the German lines.

That helped her a little but it was still difficult. The precious fuel from the shed was running low and they'd decided that they couldn't have a fire every night but only on special occasions.

'Maybe on Nan's birthday,' suggested Evie. 'That's not so far off, now, is it?'

Nan needed cheering up because Chas hadn't

been available for many dates recently and he was unusually tight-lipped about it. 'Things are coming up, big plans and so forth,' was all he would say. 'I'm sorry, darling. I'll see you when I possibly can, you know that. And nothing will stop us getting married. But before then, I still have to do my job.'

When Carrie got back from dinner that evening, she found Evie on her own in Southgate Lodge. 'Where's Nan?' she asked.

'She's off being love's young dream. Chas turned up unexpectedly. You couldn't see her for dust. Lucky we weren't on lates tonight.'

'Where've they gone?'

'I don't know. The pub in Little Modeley, perhaps? Or there's another place that Nan said they'd found, so they've probably gone there. Nan doesn't like risking seeing that old man who told her about Cecilia. She says he gives her the creeps, poor old thing. He's just telling old folk tales. I'm sure he doesn't mean for Nan to take them so seriously. Listen, Carrie, I was thinking – why don't we go down to the pub tonight? I've written a letter to Bob but my hands are so cold I can't do it right. It's bound to be a bit warmer in there and it'll be a bit of a treat, don't you think?'

'How'll we get there? We can't walk in this freezing weather, but I can't take any transport from the motor pool. It wouldn't be right.'

'Oh.' Evie's face fell. 'Are you sure? I thought you might be able to use the pick-up.'

Carrie shook her head. 'I couldn't. I'd be up on a charge if they found out. Tell you what though – Freddy showed me something a couple of days ago. He found some old bicycles in the stables and said he was going to clean and oil them, because you never know when they might come in handy. Shall we see if we can use those?'

'Brilliant idea!' cried Evie, her face clearing. 'I knew you'd think of something, you clever puss.'

They ran up to the stable block and found the bicycles under some old tarpaulin, all gleaming and freshly oiled to Freddy's usual high standards. There were four of them, in different sizes, but all with decent leather saddles that were still a bit springy, and without too much rust.

'It'll be cold, cycling. And we can't use any lights,' said Carrie, already chilled to the bone despite her coat, hat and gloves.

'No, the exercise will warm us up, you'll see. We'll be toasty by the time we get to the pub. And we'll be able to hear anything coming through the blackout . . .'

'Except for foxes, stoats, pheasants . . .' pointed out Carrie.

'All right! Come on, we'll be fine.'

It was a curious feeling, riding a bicycle through the pitch blackness, the freezing air flowing across their cheeks and over their ears as they followed the road as best they could. They couldn't go fast, but occasionally the moon appeared from behind the clouds and lit their way for a few minutes. It seemed like much further to the pub than they remembered but after a while, they made out the low stone building, its windows carefully blacked out but a plume of fragrant smoke emerging from the chimney.

They parked the bikes at the side of the pub and then let themselves in to the interior. As Evie had promised, they instantly felt warm, a wonderful feeling that enveloped them all over. They found themselves a table to sit down at.

'Drinks on me,' Evie proclaimed, and went up to get them. She came back with two glasses. 'Look – cider! The publican said he'd kept some under the counter for the armed forces. Isn't that lovely of him?'

'What a treat,' said Carrie gratefully. 'This was a splendid idea, Evie. I'm glad we came. Nice to have a change of scene, anyway.' She looked about. 'No sign of the lovebirds.'

'No, they must be in that other place, wherever that is. No doubt they'll keep it to themselves for as long as they can, so they can be all nice and private.' Evie took a sip of her cider. 'Oh, *that* hits the spot! How delicious. I bet it's made around here, it tastes so appley.'

Carrie drank a little of hers, enjoying the faint tingle over her tongue. 'Mmm – you're right. Gosh, this is a treat.'

Evie paused a moment and slid a glance over towards her friend. 'Talking of lovebirds, Carrie – what's happening with you and Jeffrey? You haven't really said anything at all since you got back from leave, and that was ages ago now. Have you heard much from him?'

'Oh, yes. I've had some letters, of course. He doesn't have all that much to say really. I think he's enjoying himself on *HMS Adventurer*. After all, he doesn't have to worry about being attacked because he's not actually sailing anywhere, and he likes the work. He was even a bit indiscreet to me and told me a bit about what they're all working on up there in Scotland, even though he didn't exactly say where he was or what he was doing.'

'That's not so good. We're not supposed to say anything to anyone.'

'I know – but it's difficult, isn't it? Things just slip out sometimes, even when we really don't mean it to. I was talking to Mother and she was badgering me to tell her where I'm stationed and even as I was explaining that it was just "somewhere in England" and that I couldn't tell and she shouldn't ask, the word "Heronflete" came out – just like that! Even though I was absolutely determined not to tell her anything.'

'I know. It goes against everything to keep secrets from our nearest and dearest, doesn't it? But we simply have to hold our tongues. It's a matter of national security, after all.'

'Of course! And if it's any comfort, Mother has no idea where Heronflete is, so she can't go telling anyone where we are.'

Evie gave her a curious glance. 'You really don't

want to talk about Jeffrey, do you? At least, not about getting married. Is there anything you want to get off your chest? You know I'm a good listener, Carrie, and I certainly won't be making judgements of you, if that's what you're worried about. It's just that I've noticed that even though you're engaged, there's no more talk of you and Jeffrey getting married. And that engagement ring isn't even round your neck any more. You're wearing your gold ring instead.'

Carrie looked down at the heavy gold ring on her engagement finger. 'It means an awful lot to me. My father and I had the same initials and they're engraved on the front, can you see? CT. Christopher Tiptree. Or Caroline Tiptree, now.'

'Isn't it funny,' Evie said hesitantly, 'that you don't want to wear the ring that says you're going to become Caroline Frobisher – your engagement ring. But you *do* want to wear the ring that has your name and your father's name on it.'

Caroline laughed awkwardly. 'Don't go getting all deep on me, Evie, and finding hidden motives in everything. It's purely practical, you know. This old thing is solid and can't be damaged when I'm changing tyres and things like that.' She paused and looked at the burnished shine of the old gold ring. 'But . . . can I tell you something, Evie? Something private?'

'You know you can.'

'I've found out that Jeffrey hasn't finished paying for my engagement ring.'

'Yes?' Evie frowned. 'Is that so bad? I know lots of young men who can't afford to pay for a diamond ring up front. They cost quite a bit, after all.'

'Of course,' Carrie said hastily. 'Please don't think I mean that I look down on Jeffrey for that. I don't – I know not everyone has inherited money and a house like I have. But that's the point, you see. Jeffrey didn't tell me that he'd borrowed money to buy the engagement ring. And he hasn't told me that he knew I would inherit Jackmans Cottage and the money, even though Mother let it slip that he's known for ages – even before I had any idea at all of what was coming to me. That's the problem, do you see?'

'Of course I do. He hasn't been honest with you,' said Evie with a worried look.

'Well, he hasn't exactly lied . . .'

'No – but he hasn't been open about things. And that must make you a little bit suspicious. I can quite see that. Oh dear, Carrie. The more you tell me about this situation, the more certain I am that you and Jeffrey are not supposed to be married.'

Seeing Carrie's face, Evie rushed on. 'I know you don't like me talking this way, and you think it's none of my business, but when you confide in me like this, I feel I must at least give you my reaction to it. You're perfectly at liberty to ignore everything I say, and I won't mind a bit. If you're going to have a successful marriage, you must love your husband, of course, but almost more important than that, you must absolutely trust him. I think that is probably the most vital thing. It seems that your faith in Jeffrey is wavering, to say the least. If I'm honest, it sounds as though you suspect his motives in marrying you.'

Carrie flushed angrily. 'I didn't say that!'

'I know, I know. But if it's at the back of your mind, you should think carefully before you actually do walk down the aisle.'

Carrie's heart raced and she took a few deep breaths, staring in the glass of cider to calm herself down. 'I *am* thinking about it,' she muttered through clenched teeth. 'I'm sorry if I get angry when we talk about it but you must understand this is difficult for me. I've known Jeffrey for so long. And I *do* love him, in my way. It's hard to contemplate the kind of things I've been thinking about recently. It makes me feel . . . as though I'm just as bad, just as low, to suspect him of such dreadful things.'

'Not if you're right,' Evie pointed out. 'That's the crucial thing, isn't it?'

'Yes. And when he walked to the church on the day the banns were read, my first feeling was one of dread. I can't forget that. Well, one thing I am determined about – there's not going to be any New Year wedding, not yet at least. And I'm not going to let anyone bully me into that. I've got to be sure in my own mind, and I know I will be in time.'

'Good for you! I'll drink to that!' Evie lifted her glass to her lips, and Carrie joined her, both enjoying the mild tingle that the cider gave them.

As they drank, Carrie looked about at the interior of the old pub. The walls were stone and wooden beams hung low over the lounge room. A fire glowed in the hearth.

They must go out to the woods and get these great logs, thought Carrie, watching the wood in the fireplace crackle slightly and pop sparks up towards the chimney.

Her eye was caught by the sight of a man in a dark suit standing at the bar. She could only see his back but something about the broadness of the shoulders, the strength of the back, and the dark hair cut very short at the back, told her that this was an intriguing young man.

Not in uniform, she thought, surprised. He looks like the right age to be in one of the services, and he certainly looks fit enough, from the back at least. I wonder . . . perhaps he's already been injured and is recovering, or isn't fit enough for service. I can't see his face after all. He might be burned or disfigured or blind. He might be in a reserved occupation. Still strange though, to see someone of his age who isn't wearing the colours of one of the forces.

As she studied him with interest, the man at the bar raised his head as he drained the last of his drink, put the glass on the bar, and turned. As he did so, he and Carrie locked gazes, his brown eyes fixing on her blue ones. Carrie gasped.

'What's up?' asked Evie. 'Here, are you all right, Carrie? You've gone absolutely white.'

'I-I-I –' stammered Carrie. 'Oh my goodness . . .'

She stood up as if in a dream. The man walked forward a few paces from the bar, evidently as shocked as Carrie. He stopped and looked at her awkwardly.

'Carrie?' he said in a wondering voice. 'Is that really you?'

'Todd!' she gasped. 'I thought it was you! How incredible. What on earth are you doing here?'

Scanning his face, she could see now that the fourteen-year-old boy she remembered was still present: he had the same dark brown eyes and thick dark hair, but his boyish curls were gone and his face had a sharper, more chiselled quality. He certainly was not blind or disfigured or any of the things she had wondered about. So why wasn't he fighting?

Todd said, 'I just can't believe it. Caroline Tiptree. You haven't changed a bit.' He came towards the table.

Carrie fought to get control over herself and seem as normal and calm as possible. 'Evie, let me introduce you to Todd Coverdale. Todd, this is Lance Corporal Evie Turner. Evie and I are in the ATS together.'

'Pleased to meet you,' Evie said with a smile.

'And you too, Lance Corporal,' Todd said politely. 'Carrie and I are old friends. In fact, I used to live at Jackmans Cottage when I was a boy, didn't I, Carrie? So we know each other well. Did your mother really let you join up?'

'Yes, well, let's just say that I took matters into my own hands.' Carrie smiled back at him. 'She wasn't all that thrilled to be honest. Todd – this is amazing. I can't get over it. You, here in the pub at Little Modeley! How do you come to be here?'

An uncomfortable look passed over Todd's face, and he came closer to the table. 'Listen, Carrie, I can't talk about it now, all right? Sorry and all that. But I can't. I'm amazed to see *you* here. Are you based locally?'

'Yes.' She nodded. 'Not far at all.'

'It's the strangest thing. Listen, I have to go now. I say, Lance Corporal, do you mind if I steal your friend here for a moment?'

'Not at all.'

Carrie got up and went where Todd beckoned towards the door.

'Carrie,' he said in a low voice that only she could hear, 'we must meet again and I'll be able to tell you more. And I want to hear about *you* and what you've been up to. Could you meet me here again one night?'

'Yes . . . yes, I'm sure I could.'

'Well, look, nothing is certain. But how about we say Friday night, at nine o'clock. Do you think you could manage that?'

'I can try.'

'Excellent. I'll be here if I possibly can. When I see you, I'll explain. All right?'

'Yes,' said Carrie, still in a daze that she should have met Todd right here, in the pub, a few miles from Heronflete.

'Good.' He gave her another warm smile. 'Good night then.' With a few strides, he was at the door, and then gone into the bitter cold night outside. Carrie went back to the table.

Evie gave a low whistle. 'My goodness, Carrie Tiptree. Who on earth was *that*?'

Carrie sat slowly down, shaking her head, unable to muster her thoughts at all. She held up a hand and saw that it was shaking.

'He's certainly had an effect on *you*,' grinned Evie. 'I don't blame you, he's ever so nice-looking. Bob's dark like that, and I always think it's the most romantic look on a man. And with those dreamy brown eyes. He's quite a dish, isn't he?'

'Oh, dear, Evie. I don't know what to say, I'm so confused! I haven't seen Todd for seven years and now . . . here!' Carrie shook her head, frowning. 'It's just . . . so odd.'

'A very strange coincidence,' agreed Evie. 'I want to hear all about this Todd.'

Carrie looked at her watch. 'Oh my goodness, we'd better get back. We have to be in by twenty-three hundred hours or we'll be for it. Come on, let's get the bikes and head back.'

* * *

They got back easily enough, with plenty of time to spare before the curfew. The ride home undid some of the benefits of the warmth of the pub as they had to cycle too slowly to work up any real heat from the exercise. After returning the bicycles to the stable block, putting them snugly back under their tarpaulin covers, they walked back as briskly as they could to the Lodge, hoping to prevent their toes turning to ice.

'D'you think it's going to be like this until Spring?' asked Evie, shivering as they went inside. 'I've never known it this cold in November! Oh well – look, Nan's not back yet. She's cutting it finer and finer, getting back from seeing Chas. One of these days she's going to regret it – she'll get caught and the sarge will let her have it.'

'They'll calm down after they're married, I should think,' said Carrie, taking off her cap and gloves. 'Shall I get the kettle on?'

'Oooh, yes. And don't be too sure about them calming down, as you put it. Bob and I were still as desperate for a private kiss and cuddle after the ceremony as we were before. I suppose there's one thing to be said for this awful war – it's certainly keeping the heart fonder, with all the absences we have to put up with.'

They filled their hotties, wrapped their pyjamas round them to warm them up for a few minutes, and then got changed, trying to keep the heat in by tying their dressing gowns tightly round themselves.

Carrie put on her woolly hat and bedsocks, and went to sit on Evie's bed for a while with her mug of cocoa.

'Todd was the first boy ever to propose to me,' she confided shyly. 'He was the one I told you about. He and his mother came to live with us, because his father saved my father's life in the Great War, so Daddy felt that he owed it to him to protect his family. My mother never liked it, of course. And after Daddy was gone, and Marie Coverdale died, Todd was sent away. But before then, he was my best friend. He lived with us for five years, and I loved having him and his mother there. The place was never the same after they were gone. It felt as though all the life had drained out of Jackmans Cottage. Instead of games and fun, there was quiet and order and everything just so, as Mother likes it. When Todd was there, we ran about the garden and explored the woods and invented stories and adventures. Afterwards, when he was gone, I wasn't allowed out so much any more, and I was only permitted quiet lady-like activities like sewing. I hated it.'

'No wonder you ran away to join the Army,' said Evie, snuggling under her blankets. 'What about Jeffrey? You said you grew up with him – did he know Todd as well?'

'Oh, yes. It was a strange thing because we all played together at times, and sometimes Todd and Jeffrey could be in cahoots, teasing me and frightening me with ghost stories. But most of the time, there was a kind of rivalry and hostility between the two of them.'

'Ooh – do you mean like the two boys fighting over you?' Evie grinned. 'This is as good as a penny romance!'

'No. Not really. At least – I don't think so.' Carrie thought back. It had never occurred to her that the boys had been possessive of her, each wanting to win her, but now she could see that perhaps there had been an element of that. But there was also more to it. She could remember the cold disdain in Jeffrey's eyes when he looked at Todd, and the burning resentment in Todd's face when he had to take yet another of Jeffrey's insults.

'I am a Frobisher,' Jeffrey used to say haughtily. 'I don't take orders from the son of a servant like you, Coverdale. You do as you're told. There's only one gentleman here, and it isn't you.'

Todd would smoulder with concealed anger, unable to let his temper burst forth.

She said to Evie now, 'There was more to it all round. It was hard for Todd – everyone thought of him as a charity case because my family had taken him in. But he was always a clever, energetic soul who I felt could go as far in life as he wanted.'

'So you didn't look down on him then?'

'Oh no!' cried Carrie. Her cheeks flushed pink and her eyes sparkled. 'It was quite the reverse! I looked *up* to him. He was my hero. He could do anything – and he could take Jeffrey on and win whenever he felt like it.' She remembered a day when Jeffrey had piled on one insult too many, and Todd had challenged him to a fight, right there, in the woods.

'Do you know how *gentlemen* fight, Coverdale?' sneered Jeffrey.

'Course I do,' retorted Todd. 'Now, are you good for it? Want to give it a try? I'm ready whenever you are.' And so saying, he had stripped off his rough tweed jacket, rolled up his shirtsleeves and raised his bony white fists. Carrie could see him now: slender and still boyish, no real match for Jeffrey's tall, well-nourished frame, but more than equal to him thanks to his burning desire to stand up to the bigger boy.

Jeffrey had stripped to his shirtsleeves likewise and they circled each other warily. Todd jabbed his fists towards Jeffrey, who laughed mockingly and then landed a sharp punch to Todd's cheek without much trouble.

'Oh, don't hurt each other!' Carrie cried, wanting them to stop.

'Shut up, Carrie,' said Jeffrey. 'It won't take me long to deal with this little upstart.' He put another hooked jab on Todd's face, raising a red mark where his fist had hit. It wasn't long before it seemed as though the bigger boy would win. Just as Carrie was almost crying, desperate for them to stop, Todd, given extra strength by his anger, suddenly launched a flurry of punches that landed Jeffrey on the ground, panting for breath and agonised amid the crushed bracken stems.

'Want any more, Frobisher?' Todd had shouted triumphantly.

'No – you . . . *beast*,' Jeffrey managed to say, as he tried to catch his breath. 'You're just lucky. Anyone can fight like that.'

'Can they? So why didn't you?'

'I told you. I fight like a gentleman.'

'Then I suppose gentlemen must lose all the time,' said Todd. 'Gentlemen like *you*, anyway.' And he laughed.

Carrie laughed now, remembering his triumphant face and the sight of Jeffrey squirming in the undergrowth.

'What are you giggling about?' Evie asked. 'You know what, Carrie? This Todd doesn't just sound like a hero to me. He sounds like a first love. Am I right?'

Carrie didn't say anything. Then, with a small smile, she said, 'I'd better get to bed. That ride has bushed me completely. And listen! I think I can hear Nan coming up the path. I'll go and let her in.'

And she slid away without answering the question, leaving Evie with one eyebrow well and truly raised.

NINETEEN

Nan sat on her bed, the tip of her tongue protruding from the side of her mouth with the effort she was making. She was writing carefully in her best handwriting, not wanting to make a mistake and waste the precious paper and have to start again. There wasn't so much notepaper about that she could afford to throw it away, and she didn't want to send anything with crossings out and spelling mistakes in it.

Dear Auntie Mim,

Things are full of excitement here. As you know, it is my birthday in a week or so and the girls say they are planning a little treat for me. They are such loves to me and I couldn't wish for better friends, so I'm sure it will be something nice. After that, it is my wedding. I will be going down to Shrewsbury on the Friday and Chas and I will be married on the Saturday. Then we have a week together at his mother's house before we are both back. If you would like to come, you would be most welcome and it would mean a lot to me. I am enclosing Chas's mother's address so you can write to her and let her know if you can come . . .

At that moment, Evie burst in. 'Hello, stop your writing, Nan. Look what's arrived!' She held out a bulky parcel wrapped in brown paper and string.

'What is it?' asked Nan, frowning.

'What is it? The wedding dress, of course! Come on, don't you want to try it?'

'Ooh, yes! I didn't expect it so quick.'

'I told you Mum would send it as soon as I asked. Let's open it.' Evie started pulling at the knots with her fingernails.

'Your mum's good at parcels, in't she?' grumbled Nan, as they picked at the tight twists of string. 'Can't we just cut the blessed things?'

'And waste this good string? Not likely. Come on, a bit of persistence is all we need.'

At last Evie managed to get a fingernail into a knot and loosen it, and eventually the parcel was free. They pulled away at the paper and found tissue paper underneath.

'Gawd, this is fancy. Tissue paper! Where'd your mum get that from?'

'This is the original tissue,' explained Evie. 'It's what the fabric came in. We got it from John Lewis.

Only reason we managed is that we bought it before the war started.'

Nan could already see the beautiful sheen of oyster-colour silk and the luxurious edging of cream lace.

'Come on, let's get it out.' Evie lifted the dress up and shook it out, letting it fall to the floor.

'Oh! Oh, it's beautiful!' breathed Nan, overcome. 'Was this really your wedding dress?'

Evie grinned. 'It certainly was. It looks the height of luxury now, doesn't it? You're lucky these days if you can find parachute silk to make a wedding dress out of, and a scrap or two of taffeta for the bridesmaids. We didn't know how fortunate we were.'

Nan was struck dumb by the sight of it. It was a dress, but the way it was sewn, it looked like a jacket over a skirt. The jacket top was smart, with mother-of-pearl buttons and long sleeves slightly puffed at the shoulder, coming tight in at the waist with a silk belt. Below it, the silk skirt fell elegantly to the ground in lavish folds of material.

'Oh look, Mum's even put in the seed pearl tiara and the veil. That was good of her. Well – are you going to try it on or not?'

'Yes please.' She was all fingers and thumbs but Evie helped her out of her jacket and skirt, so that she stood there in her khaki knickers, stockings and brassière, along with her Army regulation brown shoes.

'You're a sight!' laughed Evie. 'Now, put your arms up. The zip's hidden here at the side, you see, so I'll slide it down over your head. You can't get one of these on on your own, that's for sure, so I'll be your lady's maid.'

Nan obediently put her arms up in the air and Evie wiggled the silk dress over her head and smoothed it down. It went on without too much trouble, and Evie pulled it into place and did up the zipper under the arm. Then she tied the silk belt into a bow at the front and arranged the pleats of the jacket top so that they sat just so.

'It feels real nice,' breathed Nan, looking down. 'It's so soft! Like butter. I can't imagine what it must be like to wear this for a whole day. And to think there are ladies who can wear silk every day. Hard to imagine, in't it?'

Evie frowned. 'The fabric's lovely, that's for sure. And it suits your skin and hair no end. There's only one problem.'

'It's too big,' Nan said gloomily. She held up one arm to show the sleeve covering most of her hand, while Evie pulled at the waist where there was a good inch of spare material at least. 'I couldn't walk in it without trippin' up. If it was a bit shorter, we could pretend it was part of the style – you know, like it had a train or something. But it just looks too big, don't it? Oh, flamin' norah! I knew it was too good to be true.'

'I didn't really realise how much taller I am than you. I suppose I must be bigger all round.'

'I look like a little gal tryin' on her mum's dress, don' I? It's no good, Evie. I appreciate it an' all,

513

but I can't get married wearin' this. I'd better wear my uniform. At least that fits me.'

'Sorry, Nan. It seemed like a good idea. I just clean forgot that we were such different sizes.'

They both stood there for a moment, contemplating the over-large dress, Nan gazing down at the folds of silk with regret and Evie tutting with annoyance. Just then, the door opened and Carrie came in, bringing a gust of cold air with her. She stopped in amazement at the sight of Nan standing in a wedding dress, and gasped. Her hand flew to her mouth and she stared for a moment, as her eyes glazed over with tears.

'Oh, Nan! Don't you look wonderful! You're a real bride.'

'I'm glad you think so,' Nan retorted tartly. Her disappointment was making her sharp. 'I think I look like a real idiot! Can't you see I'm swimmin' in it?' She held up her hands as explanation, showing her fingers poking out of the top of the sleeves, and then hoisted up some of the loose fabric of the skirt. 'If I turned up lookin' like this on my weddin' day, Chas would think I was skittin' him or somethin'. It's a right joke, that's all it is.'

'I think this is worse than not having seen the dress at all,' Evie added unhappily.

'But it's not a disaster at all!' cried Carrie. 'All we have to do is take it in. It would be much worse if it were too small – there'd be nothing we could do for it then, that's true. But there's heaps of room in it. All that needs doing is a bit of tucking and trimming and rehemming and it'll fit like a glove. Look.'

She rushed over to Nan and in a moment had tucked back the sleeves, saying, 'We can move these buttons back', and had pinched in the waist and grabbed a fistful of loose material in the skirt and cleverly hitched it into the back of the belt to show how it would look. 'There! Isn't that a million times better? It's easy.'

A small ray of hope shone in Nan's eyes. 'D'you really think so, Carrie?' Then in a moment it flickered and went out. 'But this is Evie's weddin' dress. We can't go cuttin' it around and changin' it around an' all that. It wouldn't be right.'

They both looked over at Evie, who was frowning. 'Oh dear,' she said at last. 'It *is* hard to think about the dress being altered so that it won't fit me anymore.'

'But were you ever going to wear it again, Evie? Most women cut their dresses up anyway for Christening robes when the babies come along.'

'I suppose not. But there is my sister, you see. She's not married yet, and we're pretty much the same size. I'd like her to wear it if she can. Who knows when we'll be able to afford material like this again, even if the war was to end tomorrow.'

'Evie's right,' Nan said sadly. 'We can't cut her dress up, we just can't. I wouldn't want to anyway. Besides, who can we get to do it?'

'I never thought I'd be pleased about the hours my mother made me spend sewing,' said Carrie with a grin. 'But there is one good outcome. I'm a demon with a needle and thread. And you know what, Evie, I'm sure we can do all this without cutting any of the material out. It'll mean a bit of extra work, but I'm certain I could do it. With some cunning folding and tucking and double-stitching, it'll work a treat. Then, when it's served its purpose for Nan, I can let it back out again, and Bob's your Uncle. It'll be back to how it was.'

'Won't it be marked?' queried Evie.

'Not if I stitch finely enough – and believe me, I can do it. But I'll have to get a move on if we've got just over a week to do it in. What do you say, Evie?'

Hope was shining again in Nan's eyes as she turned to the lance corporal. 'Don' say yes unless you really mean it, Evie. You know I won't hold it against you,' she said bravely.

'If you're sure you can do it, Carrie . . .'

'Of course I am!'

Evie smiled broadly. 'Then you have my permission to make my wedding dress fit for Nan Morrissey to get married in!'

'Oh thank you, thank you,' cried Nan, not knowing who to hug first: Evie, for her generosity, or Carrie for her inspired vision and willingness to do the work. 'It's a dream come true. I mean it. It'll be the weddin' I never thought I'd have.'

Carrie was working hard, overhauling one of the vans in the motor pool. It was a dirty job but she didn't mind. Not only did she enjoy a bit of hard work but it gave her time to think about the extraordinary event that had happened just the other night. She could still hardly believe it – Todd Coverdale, in the bar of the Black Bull at Little Modeley! Sometimes she wondered if she had dreamed it, but she knew really that she hadn't.

I couldn't mistake him. He was still the same after all these years – except that he's a man now, of course. Not a boy any longer. Not the Todd who used to live with us at Jackmans Cottage much to Mother's disgust, and who had all the onerous, dirty jobs that she considered me too delicate and ladylike for. Jobs like cutting the wood, cleaning out the garage or the hearths, and blacking the stove. That's what Todd did – while his mother did all our cooking and cleaning and mending. She made it a lovely home really, and her food was delicious. Gosh – I can remember how we used to eat before the war. I can remember Todd and me falling on our breakfasts, like we'd never seen food before. Eggs and bacon and fresh-baked bread with lashings of butter, and marmalade made with heaps of sugar, and coffee and tea whenever we wanted it . . .

As she thought back, it seemed to Carrie that Todd was unmistakeably related to those days of peace and plenty and happiness when she was just a girl and the whole world seemed to be confined to Nether Hutton. Not like now, when, thanks to the war, she'd learned just how big and dangerous the world was, and how dedicated mankind could be to cruelty and killing, instead of letting everyone live in harmony together.

Still, she had found a different kind of freedom and happiness in the Army, far from her mother's meddling, and devoting her energies to the cause they all believed in – defeating Hitler and his tyrannical aims and making sure they would have a decent world to live in and bring children up in afterwards.

That set her thinking on Todd again. Why wasn't he in uniform? Whatever else you said about Jeffrey, he hadn't been slow at joining the Navy and doing his bit for the effort, even if it meant sitting in relative safety on the shores of a Scottish loch, transmitting signals and watching some of the secret submarine trials that he really should not have mentioned to her. After all, he hadn't known that he would draw that straw, even if he was convinced that he was a lucky sort who always fell on his feet. He could just as well been assigned to a battleship like the HMS *Hood,* and perhaps lost at sea along with all those other brave souls.

So what on earth was Todd doing? It just wasn't normal to see a fit young man out of uniform. He couldn't be a conscientious objector, or he would be in prison, along with all the other types who refused to fight for reasons of conscience. Carrie wasn't sure how she felt about that: it was everyone's right, she supposed, to have their own opinion and perhaps it was wrong to force someone into the army and killing and so on if they didn't want to. But what about protecting the country where they were allowed to express themselves so freely? Everyone could do their bit, after all. It didn't have to involve combat. But if you allowed a few to avoid the draft, where would you stop? She could see why, perhaps even for their own safety, the objectors had to go to prison.

That wasn't Todd. She knew that for sure. No – there was something else. Some other explanation. Was he in a reserved occupation? Perhaps he was breaking codes or something – she had heard of places where that happened, where all the brains from the top universities worked together to unscramble German messages and break into the enemy communications, so that they could save convoys under attack and plan counter-actions.

Perhaps that was what was happening here at Heronflete – after all, it made sense. Evie had said that all messages to and from the house were scrambled. Even internal calls were coded so that no one could listen in, not even an ATS switchboard operator, who you would think would be trusted. There had to be something unusual and special going on.

Carrie liked to think that Todd had been drafted in to help this kind of secret work. It meant that her instinct about him had been right – she had always been sure that he was clever: he had won a scholarship to the grammar school when he'd lived in Nether Hutton. Perhaps he'd gone to another good school where his Aunt Hilda lived, and won himself a place at a university and now he was helping the war effort at its most complicated and demanding.

Oh Todd, she thought, cleaning surplus axle grease away on an old rag. Is that what you're doing? I hope so. I hope it's something like that. Perhaps you can solve the mystery of Heronflete for me. I don't think I'll be able to wait until Friday night. Oh, I hope, *hope*, he'll be there.

The mysterious appearance of Todd Coverdale had driven all thoughts of Jeffrey and her impending wedding out of her mind. But then, this morning, there had been a letter from her mother. After talking about her health and village matters, her mother had written:

Now, when are you going to get this leave sorted out? It's simply not fair on any of us to keep it hanging like this. Surely the authorities can tell you whether you can have leave to get married or not? As I understand, it is a straightforward matter to get permission, particularly if there is a ceremony arranged. Ethel and I need to get on with the planning, and it is hardly fair on the vicar either. He needs to know what is happening and I'm sure you're aware that Christmas is one of the busiest times in his calendar. Please, Caroline – get this arranged as soon as possible. I need to think about your dress at the very least. I can't bear the thought of your being married in that horrid uniform.

A wedding dress! thought Carrie. After everything she had said to her mother about having a wedding in uniform because it was most appropriate considering the circumstances. But that was always the problem: Janet Tiptree simply wouldn't listen. If she'd set her heart and mind on something, then she would do everything in her power to make sure it happened. She wanted Carrie in white silk, or at least something a bit dressy, with a bouquet and a veil, and she wouldn't stop until she'd got it.

Carrie laughed to herself. It was rather ironic that she was spending every spare moment carefully stitching Evie's wedding dress so that it would fit Nan, but she had no intention of doing any such thing for herself. She'd never sewed as finely as she was doing at the moment, with tiny stitches only a doll or a Beatrix Potter mouse like the ones in *The Tailor of Gloucester* ought to be capable of. It was a bit ridiculous really: by day, cleaning engines and driving trucks, and by night, sewing the finest oyster-coloured silk. She'd never realised she was capable of so much. It was really rather heady stuff.

'Oy, Carrie.' It was the voice of Corporal Finnigan. 'Are you nearly finished?'

'Just done, Freddie.' Carrie stood up. 'Is it tea time?'

'It certainly is. I'm parched. Be a good girl and get the brew, will you?'

'You know you don't have to ask. By the way, I wanted to ask you if it's all right to drive Evie and Nan into Lincoln tomorrow? It's Nan's birthday and wedding coming up, and they've got nearly a day free, so I was hoping to take them in so we can buy some bits and bobs, if we can find anything.'

'Fine by me. Take the truck as usual.'

'Thanks, Freddy. I'll get that tea.' Carrie walked away, with a shiver of anticipation. Not only would she enjoy the trip to town, but in the evening was the event she had been waiting for with such eagerness. Her rendezvous with Todd in the Black Bull. Always assuming he made it, of course . . .

'Are you looking forward to your birthday tomorrow, Nan?' asked Evie. They had just arrived in Lincoln, and Carrie had parked behind the barracks as usual. Now they were wondering what to do with their precious hours of leave.

'Yes,' said Nan, 'but it don't seem like a patch on what's to come. Birthdays don't seem so important when you put them beside a wedding, do they?'

'No,' agreed Evie. 'After all, you get your birthday every year, but a wedding day only comes along once.'

Nan smiled. To be honest, she just wanted tomorrow over with. And the next day, and the next. She wanted them all to disappear as fast as possible until she woke and it was Friday and time to leave for Shrewsbury with the precious dress with its veil and tiara – she hoped that Carrie would have finished sewing it by then. She had taken all Nan's measurements very carefully and was now spending almost every spare moment hunched over the oyster silk, sewing with such tiny stitches that Nan could barely see them although Carrie shooed her away every time she tried to look.

No, birthdays didn't matter a hoot, now, when all she could think of was Chas. What was most difficult about the waiting time was how little she was getting to see him at the moment. They seemed to stepping up operations at RAF Modeley and it was harder for him to slip away and see her. Two nights this week, she'd waited in vain, shivering by Priest's and longing to hear the ridiculous noise that Boadicea made as she approached, but it hadn't happened. Then, last night, Chas had arrived only to find that she wasn't there – they were on late shifts. He had managed to leave a note with Lenice, who'd brought it down to Southgate without so much as a grumble, which was unusual for her, and Nan had snatched a brief word with him that morning when she'd called the sergeants' mess from the NAAFI and luckily he was there and able to say a quick hello followed by a whispered 'I love you, darling' before he had to go. It was terrible, being apart from him like this. The only thing that kept her going was the knowledge of next week and the fact that they would be joined together for ever.

A letter from Auntie Mim had cheered her up. It had said that her aunt would make her very best effort to be at the wedding. It would be a difficult journey and she had wondered whether she ought to attempt it, especially with the Government posters everywhere asking 'Is your journey really necessary?', but having thought it over, Miriam Simpson reckoned that her niece's wedding *was* necessary, especially when there was no other family to go. It had brought tears to Nan's eyes that her aunt was willing to make the journey, especially when trains were hardly the height of luxury these days. Late, dirty and crowded, they were not much fun and it took a lot of determination for a civilian like Auntie Mim to use them.

The three girls strolled about, not looking for anything in particular but keen to see if they could find any small treats that might brighten a birthday or a wedding. In the chemists' shop, Nan was delighted to find a lipstick – 'and it's just your colour!' said Evie. 'It'll look lovely on the big day' – and later, in a small teashop, they were lucky enough to be given an iced bun each, on account of their uniforms.

'We should keep them till tomorrow,' said Carrie, 'and eat them on your birthday. There won't be any cake, I'm afraid.'

'I don' mind a bit,' Nan answered stoutly. 'Birthday cake an' all. It seems a bit silly, somehow. An iced bun here with a cup of tea is a treat enough for me.'

'We were sorry to hear you missed Chas last night,' Evie said cautiously, as she didn't want to upset Nan.

'Yeah. Bad luck or what? After two nights shiverin' me boots off waitin' for him and he turns up the night I weren't there. Still, he left me a very nice note. And it's bad luck to see each other too often before the weddin', so they say! So I've gotta look on the bright side.'

'That's the spirit,' said Evie.

Nan smiled at her, remembering how lucky she was. She could see Chas almost every week and speak to him on the phone if he couldn't make their dates, whereas poor old Evie could only rely on letters from Bob, who she hadn't seen in so long, and sometimes even those letters took such ages to reach her that they could only give a brief comfort before Evie was back to worrying whether something had happened to him since he had written. They could only tell each other about their love knowing that the censor would be reading every word, and as for the kisses and cuddles they must be missing! It didn't bear thinking about.

Of course, they were also husband and wife and Nan knew that they must have made love – did that make the physical longing for each other harder? Now that they had known what it was to belong to each other completely? She couldn't guess. A shiver came over her as it occurred to her that in only a week she would know what it was like. There was a sense of delicious anticipation: she couldn't wait to be alone with Chas, to let their bodies do everything that they urged to do, every time they got close to each other.

'You're very quiet today, Carrie,' said Evie. 'Everything all right?'

'Oh, yes. Fine.' Carrie looked startled, as though she had been miles away. 'Listen, I was thinking – we ought to be getting back if we can. I don't want to be driving in the complete dark if I can help and you know how quickly the sun goes down these days. Has everyone finished what they want to do?'

The other two nodded.

'Right, well, let's get on our way then.'

Carrie took one of the bicycles in the stables for her trip to the pub. There was something sneaky about setting off on her own like this but she hadn't wanted to tell the others what she was doing. She had even asked Evie to keep quiet about their meeting Todd in the first place. It wasn't something she wanted even Nan to know about, she didn't know why. It just felt very private and over the last few days she had become certain that Todd was involved in something secret that she ought to keep hush-hush as well. She had no reason for thinking any such thing but it was an instinct she had decided to obey. There was no harm in being cautious.

As she rode along slowly in the darkness towards Lower Modeley, she realised that she had become convinced in her own mind that Todd was somehow connected to Heronflete. All the secrecy of the operation they were part of seemed to fit with his appearance and his reluctance to talk much about what he was doing. Perhaps he would tell her more tonight. She hoped so. So many questions raced through her mind.

She arrived at the pub out of breath, despite the slow ride, as much with anticipation as anything else. She put the bike at the side of the pub as before, and went in to the light interior. The old pub had such a warm and welcoming atmosphere that her spirits lifted at once and she felt herself calm down a little. A quick scan of the lounge bar told her that Todd wasn't there.

There you are, Caroline Tiptree, she told herself sternly. That's what you get for letting your imagination run away with you. He isn't here and he probably isn't going to come. People can't just do what they want to anymore – there are more important things going on than your social life, that's for sure!

Almost sure now that Todd wouldn't show, she decided to make the most of her evening anyway and have a drink. She'd brought a book along with her just in case he wasn't there, so she would get a small glass of beer and sip it slowly while she read by the fire. That would do her just fine.

She didn't think she would be able to take her mind off Todd's arrival even for a second, but before long she was absorbed in her book and hardly noticed when the door opened. A few moments later, a tall figure towered over her.

'Evening, Carrie,' said the man softly, and Carrie looked up, startled, to see Todd Coverdale gazing down at her. 'I've made you jump. Did you think I wasn't coming?'

'Todd, hello – you made it. I wasn't sure if you'd be able to, so I decided the best thing to do was not to expect you at all.' She smiled up at him. As soon as he was there, he became just like that familiar boy who lived with them in Jackmans Cottage, who'd been like a brother to her.

'Can I get you a drink?' he asked.

'I'm all right, thanks. I'm managing to make this one last very well.'

'Well, I shall just get one myself.' He strode off to the bar, giving Carrie time to put away her book and collect her thoughts. So he had come! Now, she hoped, at least one or two questions would be answered.

Todd returned a few moments later with a tall glass of foaming beer, and he sat down at the table opposite Carrie. After a few moments of small talk, he looked at her seriously.

'Strange coincidence, isn't it, Carrie? Us meeting like this? I must say, I've thought about little else since I last saw you. It seems so very odd – but as though it was meant to happen. We were such pals in our childhood, weren't we? But circumstances took us away from each other. It seems that fate still wanted us to be acquainted.'

'Circumstances,' said Carrie grimly. 'You mean, my mother. She's the one who sent you away. I don't think I ever had the chance to tell you how sorry I was about that.'

'It wasn't your fault. You were only thirteen – what choice did you have in the matter? And you mustn't be too harsh on your mother. She never wanted to have Mum and me living in her house – it's not surprising that she didn't feel she could keep me on after Mum died. A young boy is quite a responsibility, particularly if you never wanted it.'

'That's kind of you, Todd. But it was a debt of honour, as I see it. Your father saved my father's life, giving up his own in the process. Looking after you and your mother was the only way my father felt he could repay yours for his actions. It was wrong of my mother, I think, to send you away. It was only a few more years before you would have been independent anyway.'

'It was hard to leave Jackmans Cottage. I'd grown to love it very much,' he admitted. 'But it was also good for me to live with Aunt Hilda. She's a very kind lady and she is my true family. Dear old Auntie. Life isn't too bright for her at the moment – our house in Bradford was bombed during the raid in March and it's not safe to live in. She's staying with friends, poor thing, until they can either make it secure or pull it down. She isn't downhearted though – she's so positive. That's Aunt Hilda all over. She's seen me right, encouraged me to work hard and learn. I've done well.'

'Have you?' asked Caroline cautiously. This was the part of Todd's life she was so eager to know about. 'I know you may not be able to be frank with me about what you do, Todd. I've already made several guesses about why you aren't in uniform and what you're doing round here. One of them may be right, I don't know. Can you tell me?'

Todd looked anxiously about. There was no one near them. He lowered his voice and gazed earnestly into Carrie's eyes. 'You're probably pretty close with your guesses. Listen, I wouldn't normally tell a soul about this, but I trust you, Carrie. I think we've met up again for a reason and part of that is because I need a friend at the moment. I shouldn't be in the pub at all – I shouldn't have been here that other night when you recognised me. But I'm about to do something very dangerous, something I may not return from, and I wanted to experience the simple pleasure of a pint of beer in an old English pub before I went. So I came down here. It's close to our base, you see.'

'Is . . . is it Heronflete?'

He looked startled. 'How on earth do you know that?'

Carrie whispered back, 'Because that's where we are too! We're providing communications back-up to the big house, and so is the Navy. It's all been very puzzling. No one's allowed near the house itself, we work in a signal office near the stable block.'

'I can't say much,' said Todd solemnly. 'But have you heard of the Special Operations Executive?'

Carrie shook her head.

'I am an agent for them. We are covert fighters, organising resistance and sabotage, undermining the Germans' war machine in any way we can. Some-times it's blowing up bridges, or depots, sometimes it's sending false information or setting up accidents that look real but are planned so that the Germans will make wrong assumptions about what the allies are up to. I can't be more specific but I hope you understand the kind of thing I mean.'

'Yes – yes, I think I do.'

'It's dangerous work. It involves a lot of thinking on your feet and a dash of madness, I think. It's deeply exciting but highly dangerous. It's also very effective. A few clever, well-placed agents can disrupt whole battalions and send entire armies off in the wrong direction. But the downside is the danger and the great cost there can be in lives. The Germans are ruthless. They will execute innocent hostages in revenge for being made fools of by special agents. And if they find an agent . . . well, it's not pleasant to think about.'

Carrie went white and her stomach churned. 'Oh Todd – is that what you're doing? Are they about to send you off on a mission?'

Todd paused and looked at her seriously. At last he said, 'I'm proud to do what I can for victory in Europe. I'm honoured that the SOE think I'm up to the task. I'm determined to help.'

'And they've been training you here?'

He didn't answer but said instead, 'Soon I'll be leaving on a mission. I can't tell you where or what I'm going to do, but it will be highly dangerous. The chances are that I won't come back. At first, I didn't care. I don't have that much to live for, you know. It's not that I want to die – not at all. I love life. But I value freedom enough to be able to die for it. And I don't have a wife or children, or even a sweetheart. My parents are dead. The only person who'd miss me is my dear old aunt, but that doesn't seem so bad. Much worse for a fellow with young ones to provide for and a wife he adores to go and be killed.'

'Oh, Todd . . .' Carrie's eyes filled with tears. It seemed inexpressibly sad for this young man, so handsome and so fit, with everything to live for, to speak so casually of dying and not being missed. But so many young men – brothers, husbands, fathers, sons – were being killed every day. It was a terrible fact of life, and perhaps it would take more men like Todd to make the ulti-mate sacrifice to stop the awful slaughter from continuing. But it was so horribly sad!

'That was before I met you again, Carrie,' he said gently. His eyes searched her face. 'I'd forgotten how beautiful you are. Or perhaps I hadn't, perhaps it's just that you've grown into a woman now and you're not that little girl any longer. You know, you've always been the girl of my dreams. That's why I feel as if it's Fate that's brought us back together again.'

Carrie felt herself flush, a hot wave creeping up her face. She had always been the girl of Todd's dreams! She felt pleasure at his words but hardly knew what to think. Instead she said, 'All this time, Todd! All this time you've been right here at Heronflete. Imagine that.'

She remembered all the times she had stood at the window of Southgate, gazing out on the moonlit outlines of trees and buildings, watching foxes slink through the garden. Perhaps, only yards away, Todd had been standing at his window, looking out on the very same view: seeing the roofs and treetops, just as she did. How curious that was! Perhaps he was right – maybe something did intend them to meet again.

'What about you, Carrie? How has life treated you since we parted?'

She stared at the table, her hands clasped together on her lap, out of sight.

'Do you have a sweetheart?' he asked softly. 'I bet you do. I can't imagine how a lovely girl like you wouldn't have.'

'Actually . . .' She swallowed hard. More than

anything she wished she didn't have to say it, but she knew she must. 'Actually, I'm engaged.' She slowly drew her hands out from under the table.

Todd looked at her ring finger. 'That's not an engagement ring, is it?'

'No, it's my father's signet ring. He left it to me and it makes sense to wear it – I'm a driver, you see, and the work is often dirty. My engagement ring is in a strong box at Jackmans Cottage.'

'Who is the lucky man?'

'It's . . . it's Jeffrey Frobisher.'

Todd's face took on a strange expression and then he smiled a tight, lop-sided smile. 'Ah. My old friend Jeffrey. Fancy that.' He laughed. 'You know, Carrie, I always thought you were going to marry me. You said you would. Don't you remember?'

'Yes. Yes, I do.'

She had never forgotten it. They been sitting in the orchard underneath a cherry tree in blossom. White petals, loosened by the gentle breeze, floated down upon them. She couldn't remember now why they were there, or how long they stayed. But she knew that they had just learned that Todd was to be sent away and both were stunned by the news.

'I'll come back,' he had said, his chin set with determination. 'I'll come back before too long, Carrie. And you'll marry me then, won't you?'

They were words that would have sounded childish from anyone else. But from him, with his blazing brown eyes and boyish strength, they sounded heartfelt. More than anything at that moment, she believed him.

'Of course I will, Todd,' she cried, unable to imagine what life would be like without him. 'I will. You must come back.'

Thirteen, she had been. A child. But she had meant it just as sincerely as he had. Perhaps Evie was right: Todd *was* her first love.

She blushed as she thought it.

'So when are you and Jeffrey going to be married?' Todd's tone was casual but she could sense that there was a new distance between them.

'I . . . I don't know. After Christmas. That's what Jeffrey wants, anyway.'

'And you? What do you want?'

She tried to look into his eyes but there was a kind of intensity in them that was too much for her. She stammered, 'I'm not sure. It's very complicated.'

'What's so complicated? You fall in love with someone and then you get married.'

She wanted to say so much more, to confide all her doubts about Jeffrey to someone who actually knew him as Todd did, but she couldn't. She had a loyalty to Jeffrey and she couldn't be so wretched as to speak evil of him behind his back, when she was engaged to be married to him.

'I don't want to be married quite yet,' she said at last. 'I want to do my bit in the army. I don't want children until the war is over.'

'I see.' Todd looked at her thoughtfully for a

few moments. Then he leaned forward towards her and spoke fast. 'Listen, Carrie. You're an engaged woman, I quite appreciate that. I'm not asking anything of you that it wouldn't be proper to ask of someone in your situation. But you're an old friend, and I'm asking you to be just that for me – a friend. The chances are I'll be going to my death very soon. Will you be my friend until I leave? Perhaps meet me a few more times? Even dance with me? I could get away and we could go into Lincoln and find somewhere with a band. I'd love to dance before I go. It would all be above board, you needn't worry that I would compromise you in any way, you know that. But, if you wanted to, you could do a little to comfort me before I leave. Would you, Carrie?'

His strong hand, lying on the table, clenched as he spoke and she had the impulse to cover it with her own, but she didn't. Instead she said in a low voice. 'Of course I will. It's very little to ask, Todd, you know that. I would be proud to be your friend until you go. And I'll be your friend in spirit afterwards, wherever you go, and after you return, you can be sure of that.'

'Thank you. Thank you.' He smiled at her. 'Bless you, Carrie.'

TWENTY

'Eighteen today!' breathed Nan. 'Fancy that.' Then she wrinkled her nose. 'Don't mean I get a break though. On early shift, just like usual.'

'You're off on leave in less than a week!' called Evie, as she hurried by in her slippers to the little kitchen to boil the kettle for a wash. Carrie would be arriving soon to take them up to the signals office. 'Aren't you looking forward to that?'

'Course I am!' retorted Nan, shivering and pulling her blanket up round her neck. 'It's just that it's bloomin' cold outside and it don't feel much like a birthday when you've got to get up and put on the same old uniform and do the same old work.' Even if I am gettin' married soon, she said quietly to herself, smiling a little smile. If anything could make her feel better about putting her feet in the freezing air outside her bed, it was that.

'Well, we'll see what we can do to make it special,' Evie said from the other room, running some water to clean her teeth with. 'How about a fire tonight? We can use the last of our coal.'

'That'd be nice,' conceded Nan.

'Then get a move on, Private! Birthday or not, Carrie will be here soon and we'd better be ready for her. I don't want us on a charge for being late! I've got the rank up and I'll get the blame, so come on.'

Once Carrie had bumped them up the lane to the signals office, it was good to get inside into the warmth, even if Yeo's cigarette fug from the night shift gave the place a stifling air.

'Happy birthday, Morrissey,' greeted Sergeant James. 'As it's your birthday, you can go to the cookhouse first. I think they've got sausages today. Now there's a treat for you.'

'Thanks, Sergeant,' grinned Nan, and dashed off, leaving Evie to man the switchboard once she'd made the all-important pot of tea.

I hope Chas will try and reach me today, she thought. They were spoiled really – so many sweethearts never saw each other at all in wartime. Look at Evie and Bob for one. But she was used to having a kiss from Chas every few days and she was missing her cuddles like billy-oh.

That's enough complaining. You've only a week to wait, she told herself sternly. Just concentrate on other things and you'll be fine.

The day went quickly enough. Once she was back from breakfast, she soon lost herself in the usual daily routine. If anything, it went quicker than usual because it was a bit busier than they were used to.

'There's quite a buzz, isn't there,' commented Sergeant James dryly, as the teleprinter churned out another message and Evie was kept busy picking up the calls on the switchboard and transferring them to wherever was necessary. 'Must be things going on.'

'What do you think it is, Sergeant?' ventured Nan.

'I've no firm information but I've heard that the Army in North Africa has started some major attacks on the Germans and Italians there. And now that General Sir Alan Brooke is in charge . . . well, I think we'll see some activity going on.'

'Is that good?' asked Nan. She hardly ever read the papers. So much of it meant nothing to her. All she knew was that they were *against* the Germans and the Italians, and *for* the Russians and the French. But even she knew that, the way things were going, it would be hard for Britain to stand all on its own against the might of the Fascist powers. Even with the Russian Front and the perils of the bitter winter approaching, the Germans didn't yet show any signs of weakening.

'It's all good, Morrissey,' snapped the sergeant. 'We're pushing on, just as Churchill says. Now let's get on. Birthday or not, there's work to be done.'

They finished their shift at two pm. Carrie gave them a wave as she dropped off Lenice and Ailsa, but she didn't stop to chat.

'What shall we do now?' asked Evie. 'What do you feel like doing?'

'It's cold – let's go to the NAAFI and see what they've got. I might try and ring Chas, see what he's up to.'

'I'm sure he wants to wish you a happy birthday.'

'He said he has a present for me. Can't think what it is. I hope he'll be free tonight so we can meet up. Come on.'

They walked quickly to the NAAFI, eager to be out of the cold, and while Evie got them some tea, Nan tried to telephone the sergeants' mess.

'Any joy?' asked Evie, coming over with a couple of mugs of tea. 'Look – some biscuits. Want one? They're only plain.'

'Thanks,' said Nan, gloomily. 'No. The operator won't put me through. I don't understand it. They can't be flying ops all ready. It's too early, isn't it?'

'Perhaps they're training, or doing practice runs or something. What was that thing you said they did?'

'Circuit and bumps. It's when they test the aircraft. It almost always happens when they're flying that night.'

'That must be what they're doing then.'

Nan's big brown eyes filled with tears. 'But it means I won't be seein' Chas tonight – again! It's been ages, and I thought that on me birthday . . . I'm sorry, Evie, I know it's right selfish of me, considerin' how you never get to see Bob at all. But I was so lookin' forward to it.'

'I know,' comforted Evie. 'Of course it's not easy, especially when you're in the first flush, like you two. I'm sorry, Nan. You'll see him soon, I'm sure.'

'I hope so. I just dunno how long I can keep on without him, that's all.'

'Come on, fancy a game of cards to cheer yourself up?'

They played cards and board games, sipping their tea and munching on biscuits until Carrie came in later and asked them if they were going to the cookhouse. 'It's one of your favourites, Nan. They must have known what today is. Toad-in-the-hole with onion gravy, and then jam-roly-poly and custard to follow.'

That managed to bring a smile to Nan's face and they all went off to enjoy a good hearty dinner that would help to keep the cold out, though Nan couldn't help thinking all the time about Chas, freezing in the back of a Wellington bomber, even inside his flight suit and jacket, sitting hunched in the dark, directing the pilot towards Berlin, or Cologne, or Mannheim, or wherever it was that they were heading that night. He wouldn't be enjoying a warm meal with good friends, before going back to his billet to sleep. She hated to think of it.

They lingered over their food for as long as they could before they braved the cold walk home.

'Want to go back to the NAAFI?' asked Caroline. 'At least it's warm.'

'I want to write some letters to Bob,' answered Evie. 'So I think I'll go back to the lodge.'

'Yeah, let's go back,' said Nan. 'A last cup of cocoa and bed is all I want.'

They walked back, staying close together in the cold and darkness. There was the distant hoot of an owl, and rustles in the undergrowth along the path, though they couldn't see a thing. As their eyes grew accustomed to the dark, they could make out odd shapes, and saw the stable block looming up beside them on the left as they followed the path.

Nan suddenly stopped dead, and said in a tight voice, 'I've got a real bad feelin' about this.'

'What?' whispered Carrie, though she didn't know why she needed to keep her voice down.

'It doesn't feel right!' hissed Nan. 'Can't you feel it? There's an 'orrible feeling in the air! I'm chilled right through.'

'But it's cold,' ventured Evie.

'Not like that. Like a goose walkin' over me grave. Cold, right to the bone. Can't you feel it?'

'Now you mention it,' Carrie said slowly, looking about her, 'it *is* a bit eerie, isn't it?'

'What's that?' cried Nan suddenly, her voice high and frightened.

'What?' said Evie.

'That! Can't you see it?'

The other two looked where Nan was pointing but they couldn't see a thing in the darkness.

'I'm sure it's . . . it's a shape! Something in black
. . .'

'I can't see anything,' hissed Caroline, her eyes
searching the darkness.

'Oh Gawd! It's Cecilia! It must be!'

'Oh crumbs,' said Evie faintly.

'It's just not true, there's no such thing as ghosts
. . .' protested Carrie, but she didn't have time to
say any more because the other two started running
as fast as they could, and she hurried off to catch
up with them. There may not be any such thing
as ghosts but Carrie certainly wasn't going to stay
there on her own, and risk being proved wrong.
They all dashed as fast as they could down the
lane, and let themselves into the lodge, panting
from the unexpected run.

'That was horrible!' said Evie, taking off her
coat. 'Let's get the kettle on. I think we need some
cocoa to cheer us up.'

But Nan's face was dead white and her eyes
still terrified. 'It was just like the old man said,'
she whispered, slumping down on to her bed. 'He
said she'd walk on my birthday and she did. But
it was much worse than I thought . . . it was
awful.'

'I think we may be suffering from a case of
over-active imagination,' Carrie said firmly. She
didn't like to see Nan so upset and she was sure
that there had been nothing there. They had simply
spooked themselves, as anyone would be in the
pitch blackness.

'No,' said Nan, in the same hushed voice. 'Don't you see? She was tryin' to tell me somethin', Cecilia was. She's tellin' me that somethin' bad is happenin'. I'm sure of it. She's come to warn me. Oh, Chas, oh Chas . . . where are you?'

Carrie and Evie were the frightened ones now, gazing at each other helplessly over Nan's head, as the younger girl burst into despairing sobs, rocking backwards and forwards on her bed.

With a shaking hand, Nan held the receiver close to her ear as she made the phone call to RAF Modeley's Sergeants' Mess. The operator put her through – so they were not flying ops tonight. She had spent the day in the grip of an awful depression, convinced that something terrible had happened, even though Carrie and Evie had done their best to cheer her up and convince her that it was all in her mind.

'Hello?' It was a crisp voice, not like Chas at all. Well, what were the chances he would answer?

'Caller, you're through,' said the operator.

'Hello,' said Nan in a quavering voice. 'Can I speak to Sergeant Charles Lawson, please?'

There was a pause before the cut-glass tones were heard again. 'Who is this, please?'

'Private Nan Morrissey.'

'Oh –' the voice softened. 'Oh, you're Lawson's fiancée, aren't you?'

'That's right. We're gonna be married next week. Is he there? Can I speak to him please?'

'I say . . . this is really dashed awful. I don't quite know how to break the news, I'm not trained for this sort of stuff like the senior bods are. I'm terribly sorry. I truly am.'

'Can I speak to Chas?' Nan implored, her voice rising higher, as if she could somehow persuade this strange airman to get Chas for her even though she knew now that her worst fears were about to be made real.

'You see, Private, Lawson didn't return from ops last night. None of his boys did. The Wellington went down over the Channel, badly holed and burning. Another crew saw them go down. I'm so very sorry. I hate to be the one to tell you.'

Nan had thought that when she heard those terrible words she would scream and howl but now that it had actually happened, she didn't do that. Instead, she said politely, 'I see. Well, thank you for telling me. Goodbye.' She went to put the receiver back, when she heard the sergeant say hurriedly, 'Here, wait a minute! Give me your address. If I hear anything, I'll write to you.'

Mechanically, Nan gave the address of Heronflete and then carefully replaced the phone. She turned round to look at Evie, who was waiting anxiously, sitting on the arm of one of the chairs.

'He's gone,' she said briefly. 'The plane went down last night.'

Evie's hand flew to her mouth as she gasped, 'Oh Nan! Oh no!'

But Nan didn't hear her. For the first time in her life, she had fainted.

'Oh, Carrie, it's just too terrible. Poor, poor Nan.' Evie looked up at Carrie with solemn eyes.

'I know. I can't believe it.'

'Sergeant James has sent her to the sickbay. She's under sedation apparently. They think it's best until the worst of the shock has past.'

'It's terrible. She was going to be married next week! How can fate be so cruel? Why did Chas have to be killed *now*? At least they could have had a little happiness together before they were parted, just a brief moment.' Carrie was filled with impotent rage that such a thing could have happened. War was so cruel! She gestured towards the wedding dress, sitting almost finished on the table beside her bed. 'I suppose there's no point in finishing that dress for poor Nan now. How on earth will she go on?'

'He's only missing. We can't give up all hope,' said Evie but her voice gave away her lack of optimism.

'Nan said they went down in the Channel. It's a freezing November, they'd only survive for an hour or two if they managed to escape the plane and the flames at all. I fear that poor Chas didn't have a chance.'

Both the girls sat solemn-faced in silence for a while as they both thought of their loved ones. Evie's mind was far away with Bob, while Carrie thought of Todd, so close, up in the big house, but soon to be sent away on his own perilous mission.

Then she was aghast at herself. How could she think of Todd? What about Jeffrey, the man she was engaged to and who was expecting to marry her in only a few weeks' time? Todd wasn't her fiancé, he wasn't her beloved. It was Jeffrey who was all those things. Wasn't it?

But even as she told herself that, she realised that it wasn't true. She tried to imagine hearing the awful news that Jeffrey had been killed. Yes, it would be terrible – but would she be so overwhelmed with the pain of it that she would need to be sedated, like Nan? Would it mean the death of all her hopes and dreams and everything she had wanted to live for? She didn't even want to ask herself that question.

And then – thinking of Todd, and what it would mean if a ghastly fate befell him . . . well, she was astonished by the stab of anguish that she felt. How could that be? She had only seen him twice now, and yet it seemed that the connection that had once been between them was as strong as ever.

Oh my goodness, Carrie thought, this is something I need to think about. I can't keep running away from it. I must make my mind up about Jeffrey. That's all there is to it. She said suddenly, 'How long do you think it will be before we know what's happened to Chas for certain?'

Evie said sadly, 'He's been reported missing. I

suppose if they find his body, he'll be listed dead. But who can tell how long that will take . . . I'd better write to her Aunt Miriam and tell her that there's not going to be a wedding on Saturday and not to go to Shrewsbury. Oh poor Nan. If she's ever needed her friends, Carrie, she needs us now.'

Carrie nodded. 'We'll do everything we can. Of course we will.'

Even with the terrible events of the weekend, life went on as normal. It had to. And, strangely, it helped. With so many people facing loss and grief every day, there wasn't any other way. Everyone had to do their bit no matter what.

The post brought Carrie three letters, one from her mother, one from Mrs Frobisher and one from Jeffrey. All were on the same theme.

Caroline, *wrote her mother,* I simply do not understand why I haven't heard from you about the wedding. Can't you see it is your duty? Please let us know immediately what your plans are. I don't understand why you are the one Private in the entire army to be denied leave to get married.

Mrs Frobisher took a gentler tone but even so, she left Carrie in no doubt of what she expected.

We are all very eager to have you in the family, my dear. Please write and tell us that

our fondest hopes are to be fulfilled after
Christmas and we can do everything neces-
sary to ensure a perfect day for you and
Jeffrey.

It was Jeffrey who was least able to contain his
irritation.

For God's sake, Carrie, what on earth is
going on? The chaps here are beginning to
laugh at me. I can't tell them whether I'm
going to be married or not, and I've arranged
a leave specially! This really can't go on, I
can't tolerate it. Please obey my instructions
at once and get confirmation for your
compassionate immediately. There is no
reason at all why we shouldn't be married in
the last week of December, and I shall go
home fully expecting that to happen. Please
don't let me down.

Carrie put all the letters under her pillow, sighing
with annoyance. Well, they were all right about
one thing. She had to let them know her inten-
tions, and soon. But couldn't they see that bullying
her was the worst way to go about it? It simply
made her want to dig her heels in and refuse to
do anything they said. She was feeling unsure about
her future, and in need of support and kind words
– not this browbeating. She would write to them
all and explain that the wedding they had all

planned for the last week of December would not be happening and that was that.

The whole idea of a wedding now made her feel terrible. In a few days time, it would have been Nan's wedding day – a truly happy occasion that both the bride and groom clearly lived for. Now it was going to be a bitter day, marked by the awful sense of loss and waste. Carrie hardly wanted to mention her own wedding plans, it would be the most deeply insensitive thing she could do.

Instead, she took out her writing paper and sighed deeply. Then she took up her pen and started writing the first of her letters.

Dear Mother,

I am sorry to break the bad news to you, but I won't be coming home over Christmas and the wedding will have to be postponed. I know it's not what you want to hear but that's the way it is. We are very busy at the moment and every hand is needed. I cannot justify taking leave to get married and there is no reason at all why Jeffrey and I have to be married at once. In the circumstances, it will make no difference if we wait.

She stopped writing as Evie came into the room. 'Writing home, Carrie?'

Carrie made a face. 'Yes. I'm confessing. Telling

everyone I won't be getting married after Christmas. I hate even talking about it, actually – it seems somehow wrong with poor Nan suffering so much.'

'If it's any help, I'm sure you're doing the right thing.'

'Thanks.' Carrie grinned. 'It does help a bit.'

As Evie settled down to write to Bob, Carrie finished her letter to her mother, asking after her health and hoping that everything at Jackmans was well, and put it in the envelope. Then she wrote a polite note to Mrs Frobisher, before taking up her pen again and a fresh sheet of paper to write to Jeffrey.

What to say? Should she tell him about Todd? She knew that she wasn't going to do that. It was private. She didn't want to share it, not even with Evie, not yet at least.

My darling Jeffrey . . .

She thought for a moment and then changed it.

My very dear Jeffrey,
    I'm sorry to bear bad news but I'm afraid that a wedding this December is completely off the cards. I want to tell you right away so that you don't get your hopes up and then feel more disappointed. I can't really explain why but getting leave at the time you want

me to is just very difficult for lots of reasons I can't go into here.

Carrie Tiptree! she told herself. Look at the way you can lie so easily! When did you become such a practised deceiver?

As she reread her letter, she felt the urge to explain more, make more excuses, perhaps even tell more lies.

No, she admonished herself sternly. You don't need to justify yourself. If you don't want to get married, that should be that. It should be more than enough. If Jeffrey loved you properly, he wouldn't bully you or be rude or send letters like the one I got from him today.

Look how far I've come – when I got to Heronflete, I was sure that eventually I would marry Jeffrey. Now I can see that it is less and less likely. I am beginning to understand that it is not what I want . . .

Just then, the door opened and a pale figure appeared in the doorway.

Evie leapt to her feet. 'Nan! What are you doing here?'

'Nan, are you all right?' Carrie got up as well, and they both hurried to the door, where Nan stood.

'I'm all right,' she said weakly as the other two went up to her, each taking an arm.

'You look terribly frail. Shouldn't you be in sickbay? You don't look well at all.' Evie looked her over with concerned eyes.

'I can't stay there another minute!' declared Nan, with a trace of her old spark. 'It's worse than being up and about. Besides, I can't lie in bed forever, taking medicine when I'm not really sick. I've got a broken heart but that's something different altogether. It doesn't stop me doin' my bit. It won't help Chas any if I flop – and he would never have wanted that, I know that for sure.'

'Come and sit down. I'll make us some tea,' said Carrie, and they bustled about trying to make Nan comfortable.

'You're gonna have to treat me like normal, if you can,' said Nan. 'I know you're bein' kind but it's gonna make it worse if you're all sympathetic and everythin'. I need to buckle down and get on with things, so we just have to be like we've always been.'

'Understood,' said Evie gently. 'But you've been through a terrible shock, you know, and we want you to know how sorry we are.'

'I know you are,' whispered Nan. 'That's why I need you to be the same you always are. I won't think you don't care.'

'All right, Nan,' Carrie said, and smiled. 'We'll do what we can for you. Promise. Now, where's that tea?'

Even though Nan had demanded that she be given no special sympathy in the face of her enormous loss, it was hard for the other two to treat her anything like they would normally. They were too aware of her pale face and the way she seemed to have lost weight in the last few days, and that her eyes looked enormous and haunted. They could hardly bear to think what she must be going through.

It was Sergeant James who brought Nan comfort. When Nan and Evie arrived for work on the early shift, it was Evie who was sent off to the cookhouse, while Nan was deputed to make the tea in the little stuffy kitchen.

'How are you. Morrissey? All right? I hear you've had a couple of days in sickbay,' the sergeant said briskly.

'Fine, thanks, Sergeant,' said Nan. The no-nonsense of the sergeant's voice made her somehow secure, as though things were normal after all and everything was going to be all right.

When they sat down with their tea, Nan in her position at the teleprinter, the sergeant said more softly, 'I've heard you've had a loss. Very bad show. You have my sympathy. I'm going to tell you something I don't tell many people, and that is that I know what you're feeling. I've been through it myself. I've lost a loved one too – my Joe. He and I were also going to be married but he was killed. It's terrible, heartbreak, I know that as well as anyone, and I know what you're suffering. What I'm going to tell you is that it's best not to dwell on it. You can go mad that way. Life goes on – it has to. And there's nothing like hard work to help you forget – not forget that you were in love and what you shared together, because you'll never forget that, but to numb that pain until you're able to cope with it a little better. Does that make sense?'

Nan nodded, not able to trust herself to speak.

'Good. Let's press on. It does all help, I promise. And we need to get on with this war and win it, and put a stop to all this grief and loss.' The sergeant stood up, now back to her usual self. 'Come on, Morrissey. We need to be our best at all times. Understood?'

'Yes, Sergeant.' Nan turned back to her teleprinter, her heart raised just a tiny amount from the pit of despair where it had been since she had heard the dreadful news.

'Nan! Nan! You'd better come quick.' Evie burst into Southgate Lodge, puffing with the effort of running. Nan was lying on her bed. She hadn't gone to the cookhouse for dinner. Her appetite had gone, along with every smile or vestige of happiness about her. As Evie came in, Nan propped herself up on her elbows.

'What is it? What's the fuss?' she said wearily. What could matter now? Nothing was of any importance at all any more, or ever would be again.

'I just took a call for you in the NAAFI. It was that Sergeant you spoke to, the one who told you about Chas. You weren't there, so he talked to me instead. Goodness knows how he found our number. Oh Nan!' Evie flew to Nan's bedside and grasped her hand. 'It's Chas! He's alive! They've found him.'

'W-w-w-hat?' stammered Nan, unable to take in what Evie was saying.

'Don't you understand? Chas isn't dead! Apparently he bailed out of the plane before it went down. He's hurt but they don't know how badly yet. He was picked up by a fishing boat and taken into Portsmouth. He's still there, in hospital. Isn't it wonderful?'

The news was just beginning to sink into Nan's befuddled brain. She could barely grasp what Evie was telling her: what had she said? Chas wasn't dead? That was impossible, he had gone down with his plane into the icy waters of the Channel, they all knew that. But . . . he had bailed out! She had a sudden vision of her beloved boy leaping from the door of the burning aircraft as it plunged downwards towards the sea, his parachute suddenly breaking free and filling with air, pulling him safely out of the way and dropping him gently, gently on to the surface of the water. And then . . . miracle of miracles, a boat, finding him and picking him up and taking him to safety.

Nan felt her hands start shaking, and then her whole body seemed to be trembling, her breath coming in short pants. 'Wh-wh-where is he?' she managed to say between her shaking lips.

'In Portsmouth, that's what the sergeant said. In the hospital. Isn't it wonderful?' Evie's face was alight with joy and she held Nan's hand tightly as though to stop the tremors with her own strength.

'Yes, it's wonderful. I can hardly believe it.'

'You must believe it! Now all we have to do is find out exactly where he is, and you can still take your compassionate leave. You can go to him, Nan! Won't that be the best thing?'

'Yes . . . yes, I must find Chas. I must go to him. You're right.'

'Do you have his mother's telephone number? Can you call her?'

Nan remembered the smart writing paper on which Stella Lawson had written to her. It had been engraved with the address of Gardener's Cottage, and there had been a telephone number underneath. She could telephone – surely Stella Lawson would know better than anyone else in the world what had happened to Chas.

'I'll call her now,' said Nan, excitement beginning to build in her. 'I'll go to the NAAFI right now, and telephone her.'

'Wait, Nan, it's nearly ten thirty at night. Best wait till tomorrow.'

'How can I wait till then?' cried Nan, anguished. 'I need to know now!'

'Of course you do, darling, but isn't the best thing that Chas is alive? It won't make any difference now where he is, you can't go till Friday anyway.'

'Chas is alive,' repeated Nan, frowning. Then, her huge brown eyes shining, she looked up at Evie and shouted, 'Flamin' Norah, Evie! Chas is alive!'

They both started laughing as hard as they could and then Nan jumped up and began dancing round the room, followed closely by Evie. The door opened and Carrie walked in, stopping short astonished when she saw the sight in front of her, of Evie and Nan prancing round the room like they were possessed.

'What on earth . . . ?' She had left Southgate with a dull, depressed Nan lying in silence on her bed, and now had returned to find a party going on. 'What's happened? Are you both all right?'

'We're fine!' shouted Evie. 'It's good news! Chas is alive!'

'Oh Carrie, he's alive, he's alive!' cried Nan, still jumping about.

'He is?' Carrie absorbed the news in a moment, a huge smile spreading over her face. 'But that's wonderful!' A second later, she too was leaping about, laughing and cheering.

Oh thank God, she thought. Thank you for bringing Chas back and giving Nan a second chance at happiness . . .

TWENTY-ONE

The next day, Nan made a long-distance call to Gardener's Cottage.

'Mrs Lawson? It's Nan!' she said, when the operator put her through at last.

'Oh, Nan! How wonderful. I'm so pleased you telephoned, I was about to write to you anyway. Have you heard the news? Charles is alive, he's been picked up.'

'Yes, I have. It's the best news in the world.'

'We must be quick – we only have three minutes, so I'll tell you what's happening. I don't know how badly Charles is hurt, but it can't be that bad, because I've managed to speak to some high-up people I know and the excellent news is that we've arranged for him to be moved to the Manor House for his convalescence. There's everything he needs right there and of course I'll be on hand to look after him. They're bringing him up from Portsmouth by ambulance on Friday.'

'That's splendid,' said Nan.

'Yes – but I can't help also thinking about how this was supposed to be the week you were married. We mustn't dwell on it though – it could have been so much worse. Now, do you think you can still come on Friday? I'm sure that seeing you would do Charles the world of good.'

'I don't see why not,' replied Nan, her heart lifting. 'I've not cancelled my leave or anythin'. I'll ask the sergeant but I can't see why she would say no, especially under the circumstances.'

'Wonderful. Just write or telephone and let me know for sure. That's our time nearly up, Nan. See you on Friday!'

'See you then!' called Nan, and returned the receiver to its cradle.

Carrie could not fight the sensation that she was being very sneaky indeed when she took the bicycle from its tarpaulin in the stable block once again, and set off towards Lower Modeley. Instead, she tried to forget about it, and concentrate instead on the pleasure of seeing Todd again.

He was there waiting for her in the pub and it gave her a rush of excitement to see him as she came in, red-cheeked. Seeing her, he got to his feet.

'Carrie, you made it.' He kissed her politely on the cheek and motioned for her to sit down at the small table near the fire. 'I'll get you a drink.'

When he returned from the bar with her drink, Todd took his place opposite her. 'So, how have you been?'

'I've never known such drama and upset. It was Nan's birthday – she's a private who shares the billet with me and is a love, only eighteen – and she was convinced she'd seen the Heronflete ghost, a nun called Cecilia. That was our first drama, though it rather paled into insignificance after what came next. We heard that her fiancé had been shot down over the Channel, presumed dead – and they were due to be married on Saturday.'

'Oh that *is* awful,' said Todd sincerely. 'That poor girl.'

'Yes. We were all very upset for her and she just went to pieces, had to be sedated in sickbay. So it was a very bad few days, as you can imagine. Then a couple of nights ago, we heard Chas – her fiancé – had been picked up, injured but alive. So then we were all celebrating, and Nan is going to see him this weekend after all, though the wedding is off, naturally. No one knows yet how badly he's been hurt.'

'I hope he's one of the lucky ones,' remarked Todd. 'They can do wonders these days. The medical advances lately have been astounding. But it's bad luck all the same.'

'Yes,' said Caroline, suddenly self-conscious. She'd been lost in telling Nan's story, and was always at ease with Todd, whom she'd known for so long. Now, unexpectedly, she felt on edge. 'It makes you think, doesn't it? About how we don't know how long we'll have with our loved ones.'

'These are dangerous times,' agreed Todd.

'It . . . it made me think about things myself. About Jeffrey. And about marriage. I felt that . . .' she took a deep breath. She didn't want to blush or stumble or make a fool of herself but she'd been thinking hard about things lately and certainly since what had happened to Nan. 'I felt that we have to grasp our opportunities, grasp life. Not let chances pass us by.'

'Yes?' Todd gazed at her intently.

'I . . . I wrote to Jeffrey. I told him there was no way I will marry him at Christmas, as he wants.'

Todd's eyes glittered and a small flush of red showed on his cheekbones. 'You mean, you've broken off your engagement?'

'Not exactly . . . no. But I said I can't get married in December and that's for certain.'

The light in Todd's eyes died. 'I see.'

Carrie was instantly terrified. What was she trying to tell him? Was she leading him on with no reason? Could he possibly want to be more to her than just a friend? Yes, he had said she had always been his dream girl, but he was talking about a childhood love, not an adult one. No matter the connection they felt between them, the grown-up Todd and the grown-up Caroline didn't know each other at all. Could she really break off her engagement to Jeffrey because this man had suddenly walked into her life, when he was just as suddenly about to walk out again, probably never to return?

And yet the idea of Todd turning away from

her, leaving her believing that she was going to marry Jeffrey, was something she hated.

What do you want, Carrie? What? she asked herself. But her thoughts continued round on the same whirl that they had been in since she'd met Todd again.

She said in a low voice, 'Todd, there's something you must understand. This engagement – it's been on the cards for years. I almost didn't have a choice in the matter, our mothers decided it all between them. I'm only just beginning to entertain the idea that I might have a say at all. You mustn't blame me if I'm slow in coming to realise certain things. I have to do it in my own time, that's all.'

'I understand,' he said. 'The last thing I want to do is step into your peaceful existence, with the future all mapped out, and disrupt it for you. If you want me to, I can leave now and we can pretend that these strange meetings of ours never happened.'

'No, oh no! I don't want that, not at all! I already disrupted my own future, Todd, the day I walked out and signed up for the ATS when I knew my mother didn't want me to. If I'd wanted to marry Jeffrey and live at home and have babies – well, I could be doing that right now. But I'm not, am I? I'm here, through my own choice.'

'Yes, you are,' he said warmly. 'And I admire you for it. Not every girl would make that choice.'

'We're all called up now, anyway,' said Carrie wryly.

'Yes, but you went before that, before you were ordered to. It makes the difference.'

'We get on so well, Todd. We're so at ease together. I really feel that you know me. We laugh and we talk like friends, like equals, and I treasure that. We've only spent one other evening together but already I feel like we're true companions. But it also frightens me, because I'm worried that I'll feel . . . more than I should. More than I ought to, under the circumstances.'

Todd stared at the table for a moment, and then looked up at her. 'Please don't look ahead, Carrie. Where's the good in that? Look at your friend and her fiancé – think about seizing the moment and enjoying it. Don't fret about what might or might not happen. I'm leaving in a week or two – let's not bother ourselves with pointless worrying. Let's just enjoy the time we have left together.'

Carrie smiled. 'You're right. Very well – I'll do as I'm told and I'll stop trying to peer into the future.'

'Good. Just be my old Carrie, my childhood friend, and bring some light into my life before I go. That's all I ask.'

'I'd be happy to.'

'Shall we have another drink then, and talk about something quite different – perhaps something frivolous and silly? Let me tell you about Aunt Hilda and her stories about living with her neighbours in Bradford. She's very funny, dear old thing.'

'Yes, do – I need to laugh.'

'And I meant to ask – I heard about a dance in Lincoln just lately. Would you like to go with me? Do you think you could get a pass? It's in a couple of weeks, not long before I have to leave.'

'I'm sure I could get a pass but what about transport? If it's not an army do, it'll be hard to get there. I don't think I'm up to cycling all the way to Lincoln!'

'Don't worry, I'll handle that. You get the pass and I'll do the rest. Now, I'll get those drinks and you prepare yourself for my aunt's latest antics . . .'

She watched him go. What is my heart trying to tell me? she asked herself. I've got to guard against the romanticism of all this. What if I'm simply caught up in the adventure of it all? Meeting Todd, his going off on this secret mission, all the drama of it . . . what if I ruined my life because of a silly childish passion for someone I hardly know? Oh dear. If only I knew the right way to go.

Then she laughed at herself. A moment ago, I promised Todd not to peer into the future and here I am, worrying away again. I *am* silly sometimes! I shan't think about it again. I shall live for the moment, just like we said, and enjoy this evening.

It was late on Friday night when Nan finally arrived at Gardener's Cottage, her face and hands dirty from the trains and all the smuts, and utterly exhausted.

Perhaps it's a good thing I'm not getting married tomorrow after all, she thought dryly. Because I wouldn't really be in the mood for dressin' up and puttin' on my best smiles after a journey like that.

But really she knew that she would have borne the whole thing with humour if she had been going to be married the next day.

She walked from the station, remembering her way back to the cottage with no trouble. The door opened in response to her tired knock, and Stella Lawson came out at once, enveloping her in a warm hug that at once made her feel better.

'Oh Nan, you're here! I'm so pleased to see you. You must be absolutely bushed. Come on in, I've got some tea just brewing for you. Come and sit by the fire.'

It was wonderfully comforting to go into that bright, homely interior with the thick carpets and warm fire. Nan felt as though a terrible weight had been lifted from her shoulders as she sat down in the soft armchair by the hearth. If anyone could make it all right again, it was Stella Lawson, who was so kind and motherly and capable.

She brought Nan a cup of tea, which was exactly what she needed and she sipped at it gratefully. Stella sat down opposite her.

'Are you hungry? You must be. I've got a pie made – mostly vegetable but with a dab of meat in it. It's staying warm in the oven. As soon as you've had your tea, I'll get it for you. I thought it was going to be eaten under more propitious circumstances' – her eyes were sad for a moment – 'but we can't change what's happened. We can only be grateful for the great mercies we do have.'

'He's alive, isn't he? That's what counts,' said Nan.

'Exactly,' replied Stella. 'That is what we must hang all our hopes on now.'

'How is he? Can I see him?' Nan was ready to put down her tea and run to the Manor at once.

'Not tonight, Nan. He'll be asleep by now. He badly needs his rest. He only arrived from Portsmouth yesterday and the journey was a rough one for him. It completely wore him out.'

'But you have seen him, haven't you?' Nan gazed at her beseechingly. She longed to know how Chas was – it had been the not knowing that was making her so tense. 'How is he? Is he badly hurt?'

Stella Lawson hesitated. She knew that in Nan's mind, Chas was still the healthy, whole boy she had said goodbye to when they had last met. It was going to be hard to make her understand that he was gone now, that lad. And would probably never come back.

She said tentatively, 'The first thing you must realise is that Charles is very lucky indeed. He was the only man to survive from his plane – the rest of the crew perished. We must always remember that, and how close we came to losing him. But he was hurt. The plane was in flames and he was burned.'

'His face?' asked Nan, remembering that she had seen badly burned boys on her last trip, with their taut, shiny skin amid the bright red wrinkles, whole faces melted into a terrible waxy mess. 'I don't care,' she added. 'I'd love him no matter what he looked like.'

'No, thank goodness, his face was spared. He looks just the same. But his hands and legs, they caught the brunt of it. He should heal well, in time, but he's heavily bandaged. And . . .' Stella hesitated.

'What? What is it?'

'His right leg. It was so badly burned on the lower leg that there was nothing they could do to save it. It was amputated, I'm afraid. They did it in Portsmouth, just after he was brought in. They could see immediately that it was beyond repair and that it was likely to cause blood poisoning if they didn't take it off. So they did what was necessary. It's gone, just below the knee.'

'Oh,' whispered Nan, trying to understand this new version of Chas that suddenly existed, one with bandaged hands and a stump where his right leg used to be. 'Oh, poor, poor Chas. What an awful thing for him – he's so fit and healthy, he loves to run and to . . . to dance.' Her voice broke, as she had a crystal-clear memory of the two of them dancing and laughing, Chas stumbling a little as she counted, 'One, two, three – bump-sadaisy!' and they bumped bottoms before returning to each other's arms. 'He enjoyed dancing so much, and we had such fun when I was teachin'' him what to do . . . oh, dear, I am sorry!' – as the tears welled up and began to spill down her face. 'Please don't get me wrong – I'm so happy he's alive, you can't think! And I don't care if he's lost a leg, it don't mean I won't love him still. But I can't help it when I think of what he's suffered, and how much it will mean to him.'

'Nan.' Stella came over and put an arm around her, making Nan sob still harder, this time dripping tears into the soft wool of the older woman's cardigan. 'There, there. It's going to be hard for all of us, but particularly for you. After all, you two were not even married yet. It's going to change your future.'

'No. No, I won't let it. We won't have all our happiness taken away from us! I won't let this destroy what we had.'

'But Nan – Charles is a different person now. When you meet him, you'll see what I mean. I don't mean that you can't be in love but it won't be the same.'

'I want it to be the same!' cried Nan, and started sobbing again. 'Why does it have to change?'

'I don't know, sweetheart,' said Stella, her own voice quavering with emotion. 'It doesn't seem right or fair or just, but it does change. Everything and everyone – nothing stays the same. That is just life and even more so in war time. I wish I could make everything all right again, and magic it all back the way it was. But no one can do that. We must live with what we're given.'

'I know,' said Nan. 'But it's very hard.' Her sobs quietened and she wiped away her tears with one hand.

'Of course it is. But you're strong and you're determined, if I know you. Now, you're going to need all the strength you can get, so let's go and have some of this pie I've made and then get you to bed, all right? Something tells me you need your sleep.'

Gently, she led Nan out of the sitting room and into the kitchen, calming her down with all the love and comfort she could offer, along with hot pie and a cosy bed.

The next day Nan woke full of apprehension. Today she would see Chas. It was a moment she had longed for but now it was here she was scared. Perhaps she didn't really want to meet this new person who had taken her beloved Chas's place. Perhaps it would be easier if she simply went away and just pretended that her own boy had been lost for ever so that she could remember the way he was.

'Shame on you, Nan Morrissey!' she whispered to herself sharply. 'How could you even think of such a thing? You've got Chas back and that's the answer to your prayers. If he's hurt, then it's up to you to be the strong one and help him through it. If I know Chas, he'll come round. He's too strong not to.'

She got up, feeling a great deal warmer than she did when she crept out of bed in Southgate –

it must be the carpets, she thought. Aren't they good at keepin' it all nice and toasty? – and put on the dressing gown Stella had left for her. It was wonderful to be back. She had only happy memories of Gardener's Cottage and despite the circumstances she was filled with a kind of peace now that she was back there.

She crept down to the kitchen where her uniform was hanging up near the stove. Stella had sponged it down the night before, cleaning out all the dirt and smuts from the awful train journey, and then carefully pressed it. Now it looked as good as new. Nan took it back upstairs and went to the bathroom. Stella had said that there would be plenty of hot water first thing, so Nan ran herself a steaming bath – although no deeper than the regulation six inches – and climbed in with a sigh of enjoyment. This was luxury! No quick wash standing in a tiny kitchen, freezing to bits while the water cooled quickly to less than tepid; or a run through a dark, icy morning to ablutions, when all the good of the heat was lost immediately you stepped back out into the freezing air.

Once she was washed and dressed, her long hair carefully pinned up as she did it every day, she went back down to the kitchen to wait for Stella. She didn't like to make tea without her hostess there, in case the ration was low, so she had a cup of hot water instead while she waited. It seemed like hours before Stella finally arrived, dressed in her dressing gown and pyjamas.

'Oh, Nan!' she said in surprise. 'You're up already. And dressed.'

'I got up at the usual hour. Hard to break a habit, and besides I couldn't wait. Can we go and see Chas now?' she asked anxiously.

'My dear girl – it's barely seven-thirty. You must have been up for ages. But we can't go over to the Manor yet. They don't really have visiting hours as such, but they certainly wouldn't want us over at this time. They'll be getting all the patients up, washing and dressing them and giving them their breakfasts. We can't really go over till later – ten o'clock at the earliest, I should say.'

'Ten o'clock!' cried Nan, agonised. 'I can't wait all that time!'

'We'll make it slip away more easily than you'd think,' smiled Stella. 'First things, go and take your uniform off and put on some of the clothes I've left in your room. You can keep it nice and smart that way. Meanwhile, I'll make us a nice cup of tea and then we'll have breakfast. That will take us up to at least half past eight, I should think. Then we'll tidy up, make up the fire in the sitting room so it's ready to light later, and do those little bits and pieces that make the time pass. Then you can get changed again, if you want to wear your uniform, and we'll go off to the Manor.'

'Well – all right,' said Nan, as she didn't have much choice. Despite Stella's efforts, every minute seemed to tick by twice as slowly as normal ones.

Even a late shift didn't drag like this! she thought. But it was nice to be in the soft trousers and fluffy white woollen jumper that Stella had put out for her; and it was lovely to eat hot toast with a smear of jam over it, with another cup of tea squeezed out of the pot. In a way, she was grateful for the time that allowed her to settle her nerves and calm down a little. It would be no good going in to see Chas on edge – he would need her to be serene.

At last, it was time to go over and see him.

'Are you all right, Nan?' asked Stella gently, as they put their coats on.

'Yeah,' answered Nan in a tight voice. 'I'm all right. I'll be fine.'

'It's just that . . . this was going to be your wedding day, wasn't it?'

Nan breathed in sharply. 'You know what? I'd forgotten that. Isn't that funny?'

'It's amazing how quickly we get used to the new way of things. Don't dwell on it, but let's go and see our boy.'

They walked up through the cold morning air towards the Manor. It was just as Nan remembered it: a large brick building with white-painted windows that seemed to have an enormous number of rooms behind them. But this time they went up the drive, and then up the flight of stone steps that led to the wide wooden front door. Stella rang on it.

'Must be strange, ringin' the bell to your own house,' remarked Nan, trying to keep a hold on her nerves. Her hands were shoved deep in her pockets, where no one could see how tightly her fists were clenched.

'I don't even think of it as ours any more,' said Stella, looking up at the old place. 'It seems to be much better suited to its present purpose. It was rather big for Charles and me to rattle around in on our own.'

The door opened and a smartly uniformed nurse with a starched cap stood just behind it. 'Morning, Mrs Lawson,' she said politely.

'Hello. I've come to see Charles. Is he up?'

'You'll have to ask Matron, ma'am,' replied the nurse and nodded down a long hallway.

'I'll find her in her office, I expect. Come along, Nan.' They went into a large square entrance hall with a black-and-white chequered floor, with wheelchairs and other hospital equipment all around the sides. Then Stella led the way down a wood-panelled hallway.

'Matron's office used to be the butler's pantry,' she explained, 'but it does very well for Matron, with a desk and a telephone.'

They stopped in front of a panelled door that was almost invisible in the wall panels and Stella knocked.

'Come in!' came the business-like reply. 'Ah, Mrs Lawson,' said the matron, 'we were expecting you. Charles is awake. He's doing very well today. Would you like to see him? He's in a room of his own at the moment, while he's still vulnerable to infection, but we'll move him on to the ward in a few days.'

'Thank you, Matron. This is Nan Morrissey, by the way, Charles's fiancée. I trust she's allowed to visit?'

'Of course. How do you do. Now please follow me.'

Matron led the way to a back staircase, and they followed her up it, making way for nurses as they came running up and down, carrying pans and kidney trays, bandages, crutches and bowls of hot water.

Nan had no idea of where they were going. She just followed the white of Matron's uniform until they were walking down a corridor and then stopping outside another door.

'Here we are,' said Matron. She knocked smartly and then opened the door at once. 'Visitors for you, Sergeant!' she said brightly, ushering Stella and Nan into the room before shutting the door behind them, murmuring, 'Half an hour at the most, I'm afraid.'

Nan's heart was pounding as she went in, and her breath was coming so quickly that her head felt light. Stay calm, she told herself.

The room was neat and clean, with a freshly made bed in it. Over by the window was a wheelchair with a man sitting in it, his back to the room as he stared out of it on to the bleak winter landscape beyond.

'Good morning, Charles,' said his mother

cheerfully. 'Look who I've brought to see you – a wonderful surprise!'

Chas didn't move but carried on staring out in front of him.

'H-h-h-hello, Chas,' said Nan in a small voice. 'It's me, Nan.'

At that, a shuddering movement seemed to go through Chas's frame. Then his head moved slowly round in her direction, but not so that he could see her.

'Chas?' she ventured.

There was a long pause. Stella took her hand and held it tightly.

'Why did you come?' demanded Chas suddenly, his voice rough. 'Don't you think this is hard enough for me as it is?'

Nan's stomach contracted with horror at the sound of his voice. Where was her gentle, tender Chas? 'What do you mean?' she asked in a quavering tone.

'This was supposed to be our wedding day! What a joke. I don't know why you came, Nan. You might as well have stayed in Heronflete and got on with your life, and left me to mine.'

Nan looked up at Stella with frightened eyes. Why on earth was Chas talking like this? It was worse than anything she could have imagined.

'Charles, that's enough,' said his mother in a firm voice. 'You're to be nice to Nan. She's come all this way and the least you can do is turn round and look at her. Now I'm going to find Matron

– I've got some things I need to talk to her about and I'll be a while. You two need some time alone, I think.'

She let herself quietly out, leaving Nan alone with Chas, who had gone back to staring out of the window.

Desperate to break the uncomfortable silence, she searched for something to say. She had hardly been able to wait for this moment, and now her mind was blank. At last, she said, 'I was so happy when I heard that you were alive.'

It sounded weak and silly. This was not how she had imagined their reunion! She had thought that there would be tears and smiles and embraces – not this strange coldness.

'You needn't have bothered,' said Chas in a dull low voice. 'It would have been better for me if I had died.'

'What do you mean? How can you say that, Chas?' she cried. 'That's a terrible thing to think!'

'Is it? Look at me!' He turned his wheelchair round to face her, and held up his hands. They were heavily bandaged, thickly wrapped in white so that he seemed to be wearing over-sized mittens. 'My hands are fried, burnt to pieces. We'll have to see if I can ever do anything again – feed myself, dress myself, wash myself. And then there's this . . .' He gestured at his leg, which ended just below the knee in another dense swathe of bandages. 'I've lost my leg, Nan.'

'I know,' she said softly. 'It's a terrible loss –

577

but you're alive. That's the thing that matters. You're still here, and you're still my Chas.'

'But I'm not.' His voice dropped back to its dull monotone. 'Can't you see? I'm not your Chas. I'm not the man I was. I'm this cripple, who cannot care for himself, cannot be any use or any good. It would have been better for everyone if I'd died. Then at least you'd have had the chance to meet a proper man, a whole man, who could love you properly and not need you to nurse him. Now I'm a useless thing. Can't you see, Nan? It's better if you leave me now, go home and forget about me. The life we dreamed of can never happen now.'

'But it's not true . . . don't send me away!'

'No, it's for the best,' said Chas plaintively. 'Best if you go and leave me to my misery. We'll never be able to dance now. Never again.'

Something in Nan snapped and she felt anger rush up and fill her. She frowned and marched up towards him. 'I thought you were stronger than this! I didn't expect to hear such self-pity from you, Chas. What about those boys with you who died? Wouldn't any of them have given anything to trade places with you? To *live?* You were the luckiest of them all! What have you really lost? You've still got your home, your mother. You've still got me. You've lost a bit of your leg – but that's not the end of the world. They make clever pretend legs now that fit on to the stump and look just like the real thing. You can even learn to walk on them – even dance on them! I'm not listening to all this bleak talk, when there's so much to be thankful for. You're not even twenty-one yet, your life's only just begun.'

For a moment, there was a spark of the old Chas in his eyes. 'Do you think so?' he said hesitantly.

'Of course! You're only starting out, we both are. We're going to spend our life together, just like we planned.'

He seemed to respond to her, just for a moment, but then he looked down, seeing his bandages and the leg that ended at the knee. To her despair, she saw the little light in Chas's eyes flicker out and die. 'No,' he said flatly. 'It's no good, Nan. You'd better go. Don't you see, my life's over now, at least the way I thought it was going to be. You may as well leave me alone.'

'Don't you let yourself be like this, Chas! Please!'

'There's nothing more I can do, not for you and not for my country. Can't you see how frightful that is for me?'

'Yes, but . . .'

'No buts, Nan. You're still the same – fit and healthy and doing your bit for the war. You can't possibly know how it feels to be like this. I want you to leave now. I mean it.' With that, he turned his back on her and stared again out of the window.

'No, Chas, you can't mean it . . .' she whispered, her heart aching.

'I do. Goodbye.' The set of his shoulders was obstinate.

'I . . . I . . . please, Chas! We were gonna be married today!'

'Then you're lucky this happened before we did, or you'd be married to a useless cripple.'

She hated to hear him speak of himself like this – it wasn't true! And it wasn't the Chas she knew! But he still sat with his back to her. She was helpless, not knowing what to do or how to reach him.

'All right,' she said at last. 'If that's what you want, what you *really* want. You're breakin' my heart, Chas, as long as you realise that. You're not a useless cripple to me – you're my boy, with everythin' to live for. I don't understand what's happened to you but I want you to know that I'll be waitin' for you when you change your mind.'

'Don't waste your time,' he said harshly.

'Goodbye, Chas,' she whispered, then turned and ran for the door, struggling with the handle to let herself out. Once she was out of his sick room, she leaned against the wall in the corridor and sobbed and sobbed, hardly able to bear the pain of realising what had happened to her beloved Chas. He was a stranger to her, not the man she'd known and fallen in love with. Not the man that she had been hoping to marry this very day! Was he gone for ever?

Stella found her in the corridor a few minutes later, and they went back to the cottage for a reviving cup of tea.

'It was awful,' Nan said, wiping her red, swollen eyes. 'He's changed.'

'I tried to warn you, but I hoped that your appearance might bring him back to himself.'

'No. It didn't help at all – he just didn't want to know. He told me to go away and find someone else. I couldn't believe it.'

'Oh, Nan, I'm so sorry,' said Stella, her eyes full of sympathy. 'I didn't want it to be like this.'

'In some ways, it's worse than if he'd died, that he's changed so much and doesn't love me any more. And he says he's a useless cripple!'

'He's coming to terms with his injury – you must be patient. It will take time for him to stop being so angry and so unhappy about losing his leg. Can you wait for him, Nan?'

'Of course I will,' said Nan as bravely as she could. 'But it's hard work when he's so sure he doesn't want me.'

'He says that now – but he'll change, I'm sure of it. The old Chas will come back.'

'I wish that would happen,' said Nan with longing.

'It will!'

'If I could believe that, I'd wait for as long as I had to. But he's so different! It's hard to believe he'll ever be the same.'

'Keep the faith, Nan. Keep it with me and we'll win through, I promise.'

TWENTY-TWO

'The second Christmas of the war,' said Evie idly, as they prepared for bed in Southgate Lodge.

'Third,' corrected Carrie. She was boiling the kettle to fill her hottie. She'd already filled it once to warm her sheets and pyjamas but she wanted to refill it before she went to bed. As much heat for as long as possible, that was the idea. '1939, 1940, and now 1941.'

'Oh yes,' said Evie. 'But the first one didn't feel like wartime, really, did it? It hadn't kicked off properly. Imagine – we hadn't even had an air-raid. It wasn't the way it is now.'

'But, when you think about it, it was much worse then. Now we've got the Russians on our side. And the Americans, at last.'

'Thanks to the Japs anyway. That's what the sergeant said – if they hadn't bombed Pearl Harbor, America might still be neutral. But now we're at war with Japan as well.'

'The important thing is that America is with us – it means we have a real chance.'

'Yes – but, Carrie, it's not going to be over tomorrow, is it? There's still months to go. Years of war and bombings and rationings and Bob so far away . . . I don't know how I'll cope with it.'

'We will,' said Carrie, trying to be cheerful. 'I know it's hard with Christmas coming – it's always when we miss our loved ones the most, after all – but we've got to keep on, haven't we? There's no other way.'

'What about poor Nan?' asked Evie, dropping her voice. Next door, Nan was already curled up in her bed under the blankets, staring into the small cold fireplace opposite.

'Yes, she's having a terrible time,' agreed Carrie in a low tone. 'She's going through the motions well enough, doing her job and so on, but all her spirit has gone. She must have had an awful experience with Chas, though she won't say anything about it. She's not said a word since she got back, and that was a fortnight ago.'

'There haven't been any letters for her either, apart from one from her aunt. So Chas isn't writing.'

'Perhaps he can't. He burnt his hands after all.'

'Yes. But I have a feeling the story is more complicated than that.'

Carrie glanced through the small kitchen doorway towards the bedroom. 'Well, we can't press her. She'll tell us in her own good time.'

Evie gave her a sideways look. 'And what about you, Carrie? Are you going to tell me *your* secret?'

'What do you mean?' asked Carrie, flushing slightly.

'It hasn't escaped my notice that you've been off several times in the evening lately without saying where you were going. It doesn't have anything to do with a certain handsome childhood friend, does it?'

'Evie . . . would you mind if I didn't talk about it? Not yet, anyway. I'm confused in my own mind. I know you mean Todd – and yes, I have met him a couple of times. But it's not as simple as it sounds. I don't mean to be secretive –'

'Don't worry at all, old love,' said Evie breezily. 'Whenever you're ready, I'm all ears. Until then, keep it to yourself.'

When Carrie was in bed, she remembered back to her last two meetings with Todd. Each time, they had a lovely evening, full of laughter, reminiscence and conversation, but staying very carefully off the subject of Jeffrey and the engagement. Now, tomorrow night was the dance in Lincoln and she was both looking forward to it and dreading it. Looking forward to it because she now had to admit to herself that she'd never been so happy in her life as she was with Todd, and dreading it because it was going to be their last meeting. Soon he would be leaving on his mission and it was doubtful that he'd ever come back –

the very thought was appalling, making her feel sick and weak with fear.

And what of Jeffrey? she asked herself miserably. What about her fiancé? The last letter she had received from him had surprised her. It was the reply to her note explaining that they were not to be married at Christmas.

> Don't worry, darling, *it read,* I don't want you to be rushed into anything. Of course I'm sad, because I long for us to be married – but I also know that doing your bit in the army is important to you. So why don't we have a spring wedding instead? It will give the mothers all the more time to squirrel away wedding cake ingredients . . .

She hadn't expected such a reasonable, affectionate reply and it had filled her with doubt and confusion again. It had almost made her pull out of a meeting with Todd, but at the last minute she had gone ahead with it because she couldn't bear not to see him. What kind of girl went behind her fiancé's back to go out with a man who, she had to admit, was beginning to spark feelings in her that were most definitely more than friendship?

I can't question it, she thought, turning over and punching her pillow to find a soft place for her head. I just have to do what I have to do.

*　　*　　*

The next night she stood at the gates to Heronflete by the drive that led up to the big house. It wasn't possible to see the soldiers on duty in the darkness, but she knew they were there. It was cold and she stamped her feet to keep warm, occasionally switching her torch on just for a moment to see if there was anyone about. Then she heard the rumble of an engine and saw the pinpoint lights of blacked-out headlights, and she lit her torch for an instant to show where she was. The next moment, the car had drawn to a halt beside her and Todd said cheerily, 'Jump in!'

She got quickly into the passenger seat, and then they were off, driving through the blackness.

'Where'd you get this?' asked Carrie, laughing.

'Borrowed it from a man who not only has a car, but a heart, and knows that a dance in Lincoln with a beautiful girl is just about the most important thing there is at the moment.' Todd was hardly more than a dark shadow next to her, but she knew his brown eyes were sparkling and he was smiling his broad smile that showed his straight white teeth.

'You're such a charmer, aren't you?' she joked.

They chatted and laughed all the way to Lincoln, and then Carrie directed him to a good place to park the car.

'The dance is in the middle of town,' explained Todd, 'in a hall. A Christmas knees-up.'

'It's not Christmas for days!'

'So they're starting early . . . who can blame

them? We all need a bit of Christmas cheer, don't we?'

They left the car in a quiet street and walked together into the town centre.

'You'd better take my arm,' said Todd, 'it's safer in the blackout.'

So they went arm-in-arm, his large hand clasped over her small one, until they got to the hall in town. Despite the blackout, they could hear band music coming from the inside, and saw couples running up the stone steps to go inside.

'A real dance!' said Carrie happily. 'I can't believe it, it's been so long.'

Inside there was a band playing, a good one. The musicians were middle-aged men, too old to be called up, but dapper and professional-looking in their dinner jackets. They were playing lots of current favourites like 'The Chattanooga Choochoo', and Carrie itched to get dancing right away.

There were tables all around the dance floor, and couples talking and drinking together as they watched the others dancing. Some were already getting close and smooching a little, despite the early hour.

'Would you like a drink?' asked Todd, after they'd given their coats to the cloakroom girl.

Carrie shook her head. 'In a minute. I want to dance first.'

Todd grinned. 'Me too.'

Then next minute they were dancing and spinning on the dance floor. Todd was an excellent dancer, expertly turning her while keeping perfectly in time. When the music ended, Carrie was out of breath but exhilarated.

'Again, again!' she said, laughing.

'Again? Right you are.' The music started up and he whisked her off again, guiding her gracefully as they whirled about. They danced five dances in a row before Carrie wanted to sit any of them out – every time the music started it was too hard to resist.

'Come on, I'm puffed even if you're not. Let's get a drink and have a rest,' said Todd, taking her over to a table and pulling out a chair for her. He returned with two glasses of punch and they drank them, thirsty after their exertions.

'It's fun, isn't it?' said Todd.

'Marvellous fun!' cried Carrie. 'I'm having a wonderful time.'

'Good.' He looked at her seriously. 'So am I. But anywhere would be wonderful with you, Carrie.'

'Todd . . .'

'No, Carrie, let me speak. There're only a few more dances we can dance before we have to leave. And then I'll be gone and I'll never have the chance again.'

Carrie nodded, biting her lip. It was the last thing she wanted to think of, that Todd would soon be going. It took the joy out of the evening and she didn't want that to happen yet.

'I know you're an engaged woman. I can never

forget that – even if you don't wear your engagement ring. It makes it much harder, but I can't leave without telling you how I feel.' He looked down at the table and then up into her eyes. 'You must know I'm very fond of you, Carrie. You've grown into the woman I always dreamed you would – you've always been the one I've wanted all my life. Don't worry, I'm not going to spoil your life and your plans because soon I'll be leaving and the chances are that I won't come back. But you have to know that . . . I've fallen in love with you. There. I've said it.'

A kind of excitement built up in her stomach and made her heart pound. As soon as she heard the words, she knew that she had longed to hear them and that the feelings she had been experiencing were real. She was in love as well – she had fallen in love almost as soon as she and Todd had met again, and had been falling just a little deeper each time. Now, after they had spun in perfect unison on the dance floor, she knew that he was the one she wanted.

'Oh Todd.'

'I know. It's made things difficult. And I promised I wouldn't. I don't want to compromise you or embarrass you, when there's Jeffrey . . .'

'No, no, you don't understand. It's not you – *I'm* the terrible one. Because I've fallen in love with you as well, and I'm engaged to someone else and it's a terrible betrayal.'

'What did you say?' said Todd, his eyes bright.

'I said, I've fallen in love with you too . . .'

'Oh Carrie,' he said, smiling as though he would never stop. 'I've so longed to hear those words.'

'But there's Jeffrey,' she said wretchedly. 'I must break it off with him, of course. I can't marry him now. But I feel so low and dreadful! And . . .' She faltered and then looked into Todd's eyes. 'There's something else as well. Something I have to tell you. Before I joined the army, Jeffrey and I were together, already engaged, and one night . . . well, one night we were . . .' She struggled over the words. 'We were . . . intimate, Todd. We were lovers. I never dreamt I'd tell anyone about it in this way, but I have to tell you that I'm not all you might think me.'

He clasped her hand and looked deeply at her. 'Do you think I care about that, Carrie? You were engaged, you thought you were going to be married. But that was before we met again, and fell in love the way we have. I don't care what happened before! You're my girl, my precious girl, and I wouldn't have you one jot different.'

Tears filled her eyes. 'Todd, if you knew how much that means to me.'

The music struck up again in an infectious melody that they could not resist.

'Come on!' cried Todd, taking her hand. 'We don't have much time left. Let's dance.' So they got up and spun and whirled until at last it was time to leave.

The journey home was strange. It was full of

desperation because they were going to be parted, but also with a joyfulness because at last they had admitted how they felt about each other. When Todd brought the car to a stop just near Southgate Lodge, they sat for a moment in the darkness before Todd spoke.

'You've made me very happy, Carrie,' he said softly. 'I'm going off tomorrow night and I'll treasure this memory. It will help me through the hard times ahead. You can't imagine how.'

'You've made me happy too, Todd,' she said, her heart pounding again. 'I've never known anything like this.'

He moved closer to her and then his lips were on hers and he was kissing her with great passion and she returned it, as his arms wrapped around her. They kissed for what seemed like forever, before they finally had to break apart, both left breathless.

'Oh, Todd,' she said.

'Carrie, I've got to leave you now. But when I can, I'll be in touch. When my mission is over and I'm safe, I'll send you a card to let you know that I'll be back and I'll find you wherever you are. Do you understand?'

She nodded, filled both with wild joy at their kiss, and despair that in a few minutes he would be gone, perhaps for ever.

He went on, 'Do you remember the path to the woods? Do you remember when I first arrived and you told me how to get to Jackmans? It was springtime.'

'What did I say?' Carrie asked, puzzled.

'You said: it's easy – you just turn left at the daffodils.'

'Oh yes – the big bank of daffodils just by the stile! What a sight that was at Easter time. Dear old Nether Hutton. We'll be back there together one day, won't we, Todd?'

'Of course we will. And when I write to you, that's what I'll say on my card, to remind you of my promise that I'll find you wherever you are. And we'll never be parted.'

'Yes – yes. Todd, please, you will take care, won't you? For me?'

'Yes. Because now I have everything to live for,' he said vehemently. 'Now I have you and I'm the happiest man in the world.' He kissed her again passionately. They pulled apart at last, reluctant to let each other go.

'I promise I'll be back,' he said softly. 'I promise, Caroline Tiptree. And I keep my promises.'

Nan went through all the motions required of her but it felt sometimes as though she were living underwater, with all normal sounds and sights muffled. She was sunk deep in her misery, tormented all the time by the memory of the way Chas had spoken to her, and the way all her hopes and dreams had been so cruelly shattered. She'd stayed at Gardener's Cottage almost a week and had tried to visit Chas, but he simply refused to see her. Each day she hoped that he would have changed his mind, but each day Stella came back from the Manor with the same message: he didn't want her to visit.

'I'm so sorry, Nan,' his mother had said. 'I don't understand him. This isn't my Charles! But it's early days – we must be steadfast.'

That was easy for her to say, Nan had thought bitterly. Chas still loved *her* and valued her. It was Nan he'd rejected in this awful way. Perhaps, she'd begun to think, it was better that they hadn't got married, if this was what he was really like . . . But all it took was for her to remember the dancing and the laughter and the tender kisses for her to long for him again, and to weep with grief for the lovely man she had lost.

Auntie Mim had written to her. It was a sympathetic letter saying how sorry she was the wedding had been cancelled but that it was lucky Chas had been rescued, and she wouldn't put her best coat in mothballs quite yet, as no doubt there would be another wedding soon.

Ha! That was a laugh. If Auntie Mim could've seen the way Chas treated her – it was hardly love's young dream, the two of them. The man staring out of the window while he told the girl to get lost. Very romantic. They weren't making Hollywood pictures with *that* scene in it.

It was going to be a terrible Christmas this year, although at least she would be at Heronflete where she could lose herself in work, and be with Evie and Carrie, who were both being very good and not asking her about what had happened. She couldn't bring herself to talk about it, not yet. She was ashamed of it, if the truth were known. She felt ashamed that Chas no longer wanted her and that the wedding was cancelled for good – after Carrie had spent all that time sewing that bluddy dress! No, she didn't want to admit it yet, though she would have to some time. She'd have to say, 'Oh, by the way, Chas has lost a leg and doesn't want me anywhere near him ever again. Says I have to find a new bloke, so I s'pose that's what I'd better do.'

Maybe one day she'd make that speech. In the meantime, she got on with her work. The sergeant had never been so pleased with her. 'Nan, you're very conscientious these days – well done. That's the kind of effort that will help win the war.'

Losing herself in activity was one way of forgetting the pain of her broken heart. Southgate had never been so clean: Nan was always up first thing, stripping off her bed and folding all the bedding just so, in case the sergeant did an inspection. She was often in her overalls, sweeping and mopping the billet. Her uniform was perfectly pressed and her shoes, buttons and hat badge gleamed like mirrors from all the polishing she did. She was always looking for something else that would take her mind off things, and she didn't want to talk anymore. The chirpy, bubbly Nan had quite vanished.

As Christmas approached she found it hard to muster any enthusiasm at all, but did her best to join in when Evie and Carrie suggested hunting about for something to decorate the lodge with. As it was Christmas they were allowed to put a few things in the billet to make it more festive, and they found a big holly bush, which meant they had lovely sprigs of bright berries and dark green leaves pinned up at all the doors and windows and arranged over the fireplace, where pine cones they'd found gave out a wonderfully Christmassy scent.

Carrie received a Christmas parcel from home that included a big tin of Canadian sweets – 'from our cousins in Ontario!' she explained as she handed them around – some more cocoa and a present from her mother wrapped in brown paper. 'A knitted scarf, I should think,' Carrie said, squishing it thoughtfully. Evie and Nan also got a small parcel each from their families, and Nan got one from Gardener's Cottage as well.

Christmas Day dawned bright and clear but cold.

'What a luxury!' sighed Evie. 'A lie-in. How about that . . . We can stay in bed till eleven if we want to!'

They weren't on duty at all that day, and the only thing they had to show up for was Christmas lunch. Carrie made them all a cup of cocoa and they sat in bed, opening their presents.

'It *was* a scarf!' said Carrie, holding up a pale blue knitted strip of wool. 'That was sweet of her. What have you got, Evie?'

'Mum's sent me a book and a photograph of her and Dad. What a love! Oh, it's lovely to see them.' She handed round the photograph of her smiling parents dressed in their Sunday best, standing stiffly against the backdrop in the photographer's studio.

Nan had a calendar in her parcel from Auntie Mim. Inside the package from Gardener's Cottage was the soft white fluffy jumper she had worn over her stay.

This suited you so much, I thought you might like to have it, wrote Stella. *Wishing you a happy Christmas and that we will soon meet again. Much love, Stella Lawson.*

Nothing from Chas, of course.

'What a pretty jumper!' exclaimed Carrie when she saw it.

'Don't know where I'm gonna wear it, though,' replied Nan. But she tried to have a laugh for the sake of the others. They all went up to the cookhouse for their celebration lunch, and were delighted to find Sergeant James was serving them all.

'Officers serving!' laughed Evie, once she'd been handed her plate of turkey and all the trimmings.

'Don't get used to it, Turner,' warned the sergeant.

After a big dinner followed by Christmas pudding and custard, they all went to the NAAFI to settle down and listen to the King's Christmas speech. All too soon, they were back in Southgate Lodge and Christmas Day was over. Tomorrow, it would be business as usual and all the frivolity and enjoyment of Christmas well and truly behind them.

* * *

Just after Christmas felt like the bleakest time of all and life in Southgate Lodge was distinctly cheerless. It seemed as though it was always night time, as they struggled through the darkness to the ablutions and the cookhouse, and then shift and off shift. Spring was so far away and the war, it seemed, was endless. Now that the whole world was fighting itself, when would the finish ever come? It dulled all their spirits – especially when news came through of heavy Allied losses and of the terrible suffering of the people in Russia.

Nan struggled through every day, desperately trying to forget her broken heart, while Carrie was feeling deeply bereft now that Todd had gone. It was as though a light had gone out and she was overwhelmed with a terrible sense of loss. When she wasn't mourning the loss of Todd, she was berating herself for falling in love with someone else when she was engaged to Jeffrey. All her doubts and suspicions about him now seemed to melt away in the face of her own behaviour, which was just about the most treacherous thing imaginable.

She had kissed Todd – really kissed him – and it had excited her and thrilled her in a way that had never happened with Jeffrey. With Todd, her whole body tingled with excitement when she simply sat next to him. The touch of his lips on hers was a pleasure like nothing she had ever known, and her body had urged her to carry on, to go further, to obey the deep impulses that came over her.

It was nothing like the cold, miserable detachment she had felt when Jeffrey had had his way with her that night. It was so different, she could hardly believe that the two events were in any way connected. But they were: one was sexual desire driven by someone else's lust. The other was the same but driven by her own enormous attraction and deep feeling for Todd. That was the key.

This is what Evie means, she thought. I couldn't see it before! I didn't understand. I can see now why she was so adamant that I wasn't to marry Jeffrey. I thought love was something you could feel if you tried hard enough. I never realised it was something that swept you up and carried you off to such bliss. Oh Todd!

Just thinking about him made her stomach somersault wildly and her fingertips tingle. Her longing for him was so intense that it was a physical ache.

I must break off with Jeffrey, she told herself. And I must do it as soon as I can. It's not right to keep him hanging on like this. There's going to be music – not least from Mother and Mrs Frobisher – but I have to face it and that's that.

But somehow it seemed easier to let things slide, and not really do anything about it, than it was to write that awful letter saying that she had changed her mind entirely, and couldn't get married after all.

Poor Jeffrey, she thought. He doesn't deserve this, he really doesn't. I can't do it to him. I'll break his heart.

TWENTY-THREE

Boxing Day was the worst day so far for Nan. It was Chas's twenty-first birthday and the whole day was filled with despair for her, as she thought of him almost every minute, wondering what he was doing and if anyone was giving him a birthday treat. She wished she was there to make sure he was treated special on his big day, when he came of age. She felt very powerless far away from him at Heronflete, and in the evening she sat down to write him a letter, letting all the emotion and torment of the last few weeks come pouring out.

My darling Chas
I have thought of you all day, wishing you a happy birthday and hoping you are well. I cannot let this day pass without telling you, maybe for the last time, how I feel and how you have broken my heart by turning me away. I love you, Chas, and I always will, no matter what. You say you are

useless but it's not true. You are only just
21 with your life ahead, and so much you
can do. Besides making me happy by loving
me again, you have many things to offer
the country and the war effort and I can't
bear to think of you suffering alone when
you don't need to . . .

She wrote down everything she had longed to
say, filling two pages of writing paper. By the
end, tears were falling down her face as she
wrote. Then, before she could change her mind,
she folded up the letter, put it in the envelope
and sealed it. She would send it to Chas no matter
what.

Then, when it was gone, she waited, as New
Year's Eve came and went and January 1942
dawned, bringing with it hope but also a certain
knowledge that further suffering and effort lay
ahead. But no answer came from Chas.

It was a couple of weeks later that a letter
finally came from Shrewsbury. But it wasn't from
Chas – it was from Stella.

Dear Nan,
If you possibly can, I think you should come
at once. Charles is sinking daily into a very
bad depression and you are the only person I
can think of who could help him. Your letter
touched him, I believe, but he is unable to
muster the strength to do what you ask, and

get back his old self. If you could be here, I believe there might be hope . . .

As she read it, Nan gasped. The very slimmest chance was better than none – she had to do whatever she possibly could. She went to the sergeant immediately and asked for a 72-hour pass, so that she could get to Chas. Very carefully, she explained the circumstances, while the sergeant regarded her coolly.

'You want to leave at once, do you?'

'If I can, yes please, Sergeant,' said Nan, breathless from her speech.

'Well . . .' Sergeant James tapped her pencil on the desk. 'I'm not unaware of what you've been through, Morrissey, and I admire the way you've coped. You've become my best-turned-out private and you've not shirked a minute of work. Nor have you let your personal troubles turn you into a moaner or someone who will bring the rest of the girls down. I respect that. I think you've earned this chance. I don't know about leaving immediately – I've got to sort out permissions and so on – but I think I can safely say that you could go the day after tomorrow, for seventy-two hours. And as you're on earlies, I'll arrange for Tiptree to take you to the station immediately you're finished, and that way you'll get a head start. All right?'

'Yes, Sergeant. Oh, thank you, thank you!' cried Nan.

'That'll do. You're dismissed.'

Nan saluted and ran all the way back to Southgate as fast she could, a smile on her face for the first time in weeks.

Carrie drove an excited Nan to the station the next evening.

'You have a good trip, do you hear?' she said as she dropped Nan with her kitbag.

'I'll do my best,' grinned Nan. 'I don't know why I'm so cheerful, considerin' that his mum tells me Chas is just as low as he can get. But somethin' tells me that if I can only get there, we have a chance . . . that I'm the one that can make a difference. This is our last hope, I can feel it.'

'We'll be rooting for you both!' called Carrie as Nan hoisted up her bag and headed for the platform. 'Goodbye!'

By the time she turned around and headed back towards Heronflete, it was already getting dark. It made the progress slow and careful, but Carrie didn't mind. She wanted to be alone, so that she could think about Todd, and wonder what he was doing now and if he was safe. She hoped that, wherever he was, he was among friends, and with somewhere comfortable and dry to sleep, and hot food to eat. She longed to care for him herself but that was impossible. She could only send her prayers and good wishes instead, and her love.

Love! Yes, she was in love! She knew that now. It made it all the harder that she was getting such affectionate letters from Jeffrey all the time. He had quite stopped his bullying tone and instead was warm and open, writing sweet letters that always told her how much he loved her and longed to marry her but didn't try to push her into naming a date. It made her feel quite rotten. He didn't deserve this from her, he really didn't. He was a good man at heart, and she shouldn't have betrayed him. But she couldn't help where her heart led her . . .

Her mother was another matter though. The letters from Janet Tiptree were getting hysterical, ordering Carrie to arrange a wedding date.

Don't you think that just because you're twenty-one now, and own this house, that you can do whatever you like. You still have to obey me, you know! I demand you set the date for this wedding at once . . . she had written. Poor Mother – she wouldn't like it at all when Carrie told her that there wasn't going to be any wedding day. Even less would she like it when Carrie revealed whom she had given her heart to. Janet Tiptree had always scorned poor Todd – when he was worth ten Jeffreys at least!

Carrie dreamt all the way back to the stable block, returned the truck and then went off duty. She had something to eat in the cookhouse and then decided to spend a quiet evening reading in bed. When she got to the lodge, it was very quiet without Nan or Evie. Nan, of course, was aboard a train somewhere, and Evie must be in the NAAFI, playing cards with another friendly soul.

603

On her pillow, Carrie found a letter. Evie must have put it there earlier when she collected the post. It was another missive from Jeffrey. She knew his sloping handwriting very well by now. Oh dear – another loving little note that would make her feel like the lowest form of life that there was.

She sat down, opened it and began to read.

Dear Mumsie, *it began.* Sorry I haven't written in a while – been busy with all the usual. Can't pretend I'm not worried about the Carrie situation.

Mumsie? she thought. Oh no, this letter isn't for me . . . it's for Jeffrey's mother. He must have put it in the wrong envelope.

She ought to stop reading but she had seen her name now, and she could see it again further down the page. There was no way that she could stop now, so she continued.

The truth is, Mumsie, I'm in Queer Street. If Carrie doesn't agree to marry me soon, I don't know what I'm going to do about money. There's her damned ring, which is still hanging over my head, though I know you won't rush me for payment. You know I've been banking on getting some of her dough to settle these debts of mine – they're not getting any smaller. It would have helped if

Dad had left us something, but he hasn't, so I'm going to have to marry for money. A man's got to live in the way he's become accustomed to. My worry is that, now she's twenty-one and in charge of her own affairs, Carrie might take it into her silly head to do something with her inheritance that means I can't get my hands on it . . . I've been sweet-talking her as much as possible so that I can at least get the damned date out of her. When she cancelled the Christmas idea, it was a real blow. But I'll be able to keep the bank manager happy if I can just get a firm day for the wedding. Anyway, I'll keep you informed, dear Mumsie. Hoping all is well with you.

   Your loving son, Jeffrey

It was strange, thought Carrie, that when something like this happened, you didn't react to it in the way you had thought you would. When she'd finished Jeffrey's letter, she began to giggle. Then she read it through again, and by the end she was laughing so hard that tears were falling down her cheeks and she was gasping for air.

'Oh poor Jeffrey!' she said out loud, when she had the breath. 'Fancy sending this to *me*, of all people! When he finds out, he'll be absolutely livid with himself.'

She smiled again, because the truth was, she was grateful to him. Of course, it made her sad to think that her engagement had been little more than a sham and that Jeffrey had, it was now clear, only wanted to marry her for her money and inheritance. She had been right all along about his motives and should have trusted her instinct. Something in her was terribly sad – especially when she remembered that he had made love to her even though he had never really felt the things he claimed to feel for her – but mostly it was as though a great weight had been lifted off her shoulders. She could finish with Jeffrey now and her conscience would be clear. She wasn't dumping him for another man. He had revealed himself as someone she couldn't possibly ever dream of marrying now.

More than anything, it was an enormous relief!

She quickly got a piece of paper and her pen, and wrote a few lines in her quick, tidy hand. Then she refolded his letter to his mother and put it with her own into an envelope, sealed it and addressed it. 'Thank you, Jeffrey,' she murmured as she did it. 'I just hope your bank manager will be understanding, that's all.'

She put the letter on the windowsill to take with her when she went up to the NAAFI.

Her note read:

Your ring is ready for collection any time you like, Jeffrey. That should be one less debt to worry about, anyway.
Caroline Tiptree

When Nan got to Gardener's Cottage late at night, Stella Lawson was waiting for her with a warm supper and hot tea, just as she had been on the previous visit. But this time, Chas's mother looked tired and drawn, her face anxious and her eyes haunted by anxiety.

'I'm so worried,' she explained, after she had welcomed Nan in, asked after the journey and made sure she had everything she wanted. 'I've never known Charles like this. He feels so worthless, I fear he's on the brink of doing something stupid.'

'Could he hurt himself?' Nan asked, worried.

'I don't think so – he's on the ward now so he's seldom alone and there's no way he can get about without help. There's talk that he'll soon have a prosthetic leg so that he can get up and about and practise walking, but it won't be for a while yet. The wound is not yet properly healed and it will need to be completely sealed and strong before he can begin to put his weight on it. Until then it will be wheelchairs and crutches. The problem is that where there is a will, there's a way. If Charles decides he wants to . . . hurt himself, I'm certain he would work out a way. And he's got the advantage over the nurses that he knows the place like the back of his hand. He grew up there after all.'

'So we'll go and see him tomorrow?'

'Yes. He doesn't know you're coming, I thought it best not to say. He got your letter and I could tell it touched him deeply – but not quite enough to penetrate his black despair. That's why I think you are the one who could reach him. I think you've got the words that will get to him.'

'I hope you're right,' said Nan fervently. 'But he wanted nothing to do with me last time. I don't wanna let you down, but I might not be able to do any good.'

'I would never blame you, whatever happens. If you can't reach him, no one can. It is as simple as that.'

They turned in soon afterwards, both tired and both eager for the next day to begin.

Matron had arranged for Chas to be moved somewhere on his own so that Nan could see him in private.

'He's in the conservatory,' she explained, leading the way towards the rear of the house. 'It's a great favourite with the men, especially in the cold winter months. It's always warm in there, and there's a lovely view of the garden and the hothouses. Only Sergeant Lawson is there today though.'

Nan nodded, her mouth dry with anxiety. Stella Lawson had left her at the door of the Manor, saying, 'You don't need me today. Good luck, dear.' And now she was being led towards Chas, whose last words to her had been harsh and cruel. She, Nan, had the responsibility of rescuing him from the dark place he had gone to, and bringing him back to the land of the living. How was she going to do that?

At the far end of the iron and glass conservatory, she could see a figure in a wheelchair, gazing out across the bleak garden. In the distant hothouse, there was greenery and a splash of colour, which Chas seemed to be fixated on.

'I'll leave you here,' said Matron gently. 'Come and find me when you're ready. There's no hurry.' The next minute, she was gone and Nan was on her own. She went forward tentatively into the thickly warm air of the glass room. Funny how hot it was, even on a winter's day.

She stopped when she was within speaking distance of Chas, and looked at the back of his head. His fair hair was cut as short as usual, and neatly combed, and he was wearing the blue uniform of the convalescent airmen. His back was stiff and straight in the chair, and she could see that the bandages round his hands were gone. That was good.

Suddenly he spoke, in a flat voice. 'Isn't it peculiar how the flowers keep on growing, even when there's nobody looking after them? There's only one old gardener here now, and he can barely manage the kitchen garden. But the hot houses go on doing their job, and all those exotic lilies and orchids are blooming away as though there wasn't any war. We should have them all dug up, I suppose. Throw them on the compost heap. That's all they're good for. Funny to see them blazing away down there all alone, with no one to enjoy them.'

'Hello, Chas,' Nan said softly.

He started slightly and half turned his head. 'Oh, it's you!' Then he sighed and turned away again. 'Why'd you come, Nan? Didn't you understand what I said to you?'

'Yes. But this isn't all about *your* problems, Chas. You got my letter and I know you read it. I'm suffering too, in a different way. I had to come and see you, to be sure once and for all that you know your mind and that it's all over between us.'

'Well, if that's all! You could have saved yourself the journey, and all the bother of the leave you must have had to arrange. Yes yes . . .' He waved his hand dismissively. 'It's all over. On your way now! Toodle-oo, cheery-bye.'

She swallowed and tried to fight the rising anger in her. Part of her wanted to slap his face and say, 'Stop all this self-pity! You're better than this.'

But she didn't. She did want him to look at her though, so she walked round to the front of his chair and faced him. He stared up at her, his blue eyes cold and his face expressionless.

'Are you still here?' he said. 'You're persistent, I'll give you that.'

'Yes,' she said in a quiet voice. 'I *am* persistent, because there's too much at stake here to throw it away without bein' sure. Two people's lives and happiness, wasted for nothin' but because a boy who's luckier by far than many in this war can't get over feelin' sorry for himself.'

Chas's eyes flicked downwards and then away,

so that he was staring at a green-fronded fern on the table by his chair.

'You can't even meet my eyes, can you? Because you know it's true. You're letting yourself rot. You're sending away everyone who loves you and wants to care for you because you can't accept their sympathy and accept the truth. You lost a leg, you got hurt. Your life will never be the same again – but you're not the only one. Haven't you been to the pictures, Chas? Haven't you seen London and Liverpool and all them places bombed into next week? People who've lost everything they've owned along with the clothes off their backs, parents who've lost children, wives their husbands, babies their families? No one's untouched by all this madness. I lost me own dad only nine months ago – don't you think I'd have wept for joy if he'd come out alive with only his leg missin'?

'I know that you're not selfish or wicked, I know that better than anyone. And I'm not sayin' it's wrong to be sad about what's gone for ever. But you could waste your life lookin' back when there's so much waitin' out there for both of us.'

She stopped for a moment, overcome. It was hard to understand how Chas could turn away from a bright future, to one of loneliness and despair.

'I-I-I know you want the best for me, Nan,' he said at last, still unable to meet her eye. 'But it's partly because you're so good and strong that I don't want you to have to spend a lifetime caring for me. It's because you're of sterling stuff, and it turns out I'm not. You can go and be useful still, and I can only sit here, staring out of windows, powerless. You must realise that's why I'm the way I am now. I hate what I've become.'

Nan knelt down beside him and clasped his hands. Her heart began to beat fast and the words rushed out of her. 'But don't you see, Chas, that it won't be this way forever. The war is going to be with us for months – years, probably. You're needed, desperately. Once your leg is better and you can get about, there's no limit to what you can do. Look, your hands have healed wonderfully.' She turned one over and looked at it. It was still scarred but the new skin was there, sealing over the old wounds. 'Think of what you can still offer. You've flown dozens of missions, you know how it's done. You've navigated your way all across Europe. Your knowledge is priceless, you must see that. There's sure to be lots of jobs you'll be wanted for as soon as you're fit, that will help bring all this to an end.'

He stared at her. 'Perhaps you're right, perhaps they do need me,' he said in a wondering voice.

'They do, I'm sure of it!'

'But that doesn't change what's happened between us,' he said sadly. 'It doesn't change the fact that you should find a better man than me, a whole man.'

'Oh Chas. When I last saw you, it was goin'

612

to be our wedding day. I was prepared to make those vows and promises to you – "in sickness and in health", that's what I was going to say and I meant it, whether or not we was already married. So the sickness came along a little sooner than we thought. That doesn't change how I feel about you. It doesn't make me want to abandon you – why would it? Just because you're hurt doesn't mean I want to give up all my love for you, and I couldn't even if I wanted. Because I love you. You're a whole man to me, and always will be, don't matter if you lose your other leg, and your arms too. You know that really, don't you?'

His hand clasped round hers and he spoke roughly. 'But I have to give you the chance to go.'

'You've done that. Every time you've said Leave, I've said I don't want to. What do I have to do before you believe me?'

'You mean . . . you'd really still want me? Want to marry a cripple?'

'I want to marry Chas Lawson, my sweet funny boy who captured my heart the first night I saw him. I want to marry the Chas who looks to the future that the both of us will share no matter what. All you need to be is yourself.'

'Oh Nan.' His voice broke for a moment and he twisted his face away from her. When he looked back, his eyes were shiny. 'I don't deserve this loyalty. I've been so unhappy, and I've punished you for it. I'm so sorry.'

'Don't be silly,' she said softly. 'It doesn't matter any more, as long as we get through it.'

'Do you believe we can?'

'I know we can.'

His hand tightened around hers. He said slowly, 'You're so sure of yourself! It makes me begin to believe that all this can work out, that we'll be all right.'

'Of course we will,' she cried. 'All we have to do is want it.'

'Yes. Yes, I can see that now.'

'Can you? Can you, Chas?'

'I believe I can!' He started to laugh. 'Oh, God, Nan Morrissey, I think you've just shown me the way back. You clever good girl! My own dear Nan.'

'Oh Chas,' she sobbed, her heart suddenly bursting and then his arms were round her and they were hugging tightly, as though they had been away from each other on a long journey and now, at last, were reconciled. 'Will you ever leave me again?'

'Never, never,' he whispered into her hair. 'Never.'

She closed her eyes and breathed in deeply. She was home at last.